Praise for

Catch a Shadow

"This is one good deed that definitely rebounds, throwing the heroine into a dark and extremely treacherous world. A master of both plot and characters, Potter weaves together a story that's both exciting and intense. It's not to be missed!"
—*Romantic Times*

"The latest from Potter is a well-paced and smartly told romantic thriller."
—*Publishers Weekly*

Beloved Warrior

"Pure pleasure . . . Proof to what her fans may already know: Potter keeps getting better with every outing."
—*Publishers Weekly* (starred review)

"[A] superb romance . . . It's Potter's unique gift for creating unforgettable characters and delving into the deepest parts of their hearts that endears her to readers. This is another masterpiece from a writer who always delivers what romance readers want: a love story to always remember." —*Romantic Times*

Tempting the Devil

"A finely crafted book, written by someone who, for all her numerous accolades and her many years of experience, is still working hard to master new tricks." —*The Romance Reader*

"The story line is action-packed . . . Fans will appreciate this romantic suspense with the emphasis on the action."
—*Midwest Book Review*

continued . . .

Beloved Stranger

"An absolutely stunning read, rich in historical details, fast-paced, and riveting in suspense . . . An emotional tale that will leave you with a lump in your throat and a tear or two in your eyes. Potter brings together a cast of new and fascinating characters as well as old friends from the first book in this wonderful historically set series of the Maclean family."　　　　　　　　　　　　　　　*—The Best Reviews*

"The action-packed story line moves forward at a fast pace, but it is the lead pairing that drives a fine return to the Maclean clan."　　　　　　　　　　　　　　　*—Midwest Book Review*

Tangle of Lies

"Fast-paced . . . A fantastic suspense thriller."
　　　　　　　　　　　　　　　—Midwest Book Review

"A chilling, complex tale of revenge, betrayal, and long-kept secrets."　　　　　　　　　　　　　　　*—Library Journal*

"A tangled web of clues [with] a touch of spice thrown in for good measure."　　　　　　　　　　　　*—A Romance Review*

"Great characters, a compelling story that's almost impossible to put down, lots of plot twists—*Tangle of Lies* has it all."
　　　　　　　　　　　　　　　—Romance Reviews Today

"Exciting mystery with hot romance make this a winner."
　　　　　　　　　　　　　　　—Fresh Fiction

Beloved Imposter

"Ms. Potter has given us another thrilling drama. Every page proves the reason for her award-winning success . . . *Beloved Imposter* travels at a fast pace with outstanding characters and an expertly developed plot."　　　　*—Rendezvous*

"A wonderful Scottish tale wrought with emotion, tender in its telling, and heart-wrenching in its beauty. Ms. Potter captures our hearts and gifts us with another beautiful story."

—*The Best Reviews*

"Ms. Potter is a very talented storyteller, taking a much-used theme—lovers from warring families—and manipulating it, adding plenty of new ideas and twists, until the end result is the original, highly satisfying *Beloved Imposter* . . . Ms. Potter very adeptly whetted this reader's appetite for more about these two Maclean brothers, but for now, there is *Beloved Imposter*, which I highly recommend." —*Romance Reviews Today*

Dancing with a Rogue

"Once again, Potter . . . proves that she's adept at penning both enthralling historicals and captivating contemporary novels."

—*Booklist* (starred review)

"Gabriel and Merry are a delightful pair . . . Patricia Potter has provided a character-driven story that her audience will enjoy."

—*Midwest Book Review*

"An entirely engrossing novel by this talented and versatile author."

—*Romance Reviews Today*

The Diamond King

"From war-torn Scotland to the high seas to the jungles of Brazil, Potter takes the reader on a roller-coaster ride as a rake becomes a hero and a courageous, resourceful woman finds love against all odds."

—*Booklist*

The Heart Queen

"This is a book that is difficult to put down for any reason. Simply enjoy."

—*Rendezvous*

continued . . .

"Potter is a very talented author . . . If you are craving excitement, danger, and a hero to die for, you won't want to miss this one."
—*All About Romance*

More praise for Patricia Potter and her bestselling novels

"Patricia Potter has a special gift for giving an audience a first-class romantic story line."
—*Affaire de Coeur*

"When a historical romance [gets] the Potter treatment, the story line is pure action and excitement, and the characters are wonderful."
—*BookBrowser*

BEHIND THE
SHADOWS

Patricia Potter

BERKLEY SENSATION, NEW YORK

THE BERKLEY PUBLISHING GROUP
Published by the Penguin Group
Penguin Group (USA) Inc.
375 Hudson Street, New York, New York 10014, USA
Penguin Group (Canada), 90 Eglinton Avenue East, Suite 700, Toronto, Ontario M4P 2Y3, Canada
(a division of Pearson Penguin Canada Inc.)
Penguin Books Ltd., 80 Strand, London WC2R 0RL, England
Penguin Group Ireland, 25 St. Stephen's Green, Dublin 2, Ireland (a division of Penguin Books Ltd.)
Penguin Group (Australia), 250 Camberwell Road, Camberwell, Victoria 3124, Australia
(a division of Pearson Australia Group Pty. Ltd.)
Penguin Books India Pvt. Ltd., 11 Community Centre, Panchsheel Park, New Delhi—110 017, India
Penguin Group (NZ), 67 Apollo Drive, Rosedale, North Shore 0632, New Zealand
(a division of Pearson New Zealand Ltd.)
Penguin Books (South Africa) (Pty.) Ltd., 24 Sturdee Avenue, Rosebank, Johannesburg 2196,
South Africa

Penguin Books Ltd., Registered Offices: 80 Strand, London WC2R 0RL, England

This is a work of fiction. Names, characters, places, and incidents either are the product of the author's
imagination or are used fictitiously, and any resemblance to actual persons, living or dead, business
establishments, events, or locales is entirely coincidental. The publisher does not have any control
over and does not assume any responsibility for author or third-party websites or their content.

BEHIND THE SHADOWS

A Berkley Sensation Book / published by arrangement with author

PRINTING HISTORY
Berkley Sensation mass-market edition / December 2008

Copyright © 2008 by Patricia Potter.
Cover design by Brad Springer.
Art direction by George Long.
Interior text design by Kristin del Rosario.

All rights reserved.
No part of this book may be reproduced, scanned, or distributed in any printed or electronic form
without permission. Please do not participate in or encourage piracy of copyrighted materials in
violation of the author's rights. Purchase only authorized editions.
For information, address: The Berkley Publishing Group,
a division of Penguin Group (USA) Inc.,
375 Hudson Street, New York, New York 10014.

ISBN: 978-0-425-22490-8

BERKLEY® SENSATION
Berkley Sensation Books are published by The Berkley Publishing Group,
a division of Penguin Group (USA) Inc.,
375 Hudson Street, New York, New York 10014.
BERKLEY SENSATION and the "B" design are trademarks of Penguin Group (USA) Inc.

PRINTED IN THE UNITED STATES OF AMERICA

10 9 8 7 6 5 4 3 2 1

If you purchased this book without a cover, you should be aware that this book is stolen property. It was
reported as "unsold and destroyed" to the publisher, and neither the author nor the publisher has
received any payment for this "stripped book."

Dedicated to those wonderful people—
and their families—
who in both life and death give hope
to others through organ donations.

1

Kira couldn't breathe as she stared down at the paper in front of her. The world stopped whirling. At least, her world did.

No, not stopped. Turned upside down. Made night day, and day night.

The words weren't true. They just couldn't be true.

Some terrible mistake. A monstrous error.

The print ran together on the paper. She'd listened to the doctor, then demanded to see the results in black and white. The form looked official. The words made no sense.

"I want another test," she said.

"We ordered a second test to confirm. Different labs. Same results," Dr. Warner said from behind his desk. "I'm sorry." He paused, then added, "You didn't know you were adopted? I probably should have said something to your mother before giving you the results, but . . ."

His words trailed off.

Kira knew, though, what he meant to say. Her mother was too ill to take any bad news.

She stared down at the results again. No match. No match of any kind. She couldn't be a donor. She'd been so sure . . .

Then instant playback. *You didn't know you were adopted?*

Her heart pounded. She put a hand on the desk to keep

standing. "I *wasn't* adopted. I know every detail of my birth. I had a hole in my heart . . . There was surgery . . . Eastside Hospital. I have a birth certificate with my footprint on it." She was babbling. But then so was he. His words . . . his conclusions . . . were incomprehensible.

She'd undergone a blood test just three days ago to determine whether she could donate a kidney to her mother. Every other avenue had failed. Dialysis was no longer doing the job. Infections occurred with increasing frequency. Her mother was on the transplant list, but they had been waiting nine months already, and she was nowhere near the top. When Kira offered to donate one of her kidneys, her mother refused to consider it, although she was in the end stages of kidney failure.

In desperation and without her mother's knowledge, Kira asked the doctor to make the tests to determine whether they were compatible. Then she would convince her mother to agree to it.

She'd been warned she might not be a match although they were mother and daughter, but this . . .

"I'm sorry, Ms. Douglas. There's no doubt. You are not Mrs. Douglas's genetic daughter. I just assumed . . ."

Not only were they not a match, they weren't even blood relatives. *According to the test.*

For the barest fraction of a second, doubt crept into her mind. Maybe that was why her mother was adamant about refusing a kidney donation from Kira.

But then she dismissed the idea. Her mother was honest to a fault. A lie never solved anything, she often said. She certainly would have known that adoption wouldn't have changed Kira's feelings toward her. It had been the two of them for thirty-two years. Katy and Kira against the world.

How could such a mistake happen? Maybe someone else's blood was sent by mistake to two labs.

"I want another test," she said. "I want blood taken today, now, and rushed to a third lab. I don't care about the cost."

"Believe me, we are very careful."

Anger boiled up inside her. It *wasn't* true, and she knew it. "Are you going to conduct another test? Or do I have to go somewhere else?"

There was nowhere else. She knew it, and he knew it. Her mother's insurance was limited at best. Memorial East was the designated hospital for the plan her mother had, and even then the insurance covered only some expenses. Duplicate blood tests at another hospital would definitely not qualify.

Kira closed her eyes for a moment, mentally seeing their checking account go down. Her mother's house had been heavily mortgaged as medical bills mounted. Kira had moved in with her to save money, and they were still in debt to the hospital.

"All right," the doctor finally said reluctantly. "I'll send in a technician for another blood sample."

"I have the birth certificate," she insisted again.

He didn't reply. He rose from his desk. "There are other patients waiting, Ms. Douglas, but I'll contact you the second the new test comes in."

She nodded.

He hesitated a moment, then added, "Stay here and I'll send in a technician for the blood." Another pause, then, "Kira, they've moved your mother up on the list."

Good news. Bad news. Good news she was closer to the top of the transplant list. Bad that she was worsening so quickly that they moved her up.

He left. Still trying to comprehend what he'd just said, she waited impatiently for the technician. She wanted to rush to her mother and ask questions. She wanted to look into her eyes and see herself in them. Disbelief still stunned her, but anger—raw and jagged—was building inside. She wanted to sweep the doctor's desk clean with her hands. She wanted to throw one of his many framed photos against the wall. He had been so calm, so matter-of-fact as he said words that made her life a lie and possibly condemned her mother.

The technician came in. She forced herself to be civil when she wanted to scream at him. How could they have messed up the last test?

When he left, she followed him out in a daze. She'd been given time off this morning for the doctor's appointment, but she had to cover a meeting at city hall. She couldn't lose her job now that medical costs were spiraling upward.

She paused outside the office door and looked down. The paper was crushed in her clenched hand. She carefully straightened it out, then glanced at it again. It was wrong. Someone had made a terrible error.

But if . . . if . . .

If she wasn't Kira Douglas, who was she?

More important, who would save her mother?

Dammit, she *was* Kira Douglas, and she could prove it. In fact, she *would* prove it.

2

Metal screeching, tearing. Blood. Pain. Mind-shattering terror.
   Mommy! Daddy!
   She woke with a scream.

Leigh Howard fought panic. It was only a nightmare. *This time*. Only a nightmare.

But so real. Nothing was missing. Not the terrible argument. Not the screams. The excruciating pain. Her mother's blood mixing with hers.

Sweat drenched the bed. Leigh wearily sat up on the side of the bed, trying to shake the images that lingered in her mind.

It was still dark outside, but a night-light made the room visible. It was ridiculous, she knew. A thirty-two-year-old woman shouldn't need a night-light, but she couldn't sleep without one.

She stood, went to the window, and looked outside at the pasture. Maude, the rescue donkey and companion to her show horse, grazed in the pasture. She always grazed, a never-ending eating machine.

Leigh looked down at her hands. They still trembled. Deep breath, she told herself. Take a deep breath. The fear will fade. But she knew it would never entirely go away.

She glanced at the clock. Only four in the morning.

Yet she knew she couldn't go back to sleep. The bed would be wet. Not damp. Soaking wet with sweat.

She closed her eyes. If only . . .

If only there were someone to call, to talk to. But there wasn't. Only Mrs. Baker, who lived a mile away. She certainly wasn't going to run crying to the family's housekeeper, even one who was almost a family member.

She went into the bathroom. Peered at herself. God, she looked a horror. Her eyes were red and tired. Her damp hair fell lifelessly around her face.

She padded down the stairs to the kitchen and turned on the light. A cup of hot chocolate might help. She heated some milk, poured chocolate syrup into it, and sat down at the large table in the sunroom. *Think about the day.* The horse show benefit that she chaired. She knew it was only an honorary position, but she wanted to show she could do more than "honorary." Maybe a cocktail party/silent auction to raise awareness of their cause.

She wanted this year's event to surpass every other one.

Maybe then she could convince Max that she could actually accomplish something important. Maybe he would loosen the strings on her inheritance.

It galled her no end that she was heiress to a fifty-million-dollar trust fund, but lived on an allowance supervised by a tight-assed lawyer. She blamed him for chasing off James Hallaway III as easily as he'd dispensed with her ex-husband. Maybe, just maybe, she and James could have made a marriage work had there not been so much interference. Dollars offered, and, she admitted painfully to herself, dollars taken.

God, could she ever pick them!

But even a gold-digging husband might be better than being so entirely alone.

She yawned. She'd had three hours' sleep at most.

She needed more. She needed to be alert and confident when she faced the lion in his den later today.

She would take a hot shower and use a bed in one of the

guest rooms. Maybe the nightmare had gone away for the night.

Maybe.

Anger came in waves. It swelled to tsunami strength, then retreated, only to return.

Kira tried to tamp it down as she walked inside her mother's cubicle. She had rerun the doctor's words all day, even as she'd struggled through a city budget committee meeting. She'd returned to the hospital last night, but her mother had been exhausted from tests.

The words made no more sense today than they had yesterday. Either the hospital had made a terrible mistake and somehow mixed her blood up with someone else's, or her mother had lied to her for more than thirty years.

She pasted a smile on her face as she approached the bed in the critical care unit. Her mother was sleeping. Kira sat down in the uncomfortable chair next to the bed.

Katy Douglas had always been a small, slender woman who was constantly on the move. Now Kira studied her mother's features as she never had before.

Kira's build was larger. She was taller and had more curves. She'd always attributed her mother's slender size to the fact she worked so hard, right up to the moment she was diagnosed with renal failure. Even then, she hadn't stopped until she'd collapsed while cleaning a house when one of her employees didn't show.

Their eyes were both blue, although her mother's were a bright blue and Kira's were more of a smoky blue gray. Her mother's hair was a honey color, and curly, while hers was a dark mahogany shade and both straight and fine.

But they thought alike. Was that genes or environment?

Had her mother lied to her all these years?

How many times had her mother told her she was a miracle baby? That when she was born, everyone—everyone but Katy—said she would die within days. But she hadn't. She'd been named Kira, Latin for light, her mother said. She'd found the name in a baby book. She'd known Kira would live, that her light would glow.

Her mother's eyes flickered open. Even though her face was wan, she smiled. The open, delighted smile that always came to her face when she saw Kira. "How long have you been here?"

"Not long."

"You should have wakened me."

"You looked too peaceful," Kira said.

It wasn't true. Katy Douglas looked ravished by a disease that was draining her lifeblood. The doctor said she didn't have much more than a month to live unless she received a new kidney.

"You look tired," Katy Douglas said. "You aren't taking care of yourself. Go home and get some rest."

"I'd rather spend some time with you," Kira said.

Another smile. "A little while, then. What did you cover today?"

Kira made a face. "A budget committee meeting. Deadly dull. Give me a good political scandal any day."

A knock came at the door, and a tall, thin man entered then with a tray full of test tubes. The technician glanced at Katy Douglas, then Kira.

"My daughter, the newspaper reporter," her mother said with pride. "She works for the *Atlanta Observer*," she explained to the technician, who placed the tray on a table, then searched for a vein in arms that were mostly purple from numerous needles. He finally found one and drew blood.

The technician nodded at Kira and left the room.

"Tell me again about the day I was born," Kira said, asking the question she'd wanted to ask since the moment she entered the room. "It was this hospital, wasn't it?"

"The best day of my life," Katy said, her gaze fixing on Kira's face. "Your father was playing drums that night. We thought . . . I thought you wouldn't come for another month. But then, you were always impatient. So impatient." Her voice started to fade.

"Was it a caesarean?" Kira asked gently.

"No. You were coming just as we reached the hospital,"

Katy said. "As I said, impatient. I just made the emergency room. The doctor . . . he said he didn't have to work . . . that I had already done everything. But then the pediatrician came in and looked at the baby. I . . . knew something was wrong."

"But you wouldn't give up on me." Kira knew the story by heart, but she had to hear it again. Now.

"No," her mother said softly. "Not my Kira." Her voice had weakened in those few moments and her eyelids fluttered.

"Time for me to go," Kira said, even as she clung to her mother's hand, trying to force her own life force into her mother. "I love you," she whispered.

"I love . . . you, darlin'," her mother replied in a voice already weakening from those few words.

Kira waited until she knew her mother was asleep, then stood. For a moment she couldn't move.

She knew one thing now. Her mother certainly believed that she had given birth to Kira. No one could relate the story with such loving remembrance unless she'd lived it.

Her mother believed Kira was her daughter, the daughter of her blood.

The hospital *must* have made a mistake. Then or now.

She hoped to God it was now.

Damn it. Damn the doctor. Damn the hospital. She knew her mother was slipping away, and Kira was being cheated of her chance to help. Perhaps her mother's only chance.

She'd been assured the doctor would call her the moment the new test results returned. She resisted the urge to pick up the phone and call him again. Persistence was a good quality for a reporter, but she couldn't risk alienating him at the moment.

She looked down at her hand. It was shaking. This time, the lab *had* to get it right.

Maybe if they were wrong about the genetic match, they were wrong about the compatibility as well.

Maybe there was still hope.

3

Max Payton raised an intimidating eyebrow. Leigh Howard
met his gaze directly.

He was impressed. Usually, she avoided directness.

She held a strange place in his professional life. Not exactly
his ward. Or his client. But someone whose life and future was
entrusted to his care. The situation suited neither of them.

He was damned tired of being a heavy.

He owed the old man—her dead grandfather—but he was
beginning to wonder whether this job was worth the aggrava-
tion. "Another horse?" he asked dryly. "You have Silver Lady
or whatever the damned horse is named."

"It's my money," Leigh Howard said for the thousandth
time.

"It's the trust fund's money," he corrected her as he had for
the thousandth time. "And it financed Silver Lady." He knew
his voice was edged with weariness. "You've gone through so
many expensive hobbies that I would like to know that you're
serious about this before investing fifty thousand dollars on
another horse."

He watched her face turn to marble. Leigh Howard was a
pretty woman. Maybe too pretty with the naturally blond hair
and striking blue eyes. Most men would consider her lovely.

But he knew her too well. She was more like a wayward younger sister to him than a desirable woman.

He liked her. He had known her since he'd been an assistant—more of a gofer—for her grandfather. He'd taken her to the zoo and driven her to dancing classes. She had always been polite except for a few tantrums, relying more on charm than temper to get what she wanted.

She exasperated him, just as she had her grandfather. She was smart; Max knew that. But underneath the polished exterior, she was still—in many ways—the six-year-old who almost died in the accident that killed her parents. That night had left more than the physical scars on her legs and arms.

"Max, just consider it. My riding instructor says I'm a natural in the show ring. She says I'm ready to start jumping."

He hesitated. "Jumping is dangerous. You know how you—"

"I'll be very careful," she broke in eagerly. "I won't take chances."

"If you get hurt again . . ."

Her face clouded. "My instructor says I have a real talent, Max. A real feel for the horse. I'm a good rider. I really am."

"I know you are. I've watched you."

She looked surprised, and he kicked himself. Ed Westerfield never praised her for anything. Neither had Max. Perhaps he'd picked up more from the old man than he'd thought. He cleared his suddenly thick throat and continued, "You're good at most things you do. You just don't stay interested very long. And I know how you feel about hospitals and . . ."

"I won't get hurt. The . . . car is just as dangerous, and I drive."

But not easily. He knew how long it had taken for her to learn to drive. She still didn't like it, and after the accident, he didn't blame her. He also knew from Mrs. Baker about the nightmares that didn't go away, and the way her face stiffened when she had a doctor's appointment.

"I'm ready," she persisted. "My instructor says this jumper is perfect. Well trained and gentle. I'm not rushing into this, Max. I've become familiar with horse people. You know I'm chairing the South Atlanta Regional Horse Show."

He knew that, too. Westerfield Industries was a sponsor. And that, he thought cynically, was exactly why she was asked to chair the committee. Yet she probably *would* be good at it. Her problem had never been lack of brains. It had been lack of confidence. If she didn't succeed in something immediately, she abandoned it. Though she would deny it forever, her grandfather had instilled a deep sense of inadequacy in her. It had led her into one very bad marriage, almost into a second, and into some terrible investments.

After buying off one husband and then a husband-to-be, Ed Westerfield put most of his fortune into an unbreakable trust for his only grandchild. She would receive the bulk of the money if and when she took a responsible place in Westerfield Industries or married someone who met Max's approval. She'd reached neither requirement. Until then she was on an allowance. A healthy one, but not enough to buy a $50,000 horse.

Max hated the promise he'd made to the old man when he was dying. At the same time, he knew how susceptible Leigh was to someone who pretended to care about her. She'd never truly been loved, and she hungered for it. He sympathized to some extent, but now he just wanted to say, "Get over it." He sure as hell had.

"Tell you what," he said. "Six months. If you still want this, then we'll talk about it again."

"Samara will be sold by then," she protested.

"There will be other horses."

Anger and disappointment clouded her face. She changed the subject. "What about Seth? Will you give him a contribution?"

He should have known that was coming. Hell, it probably had been her first goal. Make a request she knew he would refuse, and he would feel obligated to grant the second.

Good God, he was tired of saying no. He wished Ed Westerfield had just given her the money rather than establishing the damned trust and conning him into being trustee with a strict list of rules.

"Westerfield Industries doesn't give contributions," he said, citing the old man's philosophy. "You give something to one politician, then all the vultures descend. As an industry doing business with the state and U.S. governments, we can't single out one lawmaker or one party. You know that."

"This is different. He's a Westerfield. Family. People will understand that."

"He's a politician first."

"Dammit," she exploded. "It's not fair. He and David should have gotten more of the inheritance. Grandfather just wanted to bend everyone to his will and when he couldn't, he cut them off."

"True," Max admitted. "But you have a big allowance. You can contribute."

"I already have. The max." She lifted her chin. "I don't know why you're still his lackey. He's dead."

"I make promises, I keep them. It's my one virtue."

"And you believe you owe him," she said angrily. "That's bunk, and you know it. He got far more from you than he ever gave. All those years you did every nasty little chore. Hatchet man. That's all you were to him."

"Probably," Max said. "If you think that bothers me, you're wrong."

"You would have to be human to be bothered," she said, turned around, and marched out of the room.

True. He had lost his humanity when he was ten years old. A succeeding series of foster homes erased any remaining remnants. He'd resolved then never to be a victim again.

He leaned back in his chair. It was in his freshman year in college when he'd caught Westerfield's eye while he was a janitor in the Westerfield office building. He was caught reading Plato when he should have been scrubbing floors.

Ed Westerfield had questioned him at length, then become his mentor as well as employer. On his part, Max had made sure he became indispensable to his boss. When he graduated at the head of his business school class, Westerfield paid his tuition to Georgia State University Law School and slowly moved him up the ladder to corporate attorney.

The price had been complete dedication and loyalty. Whatever the old man wanted, he got. Didn't matter if Max found it distasteful. He was Westerfield's man.

Still was. Even two years after his death.

As Westerfield had known he would be.

Leigh was now his albatross.

The phone rang and he snatched it to his ear. His secretary had instructions not to disturb him unless it was about a state contract he was finalizing for the company.

He switched his mind to a different frequency.

The contract crowded out everything else.

The results of the new DNA test were the same as the initial ones. Kira could not be her mother's biological daughter. Couldn't be *any* relation.

She weighed her options now. The enormity of someone's error three decades ago was mind-numbing, and she had to act carefully. The news could kill her mother. She was that fragile.

There were no more straws left to grab. She had to find out what had happened thirty-two years ago. She had to discover the identity of her mother's genetic daughter. She had to convince that person to donate a kidney to Katy Douglas. And she had to do it within a few weeks.

The physician looked at her sympathetically, even more so than before. She knew he believed that her mother had lied to her, that she was adopted, but she knew otherwise. She'd already decided that her next step was to request her mother's medical records from the hospital. She had her mother's power of attorney, and that should give her access.

"I'll try to get your mother moved to the top of the list," Dr. Warner said. "A kidney might be available at any time."

She merely nodded. She knew the odds. So many different factors were involved: compatibility, location, need. Although her mother was critically ill, someone might be a little bit more ill.

"I'm sorry," he said. "I know how much you wanted to do this."

"Thank you," she said. All she wanted now was to leave.

She had much to do. And the first was a visit to the hospital records department.

4

Two precious days gone, and Kira had little to go on.

She was tempted to take time off, but she'd taken vacation when her mother had worsened four weeks ago, and she wanted to keep her remaining week for the transplant.

There *would* be a transplant. There had to be.

The how and why of two babies being switched thirty-two years ago didn't matter as much—at this time—as finding her mother's daughter. The need for a kidney superseded everything else. Maybe later she would think about a lawsuit to pay off her mother's growing medical bills.

She'd put together a list of babies born at the hospital on November 12, 1976. Births were a matter of public record, but it had still been difficult getting them. She had to go through several bureaucratic layers.

Twenty-one names. She didn't have the time to check them all out. Not with making her mother think everything was normal as well as tending to a job she loved, and badly needed.

Pain ripped through her, more agonizing than before. For the first time in her life, she wasn't certain who she was. Who was her natural mother? Her father? *Were they still alive?*

And her mother's blood daughter. Who was she? Where was she?

She'd been operating on robot mode, unable to think beyond the next step. Now she knew she needed help. She didn't have time to do her own investigating. Yet she didn't know where to turn.

There were friends at the paper, but then she would have to tell the entire story. She wasn't ready to do that.

No, she needed professional help. An investigator who could devote full time to finding . . . her mother's daughter.

Chris Burke!

The name kept intruding in her thoughts. She'd pushed it away, because she always hated to ask for help. One trait inherited from her mother.

Another shock ran through her. Not inherited. *Taught.* You take care of yourself. You don't ask for help. Her mother lived by that motto. She'd always refused to take government assistance or food stamps. Instead, she'd worked ten and twelve hours a day cleaning occupied houses and cleaning out unoccupied ones. She'd taken Kira with her to do the latter, carting a portable playpen with her.

She'd finally started her own small house-cleaning business, hiring four other people. But Katy Douglas—and Kira, too—often filled in when one of the cleaners had an emergency. Kira still did the bookkeeping and was trying to keep the business going during her mother's illness.

Chris Burke. Chris Burke. The name pounded at her. Maybe he was her only option.

Chris Burke was a former police lieutenant who quit his job when his wife was diagnosed with terminal cancer. The Burkes had been one of Katy Douglas's customers, and Kira's mother had often sat with Risa Burke when her husband had to be gone.

Both Katy and Kira had attended the funeral. Chris had told them that if he could ever reciprocate for her mother's kindness, he would. She also knew that after his wife's death, he'd opened a small investigative agency.

Katy Douglas's Clean Sweep still cleaned the house, although only once every two weeks.

Kira didn't think he knew of her mother's illness. Rene cleaned his house. Rene, one of their most dependable cleaners, lived near the Burke home and had taken over when Katy Douglas had slowed down.

Maybe he would help her on the cheap. Perhaps he would take five years of cleaning in payment.

She dug in her purse and found her cell. A call to information, then the number of the Burke Investigative Agency. She crossed her fingers and prayed.

Leigh sat across from her cousins, Seth Westerfield and David Crawford. The three of them had grown up together. They had bonded through their common war against Ed Westerfield.

Seth was a state senator running for Congress, and David was a pediatrician like his father. They tried to meet at least once a month. None of the three had siblings, and they had all had difficult childhoods, so they made one another their family.

Seth said it was because of the genes that so few Westerfields were born. David said it was bad luck. Whatever it was, it seemed reproduction was not a Westerfield quality.

David regarded her thoughtfully. "You look good."

"I feel good. I like riding. I enjoy working with the horse show. I've had some marketing ideas the committee actually liked."

"Good for you, Cous," Seth said. "Maybe I should have grabbed you first for my campaign."

A surge of enthusiasm ran through Leigh. She'd donated to Seth's campaign, but he'd said nothing about her doing more. She knew she was considered the family screwup. Her grandfather certainly had told her that in no uncertain terms.

"I can help with that, too," she said eagerly.

"Great. Come to the office tomorrow."

David leaned back in his chair. "What am I? Chopped liver?"

"You're too busy," Seth said with a grin. "But I'll take money from your doctor friends."

"Good luck with that," David replied. "But I'll host a small party at home. Em would love it."

"I'll help her," Leigh said. "Between the two of us, we can

pry some money away. Maybe Max will contribute more, but you know how hard it is to get ten cents from him."

Seth's grin tightened. "I doubt it."

"Well, you did better than I did. He won't buy the horse I want."

"You should consider suing him," Seth said. "It's your money."

"He'll give in. Eventually," she said.

"When do you want this little soiree?" David interrupted.

"As soon as possible. My opponent—the bastard—is self-financing his campaign."

"But you have the party behind you."

"Most of it. Others just see the money signs for other candidates."

"Hell, everyone knows you. Likes you."

Seth's grin returned. "You're right. We'll win. Money only takes you so far, and he really is a bastard."

"And we'll help," Leigh said. "One for all, and all for one."

With that, the three lifted their glasses and toasted the pact they'd made when they were teenagers.

Chris Burke opened the door of his home and gave Kira a grin. Archie, a mongrel dog of undeterminable origin, frantically waved his tail in welcome.

"Archie remembers you," he said. "Come in."

She followed him inside. She'd been in the house several times, including two visits when she took over a dish her mother had prepared for Risa. During Risa Burke's last month, she'd had little appetite. One of the very few things she could tolerate was Katy Douglas's macaroni and cheese.

Kira's gaze followed him as he led the way into his office just off the living room. He was solidly built without an ounce of fat and he moved with assurance. She sat in a chair facing the desk, and he sat on the corner of the desk. Archie plopped down next to his feet.

"Thanks for meeting me," she said.

"I have a cubbyhole in an office park," he said. "The tenants have a common secretary and share a boardroom. Good place to meet with prospective clients, but I do a lot of work here."

"Archie probably appreciates it."

"Yeah. He misses Risa. You said it was important," he said gruffly, obviously trying to hide his sudden emotion. "What can I do for you?"

"It's Mom. She's seriously ill."

His face expressed shock. "Katy?"

She nodded. "Kidney failure. Mom didn't want anyone to know. She swore her employees to secrecy. She said she feared losing business, but I think it was mostly to avoid sympathy. She never liked being the center of attention."

"What can I do?"

"Her only hope is a kidney transplant, but the list is unbelievably long. I wanted to give a kidney, but . . ." She stopped. Putting it all into words made it even more real. She realized that even now she didn't want to believe the fact she was *not* Kira Douglas.

"But?" he asked softly after a pause.

Kira had always liked him. Now she knew why. His face was creased with concern, his brown eyes warm and sympathetic. Maybe on the job, he was different. Maybe she just knew him through the prism of his wife's illness. He had been loving, and kind and caring to her.

"This is confidential, isn't it?" she asked. "Completely?"

"Unless you're about ready to commit a crime."

"My mother can't know what I'm about to tell you. Not yet. Not until I say."

He was silent for a moment. "Okay," he finally agreed.

"Another baby and I were switched at birth." She blurted out the words and realized she'd bottled them up inside. She'd been living with them nearly three days now, and not another soul knew. Not even the doctor who still believed that she'd been adopted.

His eyes didn't show anything. Not surprise. Not shock. "Why do you think that?" he asked.

"Three blood tests say I can't be her daughter."

"There's adoption."

"No," she said. "I would have known."

To his credit, he didn't look as if he doubted that statement. Instead, he waited. She wondered if that was how he interrogated suspects. Patient waiting.

She told the story in as few words as possible, how her mother had told her about her birth. The search for a surgeon. The miracle baby. "You know my mother," she said. "She doesn't have a deceitful bone in her body. If I had been adopted, she would have told me, just as she told me about my father. She's an optimist, but she never sugarcoats the truth."

"That means that if there was a switch, it must have happened immediately," he said. "A critically ill baby would be immediately known to all the pediatric staff," he said after a moment.

She nodded.

"Have you gone to the hospital authorities with this?"

"Not until I'm sure of my facts, and I definitely don't want it leaked to the news media. Mom watches the news programs."

"What do you want me to do?"

"Twenty-one babies were born that day. Thirteen were girls. I want you to find which one might be her daughter."

"Then what?"

"I'll find a way to confirm it."

"It would be simpler to go to the hospital."

"There's a giant liability here," she said. "The hospital management will stonewall at first. There will probably be denial, then a long-term investigation. Publicity will get out. Mom doesn't have that kind of time, nor can she stand the publicity. If I can find that person first and talk to her . . ."

She stopped, then took a photo from her purse. "I have a picture of my father. You know what my mother looks like. Maybe that will help."

"Have you considered the fact that this person, if she was switched, may not want to give a kidney? And that's only if we can find her."

We. She was halfway there. "I can be very convincing.

And we *have* to find her. If she was born at Memorial East, the chances are she's in this area."

"Do you have the list?" he said.

She handed it to him and watched as he scanned the printed names.

"There's something else," she said.

His gaze lifted from the paper.

"We don't . . . have much money now. I'm hoping we can offer you a year—two years—of free cleaning. Whatever would equal your time."

"Now that's just plain insulting," he said slowly.

Her heart lurched. She'd been so certain.

"After all your mother did for Risa, you think I would charge you?"

She shook her head. A Douglas didn't take charity. "No," she said. "You always paid Mom for her services. It's only right that we do the same."

"I didn't pay her for all the extra hours, all the meals she brought," he said, "but we can argue about that later." He paused. "Have you considered the possibility that her baby died? That you were adopted and . . ."

"And she lied to herself all these years? And to me?" she replied. "Of course, I considered it. I've considered everything in the past few days. But no, it's not possible. Not Mom."

Kira stood and paced the room. "I know how careful hospitals are with newborns. But I read an article a few years ago where two babies were accidently switched in California. No one discovered it until they were both young adults. It happens."

His gaze didn't leave her face. "I'll check these thirteen for you," he said. "But don't put too much hope there. It's been thirty-two years."

But she did have hope. It was all she had.

5

Leigh left the small grill. Seth and David always made her feel better. Even worthy of their friendship . . .

Damn you, girl, can't you do anything right? You'd fail basket weaving.

Her grandfather's voice was just as harsh in her head as it had been when he was alive.

I don't want to be a basket weaver.

Don't be smart with me.

She had stood silent, one of her rare bouts of defiance. He scared the hell out of her.

Not that he had been violent. But one look, one word could send grown men slinking away. She'd watched him do it . . .

Only Max stood his ground in her grandfather's presence.

She'd always respected Max for that, even as she resented him. He'd been like a big brother when she was a child, but now he was a yoke around her neck. She knew she'd made mistakes, especially with her marriage, and again—embarrassingly— with the last man she'd almost wed, but she'd sworn off men now and she wanted—needed—some acknowledgment that she could care for her own money.

The horse show association believed her competent enough to head their largest charity event of the year, and they seemed pleased with her ideas. At her suggestion, the club voted to support a horse camp for handicapped kids, a small triumph for her.

Enthusiasm bubbled up inside. She was going to show Max that she'd finally taken control of her life.

Chris Burke's awaited call came on the second morning at 11:00 a.m. "I've narrowed it down to two possibilities," he said. "I think we should meet."

Kira took a deep breath. She hadn't really thought he could move this quickly. Now she wasn't sure she was ready.

Don't turn coward now.

She looked up at the newsroom clock. "Deadline's at noon. Can we meet near here for lunch at twelve thirty?"

"You name it."

She searched her mind for a place few others in the newsroom frequented. She didn't want any questions. Not now. "There's a sub place two blocks away."

"Okay."

She gave him directions, then hung up and returned to her story. She stared at the computer. Her concentration was gone. So much depended on what Chris had discovered. Possibilities, she reminded herself. Possibilities only.

Thank God, the story wrote itself. A zoning matter that had a neighborhood in an uproar. It did have the hint of something deeper, though. The councilman representing the district had suddenly reversed himself in favor of a planned multiunit development. She made a note to look into it when she had the time.

That list was growing. She had little time for enterprise journalism these days.

She left the building at 12:15 p.m., her heart thumping harder with every footstep.

He was already there, anchoring a table in the crowded room. Two subs and two teas were already on the table. "I hope you don't mind me ordering for you," he said as he stood to meet her. "It was getting crowded and I was afraid we would be asked to leave without ordering."

"That's great. Thanks." She sat and looked at him expectantly. "You said there were two possibilities. Are you sure it's only two?"

"I'm not sure of anything," he said. "I said 'possibilities.' I'm pretty sure that it's not the other eleven, though. I eliminated some because of race or physical characteristics. Others because of time of birth. I don't think a switch could have happened even two or six hours after your birth. It had to be in the first few minutes after birth. Once the doctors determined the baby was critical, she would get immediate attention. Too many people would be involved after that."

"Who are they?"

"One's in North Carolina. She's married. Three kids."

"Her mother?"

"Her mother lives in Sarasota with her husband. There's three other children."

Sisters? Brothers? Her heart thumped even faster. She'd always wanted brothers and sisters.

She desperately wanted to know, but that question could come later. "And the other?" she asked.

"She lives in metro Atlanta. Fayette County. Married once. Divorced. I have to warn you. She looks a little like the mother who raised her. There's a lot of photos of both. They're prominent and wealthy."

"How wealthy?"

"Very," he said, watching her. "Her late grandfather was principal owner and president of a conglomerate."

"Damn," she said.

He raised one eyebrow. "Why damn?"

Her reaction was instinctive. She never really thought she was a reverse snob, but maybe she was. "If she's the one, then she has resources to fight any attempt to prove she's not who she's always believed she was."

The eyebrow went higher. "You would rather the family be poor?"

"I don't know," she said, suddenly ashamed. She was prejudging. "Where do we go now?"

"That's up to you," he said. "I could go to them and ask for a DNA sample."

"Then they might call an attorney who would then contact the hospital, and the media."

"True."

"I can try to get a DNA sample from the woman here," she said. "Then we could confirm that she's Mom's biological daughter and go from there."

He studied her intently. "How would you go about that?"

"Tell me more about her," she said, ignoring his question.

He handed her two sheets of paper. She scanned them.

The name "Westerfield" leapt up at her. She knew it well. Ed Westerfield had been a power in the metropolitan Atlanta business community, and a Westerfield was currently the favored candidate for Congress in his district.

She continued reading. Leigh Howard was Ed's only grandchild, her mother his only child. Leigh was a socialite who dabbled in several charities and was recently named chairman of a charity horse show.

Bells started ringing in her reporter's head. She was never unethical, at least she hoped to hell she wasn't, but a little deviousness was sometimes helpful, like reading a letter upside down in the mayor's office or pretending to know more than she did to get information. Reporter tricks.

"What are you thinking?" he asked. "Or maybe I shouldn't ask."

"Nothing to worry you," Kira said. She was in a hurry now. A plan was already forming in her mind.

His expression was dubious.

"Just find out everything you can about these two women," she said. "Particularly Leigh Howard. Is that her married name?"

"No. It's her maiden name. Her mother, Karen Westerfield, married Glenn Howard."

"Find out everything you can about her. Her grades, her likes, her activities. Her habits. Anything."

"I looked her up on Google," he said. "There's lots of stuff." He hesitated, then added, "She's had a lot of tragedy. Both her mother and father were killed in an accident when she was six. She was critically injured."

"Maybe that will make her sympathetic. She would be

gaining a mother," Kira said even as the impact of his words sank in and her heart dropped. If Leigh Howard was the right person, then her own biological parents were dead. She would never know them.

"If she's the right one," he warned. He changed the subject. "How's your mother?"

"Getting weaker every day." Just saying the words sent fresh jabs of fear—and anger—through her. How could her mom die when a kidney could save her?

"I'll stop by and say hello."

"You won't say anything about the blood tests?" she said, suddenly alarmed.

"No," he said, "but maybe she *should* know."

"What if this woman isn't her daughter? What if we never find her? It would be excruciating for her." She stared into his eyes. "You promised."

"So I did," he said. "And, of course, I'll do as you ask. But think about it."

She'd thought about nothing else for the past few days. If she were in her mother's position . . .

She rose. "I have to get back, but I can't thank you enough."

"I'll call if I discover anything else," he said. "I'm trying to find the physicians and nurses on duty that day. Unfortunately, personnel records are hell to get these days." He paused. "Try to find out from your mother the names of her doctors when you were born."

Kira nodded and slipped from the booth without eating. Her appetite was gone. Her mother had only a few weeks to live without a transplant.

Now she had something far more important to do than eat.

"Why in the hell do you want to do that?" her city editor asked. His brows furrowed as he studied Kira with suspicious eyes.

"A change might be nice," she said.

"You want off the city beat?"

"No," she said. "I worked for it too long, but I haven't done a feature in a long time, and a friend was telling me about this horse show. I just thought a little variety . . ."

"Now tell me the real reason," Wade Carlton said. "You fought tooth and nail to get the city hall beat."

"I know. And I want it. I'll do the other story in my spare time."

"In your spare time?"

She winced. He knew she had no spare time, that every minute spent away from the paper was spent with her mother. He'd repeatedly let her leave early or take a day off without penalty, and now he looked at her with questions in his eyes. Why would she spend some of that precious time on a frivolous feature about a debutante with too much time on her hands?

"Do you know anything about horses?" he asked patiently, still hunting for an answer,

"No, not much," she said honestly. Although she could justify withholding certain information, she wasn't going to lie. Not directly. Dammit, she wanted to tell him everything. He was her friend as well as her boss, but this could turn into front-page headlines throughout the country. She couldn't risk that yet.

"And you just picked her out of thin air in your sudden desire to write a fluff piece for the first time in five years?"

"Not very plausible, is it?" she said.

He just sat there and stared at her. "It's important to you, isn't it?"

"Yes."

"Is there more to this story than what you told me?"

"There could be."

"And you can't say more?"

"Not right now."

"I've always trusted my people," he said finally, making her feel as low as a pig's belly. "Take tomorrow and do the story. I don't think there will be a problem with the feature editor."

"I'll need a photographer."

"What time?" he asked.

"I'll have to let you know after I talk to her."

"Let me know by four so I can send down a photo assignment. Even then it's iffy. With the legislature in session, we have a shortage of photographers available for feature stories."

She nodded. "Understood. And thanks."

"Not necessary. You're a good reporter. I like your instincts."

She nodded and hurried to her desk. She had to set up an interview tomorrow. Usually organizations were more than eager for good publicity, and she planned to give it to Leigh Howard.

6

In fifteen minutes, Kira had her interview. She'd contacted the paper's sports department. The events reporter there had the telephone number of a publicity contact person for the horse show.

The word "feature" did wonders. The very enthusiastic contact person said she would call Ms. Howard immediately and set up an interview.

Ten minutes later, she had a call back. Leigh Howard would be happy to grant an interview about the show.

She could have gotten it easier herself. A phone book would have done quite nicely. But going through channels gave her a legitimacy that she needed.

She picked up the phone. Her hand shook slightly. This could be the most important call she'd ever made. What kind of person was Leigh Howard?

She punched in the number, and it was answered almost immediately. A soft, Southern-accented voice answered with a simple, "Hello."

"Ms. Howard?"

"Yes?"

"I'm Kira Douglas with the *Atlanta Observer*. We're interested in doing a feature on the upcoming horse show. I thought we would have more readership if we told the story through your eyes."

"Any publicity will be welcome," Leigh Howard replied. "We'll have some of the country's best riders here, and we have two great causes."

"Tomorrow? I realize it's short notice but the earlier we print a story, the more it should help you."

"Tomorrow will be fine," the woman said. *Not "the woman," not just any woman.* Possibly her mother's daughter.

"What about nine?" Kira tried to keep the anxiety from her voice.

"Ten would be better."

"Ten it is," Kira agreed. "At your home?"

"Sure."

"I'll have a photographer with me."

A hesitancy on the phone. "Is that necessary?"

"It'll certainly draw attention to the article."

"Okay," Ms. Howard said, but there was a noticeable reluctance in her voice.

Kira hung up. She stared at the phone for a moment. It was too easy. Nothing was ever that easy . . .

Then she picked it up again and punched in the photo department's extension. Dick Cooper, the assignment editor, answered. "Cooper."

"Hey, Coop. This is Kira. I need a photographer tomorrow morning at ten." She rattled off an address.

"What is it?"

"A feature. Woman and horse."

"Got an assignment order?"

"Of course," she answered. "It should be on its way down." She paused, then asked, "Is Dan available?"

"Why does everyone want Dan?" Coop grumbled. Silence for a moment, then, "Yeah, it looks like he's available, but if anything big comes up . . ."

"I know," Kira said. "Thanks."

After she hung up, she leaned back in her chair. She liked Dan. He was a great photographer and no prima donna. He would do what she asked, even if it sounded a bit odd.

Then she turned her attention back to her job. Calls to council members about the preliminary budget figures, whether they had questions about it. Perhaps she could stir a little controversy. Always made for a good story.

Within thirty minutes, she had one. With just a little prompting, two members declared undying opposition to the budget. Two others had stated their undying support. Great quotes from both sides. Ordinarily, she would be exuberant, but now . . .

She stayed during lunchtime, then spent the afternoon searching the paper's files for anything about Leigh Howard. She found several stories about the accident that killed Leigh's parents and critically injured Leigh.

If the Howards *were* her biological parents, they'd been dead these past twenty-six years ago. The thought was excruciating. Numbing.

Yet she felt a sharp pang of disloyalty to her own mother for even harboring such thoughts.

Long ago she'd barricaded her heart against her father, who had walked out on her when she was only a few weeks old. Her mother heard he'd died several years later. No matter how much her mother explained, Kira had never forgiven him. Now she felt as if she'd lost two more parents. Parents she'd never known.

She hadn't expected those feelings. Hadn't prepared herself for them. She should have. But events had moved so fast . . .

She swallowed the lump in her throat and continued reading. There was a story about Leigh's elopement, then divorce. Rumors in society sections about other men. There were multiple stories about Ed Westerfield and his empire, including a very long obituary when he'd died two years ago.

By the time she was through, it was four. The newsroom was emptying out.

She picked up her purse and a notebook. She would stop by the hospital, then resume her Internet search tonight.

Kira rode with the photographer. She wanted to talk to him prior to reaching the Westerfield estate.

"I want this to be really good," she said.

She saw him stiffen as if she'd impugned his ability. "You're always great," she said. "That's why I requested you. But I want a certain look here." She paused, then added, "It's for charity." That last statement made her wince. She did not admire mendacity. At the moment, though, mendacity seemed the only option.

You could try the direct approach.

But she couldn't. If Leigh Howard was *not* her mother's biological daughter, Kira could cause a great deal of unnecessary angst, and word might leak out. Her motives, she assured herself, were good.

The road to hell is paved with good intentions. She did not appreciate her conscience's reminder.

Still, she didn't feel good about what she was about to do.

"Just go along with what I ask," she pleaded.

"What's up, Kira?"

"I just want this to go well."

Another long look. She and Dan had been friends since her first week at the paper. One of her first assignments had been covering the paper-sponsored spelling bee. Dan Hayes was the photographer. They traveled together throughout the state, covering the district contests. He drove. She listened to all the paper's legends. On the two occasions they stayed overnight at a hotel, they drank together and exchanged life stories. He became a friend.

She might be testing that friendship today.

He didn't say anything else during the rest of the drive.

Her heart pounded harder as they approached the address. She'd pulled up directions on the Internet and had memorized every mile. The neighborhoods became less and less dense, and the land turned into estates, most with horses grazing within picture-perfect white fences.

Dan turned into a driveway and was barred by a gate controlled by a combination mechanism. Kira had been given the combination and Dan punched in the numbers. The gate opened.

The Westerfield house was striking. The architecture resembled Tara in *Gone with the Wind*. The movie, not the book. It was stately but not ostentatious. A smaller but architecturally similar building stood to its left. A third building, obviously a stable, was at the right of the big house.

A funny twinge ran through her. Had her biological mother lived here? Her grandfather?

So many emotions had battered her in the past week. Loyalty and curiosity. The desire to protect her mother and the desire to know who she really was. They conflicted at the moment, and she couldn't reconcile them.

But she had to. She had to be just another reporter to Leigh Howard.

Dan drove up the circular drive and stopped.

For a moment, Kira couldn't force herself to open the car door. So much depended on the next few moments. Dan, on the other hand, had opened the back door and was taking out his camera gear.

Coward.

She'd never been one before. She opened the door and stepped out just as the front door of the home opened, and an attractive woman walked out to greet them.

Too easy, she told herself again.

Kira had seen photos, but she was stunned by the real person. Leigh was attractive, with long blond hair held back by a yellow ribbon. She was small, her build more similar to Katy Douglas's frame than Kira's, and there was an elegance that Kira never had. And her eyes . . .

Kira blinked. Leigh's eyes were a striking sea blue. Like her mother's. If she'd had doubts before, they were rapidly falling away.

Leigh smiled and held out her hand as Kira approached, but there was an automatic quality about both gestures rather than real warmth.

"Hi," Kira said brightly. "I'm Kira Douglas, and this is Dan Hayes, my photographer. Thanks for seeing us on such short notice."

"Whatever helps the horse show," the woman replied, obviously not believing it necessary to introduce herself.

"Can we go somewhere for say, thirty minutes, for an interview while Dan checks out possible shots? Is it possible for him to go inside the barn?"

"Rick should be inside. He's a groom that comes over every morning," Leigh Howard replied. "He can show your photographer around. Tell him I said it was okay."

Dan nodded and headed toward the barn, his photographer's bag swinging at his side.

"I won't take long," she told Leigh.

Leigh nodded. "We'll go inside."

Kira followed her to the house, feeling gawky in her size 12 slacks as Leigh Howard floated ahead in white size 6 slacks and a soft yellow silk blouse.

Leigh obviously belonged here. Kira knew she never would.

Not that she wanted to. She wanted to be back in her own small but homey apartment. She wanted her life back to normal.

It would never be normal again. Never.

Her mouth went dry with the reminder of why she was here. Her fists clenched and unclenched as they entered a magnificent foyer. Curving mahogany stairs wrapped around it on both sides, and the floors were marble. The silk wallpaper looked hand painted.

As they turned into a sitting room, a woman dressed in a blue skirt and blouse met them.

"Ms. Douglas, this is Mrs. Baker, the housekeeper. Mrs. Baker, can you bring Ms. Douglas something to drink?" She looked expectantly at Kira. "What would you like?"

Kira hesitated, then said, "Black coffee, thanks. If you'll join me."

"Tea for me," Leigh said, and the woman left.

Kira looked around the room. Everything was perfect. Too perfect for her tastes. There was a photo portrait over the fireplace. She wandered over to it. A woman. A strikingly beautiful woman. *Karen Howard.* She was dressed in a shimmering green evening gown and stood confidently on the stairs.

Nothing about her looked familiar. A chill ran through

Kira. Shouldn't she feel something? A sense of familiarity? *If.* If, she reminded herself, she had the right family.

She heard the silence behind her and knew her behavior must seem odd. She was probably staring at the portrait with untoward interest. She turned around. "Your mother?"

"Yes," Leigh said.

"She's beautiful."

"She died in an accident," Leigh said shortly.

Don't blow it. Kira joined Leigh at a traditional sofa.

"What would you like to know about the show?" Leigh asked as they both sat.

"Your publicity person sent all the facts," Kira said. "Time. Place. Tickets. Entrance requirements. That would take about three paragraphs to write and get little attention. What I need is some human interest. I really like the idea of a horse camp for kids."

Leigh gave her a real smile for the first time. "Me, too. There's a camp not far from here that offers riding as one of its activities. I've been talking to them about reserving several weeks for kids with special needs. They'll need special instructors and more horses. Some modifications for the camp. Tuition for kids who can't afford it."

"Has the show always supported camp for special needs kids?"

She shook her head. "Last year it was breast cancer. A great cause, and we'll continue to send some money to them. But the camp—it's a natural match for this show." Animation was suddenly in her voice. "I checked out some in other states. They're really quite wonderful. They use old horses that might otherwise be put down. The kids love them. And riding gives them a control they don't otherwise have."

No more reticence now. Keep her talking.

"How long have you been involved with the horse show?" she started. It was one fact she really did *not* know.

"Just since last year," Leigh said.

"You must have impressed them."

Leigh shrugged. "Off the record?"

Kira nodded.

"It's the Westerfield name more than anything else. It magically attracts sponsors."

Kira was stunned by the answer. It wasn't only self-deprecating. There was a trace of wry acceptance in it as well.

"I don't really think we want to say that," she said gently.

Leigh shrugged. "It's true, but I'm going to make it into something more. I'm planning a silent auction of riding equipment. I'm trying to get donations of equipment—particularly saddles—used in films or by famous people. My name opens doors. We're going after new stuff as well."

The housekeeper returned with a tray. In seconds she'd served coffee and tea, along with a small platter of pastries. Kira refused the food. Her stomach was still queasy from worrying about the interview.

But she took a sip of coffee. She really needed to stretch this out. Long enough to ask to use the restroom. That was one plan. She had another one. A trickier one.

"That sounds like a terrific idea."

"We've been getting a good response."

Kira scribbled. She could—probably should—use a tape recorder, but she always preferred taking notes.

"How many horses do you have?"

"Just one at the moment. And a rescue donkey to keep her company."

"A rescue donkey?"

"Horses are social animals. They like company, and someone told me about this donkey . . ."

"I have friends who have rescue animals," Kira said. "They swear by them. One has a rescue parrot and another, Chris, has a dog named Archie. One of these days, I plan to adopt several. Right now, my schedule is a little too busy."

Leigh took a sip of tea.

"How long have you been riding?" Kira tried again. She wanted to keep Leigh talking and talking and talking. She wanted to know everything she could.

"Not long. My mother was a superb rider and had started to teach me when I was five. After she died, my grandfather got rid of the horses. I just started riding again two years ago."

After Ed Westerfield died.

Leigh looked at her watch, and Kira got the message. She'd stumbled on something painful.

More research needed.

But she needed something else now. She glanced down at the cup of tea on the table. Lipstick on the side of the fragile cup. God—or the devil—was with her.

"Ben will want some photos," she said. "I hope to have the front of the feature section, and that means color. Perhaps a riding outfit . . ."

Leigh Howard looked as if she was going to object, then nodded. "I'll be back in a moment."

Kira doubted it. She certainly hoped not.

She stood as Leigh left the room, then walked to the door where she watched Leigh climb the stairs.

She went back to the chair. The hardwood floor was covered by an obviously expensive rug. Probably a Persian. What she was about to do was a sacrilege. Her mother would horrified.

Don't think! Hurry.

She leaned over the table, her hand brushing the cup, tipping it on the face of the table. China shattered against glass. Tea spilled across the table onto the floor and onto her slacks. She scooped up a broken piece of china that had a trace of lipstick. She slipped it into an envelope in her purse. Then she took a handkerchief from her purse and gathered up the other pieces.

She glanced around. No one in sight. She hurried down the hall to where she hoped she would find the kitchen.

No housekeeper. No anyone. She put the pieces of the cup on the counter, then started swabbing at her slacks as anyone would do under the circumstances.

How much did the cup cost? She would replace it. She only hoped it wasn't part of a one-of-a-kind antique set.

She finished rinsing the spot on her slacks, turned.

And ran smack into a tall masculine figure. She looked up at his face and was stunned. Dear God, he was a fine-looking male specimen . . .

His arms went around her waist, balancing her. "And who in the hell are you?" he asked with a lazy drawl.

7

Kira was too startled to say anything. Even to breathe. How long had he been in the house, and had he seen her deliberately break a cup?

And why did he have to be so incredibly fine-looking?

She tried to move away, but bumped against the sink. His arms were still around her. Good thing. Her legs were suddenly rubbery.

She forced herself to meet the man's gaze. She felt like a thief, and that was exactly what she was. She had purposely broken an expensive piece of china and . . .

Dammit, she planned to steal even more while here. She just hoped guilt didn't radiate from her eyes.

"Well?" he asked.

"I'm Kira Douglas," she said, trying desperately to sound professional. "I'm here to do a story on Ms. Howard."

"A story?"

"I'm with the *Atlanta Observer.*"

His brows drew together and he frowned. She realized instantly his opinion of the press wasn't good.

"It's about the horse show," she said as if that explained everything.

He dropped his hands from her waist. He stepped back,

regarding her with sharp green eyes. "Kira Douglas? Don't you cover the city government?"

Her surprise must have been evident.

"I read the paper," he said wryly, "and the name is unique."

She shrugged. She hoped it looked careless. "I write other things, too. I was available."

His eyes didn't change expression, yet his silence spoke volumes. He didn't believe her.

Then his glance went to the broken china on the sink and to her stained slacks.

She told her legs to behave. She couldn't let him see her nervousness. Or guilt.

"I broke a teacup," she confessed. "And spilled tea on the carpet as well as myself. Clumsy of me, I know, but I can be a klutz at times. I came in, looking for the housekeeper," she continued, rattling on like an idiot.

A humiliating confession but better than the truthful alternative. He raised one of his dark eyebrows but said nothing.

A superb technique to get someone to say something she didn't intend to say. She'd used it herself. *Who was he?*

"Where's Leigh?" he asked after the pregnant silence.

"She's changing clothes for a photo," she replied, her voice a little unsteady.

He looked startled. "Leigh?"

"You sound surprised."

"She doesn't usually like the press."

"You don't, either," she said.

"Now why do you say that?" His green eyes were like a truth laser drilling through her.

"Something in your face when I mentioned it."

"I don't like or dislike," he said. "I'm just wary. So is Leigh. Usually."

The familiar use of Leigh's name sent a shock of reality through her. "She chairs a charity horse show. The position usually brings publicity."

"It brings money," he corrected wryly.

"You don't approve?"

"I neither approve nor disapprove. In any event, it's not my business."

"What *is* your business?" she asked. The question just popped out, but then her professional life evolved around questions. Still, she realized that this one was personal as well as professional.

"I'm an attorney," he said as a gleam appeared in his eyes. He seemed amused at the question.

She waited for him to continue. He appeared very much at home in Leigh Howard's kitchen.

"Mr. Payton?" came a voice from the door.

The housekeeper entered and didn't seem surprised to see either one of them in the kitchen.

"I was looking for Leigh," the attorney said. "And ran into this young lady, who has a confession to make."

The housekeeper looked directly at Kira.

Stunned, Kira wondered whether he'd been able to see within her head. Then she remembered her cover story. "I'm afraid I was very clumsy," she said. "I leaned over the table to get cream and knocked over the teacup. I'm afraid it broke. I came out here to tell you and ran into Mr. . . . . Payton."

His gaze met hers. "I didn't have a chance to introduce myself. I'm Max Payton. Ms. Howard's attorney."

That explained the familiarity. Maybe. Did most family attorneys make themselves at home in the kitchen?

He didn't look like a family attorney. Of course, she hadn't had much experience with family attorneys. But in the films they were always elderly and smoked a pipe. They certainly weren't eye candy and named Max.

The man standing next to her looked as if he ran five miles every morning and played racquetball every afternoon. Because he was in such good shape, she couldn't quite determine his age. His hair was dark and thick, styled short enough to keep what looked like unruly tendrils in check. Inexplicably, she wanted to reach out and run her fingers through it to see how it felt. A bubble of heat formed in the pit of her stomach.

She tried to tamp it down, but still she couldn't stop studying him. He wore a dark suit that was obviously tailored. His face was lean, all interesting angles, and his mouth had a twist on the left side as if he were laughing at the world.

And his eyes. God save her from green eyes that seemed to look through her. She was sure her lies were visible to him.

She turned back to Mrs. Baker. "I'll pay for a new cup, of course," she said.

"I don't think that will be necessary," Max Payton said in a slow drawl that made her wonder how natural it was. It didn't go with the sharp eyes, the edgy quality underneath a very definite charm. The latter had faded only briefly when she said she was a reporter.

He glanced at his watch. "I have to go. Mrs. Baker, tell Leigh I'm negotiating a lease for the horse she wants."

"Yes, sir."

He shook his head. "I just can't break you of that 'sir' thing, can I?" Then he turned back to Kira. "A pleasure, Ms. Douglas."

He strode to the door with the grace of a professional athlete. He was polished and well dressed and yet . . . there was something elemental about him that intrigued her. Intrigued, hell. Attracted. Like, big time.

Out of your league, kiddo. Her brain told her that, but she could dream.

Some other time. Why was she even wasting precious time on him?

She turned her attention to the housekeeper. "I picked up the pieces of the cup and placed them on the counter."

Mrs. Baker's neutral expression didn't break. "We have a lot of teacups," she said.

"There's also a spill on the carpet. I really am sorry."

And she was. Guilt was getting heavier inside her. She would rather someone shout at her. Swear, even.

Leigh chose that moment to walk in.

She was striking in tan riding pants, boots, and a vivid blue silk blouse. Her blond hair was now tied back with a matching blue ribbon. She was really quite beautiful. Kira felt a little like an ugly stepsister next to her. God, what was their relationship if Leigh *was* her mother's daughter?

"You look great," Kira said truthfully. She went through her explanation about the teacup.

"Doesn't matter," Leigh said. "We have a million around here."

Kira's conscience grew heavier. Why couldn't Leigh be a witch? But she didn't want that, either. Not for her mother.

"Let's go outside," Kira said. "Dan's probably picked his spots."

Leigh didn't say anything. She just led the way outside. Dan was sitting on a fence, his cameras hung around his neck. He stepped down when he saw them.

"Looking good," he said to Leigh. "Can you bring the horse out here where the light's good?"

"Rick's not inside?"

"Didn't see anyone. Just a horse and a donkey that tried to kick the shit out of me."

"She's protective of Lady," Leigh said. "I guess Rick's gone already. I told him I wouldn't be riding today."

She went inside and several moments later appeared at the door with a fine-looking white mare.

Dan snapped a number of photos. Kira went over to him. "What about suggesting that she take the ribbon off and let her hair fall around her face?"

"Good idea."

He went over to Leigh. She nodded after a few words.

"Here, let me," Kira said. She moved over to Leigh before she could protest and undid the bow in back, pulling a strand of hair as she did. She tried to make sure she had a root. "Sorry," she said as Leigh jerked. "Some hair was caught in the knot."

She backed away, clutching several strands of hair in her closed fist. She felt like a criminal.

Think about Mom. A kidney. Nothing else. Not the invasion of privacy she prized for herself.

As Dan posed Leigh next to the horse, Kira slipped the strands of hair into a second envelope, then into her purse. Two chances. Two possibilities. Chris would send the samples to a lab. An extra fee would speed the results.

"We're through," Dan said ten minutes later. "I have some great shots."

Kira went over to Leigh Howard. "Thanks for your time. If I have any more questions, I'll call."

Leigh merely nodded. Cooperative but not friendly. The family attorney had indicated Ms. Douglas didn't overly care for the press. Kira wondered why.

She left with Dan, her hand clutching the purse. She prayed she had what she needed.

And wondered whether she'd just taken a few steps toward ruining a life or, at least, changing it forever.

Late for a scheduled meeting, Max ran a few yellow lights. He'd meant to run in and tell Leigh he'd negotiated a lease for the jumper she wanted. Then he became intrigued with the reporter.

The reporter crowded out all other concerns. He'd made it his business to understand the media. It had been important to Ed Westerfield to have good press, and Max tried to be thorough in whatever he did. He'd cultivated the business reporters at the paper and had invited editors and executives to Westerfield parties.

He knew how they worked, and he knew that the state house and city hall reporters took pride in their specialties and seldom did features, particularly on a comparatively small horse show.

Kira Douglas had also been uncomfortable. Even jittery. He might have attributed the nervousness to the broken cup, yet her smoky blue eyes hadn't quite met his. Unusual for reporters who usually had few qualms about peeking into private lives.

So why was she there?

Something about Westerfield Industries? About Leigh? Maybe Seth?

He would bet his sports car that it wasn't a horse show.

He intended to discover her real purpose. He moved it to the top of his mental priority list.

8

Kira finished her story and looked at the newsroom clock. Nearly noon.

She left the newsroom and went to the feature department. Although the Sunday paper wouldn't be on the stands until late Saturday afternoon, the feature section was printed early. It was available today. Friday.

There was a pile of them on the editor's desk, and she grabbed one and took it back to her desk. The photo of Leigh with the horse took up a quarter of the page. Leigh was stunning as she looked directly at the camera. Photogenic didn't say half of it.

She resembled the early photos of Katy Douglas. The eyes were similar, and the full mouth. So was the build.

But where Leigh's movements were all grace, Kira's mother's had been all energy.

Stop it!

She was probably seeing things that weren't there, like someone looking at a newborn and claiming it looked just like the mom or dad. To her, babies were yet unformed. They didn't look like anyone, only their own small selves.

When would the test results come in? Chris had said it should be sometime today.

She had paid an exorbitant sum to have them expedited. A technician from a private lab Chris had recommended had taken a DNA sample from her mother under guise of just another test. The question was whether she—Kira—had obtained enough DNA from Leigh for a true test.

Her cell phone rang. She looked at the caller. Chris!

"You have a match," Chris said without preamble. "Leigh Howard is your mother's biological daughter."

Her breath caught in her throat. She couldn't breathe for a moment. She had thought Leigh Howard was probably her mother's daughter, but she hadn't *known*. Even though she'd wanted a match for her mother's sake, the truth was still like a kick in the ribs.

"Kira?"

"I'm here," she said with a tremor in her voice. "There's no mistake?"

"No." A pause. "What now?" he asked.

"I have to go to Leigh. It would probably be better if the feature had already been published, but every minute counts now."

"Isn't it time to contact the hospital?"

She *could* go to the hospital. But how long would it take for hospital officials to act? They would go to their attorneys first. An investigation. Meanwhile, her mother's chances dropped every day. A matter of weeks, according to the doctor. Maybe less. She felt the moments ticking away . . .

"Kira?" Chris's voice was full of concern. She'd told him about the visit, had given him her impression of Leigh Howard. Pleasant but with no real warmth. Plastic more than real. The only time she'd really come alive was when she talked about the horse camp for disabled kids. Maybe because of her own trauma years ago.

"I have to convince her to donate a kidney," she said. Her one hope for a fast resolution was to contact Leigh Howard and make a personal appeal.

She remembered the morning earlier in the week when she discovered she might not be who she thought she was. Incredulity. Disbelief. Devastation. A loneliness that couldn't be defined. A life that was a lie.

But she'd *had* her mother. She had memories. She had the comfort of love and support all these years. Leigh had lost hers when she was very young. Would she long for one now, or would anger and doubt keep her from acknowledging the truth?

"Are you still there?" Chris's voice was worried.

"I'm sorry. I was just thinking how I felt when the test results came in. In that moment, I felt as if I'd lost part of myself, that I was wandering on some strange planet."

"You couldn't lose part of yourself," he said. "Neither will Leigh Howard, not the important part. Not who she really is inside." He paused, then said, "You know this could mean something financially," he said. "I found a copy of the probated will of Ed Westerfield. He left the bulk of his estate in a trust for his granddaughter, Leigh Howard. It looks like *you* are Leigh Howard."

"He left it to the granddaughter he knew," she said, "and that's where it should stay."

"Even if she doesn't agree to a transplant?"

Kira didn't want to go there. She didn't really want to go anywhere with this. She didn't want to impact someone else's life like hers had been. It was an emotional train wreck. Only the necessity of a kidney transplant kept her from staying silent now and forever.

When she didn't answer, he continued, "Do you want me to go with you?"

Kira thought about that. He would give substance to her claim. And that was what it was now. A claim. No fact proved in court. If someone showed up on her doorstep with the story she meant to tell, she'd probably call the police. But then, this was something she should do alone. It was too personal to bring along a stranger.

"Thanks. I might ask you to call or see her later, but I think it might be better if I approached her alone."

"Okay. But call if you need me."

"I probably will," she said honestly. "I don't know what to say, or how to convince her of something that was impossible for me to believe."

"You'll find the words."

"I hope so."

I have to.

She hung up and sat for a moment, wondering whether she was wrong in refusing his help. And yet in her gut, she felt it was the right thing to do.

She used her cell phone. "Ms. Howard, please," she said when the housekeeper answered. Leigh Howard. *Her name.* Funny how that just sounded. Funny and tragic.

"Ms. Howard," she said when Leigh came on the line. Her voice shook slightly and her hand clasped the phone receiver. "This is Kira Douglas. I wonder if I can see you tomorrow. In the morning if possible."

"More for the story?"

She didn't want to lie any longer, not even for a good cause. "No. In fact it's ready. I'll bring you several copies, but there's something I need to talk to you about."

"You can't tell me now?"

"It will take a rather lengthy explanation. But it's quite important that I see you in person."

There was a pause, then, "I have a riding lesson in the morning, but eleven should be safe." Her voice was puzzled.

"I'll be there. Thanks." Kira hung up before Leigh asked more questions. Her hands trembled as she replaced the receiver in its cradle.

Max met with the president and CEO of Westerfield Indus-tries. He served as a corporate attorney and a member of the board. He also controlled—in the name of the Westerfield trust—51 percent of the shares of the privately held stock.

The CEO—Jack Melton—was not happy with the situation. If Max wanted to prevent one of Jack's proposed acquisitions, he could. And he'd stopped this one after running the numbers.

They had another fight today. "It's an obsolete business," Max said. "I checked out the financials. They just don't meet our standards."

"*Your* standards, you mean," Melton said. "I want to go in, buy bad companies cheap, and turn them around with good management."

"Some bad companies can't be turned around," Max said. Jack was competent in running the company as it existed now. He had a knack for finding good people, but he also overestimated his abilities to save companies that had outlived their usefulness. They had lost money on the last two acquisitions.

"You're tying my hands," Jack protested.

"I'm well aware of that, but Ed minimized risks. I intend to make sure the firm continues to do that."

"That's it?" Jack said.

"Bring me something more viable," Max said.

He saw the anger on Jack's face, but he was not going to let the man take risks with the Westerfield legacy. Time to go, before Jack's temper got the best of him.

Max returned to his office to find the report he'd ordered on the newspaper reporter. He'd wanted more depth than a Google search, and he'd ordered a quick investigation by Parker and Carroll, the investigative agency the company used to do background checks on high-level hires.

The report was twelve pages long. He skipped over basics, then hesitated when he saw that her mother was critically ill. Although her credit rating was good, her credit cards were currently maxed out. That was new. And she recently moved from a midtown apartment into her mother's modest home on the city's south side.

The report also noted that she'd been on the newspaper ten years and had won several awards for reporting. She was currently on the city hall beat and covered Atlanta legislation in the Georgia General Assembly. She was an Atlanta native, had graduated from Georgia State University, and had two speeding tickets.

It was the kind of report he liked to see on possible executives. Steady. Law-abiding. The maxed-out credit cards might be a warning sign, but the mother's illness might explain that.

He thought of that moment she'd turned into him, and his arms had steadied her. Blue gray eyes gazing up at him with momentary confusion, then a second of apprehension. She'd felt good.

Hell, he'd been way too long without a woman.

He punched some numbers on his office phone, reached the *Atlanta Observer*, and was passed through to Kira Douglas's phone.

She picked up on the second ring. "Kira Douglas."

"Ms. Douglas, this is Max Payton."

A short pause, then, "Mr. Payton, what can I do for you?"

"Go to dinner with me."

A longer silence, then, "Why?"

He was taken aback. It was his turn to pause. He'd never been asked that question before. The reason had always been clear.

"Because the idea appealed to me," he said.

To his surprise, she laughed, and he liked the sound. He was intrigued with the thought that he really would like to have dinner with her rather than merely tolerate an opportunity to inspect her.

"Thanks for the invitation," she said, "but my mother's ill and I don't have much time."

"I was going to suggest tonight," he ventured.

"I'm going to see my mom."

"What about afterward? You have to eat."

She hesitated just long enough to encourage him.

"We can go wherever is most convenient to you."

"I don't know how long I'll be at the hospital."

"I can wait."

"Why?" she asked again. "And why tonight?"

"I'm intrigued," he said. "I don't usually run into attractive reporters." God, he hoped that didn't sound too facile, too pushy. It had been a long time since he'd had to ask for a date twice. But then, this was no date. It was a fishing expedition. He wanted to know why she was interested in the Westerfields.

A silence told him he might have come on too strong. "Call it a sudden impulse," he added, "and I don't have many of those."

"I didn't think you would," she agreed. "I did a little research on you."

"Now it's my turn to ask why."

"A sudden impulse." She used his own words against him. "I don't usually run people down and end up in their arms."

"Should I be flattered?"

"No, research is what I do," she said, but he heard amusement in her voice.

"I didn't realize I was on your radar."

"You would be surprised how many people are on my radar," she replied.

"So it's nothing special?"

"Nope."

"So what about tonight?"

"Call me later." She gave him her home number but not the cell. Only the paper and the hospital had that.

"How did the story work out?" he asked.

"Good. It'll be in the Sunday paper."

"I'll be looking for it."

An awkward pause, and he was never awkward. What in the hell was happening?

"Good-bye," he said more brusquely than he intended, and hung up before he made more of a fool of himself.

He placed the phone back in its cradle and stared at it. He'd wanted information. That was all he wanted, but somewhere along the way seeing her again had become important.

Nonsense. It was nothing but those tingling instincts that had sensed something wrong with the interview. Nothing at all.

Kira stood.

What had she just done?

Even considering going to dinner with Max Payton was probably among the most foolish things she'd ever done. He would soon discover she had an interest in the Westerfields far deeper than a Sunday feature.

She should have said no, right off the bat.

Yet she justified her wavering. She could learn more about the Westerfields. Information was ammunition.

He's more than just a family attorney. He had been completely at home in the kitchen, as if he lived there. And he apparently did. His address was the same as the estate.

Family attorney, indeed.

She didn't know much more. She just had access to superficial stuff and hadn't had time to dig deeper. He apparently was single. He'd been featured in *Atlanta* magazine as one of the city's most eligible bachelors five years earlier. Of course, he could have married since. No ring, though. She'd noticed that.

One of Atlanta's most eligible bachelors. And he wanted to take her out. Yeah.

As much as she would like to think she was irresistible, she was a realist. She wasn't. For some reason, she'd sparked his curiosity.

She didn't usually have self-esteem issues. She was passable enough in a girl-next-door way, but she'd never attracted the football hero or basketball star or the most popular boy in the class. She'd always been more interested in books than most of the guys who asked her out. None had made her heart race, and none of her relationships had developed beyond the friendship stage. Sex, she had thought on her few attempts, was highly overrated.

Now someone *had* made her heart race, even if it had been for only a few moments, and he was the worst possible person for more reasons than she could count at the moment.

Maybe that racing was due to the circumstances, of nearly being caught red-handedly stealing DNA. And maybe she needed to know why he was curious.

Or so she told herself, even as she admitted the obvious. Max was one of the hottest-looking men she'd met. He certainly had the greenest eyes. Not to mention a definite presence. Meeting him, even for an early dinner, would be the same as walking through a land mine field. As the family attorney, it was his responsibility to represent Leigh Howard. He might even be in love with her. He would not take kindly to Kira withholding information that could rock the Westerfield empire.

She *could* tell him everything. But she owed it to Leigh to tell her first. She knew her own reaction to the news. Utter devastation. It was Leigh's right, just as it had been her own, to decide who should know. At least for the moment.

That was it, then. She would tell him she couldn't make it.

Didn't really matter, anyway. She was not his type, and he wasn't hers. And, she reminded herself again, she was, above all, a realist.

9

Kira drove home before going to the hospital. She was going to get comfortable for her hospital visit, and she changed into an old T-shirt and jeans.

The clothes fortified her decision to avoid attorney Maxwell Payton.

She ignored the ringing of her telephone. The coward's way out, and she hated to be a coward. Yet she wouldn't be tempted.

She picked up a book on the way out. If her mother was sleeping, she would read. If not, she could read to her. Her mother loved books but even holding a book seemed too much an effort for her now.

A smile spread across her mother's face when Kira entered, but she looked wan and tired. Dark circles shadowed her eyes, and she coughed, a bad sign. She'd been warned that pneumonia was a distinct possibility at this stage of kidney failure.

Kira swooped down to kiss her. "Hi, the doctor been in today?"

"Uh-huh. Said I was doing good."

Liar. Either her mother or the doctor. Her mother seemed to shrink in the bed day by day.

She sat in the only chair in the room. "Have you been watching television?"

"For a little while. It's . . . all so depressing these days." She looked at the book in Kira's hand. "Good?"

"Yep. I thought I would read to you for a little while if you're up to it."

"You and your Linus-like need for books," her mother said with a smile that was only a shadow of the familiar one. "Your security has always been books. Never . . . happy unless you had a pile nearby."

"I'm still not."

Kira read aloud until her mother's eyes closed. She put the book down, then closed her own eyes. She'd had little or no sleep during the past week, particularly since she received the result from the final DNA test. So many decisions to be made, none of them good.

She woke to a knock on the door.

The nurse had already been in. She turned around, blinked a couple of times, and focused on a tall man in the doorway.

Max Payton was even more attractive than she remembered.

"Hi," he said quietly as his gaze went to the woman in the bed.

She stood, totally befuddled. She hadn't bothered with more than a brush through her hair. No lipstick. No makeup. Old Atlanta Braves T-shirt and older jeans.

He, on the other hand, was dressed in a dark gray tailored business suit. He looked handsome and distinguished and certainly out of place in acute care, where most visitors looked as tired and as comfortably dressed as she. He looked freshly shaved and even his shoes were polished to a high shine. Yet there was a cynicism in his eyes he couldn't quite hide.

He was, in one word, formidable.

She looked back at her mother. Asleep.

Kira walked to the door. He stood aside. She walked out and he followed.

Then she turned on him. "What are you doing here?"

"I couldn't reach you about that dinner tonight."

She tried to remember what she had told him about her mother. Had she mentioned the hospital? Or which one? She didn't think so. "How did you know where to find me?"

His green eyes looked amused. "I'm good at finding things."

"I'm not a thing."

His eyes roamed over her and inwardly she winced. Why didn't she use even a touch of lipstick before coming here?

"I believe that when a gentleman tells a lady he is going to call her about dinner, he should manage to do that."

That stopped her. She had a retort but decided against it. For one of the few times in her life she was tongue-tied.

"How's your mother?" he asked, the amusement fading from his voice.

"About the same. She needs a kidney."

"I'm sorry."

He sounded as if he really was. It was disarming. She didn't want to be disarmed. She couldn't afford to be disarmed. Not for her sake. Not for her mother's sake.

He looked back at the door. "Can you get away for a bite?"

She should say no. She'd tried to avoid exactly this.

"Someplace nearby," he coaxed. "I looked up restaurants in the area. There's a small Italian place a few blocks away."

He'd done his homework. He probably always did his homework, even for something as simple as a quick meal. How much research had he done on her?

And the question was why? Her reporter's instinctive bells started ringing. She was torn between running like hell from someone she sensed was dangerous to her aims, and assuaging her curiosity about the Westerfield family. And, she had to admit, one Maxwell Payton.

Her stomach rumbled. She'd had an English muffin and juice for breakfast. Nothing for lunch.

"Lucchesi's?" she asked, going back to that "Italian restaurant" he'd mentioned.

He looked a little surprised, and that pleased her. She suspected he wasn't often surprised.

"Yes," he said. "You know it?"

"Pretty well," she replied. Lucchesi's was small, good, and inexpensive. Best of all, they treated her as family when she needed that and didn't seem to object when she read a book or newspaper while eating after visiting her mother.

"Is it as good as the comments say it is?"

"Probably better." She eyed his suit. "It's not very formal."

He gave her a crooked smile that made her legs rubbery. "You think they'll let me in with a suit?"

"Lucchesi might make an exception," she replied. He'd succeeded in making her feel completely at ease in her T-shirt and jeans. Not only that, he'd somehow maneuvered her into agreeing to go.

Then she looked at herself through his eyes and wanted to go, "Yeck."

Lucchesi wouldn't mind. But she did.

She was going to drop a bomb on the Westerfield family Saturday, and she hated looking like the little match girl today. Why had she purposely dressed down? Because she suspected this would happen?

For whatever reason, she was at her worst, and he looked as if he'd just stepped off the pages of *Gentlemen's Quarterly*.

Suddenly he smoothed back a wayward curl from her face. Her skin burned from his touch and she stepped back.

Dammit. She wanted to go with him, and not just because she wanted to learn more about the Westerfields. She needed to relax, but then she knew she couldn't relax with him. Despite his current easy manner, she suspected it was a facade hiding a ruthless interior.

But before those deep green eyes, she was helpless. "Give me a minute," she said.

"I'll give you as long as you need."

She slipped in the nearest restroom. Cold water on her face. A dab of lipstick. A quick comb of her hair. She refused to do anything else.

He was *not* a date. She wanted to know more about the Westerfields, and she suspected he wanted to know more about her interest in them. Who, she wondered, was going to get the best of the bargain?

* * *

Max was used to sleek, well-coiffed women who frequented the circles in which he moved. He'd liked several, but not enough to take the relationship to marriage. He was a workaholic, had always been a workaholic—even as a kid—and he knew that trait did not enhance a marriage. Neither did the rest of his background.

So he didn't understand now why he was disconcerted by a newspaper reporter with straight dark hair and bangs and gray blue eyes. True, the hair was more mahogany than brown, and the shade of her eyes was appealing, but she was curvy rather than sleek and her movements more impatient than graceful.

When he'd opened the door to the hospital room after being frustrated for a good part of the day, she'd rubbed her eyes. He realized he'd awakened her from a nap, and she looked tousled and sleepy, just like a woman leaving bed. Then his eyes turned to the older woman on the hospital bed. Her eyes were closed, but her pallor had a waxy look. A number of IV tubes ran in and out of veins. She hardly made a dent in the bed.

He'd learned from the private investigator that her mother was awaiting a kidney transplant. Medical records were supposedly protected but a good investigator had ways. He knew some of them himself. He'd never balked at breaking rules.

He turned his attention back to Kira Douglas. He'd rarely been turned down by a woman, and he wondered if that wasn't part of the attraction. Then he reminded himself it wasn't the woman he was interested in, but information.

When she went in the restroom, he'd prepared himself for a wait, but she apparently meant a moment when she said a moment. She was back out nearly as soon as she went in. A touch of lipstick. A quick comb. A curl around her face was damp. She'd obviously splashed water on it.

Vitality was back in her steps.

"I'll meet you at the restaurant," she said.

He realized she wanted to keep her distance. Or felt she might want to make a quick getaway from the restaurant.

"All right," he agreed, afraid she might sprint away if he didn't. "Do we need reservations?"

"Not at this time."

"Can I order you something if I get there first?"

"A glass of the house Chianti."

They walked together to the hospital entrance. She stopped to get a paper in the newsstand, and he went ahead. He didn't want to appear to be stalking her. She clearly wanted space. From him.

He'd discovered the restaurant online. He'd conducted a quick search of restaurants in the area of the hospital and settled on Lucchesi's as a possibility. He was good at reading people and suspected that after an evening in a hospital room, she would prefer something informal.

Besides, he liked Italian food. And he particularly liked small, family-owned Italian restaurants. There had been one near an early foster home. The proprietor saw him looking in one winter day when he hadn't wanted to go back to a crowded home and a tyrannical foster father who used a belt when displeased. The owner invited him in, fed him a plate of the best spaghetti he'd ever had, and let him pay for it by sweeping the place. That lasted three months until he was kicked out of that home.

Max discarded the memory and drove to the restaurant. After finding a parking space, he took off his suit jacket and pulled off his tie. He locked the car and went inside. He gave his name, said he was waiting for a lady, and was seated at a small corner table. He glanced around the room. One wall featured an Italian villa overlooking the sea. The others were painted a sea green. Pavarotti's tenor wafted through the room.

Max ordered two glasses of Chianti. He wasn't entirely sure Kira would appear, but if she did, he didn't want her to think he'd doubted it.

A few minutes later, she walked in. He watched the proprietor greet her as if she were an old friend. She saw him then and headed toward the table.

He stood. "Thanks for coming," he said when she reached him.

Lucchesi pulled out a chair for her.

"After you went to so much trouble to find me, I couldn't refuse," she said, but her eyes were wary. "I'm just not sure why you made the effort."

He gave her a disarming grin that usually served him well. "I'm not so sure, either. I usually avoid the press."

"Why? We're the good guys."

His brows lifted slightly.

"We inform people. We reveal corruption. We support good causes, such as Leigh's charity horse show." She tried to make her tone light but feared she sounded pompous. Yet she tired of the constant criticism of newspapers and reporters these days.

The glasses of Chianti arrived, so he was saved from answering. He took a sip, found it excellent, then picked up the menu.

"Everything's good, but I always get the spaghetti with sausage," she said. "Great comfort food."

He laid down the menu. "Tell me about your mother."

"Not that much to tell. She raised me alone. Built a small cleaning business through sheer hard work. Helps everyone. She's one of the good souls on this earth."

"How sick is she?"

Something flickered in her eyes and her fingers clutched the wineglass. "As sick as you can get. If she doesn't get a kidney in the next month, she'll die."

"And the list is long," he said.

"Endless. I wish more people were aware of the need and signed up as donors." She took a sip of the wine. "Now turnaround is fair play. How long have you been a family attorney?"

Damn, but her eyes were appealing. He'd never seen that smoky blue before, and he would have thought the color bland until he saw hers. They roiled with emotion. He suspected they could also be filled with laughter. They had darkened, though, when she spoke of her mother.

An odd empathy struck him. Surprised him. He thought he'd buried emotions long ago. Certainly controlled them.

Silence fell between them as he contemplated an answer,

and her gaze bored into him, interrogating him as deeply as he probed an adversary in a courtroom. There was something else there, too. An awareness. The kind of awareness that flared between man and woman. The elemental kind that shook him to the core.

"Maybe family attorney isn't quite accurate," he admitted. "I'm a corporate attorney for Westerfield Industries, but I do look after the family as part of that."

"The family being Leigh."

"Yes, I look after Leigh." He paused. "But I think you know that."

"Not exactly. I did know you were the corporate attorney for Westerfield Industries. And the most eligible bachelor in Atlanta," she added with the first hint of a smile he'd observed.

"God, you would have to find that."

"The Internet is a wondrous thing. Especially for a reporter."

"Why your interest in the Westerfield family?" he asked suddenly, ignoring her observation about that damned eligible bachelor nonsense. He wanted to break the sexual intensity growing between them. He knew from her flushed cheeks that she felt it as well.

Her hesitation told him he was right to believe she had more than a passing interest in the family he represented.

She finally shrugged. "I often get interested in different aspects of stories I write. One thing leads to another. The reporter's curiosity."

Not entirely true. She was a good liar but not good enough. He had faced too many of them not to recognize the flicker in her eyes. What else could there be? He decided to change the subject. For the moment. He would find a way back to it.

"How long have you been with the *Observer*?" He knew the answer but wanted to hear from her. He liked hearing her voice. It was soft, even when probing, with just a hint of a Southern accent. Melodious.

He liked the softness mixed with determination. And strength. He didn't doubt the latter at all.

"Ten years," she said. "Eleven if you count the summer I

interned before graduation. It earned me a ticket back when I graduated, even if it was the obituary desk."

"And college?"

She gave him that searching look again. "I suspect you know all this."

The direct confrontation surprised him. "Yes," he said, and couldn't help giving her a rueful grin. "But not the whys and hows . . ."

Pavarotti's voice suddenly went from soft to booming with "Nessun Dorma," and severed his words. As the song finished, the owner—Lucchesi—came over to them. *"Perdono,"* he said, "but this was my favorite song."

Lucchesi left and soon returned, carrying a carafe. He lit the candle on the table, then refilled their wineglasses. "On the house," he said. "The signorina is a special patron."

"Because I shamelessly love your food," she said with a smile he'd been waiting to see. "And eat too much of it."

Lucchesi beamed. "I keep telling my daughter to watch you, see how much you like to read. I tell her she'll be a reporter like you if she does."

"Or a rocket scientist," Kira said.

"Or an attorney," Max inserted.

She groaned, and he realized she held attorneys in about the same esteem as he held reporters.

Lucchesi bestowed an approving look on both of them and retreated.

Max raised an eyebrow. *"Perdono?"*

"I don't think he's ever been to Italy," she said with a conspiratorial grin. "He was born in Brooklyn. But he enjoys the words."

"How long have you been coming here?"

"Since my mother got sick. Even before going into the hospital, she came to a clinic around the corner for dialysis. I would usually grab something to eat. And they have takeout. Spaghetti was one of the few foods that sparked her appetite."

He grinned. "I pick good, don't I?"

"You pick very good."

When Lucchesi returned for their order, Max followed her lead in ordering spaghetti. Then he sat back and looked at her.

The light had dimmed where they sat, and the candle cast a red glow through her hair. She looked tired, but more relaxed than before.

So, surprisingly, was he.

The Chianti was working. Or was it Kira Douglas and her smile?

The Chianti was working . . .

The air was getting warmer. She didn't think it was on her part only. He leaned closer. His hand brushed hers, and a lightning bolt of heat rippled through her.

She took a sip of rapidly disappearing wine. Now the refill was half gone.

Emotions ran through her. Anxiety. Indecision. Guilt.

Maybe a combination of them all.

Max Payton was just too damned attractive. And disarming. Who would have thought a corporate attorney would have dimples when he smiled? Or appear delighted with spaghetti and Chianti?

A warm glow started to puddle deep inside her, and the heat was spreading through her limbs. To her horror, she *liked* him. That was truly a god-awful thing. She had hoped to dislike him. She'd hoped he was supercilious and arrogant, or were the two the same? Her mind was getting fuzzy. Probably because she hadn't eaten much, and the wine was going to her head with the speed of a runaway train.

She would swear that the electricity she felt was being experienced by him as well. His green eyes deepened. He leaned forward and the dimples were more evident.

Behave yourself! Remember what happens tomorrow. He might well be going after her with a sledgehammer.

Or he might be an ally.

She longed to tell him about her interest in Leigh Howard. He would probably find out tomorrow and believe her a liar and a fraud.

She'd been both these past few days.

So she took another sip of wine and nibbled on the toasted garlic bread the waitress brought. Time to concentrate on food rather than wine. Then she made the mistake of looking back up at her companion.

He was watching with an enigmatic smile and guarded eyes. She wondered if they were always guarded. She wanted to know more about him. Too much more.

"How did you happen to go with Westerfield Industries?" she asked.

"I worked for them when I was in school," he replied lightly. "I guess it became a habit."

Before she could ask anything else, the food came. She was a good enough journalist, though, to realize she'd heard only a crumb of the story. What was his relationship with Leigh? With the family? What had it been with Ed Westerfield? And who and what among them would he protect? Where did his interest really lie?

She started to eat, but her appetite was gone. Deep inside, she felt the two of them were on a collision course.

She looked up at him. He was watching her, and the amusement was gone. Their gazes caught, held. She felt as if he were looking straight into her soul. Worse, she suspected he was very good at looking into souls.

She quickly looked down again. She was withholding something from him that could hurt someone he was sworn to protect. Someone who, if Leigh Howard decided not to help her, could be on the other side of a courtroom from her.

Be careful, she warned herself.

She broke away from his gaze and stirred her spaghetti. Comfort food indeed. Now she felt she was staring at a dish full of snakes. She hated deceit and now she was drowning in it.

"Kira?" His deep voice seemed to caress her name. Her name had never quite sounded like that before. "Where did the name come from?"

"Mom said it's Latin for light," she said. "She found it in a baby book."

"I like it."

"I've gone through several stages with it," she said. "When I was young, I wanted to be a Susan or Mary. I always had to explain Kira."

"And now?"

"I like it, too." And she did. Even if it no longer belonged to her. The mental reminder brought her back to the moment. To the desperate need that she had forgotten for a few seconds.

She looked up at him and saw bemusement in his face. "I keep thinking I'm missing something," he said, his eyes questioning her. "You wander away from me."

"I'm just worried about Mom," she said.

"What do the doctors say?"

"They've moved her up on the list," she said, "but the chances aren't good."

"There's no one in the family who can donate?"

She felt herself stiffening. Did he know? How could he?

She shook her head. "I was tested. My kidney's not compatible."

"No other children?"

She didn't know how to answer it. She didn't want to lie.

"I don't have any brothers or sisters," she finally said, looking back at him.

She was nearly undone by the look in his eyes. For the fleetest of seconds she saw empathy there, even a flicker of pain. Then it was gone, and she wondered whether she'd imagined it.

"It must be rough," he said.

"Frustrating. Sad. To know there are people who can save her and don't."

She realized then how artfully he'd drawn her out. She suspected he was a very good attorney. Ruthless, Chris had said. She had to remember that.

But now she sensed something else. There was a quality about him that gave her pause. She'd noticed it earlier but she hadn't identified it until now. A sense of aloneness. Not loneliness. He was too self-contained for that. Instead there was something distant, a part of him standing back and watching. Never quite participating.

She took a sip of wine and tried to smother the warmth flooding her. He was a walking disaster for her. Everything she knew she should avoid. He was a forty-two-year-old bachelor who, by most accounts, was considered ruthless in business affairs and might well become an adversary.

But as she looked again, the dimples softened the harsh lines of his face and the green of his eyes deepened. Her thoughts were becoming muddled.

She'd never been this affected before. In fact, she'd always been wary of quick entanglements. Long ones, too. She'd always been aware her mother and father had met at a concert. He'd been a musician and she a groupie. They'd married five days after meeting.

He'd left when she was born. So much for one enchanted evening. Or five of them.

Sudden lust had repercussions. She put her fork on the plate. "I'm really tired," she said, hearing the tremor in her voice. She hoped he thought it was exhaustion, rather than a rampaging feminine reaction.

He didn't protest but signaled the waiter. Instead, Mr. Lucchesi appeared, his expression worried. "The food is not good?"

"It's perfect as always," she said. "I've just had a really hard day."

"Your mama?"

"She's hanging in there, but . . ."

"You come in here next time before you visit. I give you a dessert that will make her better."

"Thank you. I'll do that."

He handed the bill to her companion. He didn't pay with a credit card, but with bills. "It was very good," he told Mr. Lucchesi, and he went up another notch in her estimation, especially when Mr. Lucchesi beamed.

She led the way out. He touched the small of her back as they went outside, and she felt electricity flow from his hand through her body. The warmth turned to fire as they reached her car, and he touched her cheek. "Thanks for coming tonight," he said softly. "I enjoyed it."

The air sparked and sizzled between them like an exposed live wire. She was stunned by the heat, by the sudden need, by a craving she'd never felt before.

Then he backed away as if burned. She blindly reached in her purse for her keys. He took them from her and opened the door, holding it as she stepped in.

He closed it without another word. She glanced at him, and he looked as stunned as she felt.

She forced herself to put the key in the ignition. Her heart pounded, and her body . . . Lord, her body was a mass of sensations.

Go. Go before you do something really dumb.

10

Her heart pounding against her chest, Kira stood at Leigh's door and knocked.

It was exactly 11:00 a.m. Not a moment earlier. Not a second later. She'd used the combination to the gate Leigh had given her earlier.

She mentally ran over the words she'd so carefully planned. She'd lain awake all night, thinking about how she could explain the inexplicable. Her mind vacillated between how she would persuade Leigh to give a kidney to a stranger and the image of Max Payton's face. She knew which was by far the most important, but the latter kept intruding . . .

She wished now she hadn't refused Chris's offer. She'd never felt so alone. Not only was she going to drop a bombshell, but she would have to admit her own somewhat dubious behavior and, at the same time, beg a near stranger to donate a kidney.

Faced with the same message from a stranger, she would throw her out of the house. Or call the cops. Or Max Payton. Was he still on the premises? God, she hoped not.

The door opened and she came face-to-face with Leigh Howard.

Leigh's hair was pulled back in a long braid, and she again

wore slacks and a long-sleeved shirt. Apparently no shorts and tees for her. Did she ever not look elegant? She belonged in this house, in this setting.

Leigh had curiosity written all over her face as she led her into the same room where Kira had interviewed her just days earlier, to the same sofa. They both sat.

"Coffee?" Leigh asked. "Mrs. Baker's off today, but I made some."

Kira shook her head. "Thanks, but I'm fine." Another lie. She wasn't fine at all. *Be strong. Be strong for Mom.*

Leigh apparently read her tone and face. "What is it?" she said.

"I have some information . . . It's . . . devastating in some ways but maybe not in others."

Kira had rehearsed the words over and over again last night and this morning. Now they were all jumbled up.

A look of alarm came over Leigh's face. "Max? Seth?"

"No," she said quickly as she noted Leigh's easy familiarity with Max's name. Not like an attorney. More intimate. How intimate? It had been the first name that apparently entered Leigh's mind.

Leigh waited for her to continue.

"You're not going to believe what I'm going to tell you. I don't expect you to. I just want you to listen, think about it, check it out."

Leigh stood. "I think you had better say what you came to say."

Kira stood as well, decided to plunge in. There was, after all, no easy way to tell the story. She remembered her anger and disbelief when the possibility arose. "I think you and I were switched at birth."

Leigh's jaw fell. "You what?"

"I think my mother is your mother." What a ridiculous way to describe it. She was a wordsmith. She should be able to do better. But there were no reasonable words for a bizarre situation.

"You're insane."

Kira expected disbelief. Rage even. She realized she shouldn't have tried this herself. A hospital spokesman. An attorney. Any would be preferable, but that might take too long. And she didn't have time.

She hurried on. "My mother needs a kidney to live. I volunteered to donate a kidney, but the blood tests said we weren't related. I have the test results with me. I also have copies of birth certificates of baby girls born at the same time. You were born in the same hospital within a few moments of my birth."

Leigh stared at her. "That doesn't mean anything."

"It does because I had a hole in my heart. I would have been taken immediately to pediatric critical care. Any switch would have had to be made within a few minutes of the birth."

"Why would anyone . . . ?"

"It could have been an accident. Two babies born at the same time . . ."

"No! What kind of scam are you pulling?"

"I don't want anything other than for my mother to live. If she doesn't receive a kidney in the next few weeks, she'll die. I can't give one. My tissue doesn't match. Yours might."

"I don't believe any of this," Leigh said, then paused. "Is that why you wanted to do the story?" She turned on Kira in a fury. "Get out," she said.

"That was my reaction when I first heard," Kira said, ignoring the demand. "Anger . . . no, rage. And disbelief. I had three tests before I accepted it." Pure desperation made her go on. "My only interest is to ask you to consider an independent DNA test to prove or disprove the possibility and, if it shows you are a match with my mother, to think—just think—about donating a kidney."

The words came out in a flood. She was losing Leigh. She was doing this all wrong, But there wasn't a right way. How do you tell someone her life has been a lie?

"I had a mother and father," Leigh said through tightly clenched teeth. "I saw them both die. Get out."

Kira stood. "Just consider what I've said. I truly don't want anything of yours. I just want you to meet Mom. Think about taking a DNA test. If it proves you are mother and daughter, you gain a mother. You can give her the gift of life."

"Why did you do the newspaper article?" Leigh asked suddenly. "Is there even a story?"

"It's running tomorrow on the front of the feature section."

"But you didn't come here because of the horse show?"

"No." Kira wasn't going to lie any longer. Not overtly. "I wanted to meet you, and then it turned into a damn good story."

"You lied."

"Yes."

"And this is all supposition on your part? Because we were born a few moments apart?"

Kira paused. Weighed her options. She *had* to get Leigh to listen. She hadn't wanted to use the DNA. It had been an invasion of Leigh Howard's privacy. It might even have been illegal. But there was no time for niceties. If she was fired from a job, so be it. "There's something else," she finally said. "I took a piece of the cup you used. I had it tested. Your DNA matches my mother's. Katy Douglas's DNA."

Kira took Chris's card from her pocket and pressed it into Leigh's hand. "Chris Burke has been investigating this for me. He's a former detective with the police department. Have Mr. Payton check him out. He can confirm everything I said." She swallowed hard. "This isn't easy for me, either. I had your same reaction last week. I didn't believe it. I couldn't believe it. But I had to. I had to accept I couldn't help my mother."

Leigh simply stared at her, unblinking. Like a deer in headlights. "I went through the same shock," Kira said, her fingers knotting into a fist. "I'll sign a paper to say I won't claim any part of the Westerfield estate. My one and only concern is my mom. Think about it," she pleaded. "Just think about it."

Leigh's face paled. Her lips had thinned and yet she was quite beautiful. She went over to the phone. "Please leave," she said coldly. "You're trespassing. If you don't go, I'll call the police."

Kira started for the door. She turned. "I'm sorry. I'm really, really sorry. I don't think I would ever have told you if my mother wasn't so ill. She only has weeks to live without a new kidney." Her voice broke and she fought to hold back tears. "But you have a right to know you still have a living parent."

"And I have money," Leigh said coldly.

"I don't care about that."

"Everyone does," Leigh retorted with bitterness. She opened the door and held it open. "I'm asking my attorney to get a restraining order. I think we will also be calling your newspaper."

The door closed behind her. More like a slam.

Tears gathered behind Kira's eyes. Could she have handled it worse? Had she just destroyed her mother's last chance?

Leigh leaned against the door. There was no strength left in her.

Lies. They had to be lies.

Someone else who wanted part of the Westerfield legacy. Just like her former husband. Like her former fiancé.

Her mother and father were dead. She'd watched them die as she'd struggled to live.

She closed her eyes, and the scene came back. The nightmare that wouldn't go away. Driving home from an afternoon campaign affair held by Seth's father. There had been liquor, and her father drank a lot of it. An argument. Then the screams, the crash of metal, then moans that faded away. Her own pain. And the guilt. The terrible guilt that somehow she had been responsible . . .

The reporter's words brought it all back again. Damn her.

Hot. She was hot. She touched her face and it was burning. Max! Max would know what to do.

He would expose Kira Douglas as a liar and cheat.

She opened her hand and let the card Kira had pressed into her fingers fall onto the floor.

11

Max leaned back in his chair and put the contract he'd just reviewed on the table.

Jack Melton would be pleased. Max had few questions about the contract the CEO had negotiated with a company in Japan for Westerfield lumber. It appeared to be a damn good price.

His attention, though, was wandering. That was unique enough to be worrisome. A pretty reporter with a challenging smile kept popping into his mind.

His personal cell phone rang, and he answered. Only a few people had the number.

"Max, this is Leigh. I need to talk to you. As soon as possible."

"Go ahead," he said.

"In person. I have to talk to you in person."

Her voice trembled in a way he hadn't heard in a long time. "Can it wait until tonight?"

"No."

He heard panic in her voice. He glanced at his watch. "I have two hours before a meeting here at the office. Why don't you meet me in thirty minutes for lunch?"

"Thanks. Where?"

"Come to the office, and we'll walk over to the Grill."

"I'll be there." She hung up.

He replaced the cell on his belt. Her voice worried him. He hadn't heard that tone in a long time. Since her sessions with a psychologist three years earlier, she'd gotten on a steady course, lost some of that defensiveness. The compulsion to immediately succeed at something or abandon it had abated. Like with her riding. She'd found a great teacher, had researched horses, and had worked hard to become as good a rider as her mother had been. She'd seemed to cast aside the shadows that had haunted her since childhood. For someone who had beauty, position, and money, she had remarkably low self-esteem.

She'd even been excited about the newspaper interview. She'd become passionate about her favorite cause: the riding program for special needs kids. She'd thought the interview would help raise funds.

Maybe she was finding herself, after all. He hoped to God she was.

He wanted her happy, and God knew she'd had little of that emotion. He used to ferry her to school and various activities when she was a child. He knew how self-conscious she was about the scars from the accident that killed her parents. Plastic surgery had helped, but a number of psychologists hadn't been able to heal the survivor's guilt she felt.

He wondered if her cry for help now had anything to do with the story. And that drew his attention back to Kira Douglas and the dinner last night. He'd enjoyed himself far more than he'd expected until she'd virtually fled from him.

Her excuse had been exhaustion, and the slight rings around her eyes gave substance to the claim, but he suspected she was one of those people who ran on adrenaline.

He couldn't explain his reaction to her. Not the heat that had ignited in him, nor the desire to touch her. There was a fierce attraction—make it a sexual storm—that stunned him. It was even more surprising since she was a reporter, and he'd never been a fan of most of them.

To his surprise, Kira Douglas had challenged him in a way few women did. She was driven. Confident. Compassionate. Smart as hell.

And pretty. Not beautiful with sleek cheekbones and a straight nose, but a more interesting kind of attractiveness. Eyes that flashed with enthusiasm or clouded with questions. A smile that was real and not practiced.

She was also wary of him, and he couldn't quite figure out why. He'd been on his best behavior. But her eyes had been cautious and her responses carefully phrased, even after two large glasses of wine.

He called the investigative agency on retainer for Westerfield Industries. "Any more on Ms. Douglas?" he asked the investigator.

"Very little. She's been active lately in organ donation groups. Other than that, nothing."

"How active?"

"Press releases. Press advice. That kind of thing."

"Paper doesn't mind?"

"Not if it's a nonprofit."

"Okay, keep hunting. I want to know what she has for breakfast in the morning."

"Gotcha, Mr. Payton."

Max put down the phone and stared at the law books in his office. He loved those books. The symbol of success. He used to take pleasure in looking at them, but the glow had faded.

He suddenly felt alone, and the feeling didn't give him the satisfaction it usually did.

Leigh ran down to the pasture before leaving. Maude always made her feel better, as did Silver Lady, who came to the fence and nudged her pocket for a treat.

"You spoil them," Rick said, and she whirled around. She hadn't heard him approach.

"I like spoiling them. Did you rub Lady down after my lesson this morning?"

"Yes'm." There was the touch of insolence in his voice, but

as long as he did his job, she ignored it. He was Mrs. Baker's nephew and had worked part-time as groom for two years. He was rarely late and had never missed a day; it was rare finding someone that reliable, so she ignored his sometimes surly manner.

"I'll put them inside the barn when I get back this afternoon," she said.

"I'll be going, then," he said. "I put clean water and feed in their stalls."

She gave the donkey and mare another piece of apple, then went inside the house and grabbed her purse. In minutes she was on the interstate.

What did the Kira person want? Money? Her inheritance?

What galled her most is how she'd been tricked. She'd been flattered by the interview, had instinctively liked Kira Douglas. She'd told the other members of the board about the upcoming story, and they'd been thrilled.

What a fool she'd been. What a trusting fool. No wonder Max wouldn't give over control to the Westerfield trust.

Anger seethed inside her. She had no doubt her mother had given her birth. She'd been told that her mother had three miscarriages before her birth, and she had been a treasured child for that reason.

An ugly prank? Blackmail of some kind?

Get yourself together, she told herself. Max will know what to do. He *always* knew what to do.

She left the house early. You never knew about Atlanta traffic, even on Saturdays. Her hands trembled on the steering wheel as images flipped through her mind. Her mother singing to her. Her father whirling her around. Then the ugly parts. The drinking. The arguments.

Traffic was light today. Unusually light. She arrived at Max's office twenty minutes before noon. The security guard nodded at her. "Miss Howard. Good to see you."

On the sixth floor, she went directly to his office. Why would someone say something like this? That she wasn't Leigh Howard?

She blinked back tears. She would fight back this time. No more running and hiding. She wanted advice from Max, but no one was going to take her birthright from her. No one was going to take her name and her memories.

He stood as she entered his office. It was clean except for two manila folders. It was always clean. He was the most disciplined man she knew.

He looked at her face, and his smile faded. "What is it, Leigh?"

"Can we go out to lunch? Now?" She didn't want to be in the close confines of the office. She wanted to be in a public place where she could wear a public face. She wouldn't cry there.

"Of course." His hand touched her shoulder as they went out the door.

Was she really that obvious? Kind gestures were not in his repertoire, at least not that she'd noticed.

"That reporter," she said after they were seated in the restaurant, "the one who did the story earlier this week, visited me again."

She saw a flicker of surprise in his eyes. "Why?" he asked with more interest than she'd expected.

"She claimed that I'm not the biological daughter of my parents. That *she* is. That we were switched at birth."

Max didn't usually show emotions, but he started forward in his chair and his eyes darkened. "That's nonsense."

"That's what I said," Leigh agreed, suddenly comforted by his obvious shock. "You know all the family secrets," she said, voicing that tiny kernel of doubt. "*You* would know."

He ignored that comment. "Tell me exactly what she said."

She recounted the conversation with Kira Douglas as completely as she could, knowing she'd hit the most important points.

His eyes turned icy and a muscle flexed in his throat. She'd seen enough of him to know he was angry. Furious, in fact. It wasn't, though, aimed at her. She had been on that end before and knew the signs.

"She wants me to take a DNA test." A pause. "She wants me to give a kidney."

"And what do you want to do?" His voice was noncommittal but his eyes seethed with anger.

"Tell her to go to hell. She lied to get into my house. I have no reason to trust her. I found my birth certificate after talking to her. There's no doubt I'm a Westerfield. I wonder if she's just using the kidney story to blackmail us."

Max shook his head. "She *does* have a very ill mother on the kidney transplant list."

"How do you know?"

"A gut feeling that she wasn't just there for the interview. I ran a check on her."

She glared at him. "Why didn't you warn me?"

"I had no reason to. You made the appointment without asking me. When I saw her and the photographer, it was rather late to ask questions."

"What do you think she wants?"

"She's clean as far as public records go. She's apparently good at her job," he said.

Leigh had the sudden impression that he was not telling her everything. Her blood chilled. If she couldn't trust Max, who could she trust?

"What should I do?" she asked again.

"Don't agree to anything. Don't sign anything. I'll meet with her and find out exactly why she believes there was a baby switch and whether she has any proof. You say she got some DNA that day she interviewed you?" Then he cursed. *That damned cup.* No wonder Kira Douglas had looked so guilty.

"She says it matches her mother's."

"That wouldn't hold up in court," he said.

"What should I do?"

"I don't want you talking to her. If she phones, hang up. If she e-mails, save them for me but don't reply. Okay?"

She nodded, feeling better already. His anger was palpable, but she knew it was directed elsewhere. She would not want to be in that reporter's shoes.

"Something else," he said. "Don't mention this to anyone else. Not until I know more. You don't want the press camping on your doorstep."

"She *is* the press."

His expression tightened. "For some reason she apparently

hasn't said anything about this to anyone but you. If she had any legal proof, she would have gone to the hospital first. That's something for our side."

She liked that "our side." She left an hour later, feeling much better. She planned to do exactly as he suggested. He would get rid of the pretender.

The sense of violation, though, ran deep. She had been used. Lied to. She had invited someone into her house as a guest and her hospitality was abused.

Not only abused but trashed with an outrageous falsehood.

Max prided himself on self-control. Some, including the CEO of Westerfield Industries, called it arrogance. Perhaps they were right, because Max didn't give a damn what others thought.

He had a small opinion of most people. He'd been dumped as a kid into a group home, then foster care, and that didn't endear him to authority and courts and do-gooders.

He owed one person. No one else. He planned never to owe anyone else again, and he was wary of anyone venturing too close to him.

And no one had, not until this weekend when he'd spent a few hours with a woman he would usually avoid.

He knew now why he distrusted such emotions. Kira Douglas was a liar.

Max wanted to slam something. Instead, he finished eating. It was important that Leigh not notice how angry he was.

He had protected her now for more than twenty years. It had become more than a habit, especially when he had discovered what was behind her self-destructive actions. He related only too well.

He also felt deceived. He had been fooled by misty blue eyes and earnestness.

He looked at his companion at the table. Leigh was picking at her salad, but her eyes caught his and held. She had changed in the past year. Or maybe he had. What he used to believe was irresponsibility was really shyness and fear, and God knew she had a right to both of them.

Still, Max wanted to hurry her. He had appointments this afternoon but none he couldn't cancel. He wanted to call Kira Douglas and find out what in the hell was going on. And if she was playing games with Leigh, or was a threat to her, he would destroy her.

12

Kira spent Saturday afternoon taking care of business for the Clean Sweep. She sent out bills to clients and made out checks for employees.

She wanted her mother to come back to a functioning business. She *would* come back.

The busywork, though, couldn't quench the dread in her heart. Kira knew the roof was going to fall in on her. She simply didn't know when.

She should have told Max Payton about what she suspected. Suspected? Hell, no. What she knew. Now he probably wouldn't believe anything she said.

That thought hurt. Far more than she wanted to admit.

It had been a long time since a guy made her tingle from the inside out. Even longer since she'd been so challenged in every way. She liked him as well as being so physically attracted to him. She liked the preciseness of his mind, the trace of gallantry after they left the restaurant. She liked the ease with which he made conversation even while gently interrogating her.

But the supper had probably been their first and last social meeting. He did not seem a man who took kindly to lies. And she had lied by omission. Big time.

The phone rang and she hesitated. She felt as if she were jumping out of her skin. It kept ringing. When she picked up the receiver, she heard a very cold, very hard, clipped voice. She'd heard that words could sound like pieces of ice falling, but she'd never experienced it before. An apt description.

"There are things we need to talk about," Max said after introducing himself very curtly as Max Payton.

"You've talked to Leigh." A statement, not a question.

"Yes." Even icier if possible.

"There's a reason I didn't tell you Friday."

"Really?"

She could mentally see him raise his eyebrows in disbelief.

"When do you want to meet?" she asked.

"As soon as possible. Leigh is understandably upset. No, she's bewildered and furious. Just as anyone would be when confronted with . . . your . . . bombshell."

Time was of the essence for her as well. Maybe she could convince him, even enlist his aid. "Today?"

"Yes."

That clipped, angry tone again. She tried to ignore it. "Where?"

"My office." The answer was curt. *No intimate bistro tonight.*

"I can be there this afternoon," she said.

"Four?"

"I'll be there."

He gave directions, then hung up without another word. Her heart dropped. She'd hoped for the benefit of the doubt. But then, she hadn't given him that. She'd had supper with him as if she hadn't a care in the word, when she was really carrying around information that could shatter his client.

His office. No suggestion of her home. Obviously he meant to be in control. Well, she owed him that much.

She thought about calling Chris. She'd already reported the conversation with Leigh and planned to meet with him Sunday. But she'd asked enough of him already, and this was her problem.

She glanced at her watch. She had enough time to run over and see her mother first.

Leigh couldn't get the reporter's words from her mind. The lunch with Max had helped, but she was jumpy with anxiety. Beyond restless.

Perhaps some work at Seth's office would help while she waited for Max to report back.

Seth was talking to his campaign manager as she entered his headquarters. He grinned when he saw her, then his smile faded as his gaze met her eyes.

"Excuse me," he told the man with him and came over to her. "Hey, Cous, what's wrong?"

"That obvious?"

"You look like you lost your best friend. I would have thought you would be ecstatic after the story in the paper. It was terrific."

"You saw it?"

"Someone brought over an early edition of the Sunday paper." He picked a section of the paper up and handed it to her.

She stared down at herself. The photo covered nearly a quarter of a page and she looked good. She quickly read the story. She would have loved it had she not discovered it had a poisonous seed. She truly wanted to kill Kira Douglas at the moment.

Seth hugged her. "Good job, princess."

The gesture surprised her because Seth wasn't a demonstrative person. No one in her family was. Except her mother. She remembered her mother's cheek against her, the smell of roses. Or was that just something she dreamed? It had been so long ago.

And now someone wanted to take even those few memories away.

"Come inside my office," he said. "Jack can wait."

She followed him into the office, ignoring the look of impatience on his manager's face.

He sat on the corner of a neat desk. "What is it?" he asked.

She recalled what Max had said. *Don't tell anyone.* But Seth wasn't *anyone.* He was and always had been her friend.

She quickly told him. He was five years older than she. He might have heard rumors if anything had been odd.

His face reddened with anger as she talked. "She should be fired," he said. "You want me to call the newspaper for you?"

"I don't want you to do anything that would hurt your campaign. Max is looking into it. He's going to talk to her."

"I hate to admit it, but you're in good hands then. God, I can't even imagine what you're feeling. Forget it. You look like your mother. Everyone has always said that, particularly your grandfather."

He was right. Everyone had said she favored her mother. Another reason to totally disregard the wild ramblings of a reporter.

She brightened.

"You're an heiress," he continued. "And there's a lot of money at stake. Maybe she thinks she can get you to settle to keep a false claim out of the papers."

"Max will pound her into the ground," she said. "*I'm* afraid of him, and I think he likes me. I'm never quite sure."

"Max is a pain in the ass," Seth said. "He guards that trust like it was his. He forgets it should be yours."

"And yours," she said.

He shrugged. "I'm a grandnephew, not a grandson. And Ed didn't like my dad much. We did okay."

Leigh had always felt guilty that she'd received the bulk of the estate—through the trust, true—while her second cousins received only a token inheritance. Grandfather had said in the will that it was because she was his direct heir, but she suspected it had something to do with the fact that neither of his brothers or nephews had gone into his business. Or had succumbed to his dictates.

She also suspected that he wished Max was his son. He had left Max a life tenancy of a house on the property, a large amount of stock for himself, and control of the trust, which included the majority of corporation stock. As far as she knew, Max was the only person he'd really trusted.

Neither Seth nor David had shown any concern about

the will. But she would have, had the situation been reversed.

"It still isn't right," she said.

"Well, you don't have it, either," Seth said. "Max does." This time, some bitterness did creep into his voice.

"He'll take care of this reporter," she said, trying to reassure herself.

"Don't worry about it, Cous. If he doesn't, I will. I've fought for judge and district attorney pay raises and helped several to raise funds. They'll listen to me."

She said to him what she didn't say to Max. "What if it's true? She was so . . . convinced that it was."

"Con artists are always convincing," he said. Then he stood. "I wouldn't worry about it. I would have heard if there had ever been any question about your birth. But I'll do a little digging myself."

"Don't," she said. "Let Max do it first, and please don't say anything. Not yet."

"For you, princess, anything. But let me know if you need anything."

"I really do want to get more involved in your campaign after the horse show is over," Leigh replied. "I need to keep busy."

"Great. I'll tell Jack. You would be great with fund-raising events. You know people; you know possible venues; you're a great hostess."

Not so much. She was always terrified something would go wrong, but she'd developed a calm mask that covered the butterflies in her stomach.

Can't you do anything right?

Her grandfather's voice came from the past. Her ex-husband's voice. God, she'd tried to drown them out.

She nodded. "I would like that."

"Good. It's settled. Hey, I have a fund-raiser tonight. Why don't you go with me? Get a taste for it?"

Max would call later. "Not this time," she said. "I'm expecting Max to call."

"Okay. Let me know if you change your mind."

Slowly, she nodded. She didn't want to be alone. "I'll do that."

Kira's heart pounded as she approached Max's office. It was in a high-rise office building near Olympic Park. She noticed from the directory on the ground floor that Westerfield Industries had two floors of offices. She asked the security guard for Max Payton's office and took the elevator to the sixth floor.

A large reception desk guarded the rest of the floor. It was empty at the moment.

Then Max stepped out of an office and stood aside for her to enter.

"No one else here?" she said.

"Nervous?" he asked, baring his teeth in a smile.

"No," she lied. His face was expressionless as he studied her. For the fleetest of moments, she wished she had brought Chris along. But she had to do this herself. Especially after the dinner this man and she had shared. Regret struck her hard.

He went to his desk and sat down. She felt like a schoolgirl left to fidget before a headmaster.

To hell with that. She sat down as well.

The silence lengthened as she felt herself being taken apart piece by piece. She found it hard to believe there had ever been warmth in those cold eyes.

"What game are you playing?" he finally said. His voice was diamond hard.

"What did Leigh tell you?" she asked instead.

"That you claimed to be the real Westerfield heiress. That's impossible."

"And how do you know that?"

"Babies aren't just mislaid, Ms. Douglas."

Ms. Douglas. Not Kira. "It *has* happened," she said. "There was a case in Georgia, another in California."

"I did some quick research. A very few in many millions of births."

"So you admit it happens?"

He shook his head. "It would have been discovered by now, just as the others were."

"You know my mother is dying," she said. "She needs a kidney. I wanted to give her one of mine. I underwent tests to see if we were compatible. I wasn't, but during the test I discovered I'm not her biological daughter. The doctor suggested I might be adopted, but I was born at the hospital, and her name is on my birth certificate." She paused, then added, "I was angry, furious, disbelieving, so I know exactly how Leigh feels."

"Why Leigh? How did you come up with Leigh?"

"I hired a private investigator. His name is Chris Burke." She took a card from her pocket and handed it to him. "He's a licensed private investigator, a former captain of detectives with the Atlanta police department. You can check his reputation. He ran down all the babies born near the time I was born. I was critically ill . . . a heart defect. I was immediately taken to the prenatal unit. So the switch, accidental or planned, had to take place within a few moments of my birth. Leigh was born three minutes before me."

His cold eyes didn't change. Not a flicker of acceptance or understanding and certainly none of the ease and warmth of last night. He simply waited for her to continue. She would bet her last dollar that a recorder was running somewhere. Silence was a great interrogator technique. She'd used it herself.

"No one else?" he asked after a silence.

"Two others. Not immediately but within an hour."

"Then why Leigh?"

This was the question she really didn't want to answer. She hadn't broken any laws, at least not any she or Chris were aware of, but she'd most certainly been devious and underhanded.

"There was the timing. And then she's the only one in Atlanta. If she wasn't the one, then I would have gone to the others." She paused, then added, "The day I interviewed Leigh, I got some of her DNA," she said, hoping he didn't hear the catch in her throat. "It matches my mother's."

Something flickered in his eyes. "The coffee cup." His lips thinned into a straight line. "Aren't you the clever little reporter? You know, of course, that would have no value in a courtroom. It could be anyone's DNA for all I know."

"Why? All I want is a kidney for my mother. Nothing else. I'm just asking Leigh to test."

"Are you quite sure about that?"

She met his gaze directly. "Yes."

"Sorry, I have a hard time believing you would turn down the Westerfield fortune. Especially since we both know you're a liar. A very good one."

It was as if he'd plunged a sword through her. His eyes glittered as he said the words. His mouth curled in contempt. She had expected it, but she hadn't known it would hurt this much.

She deserved it. She knew it. He could probably have her fired for using the newspaper in the way she did.

"I didn't lie."

"By omission, you told a whopper. I don't like liars, Ms. Douglas."

"I wanted to be sure before I approached her," she said quietly. "I didn't want her to go through what I went through if it wasn't true."

"How nice of you."

He didn't believe anything she said. Going out with him Friday night had only made it worse. She could have told him then. She hadn't, and now her credibility was paying for it.

"I'm sorry," she said. "Maybe I could have handled it better. I could have gone to the hospital, to the courts, but that would have taken months, and Mom doesn't have months. She may not have weeks."

A muscle throbbed in his neck. "Well, that's exactly what you will have to do, Ms. Douglas. Leigh does not have to be tested, because she is not the person you think she is. She is a Westerfield. Hospital personnel are too careful, particularly under the circumstances you mentioned. How do you accidentally switch a healthy baby with a sick one?"

"Talk to Chris Burke," she pleaded.

"I'm not going to talk to anyone. Leigh was given into my charge by her grandfather. She's had one hell of a bad time, and I'm not going to let anyone take advantage of her."

"What if it is true?" she countered. "What if she discovers after my mother's death that Katy Douglas was her mother, and she could have saved her? Can she really live with that?"

His jaw set. "A little honesty would have helped your cause."

"I thought she had the right to hear it first," she said steadily. "I didn't know what your relationship was. Or wasn't."

"Dammit, I don't for an instant believe some conspiracy to switch children at birth."

"How do you explain the DNA match?"

"Since there's no chain of evidence, I put little credence in it. That DNA sample could have been yours, or a friend's."

The air between them was tense. Electric with accusation. She was only too aware that he was barely repressing his anger, and she her desperation.

She remembered how she felt Friday night in his presence. The thunderbolts that had struck her so unexpectedly. That made today so much more painful.

"There was another reason I didn't go to the hospital directly," she said. "Publicity. I didn't want my mother to hear what had happened. It could kill her, and once the news gets out . . ."

"And you thought Leigh would just give up a kidney?"

"No. Not like that. I knew she would want tests of her own. I want them, too. But I had to know without putting her through the anger and grief I felt when I was told of the first results. I had to be sure. For me. For Mom. For Leigh." She held back tears. That would be the worst thing she could do. Another subterfuge in his eyes.

"I probably shouldn't have used my job to make sure," she said. "But I just had to *know*, and I couldn't wait for an investigation, for the courts. There's no time." She paused, then tried again. "I truly don't want anything Leigh has except to convince her to donate the kidney. I have a great mom. I have a job I love. I don't need or want anything else." *Believe me, dammit.*

"And you'll sign a contract to that effect?"

"Yes. Anything you want."

"I want to see the DNA report," he said abruptly.

She reached in her purse and took it out. Silently handed it to him.

He read it, then stood and left the room. He was back in a moment with a copy. He handed her back the original and very deliberately placed his copy on the desk.

The tension grew even deeper, broader. His eyes were just as cold as when she'd entered his office. She couldn't tell whether he believed her or not. Whether he was accepting anything she said.

She'd thought he would understand once she explained. She'd obviously been wrong.

She sat and waited, knowing that the next few moments might mean her mother's life. And her career.

13

Max had glanced at the DNA results in the copying room.

They were explosive. *If true.*

He would check out the detective Kira mentioned, then the lab. But he really didn't buy the switched babies idea. As an attorney, he knew the liability issues and how careful hospitals were.

He tried to ignore the plea in the eyes of the woman across from him, the fingers that flexed compulsively in her lap.

He knew what her claim would mean to Leigh. If true, it would devastate her just when she was finding her own way.

He looked again at the DNA results. Kira was smart enough to know that he would ask for independent verification. As a matter of law, the paper in his hand was meaningless. But it might be enough to prompt a judge to ask for another test—a well-monitored one. That could take time, though. He could delay it. Repeatedly.

Until her mother was dead.

He didn't want to do that. Nor did he want put Leigh through the hell that might be coming her way. The publicity could destroy her newfound confidence.

There was no good course of action. He didn't like the way Kira had obtained the DNA. It had been a lie, and on Leigh's behalf he was enraged about it. If Kira had come to him directly, or to the hospital or to an attorney, then he might accept what she was saying.

"What do you plan to do now?" he asked.

"I wanted to keep this private, if possible," she said. "I don't care about the estate. I just hoped that Leigh would want to help my mom. *Our mom.*"

"And if she doesn't?"

"I'll go through the courts. If Mom dies, I'll try to get everything she has."

His eyes hardened. "Do you think blackmailing will make her prone to donate a kidney?"

"I don't have a choice. Mom has a month, if that."

"And if there isn't a match for a kidney transplant, you want her to believe you'll step away and never say anything?"

"Yes."

There was a naïveté about the short answer that stopped him. Either she was sincere or the greatest con artist in history. And where did his loyalty to Ed lie? With the granddaughter Ed knew, or the one that might carry his blood?

He didn't want to play Solomon.

He stood. "I'll talk to Leigh. It's her decision as to whether she wants to talk to you or agree to a test. You didn't exactly instill a sense of integrity in this."

She visibly winced at his words. But he was as angry as he'd ever been. He had liked Kira, more than liked her. And he felt like a fool. He certainly had been taken for one.

He stood. "I'll be in contact with you."

She stood as well. "My mother doesn't have much time. Right now, Leigh is her only hope."

He merely nodded. He went over to the door and opened it.

She paused, though. "I'm sorry," she said. "I thought I was doing the right thing by trying to make sure before approaching Leigh."

He didn't answer, and she turned and left.

He returned to his desk and sat down. He leaned back in his chair. Goddamn it. This was something that wasn't going away.

Kira Douglas obviously believed the story to be true. His

first impression after talking to Leigh was that Kira Douglas was a dishonest opportunist. No longer. He was a good judge of character, and he believed her. The fact that she went about this in the wrong way, at least as far as he was concerned, didn't change the fact that she believed she was right.

What if she had come to him, or Leigh, without any proof?

They probably would have laughed her out of the room.

"Take care of Leigh." That had been Ed's last words.

Max closed his eyes. What if he couldn't take care of Leigh? What would Ed have wanted?

She'd made a complete mess of it.

Kira leaned against a wall outside his office for a moment. She took a deep breath. Her legs didn't want to work. It was as if they'd turned to rubber. And her mind to mush. She would never forget that look of distaste in his eyes when she walked into the room.

After a few seconds, she finally felt able to walk again. She hurried down the hall to the elevator. Maybe if she reached the hospital quickly, she would see the doctor who usually stopped in around 6:00 p.m. before going home. She wanted an update on her mother's position on the donor list.

Even if her mother neared the top, so much depended on whether the available kidney was compatible. She could still have to wait months.

What if she had made a new hope impossible?

She blinked back a tear. She'd not shed them in months, but frustration forced them out. She found her car and headed to the hospital.

Leigh went down to the barn as soon as she got back home. Rick had left, and she put Silver Lady into her stall. Maude followed behind.

She checked the water and feed. As usual, both were fresh. But she always checked. There was something about Rick that had disconcerted her from the beginning. Maybe it was the way he showed so little emotion. But Mrs. Baker said he he'd been stationed in Iraq as a dog handler and had lost several friends, as well as his dog . . .

She gave both Silver Lady and Maude pieces of an apple, and leaned her head against Lady's.

What if none of this belonged to her? She would lose Lady. Maude.

Fear darted through her and took hold.

How long before Max called?

She went back into the house and to the office that had once been her grandfather's. She turned on the computer and did a Google search on Kira Douglas, something she should have done before inviting her to her home. A short biography came up, as well as a number of articles. A native of Atlanta, graduate of Georgia State University, recipient of an Associated Press award for a feature she'd written in 2005.

Nothing about her character that resembled, in Leigh's opinion, a bottom-feeder. She had never been good about people. She'd always taken them at face value, and although that character quirk had resulted in disaster several times, she'd stubbornly stuck to it. Maybe not again.

She felt betrayed. Tricked. She detested being made to feel the fool.

She took comfort in Seth's words. In Max's take-charge personality.

The pretender would be exposed.

When the doorbell rang, she dashed for it. Anyone but Max or the groom or Seth would have had to phone from the fence to gain entrance. She stilled at the expression in Max's face.

"You met with her?"

"Yes."

"She's a fraud," she said confidently. Surely Max had reduced the woman to tears and a confession. God knows, he'd done it to her ex-husband and several times to herself.

"Let's go inside," he said, and she froze. That wasn't what she expected to hear.

She led the way to the study. Max went to the bar and poured himself a bourbon and water.

"You saw her," Leigh said.

"Yes. She had the DNA test with her. That doesn't mean the DNA belongs to you. It only means that she has something to take to a judge who could order a controlled test."

"How can she do that?"

"There's a substantial claim involved. Millions of dollars."

Anger mixed with an all-too-familiar feeling of helplessness. "What can you do?" she finally asked.

"You have a choice. You can agree to take a DNA test and, if her claim is true, a test to see if your kidney is a match. In return she will give up any right to the name or estate. Or we can fight it. I can probably get repeated delays, but eventually you'll be required to submit to a DNA test. By then, Mrs. Douglas might well be dead, and if the tests confirm what Kira Douglas says, she will probably go after your throat for not helping."

"You know how I feel about hospitals," she said. She hated the tremor in her voice.

"I know," he said softly.

He hadn't been with the family when the accident happened, but he knew that she'd incurred multiple fractures and cuts, had lain beside her dead mother and father before she was cut from the car. She'd been in the hospital for months, then back again for reconstructive surgery. To this day, she couldn't go into a hospital, not even to visit someone.

Her head swam. It wasn't fair. Not now. She reached out and clasped Max's hand. "I can't," she whispered. "I just can't. I still . . . dream about the pain, the blood. I've relived it so many times. I can't . . . breathe."

He nodded as if he'd already known—and accepted—her answer.

She turned to Max. "Will you stay for supper?"

"Isn't this Mrs. Baker's day off?"

"She left a casserole."

He started to decline, hesitated, then nodded his head.

"Sounds good," Max said.

"What if it's all a lie?" Leigh said. "A fantasy she concocted?"

"A DNA test can prove that."

"Can we do one privately?" she asked. "Do to her what she says she did to me? Without anyone—even her—knowing?"

He'd been playing with the same idea. "I think so. I can tell her I need more information and offer her coffee." He paused. "You have to consider the fact it could be true. She knows we would get another test, so it doesn't make sense to lie. And a woman is dying. What if Mrs. Douglas is your genetic mother?"

She shook her head, denying the fact. She *knew* who she was. Her mother had adored her. She thought of both parents: her mother who once sang her to sleep, her father who'd tossed her up in the air as she screamed in delight.

A memory flashed for a split second, then was gone. A shiver ran down her spine.

She forced it back in her mind and walked to the kitchen. She took out a dish from the fridge and put it in the microwave.

While waiting for it to heat, she set the table, then looked at Max. He'd always had a stone face. She never knew what he was thinking. No one did.

"What if it *is* true?" she said in a broken whisper.

"She could go after the house and the trust."

"Could she actually win?"

"Truthfully, I don't know. The will bequeathed the house and the proceeds of the trust to Ed's granddaughter, Leigh Howard, who was born June 26, 1976. The question before a judge—if it came to court—would be whether he intended it to go to his biological granddaughter, or the woman he loved and believed to be his granddaughter. I did some preliminary research this afternoon. I think it could go either way, depending on the judge."

"But I can't be forced to give a kidney?"

"No," he said. "And you don't have to make a decision now."

"You'll support me whatever I decide?"

"Other than murder, yes," he said with a slight smile.

"No murder," she agreed.

Despite her taut answer, a familiar black cloud enveloped her. She tried to fight her way out. She knew what could happen if she didn't.

The microwave buzzed. She ignored it.

"Your grandfather asked me to look after you," Max said. "I intend to do just that. Try not to worry."

"I won't," she lied, straightening her back. But maybe, just maybe, she could do something to help him.

"You need to know what's happened," Leigh told David as the three second cousins had brunch on the patio. She'd phoned both of them and asked them to come, sans wives.

Both, she knew, could well be affected by a public court case. David's father delivered her. Seth was a public figure.

"Nonsense," David said after she'd repeated what Max had told her last night after meeting with Kira Douglas. "Dad delivered you," David continued. "A perfect girl, he said. A beautiful girl. I was only seven, but I remember it well. I'd always wanted a sister and you were the next thing to it."

"Where is Uncle Michael?"

David shrugged. "Someplace in Africa. We usually don't hear from him for weeks."

She knew David worried about his father, though they had not been that close. After he'd retired, his father joined Doctors Without Borders and was assigned to every armpit of the world. David bitterly resented the fact that his father had never had time for him when he was a boy, nor as an adult. Never went to ball games. Never took a family vacation. It was one reason the cousins—she and Seth and David—were close. None of them had a normal family life. Her father died when she was young, Michael's father was a workaholic, and Seth's had become an alcoholic after he lost his congressional bid.

"If she filed a suit, she would have to do it in Fayette County," Seth said. "I know the judges, several of them quite well. I helped them raise money. But maybe it'll all go away when you make it clear you're not going to fold easily."

"Max is researching the legal implications."

"I wouldn't place all your hopes in Max," Seth said. "He's a corporate attorney. He knows contracts and wheeling and dealing. God knows he wheeled and dealed with my great-uncle." Resentment crept into his voice.

But then, they'd all felt that way at one time or another. Max had been Westerfield's hatchet man for as long as the three could remember. "Go to Max," their grandfather always said when they wanted something.

"Any ideas?" she asked.

"Only a warning that Max has a stake in this," Seth says. "That trust has been a gravy train for him."

David glared at him. "You're saying it might be true."

"I'm not saying that at all. I'm saying it might benefit him if he joined forces with this woman. Only a fool—or an opportunist—would think Leigh's incompetent to take care of her own money. Once that happens, he's out as trustee and control of the stock. Maybe he thought that time was coming and . . ."

Leigh couldn't quite comprehend what he was saying. Not Max. But then, she'd been wrong before.

"No," she said.

"Just keep that in mind," Seth persisted. He took out a business card and handed it to her. "This is the name of a good attorney. You might talk to him. I'll tell him you might call."

Leigh nodded and took the card. She didn't intend to use it, but she didn't want to argue with Seth.

She looked at both of them. "Do you think I should agree to a DNA test?"

Seth shook his head. "It's a scam. It has to be." He paused, reached out, and touched her hand. "You've told us about those nightmares. I can't even imagine what you went through during and after the accident. Even if this woman's story is true, and I don't think for a second that it is, you don't owe her anything. And I doubt any judge in Fayette would rule against you. For many reasons."

His words solidified what she'd been thinking. "David, what do you think?"

He'd been silent during the conversation. "I'm not you,"

he said slowly. "I can only tell you I simply can't believe there's any way babies could have been switched. It's just not possible."

"But were there as many precautions thirty-two years ago as there are now?" she asked.

"Yes. The protocol has been there for decades."

Leigh was already beginning to feel better. Maybe Max was simply being cautions. Still, the sick feeling in her stomach hadn't receded. It didn't help that she hadn't had much sleep and that what she did get had been colored with blood.

She had a riding lesson at noon. She would have to concentrate then on the horse, and nothing but the horse. Then she would call Max and tell him she'd decided to fight. She fingered the card that she'd dropped on the table and put it in her purse.

Maybe she wouldn't need it. Maybe something would happen to keep the reporter from pursuing what David said could not have happened.

14

It was after 7:00 p.m. before Kira left the office. She'd covered several meetings at city hall, along with an important city appointment, and didn't finish the last story until long after everyone else had left.

No visit to Mom tonight. She was simply too tired, and her mother, according to the nurse on duty, was sleeping.

She walked to the MARTA station. She usually drove but she'd been late this morning, and rapid transit was quicker during the morning rush hours. MARTA didn't come to a standstill like Atlanta traffic.

The platform was empty, meaning a train had just left. Sighing, she took one of the seats on the platform and looked at the newspaper she'd grabbed as she left the office. The story she'd filed at noon led the front page. She never quite got over the thrill of seeing her byline at the top of page one. She read it over and thought about follow-up stories for the next day.

Then she stood. The next train should be coming. The platform was still nearly empty. No Atlanta Braves game tonight. Apparently no other event to draw people. A signal that a train was nearing. She moved to the area next to the track.

She became aware of someone moving toward her. She

probably would have noticed it sooner if she hadn't been emotionally and mentally drained. But suddenly a man was next to her, just as she heard the train coming.

Startled, she turned. Caught a glimpse of a Braves cap pulled down over a forehead and dark glasses. Then his hands came out just as the train thundered toward them.

"Hey," a voice some distance away yelled. The man nearing her stumbled, pushing her as he did. Her legs went from under her and she started to fall toward the tracks and the oncoming train.

She frantically reached for something, but there was nothing but air.

A hand grabbed her, swung her around just as the train slowed and came to a stop.

She landed on the ground, her arm scraping the cement. She couldn't move for a moment. Her heart thundered. Her breath caught in her throat as she thought how easily she might have been lying on the train tracks.

Several people gathered around her, including her Good Samaritan. "You okay?" he asked.

She sat up. Looked at him. He was an older man, bulky in a blue work shirt and pants. "You okay, ma'am?" he asked again.

She nodded, tried to breathe normally. "Thanks . . . to you. Did you see what happened?"

"Looked like someone was in too big a hurry. Running for the train. I saw him collide with you. I guess he panicked and ran off."

Blood ran down her arm. The fall had scraped a portion of skin from her arm.

"Thank you," she said. "You saved my life."

He looked uncomfortable. "Just glad you're okay. But I think we should call nine-one-one. Have them look at that arm."

The last thing she needed now was hours spent with the police. Long explanations. "No. You said it was an accident. And I'm not badly hurt."

Her Samaritan helped her stand and led her back to a seat. "I'll wait with you for the next train," he said.

"Thank you," she said again. She wanted to say it a hundred times. Her hand and wrist were wet now with blood. She used some tissues from her purse to stanch it. Her mind raced, even as her breathing slowed. "Who are you? You were so quick."

"Vietnam, ma'am. You learn to react fast. I ain't never forgot it. I work as a security guard at the Omni."

"I'm Kira Douglas," she said. "I work for the *Observer*. Can I get your name?"

"No, ma'am. I mean I don't want no thanks or nothing in the newspapers. Didn't do anything but grab your hand." '

"You could have gone down with me."

"Didn't happen," he said, shrugging his shoulders. He looked around, found her purse, picked it up, and gave it to her.

The platform started filling again. Not crowds, just one or two people at a time. They glanced at her curiously, their eyes falling to the bloodied blouse, then looked away.

Another train came to a stop. Her new friend gave her a hand up and steadied her. Together, they stepped inside the car.

"Are you going this way?"

"Yeah."

"Did you see what the guy looked like?" she asked.

He shook his head. "He moved too fast, and his face was partially covered by that cap. Probably about five feet eight inches or so. Thin. That's it."

Five stops later, she stepped out. "I'll come with you," he said.

"Not necessary," she said. "I live right around the corner."

He nodded.

"Isn't there some way I could thank you? Not just words . . ."

"Words are nice, miss. Just don't get too close to the edge again."

"Not to worry about that," she replied as she stepped off.

She'd parked at the MARTA station. Warily, she found her car and unlocked it. In minutes she was home. She went inside and leaned against the wall.

And shook. Quick mental snapshots of the fall . . . the train approaching . . .

She tried to recall the man who bumped her. Or had he pushed her? And if so, why?

Remember! But it was so quick. Blurred.

She double-checked the lock, then went to the bathroom, cleaned the wound on her arm, and swathed it in bandages. Then she poured herself a large glass of wine and ran steaming water in the tub with an extra dose of soothing bath oil. She took her cordless phone from the cradle and placed it beside the tub.

When the tub was full, she sank into it, protecting her arm, but relishing the heat of the water. She felt some of the tension ebbing away. She closed her eyes. Her mother's wan face floated in her mind along with Max's angry one and Leigh's bewildered one.

Had she done everything wrong? Had she ruined her mother's chances? That haunted her more than her own mishap.

The collision on the MARTA platform must have been an accident, nothing more. Someone in too much of a hurry. She probably should have reported it, but she was exhausted and didn't want to spend hours trying to explain the encounter to the police.

She glanced at the book on the tub's edge. Part of her wanted to pick it up and escape to some other world. The other part thought it would just take too much effort. She was far too emotionally and mentally drained to make sense of words.

Her eyes closed. Just for a minute.

She jerked awake when the phone rang. For a few seconds, panic played havoc with her thinking processes. Her hand trembling, she reached for the phone.

"We have a potential donor," her mother's physician said. "We need to do some more tests, but I'm hopeful."

"When?"

"It's on its way from Charlotte," he said. "It should be here in an hour."

Exhilaration replaced exhaustion. Adrenaline filled her as

she got out of the tub, threw on a pair of jeans and a shirt, and tore out the door. She was eight blocks away before she realized she hadn't locked the door. Well, hell's bells, her mother was more important. Why would a burglar pick this particular day to invade her house?

She sped down the streets to the hospital, praying that this really was the transplant that would save her mother's life. Then she could drop the whole other mess. She would never mention the switched babies again.

Her mother need never know she'd missed the childhood years of her biological child. Or did she have a moral imperative to tell her mother?

She sped to the hospital, breaking every speed limit. She wanted to be there before the kidney arrived, before they started prepping her mother. Or had they already?

She squealed into the parking lot and ran inside. The information desk was empty. So was the entrance hall. She had often scoffed at movies where a hospital seemed empty when a bad guy pursued the heroine through its halls. But she'd found it eerily true late at night.

She was the sole passenger on the elevator up to her mother's floor. Once there she ran down the corridor. She stopped at the nurse's station. They all knew her well by now.

"They're prepping her now," one said.

"Has the kidney arrived?"

"It should be here within the hour. The transplant team is already here."

Kira went down to her mother's room. Katy Douglas turned her way, her smile luminous. "I'm so glad you got here."

The surgeon entered then. Nodded to her, then went to her mother's side. "It's not certain yet. I want you to understand that. When it arrives, we have to mix your blood with the donor's blood. If there is no reaction, it means you are compatible with the donor. If there is a reaction, the kidney won't work for you because it's incompatible. Or the donor kidney might show signs of deterioration or poor function."

"I understand," Katy said. She and her physician had gone through the protocols several times.

He looked at Kira, and she nodded as well.

A technician hurried in, took several vials of blood, then left.

The surgeon left.

Katy looked at Kira, and her eyes lingered on the rather large bandage on her arm. "What happened?"

"Just a fall. You know me. I'm always in a hurry and sometimes my feet trip over each other. It's a curse."

Her mother's eyes bore into her, demanding the truth. It was damn hard lying to her, but by now she'd dismissed the incident at the rapid rail station as an accident.

"Truly it's only a small cut," she said. "Nothing to worry about."

She pulled the only chair in the room up to the bed and took her mother's hand.

Her mother's eyes met hers. "If it doesn't match, there's always another one," she said. "Don't worry about me. I'm like the Energizer Bunny. You always said so."

"It will be so good to have you home again," Kira said. "The house is empty without you."

Her mother squeezed her hand.

Minutes passed by. They talked of big and little things. Of old memories and new ones.

"I remember when you first walked," her mother said. "Earlier than any of the other babies your age. You started talking before anyone else, too."

"I think you're prejudiced." She hesitated, then asked, "You've never said much about my father." It was vital now that she learn more. Leigh had the right to know.

"He gave me you," her mother said, "and I always loved him for that. But we were both young. He was a musician, more into drugs than I thought, and a wanderer by nature. He tried. I think he really tried, but the only thing he knew was music and the only way you made music was traveling. When he took off, he left every penny he had. It wasn't much but it was a lot for him. He sent money for a year, not much, but I suspect it was a lot to him. Then suddenly it no longer came. I tried to find someone who knew something. I finally located one of the band members who was in Atlanta with him. He was killed in an accident."

"He didn't have any family?"

"He said not." She squeezed Kira's hand. "I never talked about him because of the drugs; that part was a nightmare. But you have every right to know. He was a great guitarist but a really poor husband." She paused. "Don't ever fall in love in a day."

A warning she really needed to heed.

Her mother squeezed Kira's hand. "I love you, baby."

"Ditto," Kira replied.

Her mother lay back. More technicians and nurses came in. More blood taken. Body washed.

It was really happening.

Her mother was transferred to a stretcher.

Kira leaned over to kiss her.

Watched her wheeled out.

And started praying.

15

Kira paced the large waiting room furnished with lounge chairs. A number of people slept. Others read.

She couldn't do either. She was up and down, glancing at the door when anyone entered. The hands on the clock crawled.

Even then she was startled when her name was called. She glanced at the clock. Only an hour had gone by since her mother was wheeled out. Too soon!

She went to the door.

"The donor kidney showed signs of deterioration," the surgeon said. "We had to abort the transplant. I'm sorry."

Hope plunged. The optimism that had played in her mind faded. Now Leigh's help was essential.

She had so hoped . . .

On many levels.

She waited for her mother to be wheeled out of the operating room. She was sleepy from the sedative. Kira leaned over and kissed her.

Katy's eyes fluttered open. "Is it over?"

"The kidney wasn't good," she replied. "They didn't go through with it."

"I *thought* I would hurt a lot more," Katy said with a touch of her old humor.

"I'm so sorry."

"There wasn't much time to feel lucky about it," Katy replied. The words were light, but Kira felt the quiet desperation behind them. Her mother was seldom down, at least when Kira was present. She didn't know what gremlins haunted her mother when she was absent.

"Go . . . home," her mother said. "I'm sleepy, and you probably look worse than I do."

"We'll find a kidney," Kira said. "I promise."

"Go home, sweetie," her mother said again. "I can't sleep until you do." She gave Kira a wan smile. "I love you." Then she closed her eyes.

Once out of the hospital, she turned the cell phone back on. Still no messages from Max Payton.

Her heart, already battered, sank. She had hoped he would get back to her immediately. He knew how urgent it was.

She would have to go to court, after all.

She would call Chris first thing in the morning and get the list of attorneys. It may further alienate Leigh Howard, but if she waited, her mother might die. Surely if the woman *knew* her mother was dying, she would want to help. Right now Leigh Howard was still stunned. Disbelieving.

Kira understood that. She, too, was trying to wrap her mind around the inconceivable. But she couldn't wait while Leigh dithered. If she had to use the threat of going after the woman's fortune, she would.

She wanted to call Chris immediately, but there was little he could do at this hour. First thing in the morning. Seven. Maybe even earlier. Her eyes blurred by rare tears, she stumbled to her car. There had been so much hope a few hours earlier.

But she had been warned.

She walked to her car. The parking lot was much emptier than it had been. A drizzle muted the parking lot lights. It was dark and lonely, and for a moment fear ran through her. The incident on the rapid rail platform was still very real.

She hurried her steps, unlocked the car from her remote, and stepped inside. She immediately locked the doors, not waiting this time to turn on the engine.

She'd never been afraid before. Aware, yes. Afraid, no.

She didn't like the feeling now.

She drove back to her mother's house and parked in the driveway. It had a one-car garage, and her mother's car stayed there.

Her mother had bought the small brick home at a steep discount because it was located in a less-than-desirable area, and sales had been slow. Since then, though, the area had become gentrified and property values had spiraled upward.

The house was as she'd left it. One light on in the dining room, the rest of the interior dark. The porch light was on. Keys in hand, she hurried to the porch, then remembered she hadn't locked it. She turned the knob and stepped inside. In the dim light coming from the dining room, she saw chaos. Total chaos. The room had been tossed.

Not searched. Trashed. Papers strewn across the floor. A cut across one of her mother's favorite paintings. Clothes jerked from hangers and torn. She immediately went to her room and looked for her computer. It was gone. So was her box of jewelry. Nothing really expensive but several nice pieces in the hundred- and two-hundred-dollar range. Stuff she'd carefully selected and really liked.

She checked the rest of the house. Her mother's room was equally destroyed. The room that served as an office for the housekeeping business had been tossed. That computer was gone. She searched for the index file of customers. Again gone.

A lot of the information was in her head. She knew the names, had memorized some of the phone numbers. She could re-create records. But she didn't like the idea of those names in someone else's possession. Then she looked in the drawer with the keys to their homes.

Oh God, they were gone as well. She would have to contact each one and offer to bear the cost of replacing locks.

Not only that, but what would she tell her mother?

If her mother ever returned home.

She called the police, then Chris.

"Be right over," he said.

He was there in fifteen minutes. The police hadn't arrived.

"I'm afraid a tossed house isn't one of their top priorities," he commented as he glanced around the room. "Christ. This wasn't just a burglary. This was personal."

"That's what I thought, too. Why would someone linger long enough to rip a hole in an inexpensive painting?"

"A message?" he suggested.

"From whom?"

"Written any stories someone may not like?"

"A bunch. But I can't imagine any of them pushing someone into doing this. This . . . this is pure rage." She paused. "Something else happened earlier today . . . or yesterday."

"What?"

"I was taking MARTA. It was late. After seven. Someone bumped me on the platform. I almost fell onto the tracks."

His eyes ran over her, lingered at her bandaged arm. "Christ, why didn't you call me?"

"I thought it was an accident. So did an onlooker who grabbed me. Now . . ." Her voice faded.

"What happened tonight? Where were you?"

"I had a call. The transplant people had a kidney for Mom. I went to the hospital, but it was a false alarm. The kidney had deteriorated. I just left her an hour ago."

Chris didn't say anything, but there was a very big elephant on the table. A big suspicion neither of them wanted to voice.

"How much do you want to tell the police?"

"It can't have anything to do with the Westerfields," she said. "They just found out this morning . . ."

"You can't dismiss it, either," he said quietly.

"No, but if I say anything to the police . . . it will be all over the media. It will sound like an accusation, and Leigh . . . She may never cooperate. I didn't want to call the police for that reason, but the insurance . . ."

The doorbell rang, and Kira answered it. Two uniformed officers stood there. "We had a call about a burglary."

She stood aside to let them in. "I'm Kira Douglas. This is my mother's house, but I'm staying here. She's in the hospital. I came home after . . . visiting her and found this . . ." She gestured with her arm.

"And you?" asked one of the officers as he faced Chris. He looked about twenty.

"Chris Burke," he replied. "I was formerly with the Atlanta police, now a PI."

The two officers perked up. "Heard of you," one said. "You working a case?"

"Kira's a friend," Chris said, avoiding answering the specific question. "Her mother worked for me for years and was great when my wife was sick."

The officer turned back to Kira. "When did you come home to find this?"

Kira looked at her watch. "About thirty minutes ago. I called Chris and the police."

"The hospital?" queried one of the officers.

"My mother has renal failure and is waiting for a kidney transplant. We thought she had one tonight but it . . . didn't work out."

She answered all their questions, admitting to her carelessness in leaving the door unlocked.

"I'm sorry, ma'am," the officer said. "Did anyone know you were leaving?"

She shook her head. "I just ran out when I heard there might be a chance . . ."

"Any idea as to who might have done this? Doesn't look like a random burglary."

She hesitated only a moment before shaking her head. "No."

"Anything missing?"

"Two computers, including a laptop. Jewelry. I don't know what else yet. A lot of things were just destroyed."

He took several forms from a clipboard he'd carried in. "Make a list of all the missing items. Include any registration numbers and bring it to the precinct in the next two days."

"That's all?" she blurted out.

"What about fingerprints?" Chris asked.

"You know we don't do that on a burglary."

"Ordinary burglaries, no, but there's violence here."

One of the officers hesitated. "Gotta have a good reason to call in investigators."

"Use my name."

"You can't tell me anything else?"

"I just don't like what I see here," Chris said. "I think this lady could be in danger. It's not your everyday nonviolent burglary."

The older officer made a call. She couldn't hear the conversation, but he soon returned. "A technician will be here in an hour. In the meantime, maybe you can go ahead and make out that list of missing items while he's here."

She didn't think she could make a list of anything.

She knew Chris was going out on a long limb for her in asking for more than a rudimentary investigation without saying why. That could come back to haunt both of them. He knew, though, how much she wanted to keep this out of the newspapers, even her own.

"Kira?" Chris roused her to action.

She nodded. "I'll have a preliminary list in a few moments." She went to her room, found a place among the ruins, and tried to remember all the pieces of jewelry now missing.

She had to be at work in a few hours. She needed to be a functioning human being. But she was numb. Completely numb.

Who would have done something like this? A simple burglary was understandable. But there was a viciousness here that sickened her.

Two technicians arrived twenty minutes later. She watched for several moments as they went about their work. They started with her fingerprints, then moved through the house, leaving white powder in their wake.

Forty minutes later, the technicians were gone, and she and Chris were left in the house.

"You going to be okay?" he asked. "You could come and stay with me."

She shook her head. "By the time I packed and got there, it would be time to go to work."

"Then I'll stay here on your sofa."

"No need."

His expression was implacable. "I think there is."

"I'll call Max Payton in a few hours."

"Why don't you call him now?" he said, his voice hard.

"We don't know this has anything to do with the Wester-fields."

"Maybe, maybe not, but after twenty years on the police force, I don't much believe in coincidences," he said as he picked up pieces of glass. "The Westerfields are the only thing new in your life." He paused, then added, "If you don't call, I will. Someone tried to kill you earlier today. Maybe they meant to try again tonight. He—or she—needs to be put on notice, and at this point, Payton should be asking his client some questions."

"I don't think it could be Leigh Howard. She just learned about it Saturday."

"Two days. Long enough to hire someone. She stands to lose an inheritance if you're right."

"I told her I didn't want it."

"I doubt she believed you. Few people give up a fortune, and nearly all who have one can't believe anyone else wouldn't give everything they have to get one."

She hesitated. She had Max Payton's cell phone, but she hated to be called in the early hours of the morning. Those kinds of calls always terrified her. Still, Chris was right. She had to be at the paper at 7:30 a.m.

She punched the numbers even as she wondered what she would say if he answered. It was an ungodly hour. He answered after two rings. The cell phone must be next to his bed, or he was a vampire. Or both.

"Payton," he answered in a clipped voice. Not sleepy at all.

"Kira Douglas."

Silence. Then, "Good God, do you know what time it is?"

"I would, if I had a workable clock. Someone trashed my house."

Silence, then, "Why call me?"

"I think someone tried to kill me earlier."

"I'm coming over." The phone went dead.

That was the last thing she expected. She hadn't even given him the address. Her old address and phone number were in the phone book. Maybe he would go there.

Somehow, she thought not. He would know. He would have made it his business to know. He exuded competence.

She didn't know if she was prepared for him tonight. She was too heartsick to confront that cynicism. She was still numb by the events of the last twelve hours. She'd gone through a roller coaster of emotions. Terror at the MARTA station. Then spiraling hope. The crushing disappointment that followed. Then the destruction at the house.

She was running on autopilot at the moment, and she feared anything more would send her careening into a black hole.

"Damn," she said. "He's coming. Now."

"Didn't expect you to back down from a fight."

She didn't. Never had. Never would. She was just so damned tired and frustrated. Time was seeping away. She stood and walked around the room.

"Do you have any brandy around here?" Chris asked.

"I think so. I keep it for eggnog at Christmastime. The bottle is ancient." She started to get up. "If it's even intact. I didn't look in the cabinet beside the sink."

"I'll do that."

She sat back down. "You're a very nice man, Chris."

"Not always," he said.

She looked at his hard face. She imagined he'd probably been very good at his job. And right now she was very, very thankful to have him here. She'd been so alone these past few days, especially last night as she'd waited for news at the hospital. She probably should have called him or someone, but she had her mother's horror of imposing on other people. He had given her the information she needed. She'd hated to ask for more. "Thanks for being here."

"You should have called me when you heard about the potential donor," he said. "You should have called me after the incident at the MARTA station."

"It happened so fast . . . both . . ." Her voice faded as she tried to defend her action.

"It's insulting to me, to your other friends," he continued. Then his voice softened. "I tried to do everything myself when my wife fell ill. Didn't work very well and I hurt a lot of friends by shutting them out. Don't make the same mistake."

"I didn't mean to do that . . . It's just imposing . . ."

"Christ, you sound like me a few years ago." He put a hand on her arm. "Let me help, like your mother helped Risa."

Dear God, she needed help. She nodded.

"I hope you mean that," he said, and went to the kitchen. He returned with two juice glasses half filled. She wondered whether any of the other glasses survived.

She accepted one of the glasses and took a sip. The brandy burned all the way down.

He sat on the floor. There were no other chairs left whole in the room. "Tell me exactly what was said when you talked to Payton and Ms. Howard."

She told him everything, every word she could remember. She'd called him after meeting with Leigh, but not the attorney. She should have, but she'd still felt blistered by Max Payton's words.

When she finished, he asked, "Did you talk to anyone else about the baby switch?"

"No. No one." She couldn't keep her eyes from wandering about the room. She should clean up the house. At least, start. But her mind stopped at the possibility that someone might have tried to kill her, and that someone, or someone else, viciously destroyed everything important to her mother.

She took another sip of brandy, then asked, "What do we really know about Leigh Howard?"

"Just what's been in the newspapers. I'll start digging deeper. Maybe I'll stop over there."

The doorbell rang.

She steeled herself. She recalled the frosty look on Max's face yesterday. She wasn't sure she could take it now.

It's for Mom.

She shook her head at Chris as he started for the door. Instead, she went to it herself. Opened it.

He stood tall and lean and handsome and . . . grim.

Her heart sank. Even through the chill yesterday, or was it the day before, she thought she'd made the smallest impact. But looking at his face now, she knew she hadn't.

He was an enemy.

16

Max knocked at the door of the cottage-style brick home. It looked small, but was obviously well maintained. A streetlight revealed a multitude of rosebushes surrounding the porch.

He was still stunned by the phone call. Stunned and apprehensive. He wanted to think his conversation Saturday with Leigh had nothing to do with this. Yet something nagged at him. She'd been reckless in the past. Her college days had been tumultuous. She drank too much. She experimented with drugs, and she'd certainly had a tendency to pick guys more interested in her fortune than herself.

Kira Douglas opened the door. Her cheeks were smudged, and her eyes tired and sad. The look struck straight into his heart. Then she seemed to regain strength as she regarded him warily.

He had to work at maintaining his lawyer face. He had a compelling need to hug her and tell her everything would be all right.

He couldn't do that. For a number of reasons, he couldn't do that. Most of all his loyalty to Ed, and his own integrity as an attorney. He was the opposition. His duty was to his client. And he wasn't sure everything *would* be all right.

He stepped inside without an invitation and looked around.

His eyes roamed around the slashed painting and furniture. There was a fury here that went beyond what he'd expected. It made him ill.

Then he saw the man standing in the shadows.

The man stepped forward. "I'm Chris Burke," he said. "I'm a private investigator."

"Ms. Douglas mentioned you," Max said. "A former member of the police department, I understand. A captain."

"You've done some research."

"Your client tossed a bomb in my client's lap." Max studied Burke. Mid to late forties. Early to be retired from a fast-track career. He was a tall man, taller than his own six foot two height. Big as well. Not fat, but big boned.

Max's gaze turned back to Kira. "What happened?" he said.

Burke answered instead. "A few hours earlier someone tried to tumble her from a MARTA station platform onto the tracks just as a train was coming."

Shock stilled Max. A burglary could be random. Even one this vicious. But an attack on Kira's life hours earlier? As much as he wanted to, he couldn't escape the very real possibility that it had something to do with Kira's revelation.

His anger at the way she'd approached Leigh faded as he looked at her. Her dark hair looked mussed and she wore no makeup. She looked vulnerable and pale, and yet she had the light of battle in her eyes.

"Tell me everything," he said. "From the beginning."

"I took MARTA to work this morning. There's a station not far from here, and parking downtown is always a problem." She paused, and he knew she was remembering every step. "I left work around seven. I just missed a train and was waiting for another. There were just a few people there. I heard the train coming."

Her hands balled into fists, and he saw fear—no, terror—in her eyes as she obviously relived those seconds on the platform. He wanted to kill someone at that moment.

She stopped, then started again, her words coming in spurts. "I felt more than saw someone coming close to me, then he plowed into me, his hands . . . I'm not sure whether he stumbled and grabbed me or intentionally pushed me, but I fell toward the track. I tried to grab something . . . There was nothing there. Then someone caught my hand and pulled me away from the tracks. It was all so quick I didn't really get a look at the person who ran into me."

"Did you call the police?"

"I thought it was just an accident. So did the man who helped me. I thought that until . . . I got back from the hospital and found the apartment in shambles."

"When was that?"

"Early this morning. The hospital called last night and said a kidney had been located. I was there for a number of hours."

He looked startled. "She had a transplant, then?"

"No. The kidney was deficient." The defeat in her eyes was palpable.

"I'm sorry," he replied.

"Don't be sorry. Just tell me who did this."

"I wish I knew." He couldn't say the MARTA incident and burglary didn't have anything to do with her claim. Not yet. But he sure as hell intended to find out.

He noticed the bandage around her arm. "Did that come from the MARTA station?"

She nodded.

He dug his fingers in his pocket. He wanted to punch someone. He hoped to hell that Leigh hadn't had anything to do with this. He couldn't believe she did. Fifteen years ago, maybe. Today, no.

He turned to the man standing behind Kira. "Burke?"

"Yes."

"You used to be a cop. What do you think?"

Burke shrugged. "I learned never to think anything until I know more facts. I look at who has motive. Opportunity."

"You think it's connected to Ms. Douglas's theory."

"It's a possibility that can't be ignored."

"You've called the police?"

"Of course," Burke said. "They took fingerprints." His tone was even, but the words were a warning.

"On a burglary?"

Burke shrugged. "You think this is an ordinary burglary?"

"Did you say anything about . . ."

"Leigh Howard?" Burke replied. "No. Not yet. We probably should have, but Ms. Douglas doesn't want the publicity that would result. At least not now."

Max heard the threat in his voice. He didn't like it. But then, he didn't like what had happened here, either.

"Did you talk to her about the DNA test?" Kira asked.

"I did."

"And . . ."

"She needs time to absorb this. Right now, she doesn't believe Ms. Douglas. I'm sure Ms. Douglas believes it, but . . ."

Kira started to say something, but Chris interrupted. "A blood test will determine the truth," he said. "What are you—and Ms. Howard—afraid of?"

"Leigh doesn't believe it, and therefore feels that it's unnecessary," Max said, his eyes neutral.

Kira's eyes sparked. Color came back into her face.

"Why did you come here, then?" she demanded. "To make sure I wasn't lying about the burglary? About the MARTA attack?"

"I didn't think you were," he said softly. "I wanted to make sure you were all right."

"Now you've seen for yourself. You can leave. I'll retain an attorney tomorrow and force a DNA test."

"Give Leigh a little more time."

"I don't have time. My mother—her mother—doesn't have the time."

"She doesn't accept that. How long did it take you to believe it? More than a day or two, I expect."

The arrow hit home.

But she stiffened. "Then you admit it's a possibility."

"Anything's possible. Just not very likely, and after the way you . . . obtained her DNA sample, she isn't inclined to trust you."

"And you didn't help?"

"I presented her with options." The words were pompous

and self-righteous, and he realized it the second they left his mouth. He was finding it more and more difficult to be Leigh's advocate. What if she was involved in some way here?

"I thought attorneys were all about the truth," she said in a strained voice.

"Leigh wouldn't . . ."

"You can tell her I survived. You can tell her someone did a damned good job of destroying everything my mother collected over the years. You can also tell her I don't scare easily."

Sparks darted from tired eyes, and tension filled the air. But it wasn't the sexual attraction that had so surprised him days ago. This came from anger and frustration, even remnants of this afternoon's terror. Her lips quivered ever so slightly, and he had the damndest urge to take her in his arms. To hold her close.

He took a step toward her, but Burke blocked him. "I think you should go."

Max didn't move. He didn't want to leave like this. Contempt was in her eyes. He tried not to remember the softness from several days ago. "If I can do anything . . ."

"You know what you can do," she said. "The right thing."

"The 'right thing' isn't quite that black and white." He wanted to explain. He wanted her to understand what she was asking. "Leigh was in an accident when she was six. Her mother and father were killed. She almost died. She was in the car with their bodies an hour before anyone found them, and then she went though a number of operations without either of them there, without anyone who cared. She still has nightmares. She won't go to a hospital, not even when she's hurt. Then you tell her she's not a Westerfield and, by the way, you want a kidney. You throw all this at her and want an answer in a day. You're threatening everything she knows. Everything she is. Just like that." He snapped his fingers.

He knew he wasn't being diplomatic. He knew he wasn't helping anything. But he had to make Kira understand what she was asking. "I'm damned sorry for what happened, but I don't believe Leigh had anything to do with it. And accusations right now won't help your cause."

He stopped. He wasn't getting anywhere. Both Burke and

Kira eyed him with suspicion he couldn't allay. Not now. The best thing he could do was leave, let her get some rest.

"You won't be alone tonight?"

"I'm staying," Burke said.

A sharp jolt of jealousy stabbed him with unexpected ferocity. The power of it stunned him.

He nodded and left before he did, or said, something he would regret.

"Go to bed," Chris told her as the door closed.

She looked at him. "What do you think?"

"It fits with what I learned about Leigh Howard." He hesitated, then said cautiously, "He was right about throwing all this at her and expecting an answer. I know how painful it was for you. How you fought it. Demanded another test."

She sighed. "I know," she said. "I've handled it all very badly. I just thought . . ."

He put an arm around her shoulders. Why didn't he make her quake inside like Max Payton did?

"Come on," he said. "I'll help you put a bed together. There must be complete sheets somewhere."

He was right. The burglar hadn't reached the linen closet. Together, they remade the bed and gathered the torn sheets that had been there.

"What about you?" she asked as they finished.

"I'll take the chair. It's not long before dawn and it sure as hell won't be the first time I've slept in a chair or in a car." He paused. "Maybe you should take the day off tomorrow."

"I've already taken off too much time. An hour of sleep will work."

"I'll have new and better locks installed tomorrow, along with a damned good alarm system."

"I can't afford . . ."

"A friend owes me."

"But . . ."

He put a finger to her mouth. "Don't argue. Remember what I said earlier."

She gave him a rueful grin. "Yes, sir."

He started out the door of her bedroom. "You have insurance?"

"Mom does."

"Good." He hesitated, then said, "I'd like to talk to Leigh Howard. I know about losing someone. Maybe I can help."

She nodded, and he left the room, closing the door behind him. She took off her jeans and shirt and crawled between the covers.

Defeat weighed heavily on her. She'd pushed too hard tonight.

What now? Time was slipping away like sand in an hourglass.

Why had she ever thought Max Payton had a heart? Why had she held hope? His voice tonight had been so darn neutral. His eyes so masked.

Well, if he wanted a battle, she would give him one. If Leigh Howard held her wealth and position in so much regard, perhaps the threat of taking it away would help.

17

Lights were on in the Westerfield house when Max drove through the gate. He thought about going over, but it was just past 5:00 a.m. Leigh often slept with lights on. She didn't like the dark.

He drove past the house and parked in front of his own. He sat there for a moment, fighting emotions. He hadn't had to do that in a long time. He guarded his heart well. Emotions only brought pain.

Now he was buffeted by them, pulled in two different directions.

In those few hours at dinner a few days ago, he'd found himself attracted to Kira Douglas. In fact, he'd really liked her. He still did, despite her duplicity. He understood it now, and he wasn't quite sure he wouldn't have done the same. He'd done a hell of a lot worse in the name of love. He told himself he'd been right tonight, that his responsibility was to Leigh. But he couldn't get Kira's face out of his thoughts. Nor that of a dying woman.

He parked his car and went inside to his study. *His* study. His house. As a kid, he'd never thought to have anything quite so grand. He was damned lucky he'd even survived childhood.

Ed had made this all possible. He'd made him a part of the family, and his position in the family was solidified when Ed gave him the house built for Leigh's parents. After they died, Leigh had moved into the big house, and this one had been empty for years.

Although Ed had explained to the family that he wanted his attorney close by, they all knew that it was more than that. As Ed got older, he mourned not having sons and had tried to mold Max into one.

And now Max owed him more than he could ever repay. He certainly owed his granddaughter loyalty. But which granddaughter, if tests proved Kira right?

He sat and toyed with a pen on the desk as he tried to reason out a puzzle. He had to believe Kira now. She really had no reason to press for a DNA test unless she already knew the results. That meant accepting the supposition that the babies had somehow been switched.

And if he accepted that, then did a switch happen by accident or on purpose?

One baby had been sick. Kira had told him that. How could an "accident" happen under those circumstances?

Ed? He'd desperately wanted an heir. He'd wanted a grandson, but grudgingly accepted a granddaughter. He'd loved her in his own crusty way. Unfortunately, Leigh never realized that.

He sighed. Kira might well have opened a snake's nest. Leigh had a record as a juvenile. Mostly kid stuff. Shoplifting on a dare. Reckless driving. One DUI. The records had been buried by tons of money, but he suspected that Chris Burke could find his way to it.

When the clock struck seven thirty, he called his office and canceled all his morning appointments.

"What about Mr. Melton? You had scheduled a meeting with him."

Damn. Jack had asked for it three days ago. He wanted a reconsideration of his proposal to buy the company Max had nixed days earlier. He claimed to have new information.

The answer was still going to be no. Max didn't like the company stats and cared less for its CEO, who would be part of the deal.

"An emergency has developed," he said. "Postpone the meeting until tomorrow."

"He's not going to be happy."

"Apologize for me. It can't be helped."

"Okay, boss."

He hung up and called Leigh. She usually woke about this time and went down to the barn.

"'Ello," she said sleepily.

"Good morning."

"Too early to be good."

"I need breakfast. Is Mrs. Baker in the kitchen yet?"

"I'm sure she is."

"You know what I like."

"Do you ever change, Max?"

"Nope."

"Okay," she said. "Two eggs over light, dry toast, fruit, and coffee. Boring."

"I like boring."

A pause. "Is there something new?"

"Yes," he replied.

"Good or bad?"

"We'll talk when I get there. Fifteen minutes."

"It takes me longer than that."

"Not today."

"You're frightening me."

"I don't mean to. Now go get dressed."

He hung up before she could ask more questions. He went to his bathroom, took a quick shower and shaved, then pulled on a pair of slacks and a sports shirt.

He walked across to the big house. He still thought of it that way despite the politically incorrect connotation. He remembered the first time he visited there. It seemed enormous then. It *was* large, though not nearly as big as many mansions he'd visited. Ed seldom wasted money. He'd wanted a place to entertain for business purposes as well as a home for himself and his family, but he didn't admire waste.

Toward the end of Ed's life, Max had found his mentor wandering throughout the place, obviously looking for a family that didn't exist. His wife had died early and his one child had died in an accident. His granddaughter feared him. Ed had been disappointed time and time again by family. Max didn't intend that to happen to him.

To his surprise, Leigh was in the kitchen, drinking a cup of tea as he entered. Mrs. Baker was at the stove and the minute she saw him, she dropped two eggs in a hot frying pan and started the toaster. He poured himself a cup of coffee, just as he used to do when Ed was alive.

"I hope you're eating, too," he said to Leigh. "You're getting too thin."

"You can never be too thin."

"That's a woman's viewpoint, not a man's." His thoughts immediately switched to Kira. She looked like a woman, not a shadow of one.

He wondered how she was doing this morning. Whether she'd talked to the police again, or to an attorney. He had to prepare Leigh for both possibilities.

He took a sip of coffee. He didn't want to talk to Leigh with the housekeeper present. She'd been with the family for years, but he had the attorney's obsession with discretion.

Leigh didn't press it, but her eyes were worried.

"Have anything planned today?"

Her face lit. "The new horse is arriving tomorrow, I think, and I want to get her stall ready. Fresh hay, a new blanket. Thank you for arranging it."

"I'm anxious to meet this million-dollar baby."

"You exaggerate."

"Only a little."

Mrs. Baker put a plate in front of him and another with only fruit in front of Leigh.

"Thanks," he told her. "You can clean up later," he said, effectively dismissing her.

Mrs. Baker didn't question it. She left the room and shut the door behind her.

"You do that just like Granddaddy."

"He rubbed off on me."

"Not entirely," she said. It sounded like a compliment. Unusual since she'd often been at war with him since the will was read. She'd bitterly resented the restrictions her grandfather had placed on her.

"What happened?" she asked after a brief silence. "You said there was something new."

"First, did you talk to anyone about Kira Douglas and her claim?"

"Only Seth and David. Neither believed it. David was particularly vehement. His father was at the delivery, and we all know how careful and deliberate my uncle is."

"I didn't know that," he said, but then, there was no reason he should. He'd joined the family twelve years after her birth. He filed away another interesting fact in one of his mental compartments.

"Kira Douglas's home was ransacked last night," he said without preamble. He quickly related the events yesterday and last night.

Her face paled. "Surely you don't think . . ."

"No. I don't think you had anything to do with it. But the two incidents—the MARTA incident and burglary—are too close for a coincidence. At least that's the way the police will see it."

"She told the police about what she's claiming."

"No, not yet. She doesn't want publicity any more than we do. At least, she hadn't named anyone last night." He paused, then dropped the bomb. "You have to do the DNA test, Leigh. If you don't do it informally, she'll go to a court, and it will be a circus." He held up a hand. "I know you don't think it's true. A test would confirm that." God only knew what Seth and David had said. They probably hadn't been helpful. Particularly Seth.

"Seth says any suit would have to be filed in Fayette County. He says he can block it. That he has a number of friends on the bench."

Goddamn Seth.

"He can't bottle it up forever, Leigh." He leaned forward. "Ms. Douglas's mother won't live much longer without a new kidney. Think for a moment how you would feel if she dies, then you find out she really is your birth mother. It's something you'll have to live with. And if she's wrong, well, then a boulder will be off your shoulders."

"I thought about it," she said. "I just don't believe it. I can't believe it."

"Will you take the test if I arrange it? Privately. No publicity."

"That would be admitting it could be true. It isn't."

"Then we can prove it once and for all, and Kira Douglas will go away."

"You swear?" she asked.

"Yes."

She hesitated for a moment. Then she nodded slowly. "That doesn't mean I accept the possibility. I just want to get rid of this woman."

He sighed internally. "I'll set up a DNA test immediately. It's easy. Just a swab from your mouth."

"I know. I went online and read everything I could."

He smiled. "You did?"

"I'm really not as clueless as you think I am."

"I never thought that. I just thought you were hiding from the world, and I wanted to jerk you back." He took a sip of coffee. "There's nothing I would like more than to hand over the inheritance to you, no strings attached."

"And then what would you do?"

He shrugged. "Continue as attorney for Westerfield Industries if you want."

"Not if Jack Melton has anything to do with it," she said with a sudden slyness he didn't like.

That stopped him. "What do you know?"

"Jack wants you out. He's approached me about it. He wants me to fight the trust. He knows I'm angry about Grandfather's conditions. He thinks I'm angry enough to put him in charge."

"What did you tell him?"

"I won't go behind your back. I've learned a little in the past year. I won't forget what you did for me in college or in getting rid of Adam."

But despite her words, her eyes were guarded.

"And Seth? Does he agree with Jack?"

"It really doesn't matter. He doesn't have enough stock to count."

But Seth did have an influence on her, and Max didn't need a lawsuit contesting the trust. Not now.

She abruptly changed the subject. "What if the tests prove a match? I won't give a kidney. I can't. I never want to see a hospital again." She paused. "What are my rights?"

"No one can force you to donate. As far as the trust goes, I did more research. As I said, I think it could go either way. A judge would decide whom Ed meant to be his main beneficiary. Was it you specifically? Or was it the daughter of his daughter?"

She played with her teacup. "You've checked into her background. Find anything?"

"No. She's what she seems. I really do believe her only interest is getting the kidney."

"I wonder how long that will last," she said, not bothering to hide her doubts about it.

"I don't know," he admitted, and really didn't. Money did strange things to people, and a great deal of money did even stranger things. "But I can draw up an enforceable contract."

"And she can come back and say she signed it under duress."

Another surprise. Leigh had grown up, and he hadn't noticed. "Yes," he admitted. "That doesn't mean a judge would agree.

"Leigh, I want you to think very seriously about it. The attack and burglary last night might well make Ms. Douglas go public, and I don't think you want that."

She nodded, then looked uncertain. "You're sure I should do this?"

"If not, we would only be postponing the inevitable. Once we know what we're facing, well, then there're options."

"All right, then," she said reluctantly.

"I'll call you about the time," he said.

She nodded, but her gaze wouldn't meet his, and he saw her hand trembling on the table. She saw his gaze and stood. "I have to get dressed."

"It'll be all right," he said.

"Will it?" she replied dubiously, and left the room before he could answer. He sat there as Mrs. Baker returned and cleaned up the dishes. He was surprised by Leigh's capitulation.

Had she really grown up that much? Or was something else at work?

18

Leigh felt the walls closing in on her again, just as metal had twenty-six years ago. Squeezing the life from her. She'd tried not to let Max see it. But it was there in her mind. In her reality.

She walked into the paneled den where she gazed on the portrait of her mother. There was one of her father in her own room.

"I wish you were here," she whispered to the woman in the portrait. A lullaby floated in her mind. She'd been loved, probably the only time in her life. Now someone wanted to take even that away.

She would have liked to see a more combative Max. A "Hell, no, we won't" would have been far preferable to what she believed was acquiescence. She'd given him the answer he wanted, but that didn't mean she would be available for an appointment. Even the idea of needles sent shivers through her. He should have known that. Maybe he did. Maybe he was right, but dread was a dark pit inside. The nightmares had increased in the past few days. Her mother's bloody face and empty eyes . . .

Her mother.

Not some stranger's mother. *Hers*. The one she remembered and loved and even talked to on occasion.

Kira Douglas was responsible. She hated the woman, first for the way she'd intruded in her life and now for trying to destroy it.

She went to the phone, started to call Seth, then hung up. It was time she depended on herself.

Her city editor took one look at Kira when she arrived late and called her aside. "Let's go into an office," he said.

She followed him, her heart sinking. She had to tell him what was going on. If she didn't, and kept asking for time, he would fire her. She would have to trust him.

She hated to do that. She hated putting a burden on him when it was her problem. She would be asking him to do what a reporter never did: withhold one hell of a story.

She followed him into a room. He closed the door and nodded toward a chair. "Sit."

She did. He could be formidable at times, a teddy bear at others.

"You look like hell," he said.

"That bad?"

"That bad. How long since you've had some sleep?"

"Night before last?"

"I don't need a zombie."

"The story was good yesterday."

"It could have been better. Didn't have your usual flair." He sat on the table. "Talk to me, Kira. Is your mother worse? Something else going on?" His eyes traveled to the bandage on her arm.

"A lot is going on," she said. "I need your word, though, that you won't print anything until I approve it."

"You have my attention," he said. "What do I have to give up?"

"A story that's still unfinished, but if everything works out, it could be a great story, an award-winning story. Or it could be a great story that can't ever be printed."

"You still have my attention. Why can't it be printed?"

"It could destroy lives. All of a sudden I'm questioning what I do for a living."

"Kira, you're one of the best I've seen. You can extract stuff no one else can. I don't want to lose you." He sighed. "A great story that can't be printed. You ever read those Greek myths?"

"Tantalus?" she said.

He nodded. "I'm not good at wanting something I can't have. Give me a good reason."

"A woman's life."

"Your mother's?"

"Yes."

"The transplant?"

"We thought we had a donor last night. She was prepped, ready to go, and at the last moment they pulled the plug. Something wrong with the kidney."

"Hell, Kira. That's rough."

"There's more," she said. "I might have a live donor for Mom."

"You told me there wasn't a match."

Leap of faith. "There could be." Her hand clutched the notebook she'd brought with her. "My mother's biological daughter. I just found out about it." She hesitated, then added, "The blood tests I took showed I couldn't be her biological daughter. There's one out there and I think I know who she is."

"Christ," he said. "You had no idea?"

Then she told him about the possibility of a baby swap. Then the MARTA incident and the burglary. She left out any mention of Max.

"You think all this is connected."

"I think it's a good possibility."

She explained everything, every theory she had. Everything but the name of Leigh Howard. "Mom doesn't know. She can't know. She's extremely weak and this kind of news . . . could kill her."

"How much did you tell the police?"

"Not all of it. I was afraid it would get to the media."

"And this person. She doesn't want to give a kidney."

"I don't think she believes it. No one would. I didn't at first."

"Who is it?" Then his eyes widened. "That feature you insisted on doing. Does it have anything to do with it?"

"Yes." She'd hoped he wouldn't come to that conclusion this quickly. She knew she could get fired for using the newspaper. Her throat closed in on her, but she had to tell him. "It was an opportunity to get a DNA sample."

"My God," he said as rubbed his face. "Are you saying what I think you're saying? That one of the city's most prominent families might be involved in attempted murder and burglary as well as covering up a baby switch?"

She nodded. "It was unethical using the newspaper to get to know her, but it *was* a good story. It was only way I thought I could get DNA fast without stirring up a mess. It showed a match."

"You apparently kicked up a mess anyway."

"Yes," she said unhappily.

"This is a damned good story. Switched babies. A life hanging in the balance . . ."

"I know," she said miserably. "But it could cost my mother her life."

"What do you mean?"

"I offered to keep everything quiet and not say anything or make any claim on the Westerfield trust if she donates a kidney. She would simply be a Good Samaritan. My mother would get a kidney. All would be right with the world."

"Except for attempted murder. You could have been killed."

"I wasn't."

Another line had been added to the lines around his eyes in the past few moments. But she was glad she'd told him. This could come back to haunt the newspaper, and she couldn't let that happen. Her actions were her own.

Wade Carlton shifted his teddy-bear bulk on the desk, stared at her for a moment. "Anything important coming up in city hall the rest of this week?"

"Just a few more budget hearings by various committees."

"Okay. Tell you what we'll do, though I'll have to run it by the managing editor. I'm going to put you on special assignment for the next two weeks. Keep a daily diary, and we'll do a series on the need for transplant donations. You can do it on your own time. If we can use the Westerfield angle, we will. You're right. It would make a blockbuster story, but I'm not going to risk someone's life for it. If we can't use it, the stories will make a damn good public service series."

She should have known. She'd known Wade for five years, not only on a business basis. They were friends outside the newsroom as well. "Thank you."

"I'll have to run it by Jim first. And I'll talk to him about getting you some protection, just as he did for Robin last year." He stood. "I think you should tell the police everything."

"A few more days first. I have to give Leigh Howard time to agree. If she won't, all bets are off."

He frowned.

"I promise to tell the police if I don't have an agreement by Friday."

"I'll hold you to that. Now go home, straighten up, and get some rest. I'll have Diane fill in for you at city hall. I'll talk to Jim and call you this afternoon."

"I'll keep city hall?"

"Yeah."

For the first time in several days, she felt at least part of the load lift from her shoulder. She stood. "I really am sorry about the Leigh Howard story. I should have checked with you first."

"Yeah, you should have," he said.

It was a rebuke. It sounded offhand, but she knew it wasn't. He was disappointed in her and that hurt.

She went to Diane Doza's desk and filled her in on the on-going stories at city hall. Diane, a general assignment reporter, had substituted for her before and knew the issues and personalities.

She left for home. There were calls to the insurance company. Furniture to be replaced, though most would have to wait until the insurance money came in. A computer to be replaced; that was a necessity. A visit to her mother and a call to her doctor.

Chris was still there. He handed her keys for new locks and explained the security system. "I've done some work for them," he said. "They're giving you twelve months' free service."

She wanted to say no, but she didn't have that luxury at the moment. She would pay him back sometime in the future.

"Call me if you need anything. Call if you even suspect a problem. Okay?"

"Definitely. I'm a first-rate coward."

He grinned. "I wouldn't exactly say that."

"Believe me."

"As long as you call at the first sign there's something wrong . . ."

"I will. For the moment, though, I'm going to bed."

He continued to stay there, then said, "I thought I would take Archie and pay Ms. Howard a visit."

"Why Archie?"

"He has a way of disarming women."

Kira had no doubt that could happen. Archie was a mismatched dog, as if he were composed of spare parts. He had a perpetual good nature despite, or perhaps because of, an obviously abusive puppyhood.

"You think you can convince her when her attorney can't."

"I have more than a few reservations about the attorney, but then I don't care much for attorneys in general. Cop bias."

"Go for it," she said. There seemed nothing to lose. Chris could be disarming. He'd probably been the good cop during interrogations.

He left, and she went through the house. Chris had accomplished miracles as far as cleaning up the mess. He'd stacked ruined paintings and furniture in a spare room along with boxes of broken china. The fridge, which had little in it, had been filled with several cartons of chicken salad from a deli.

There was also fresh milk and a jar of cocoa. A sign on it said, "Treat yourself."

She made herself a cup of coffee for now. She had to make

a few calls, then she would take a nap before visiting her mother. She didn't want to look like a walking ghost.

Max made a few calls, determined the best labs for the tests, then made an appointment for Leigh.

He was worried though. Leigh had agreed too easily. He wasn't sure she would go through with it. Probably she had called Seth immediately after he'd left.

Then he called the investigation agency that had prepared the report on Kira. "I want some protection for someone," he said. "Good and discreet. Do you have a recommendation?"

"Davies and Peeples. They're good. They know how to blend in, and discretion is as much a part of their training as firearms."

"Have a number?"

Twenty minutes later he'd hired someone to look after Kira.

He called the newspaper and asked for Kira. She'd left for the day.

She would probably be at one of two places. Her home or the hospital? As exhausted as she'd been last time, he opted for the former.

He went to his secretary, who was a sorceress. She could find anything. Do anything. Conjure anything.

"Do we have any spare laptops around?" he asked.

"Sure. We're always updating."

"I want a good one."

"How soon?"

"Thirty minutes."

"You're a hard taskmaster, but I'll have one."

And she did. Ten minutes later he left the office, a cleaned laptop with him.

Forty minutes later he drove up to her home. He parked, then called her on his cell.

She answered after several rings, her voice sleepy. He tried to ignore the sudden image of her lying in bed, her blue eyes half closed and her body . . .

"I have some news," he said. "I'm outside. May I come in?"

"Outside? What time is it?

"Five p.m. Did I wake you?"

"Yep."

"Sorry I woke you."

"Don't be. It's time to get up. Five in the afternoon is a god-awful time to be asleep."

He grinned at that. "Not always."

"Give me a few minutes."

"Five?"

"Make it ten."

The phone went dead. He glanced at his watch and leaned back. He was surprised at how eager he was to see her. He could have called and sent a messenger over with a computer, but . . .

Dammit. He wanted to confirm for himself she was all right. He wanted to tell her in person that Leigh had agreed to the test. He wanted to see that rare smile again.

He called himself all kinds of an idiot. He was violating every rule he'd ever made for himself. Never get involved with clients or with someone involved in a case. Hell, never get involved, period.

Yet here he was in front of someone's house like a lovesick schoolboy. It shook him to the depth of his soul.

He closed his eyes for a few moments, then glanced at his watch. Five minutes. He stepped outside, stretched, glanced up and down the street. White picket fences protected the neat houses. Several kids played in one yard.

Nothing out of the ordinary. Few cars were parked on the street. It would be difficult for any surveillance without notice. He had to believe the promises of the firm he'd retained earlier.

Another glance at his watch. Two minutes left. Not that he'd ever been the typical schoolboy.

He headed for the porch with the laptop. The door opened.

Kira stood there, her eyes swollen with sleep. She wore a T-shirt and shorts and looked as sexy at that moment as any well-groomed woman in Victoria's Secret lingerie.

She didn't say anything, merely held the door for him. Her face was tight with tension.

He walked in and looked around. Things looked far better than they had early this morning. But damage was still obvious.

He held out the computer to her. "Thought you could use this," he said.

She hesitated. "This wasn't necessary."

"No," he said. "But we had a spare one in the office and I heard you say last night yours was stolen. It's a loan," he added hurriedly before she could say no. "Return it when you have time to get a new one."

She didn't take it. "Is that why you came?"

"No. Leigh has agreed to a DNA test. I thought you would like to know."

"You could have called," she challenged.

"Yes," he said simply. "I could have done that. I just . . . wanted to make sure you were okay."

Her expression softened. "Thank you." She reached out and took the computer and set it down. "When is the test?"

"It's scheduled the day after tomorrow at two p.m."

"Where?"

"At her house. I told her that you—or someone you designate—might want to be there."

"I do."

"Even if the tests show a match, it doesn't mean she'll donate a kidney. As I told you earlier, she won't go near a hospital."

Her back straightened. "Then I'll have to convince her."

He should go. He'd done what he came to do. He felt he owed her at least a computer. He couldn't shake the feeling that the trashing of her home had something to do with the Westerfields. What and who and why he didn't know, but he was damn well going to find out.

"How's your mother?"

"Deteriorating day by day."

"I'm sorry the transplant didn't work out."

"Me, too."

His gaze met hers. He saw the sorrow there. But also the strength and determination that so appealed to him.

There was something else there, too.

He held out his hand. He didn't know if she would take it or not. After a moment's hesitation, she did. Her hand was warm, her fingers long and slender. They wrapped around his, and he felt the need in her. It wasn't sensual, or maybe a small part of it was. It was a yearning, instead, for comfort, for human contact.

He pulled her to him and held her. She trembled against him and his hold tightened.

Delayed reaction from last night's terror.

He knew it. He should let her go and get the hell out of here.

He just couldn't do it.

19

Kira hadn't meant to step into his arms.

She certainly didn't intend to look up at him and melt.

He was on the other side. And there was obviously a deep, personal relationship between Max and Leigh, a protectiveness that crept into his voice when he spoke of her.

God knew things were complicated enough. Even as she reminded herself of all that, she leaned against him, surrendered to the attraction that shimmered between them.

His scent was enticing. She wasn't good at identifying aftershave scents, but she knew she liked this one. Even more, she liked the feel of his body against hers. She fit into his angular form just right.

Stupid, she told herself. Why after her heart's long drought was she attracted to the worst possible man in the universe? Fate was perverse.

And, at the moment, irresistible.

His arms tightened around her, held her so tight she heard the beating of his heart. She lifted her head and looked into his eyes. And was consumed by them.

His lips touched her cheek. Lightly. Almost like the whisper of a breeze.

It was unlike any sensation she'd ever experienced.

He was not a man who hesitated. She'd known that the moment they met. He was strong, decisive, cynical. Yet the tenderness in his gesture was breathtaking. His fingers played with the back of her neck, not in seduction, she sensed, but in comfort, which was, in itself, incredibly seducing.

Her arms went around his neck.

Unwise. So very, very unwise.

The words hung unsaid between them. She saw he realized it as well, but they'd been on the verge of this since that night in the restaurant. Lodestones? Simply raw sex appeal?

She should move away. Too much was at stake. But her legs didn't seem to work very well.

His lips moved to hers. They barely touched, yet a conflagration started in her stomach. He hesitated a moment, then his lips played with hers. The kiss was tender at first, teasing, then exploratory.

She had not thought of him as gentle before. He'd been all unemotional competence, his face a study in reserved discipline with the slightest cynical twist to his lips.

Step back! She couldn't. Her legs were rubbery and her heart pounded and all she wanted was to meld into him, to feel the kiss deepen. From the moment his lips touched hers, she was helpless to protest, to slow the tingling of every nerve, to stop the painful longing inside.

She wanted him, although all her warning bells were clanging. She realized from the tenseness in his body that he had the same mental reservations. Neither stepped away.

She was transfixed with the essence of him. Tremors coursed through his body, and she responded with a hunger she'd never known before. His kiss deepened, and his tongue teased her mouth open. Sensations surged through her.

Heat pooled inside her as his body hardened against hers. His hands encircled her hips, pulling her up until the swelling at the apex of his legs matched the crevice at hers. The heat built inside. It was as if her blood had turned into hot, throbbing rivers of desire, painful in intensity.

She'd never felt such need, such raw desire, before.

She heard the quick intake of his breath, then his lips

pressed hard on hers, taking now because he knew she wanted this as much as he.

"Dammit," he said, his voice breaking as he moved an inch from her lips, his face taut. "This is . . ."

"Crazy," she finished, a tremor in the word. She didn't know what he'd started to say. Probably that this was impossible or unethical or stupid. All of the above.

"Nothing about this is right," he whispered, but then he defied his own words, kissing her again with a passion that crowded out any more warnings.

His hands moved up and down her back in sensuous strokes. His body, his hands, his lips made her quiver with expectation. She closed her eyes. She just wanted to feel and savor, to give up all the anxiety and fear and sorrow that racked her life in the past months and culminated in the combination of events last night.

His mouth consumed hers. His tongue tempted her mouth open again, then seduced. The kiss took on a wild, fierce quality that made everything else fade into nothingness. Passion—or was it lust?—raced through her.

It had been so long since she'd been with a man. And she'd never felt like this before. The need was primal in its intensity. He moved his lips from her mouth, downward to her throat. They lingered there as he caressed the back of her neck, then they went to her ear, nibbling the most sensitive part of the lobe. Her hands left his neck and explored the sides of his body. Lean. Hard. Sexy as sin.

She felt as if she were caught in a whirlpool, drawn more and more into turbulent, twisting currents of feelings. Drowning in them. Drowning in her need for him, for that mixture of reserve and tenderness and even a tempered violence she now felt in him.

He pulled her T-shirt over her head. Freed from clothes, her skin was alive with feeling, with wanting. She fumbled as she tried to unbuckle his belt and unzip his slacks. He helped her and discarded both them and dark briefs.

He picked up his clothes, and she led him to her bedroom. The bed was still mussed from when she'd answered his call. His eyes took it all in, and his fingers tightened around hers.

She slipped off her shorts. She was not particularly proud of her body. Her build was large and she'd never been svelte. But his gaze devoured her even as he hesitated one more time.

"Are you sure?" he asked in a ragged voice.

"Don't you dare stop now," she exclaimed.

He actually grinned. "I won't, then."

He guided her down, then he reached for his slacks and took a package from his wallet.

For the barest of seconds, the action startled her. Had he planned this? Or did he have that many chances or planned encounters? Neither choice was appealing to her.

But then he was beside her again. "That package has been in my wallet for a very long time," he said with a slow smile. "Thank God."

Her last reservation faded as he kissed her, starting with her mouth and moving, ever so sensually and lazily, downward. Her throat, her breasts, then to her midriff, and finally to the triangle of hair. The core of her became a mass of writhing nerve ends, the pain both sweet and exquisite in anticipation as he teased and explored.

Then he moved on top of her and entered her. He moved slowly, taking his time as he ignited feelings throughout her body. The air radiated with hunger, with sex, and she felt like a volcano ready to explode. A sound came from deep within her as she felt the bunching of muscles against her skin.

She caught his rhythm. He plunged deeper and deeper as if seeking the very core of her. Her body moved in response. Hungry. So hungry. Instinctively, she wrapped her legs around him, wanting him to come deeper and deeper as sensations grew stronger and wilder and more exquisite.

Then he slowed again, tantalizing her, seducing her into a primal dance that magnified all those earlier sensations until she wondered how she could bear them without screaming.

She heard her own cry, and his mouth came down on hers, his kiss snatching the sound from her as he made one last mighty thrust. Shocks of ecstasy rocked her, then climaxed in one magnificent explosion. Her body quaked with tremors as he held her.

She felt his body shudder. "My God," he whispered.

She treasured the words even as aftershocks rocked her body. His words echoed her own disbelieving reaction. She'd never suspected sex could be this earth-shattering. It had never been before.

Now she knew where music came from.

She also knew she would never be the same.

He withdrew from her, rolled over. His breath was labored. His hand took hers.

Neither of them spoke immediately. She was still trying to absorb what had happened and the ramifications. Maybe there wouldn't be any for him. She knew there would be for her.

He was an experienced lover. She knew that. Her few experiences had included precious little foreplay, or much of an effort to give her pleasure before her partner took his.

He played with her hand. "You know we just created one hell of a problem," he finally said.

"Yes." She wasn't going to pretend there wasn't one. Despite what had just happened, he still represented what could be an obstacle to her mother's transplant.

"Damned unethical," he added. "I know better."

"Me, too."

To her surprise, he chuckled. "Will you stop agreeing with me and show some outrage?"

"Only if you stop doing what you you're doing now."

"You were tired. I took advantage."

"Some could say I took advantage of you."

He put an arm under her shoulder and pulled her to him. "God, you feel good."

She nestled in his arm. For the first time in months, she relaxed. Felt as if she wasn't alone with the world on her shoulders.

She could relish it for a few moments, anyway.

He turned and ran his free hand over her body.

She inwardly flinched and wished away a few excess

pounds. She wasn't really overweight, but she sure wasn't model size, either. Not like Leigh.

Leigh's image broke the reverie. She didn't want to move. She never wanted to move, but she had to get to the hospital. Her mother would worry if she didn't appear. She also had to see how her mother was doing after the debacle last night. She'd made one call after arriving home today. The nurse said she was doing fine, but Kira didn't really trust the hospital that much.

"I have to go to the hospital," she said reluctantly.

"I'll drive you," he said.

"No." Despite the fact that the last hour was probably the most spectacular in her life, she needed her independence. Especially from him. It would be so easy to yield to him.

"Yes," he retorted, then held up his hand as she started to protest. "Just this one time. It'll be dark soon, and you're still tired. Anyone else would be comatose. I'll drive you there, wait, and then we can have supper at the Italian restaurant."

She started to protest. He stopped her with a kiss. "We have things to talk about."

They did. And he was right about her exhaustion. She'd had a couple of hours of sleep this afternoon but even less the night before. She knew she was near the breaking point, and she couldn't afford that. A good meal sounded like nectar from the gods.

"Okay. Thanks."

He ran a hand through her hair. "You're sexy as hell," he said.

She knew she looked astonished.

"Hasn't anyone told you that before?"

"No."

"Just proves most men are fools."

She wanted to ask him whether his other women friends were thin and fashionable, but she wasn't about ready to let him see that slice of insecurity.

Instead, she forced herself to sit when she really wanted to lie next to him. Forever. Certainly for the night.

At least he would be with her part of the evening.

And then?

Then they would have to stay apart. She had to get a kidney for her mother. He obviously intended to protect Leigh. That could mean a possible court case if that was what it took to force Leigh to donate a kidney.

She stood. "I need a shower."

"Me, too."

She'd never taken a shower with a man. Now was probably not the time to start.

"After me," she said firmly. "You are too distracting."

He stood, obviously a lot more comfortable with his nakedness than she was with hers. "I sincerely hope so," he replied.

He went over to her, held her easily. "This was unwise, but I don't regret it."

The hell of it was she didn't, either.

20

Chris debated whether to call Leigh Howard or just show up.

The problem with just showing up was the gate Kira had described. He might not get any farther.

He picked up the telephone. The housekeeper answered and he asked to speak with Ms. Howard. He gave his name. Lies now would definitely be counterproductive.

To his surprise, Leigh answered.

"Ms. Howard, I'm Chris Burke."

"Mr. Burke?" She obviously knew who he was. Her voice was like ice cubes dropping in crystal.

"I wonder if you could give me an hour of your time. I would like to explain a few things."

"I don't think I want to hear any explanations."

"Ms. Douglas's home was burglarized," he said. "And someone tried to push her in front of a train."

A pause, then, "Are you implying . . ."

"I'm not implying anything," he said. "And Ms. Douglas said nothing to the police about you or the Westerfields. I just want to tell you a little about Ms. Douglas. And her mother."

A stick and a carrot.

Another silence. Then, "You should talk to my attorney."

"I could, but I think there are some things you should hear." He hesitated, then added, "I realize that you're angry about the way Kira obtained your DNA. But she really did do it to avoid everyone unnecessary pain."

"I don't accept that."

At least she hadn't hung up on him.

"Understandable," he said with a charm he hadn't exercised in years. "But I would very much like to talk to you."

Another silence. He was surprised she hadn't immediately hung up. Maybe she *was* curious. "I promise not to say a word about DNA or babies or anything else you don't want to talk about."

"All right," she said, surprising him.

"When?"

"This afternoon. Around four."

"I would like to take you to an early dinner."

"I don't think so," she said.

She would have more control at home. More confidence. That wasn't what he wanted. Still, he hadn't expected to get this far. "I'll be there."

He hung up. He had time to clean up a bit, shave the late-afternoon shadow. Choose something to wear. He wondered whether he should call Kira, but he hoped she would be sleeping, and he didn't want to raise expectations. Maybe, just maybe, Leigh Howard had changed her mind.

He also called the police station and talked to the sergeant in the precinct near Kira's house. He told him what happened and asked him to keep an eye on the house. "Just ask the cops on duty to drive by several times during their watch."

The sergeant agreed. Chris would have preferred something more substantial, but private cops took big bucks, and he knew she didn't have the money. He also knew how independent she was. She wouldn't take anything more from him.

At least she was aware of a threat now and would take precautions. The new security system at the house was top-of-the-line. He knew, though, he wouldn't stop worrying.

Now why had Leigh accepted his invitation? He'd thoroughly expected to be rebuffed. It had been a long shot at best. Maybe she was rethinking her decision. Maybe Leigh Howard really wanted to know more about Katy Douglas.

Or maybe she wanted to know whether she was suspected of having any part in yesterday's events.

Max wasn't sure that driving Kira to the hospital and dining with her again was a good idea.

In fact it was a damned bad one.

But he couldn't get protective personnel there until the next morning, and he sure as hell wasn't going to let her roam alone.

He'd been stunned by the lovemaking. He'd been told he was a good lover. Like everything else he did, he tried to excel, and making love was simply another skill. He'd learned what pleased women.

But tonight had not been technique. It had been pure, explosive emotion. New to him. Startling to him. Hell, terrifying to him.

He didn't know what there was about Kira Douglas that destroyed his ordinary reserve, the wall he'd carefully built around himself as a kid and reinforced through succeeding decades. He'd seen his share of destructive marriages and dysfunctional relationships. He did not intend to add to them, and he'd never been good at sharing himself with others.

He gathered his clothes after she went into the shower. He needed one as well, but joining her, he feared, would be pushing things.

He used a half bath downstairs to wash. He dressed, then waited in the living room for her. He wandered about the room. The television screen was smashed. Bookshelves empty. Broken picture frames littered a mantel over a wood-burning fireplace. He looked through them. All were photos of Katy and Kira Douglas, or Kira alone. A graduation. A beach. A wide grin over a barbecue pit made him smile. In the joint photos, they looked more like sisters than mother and daughter.

Kira joined him. The area around her eyes was still dark with fatigue, but the eyes themselves glowed from their lovemaking.

"Ready," she said.

"That's fast."

Her hair was damp and tendrils curled around her face. She wore a pair of tan linen slacks and a short-sleeved dark brown blouse that fit in all the right places. She looked delectable.

"I'm usually fast," she said. "I've never seen the point of spending hours getting ready to go out."

"Maybe because you don't need it."

"Now that's one of the nicest compliments I've heard lately."

"That's strange. Your smile lights a room." He meant it. When he first met her, he'd liked her, but it was at supper that sparks flew between them. He hadn't understood it because at first glance she wasn't his usual type. Now he did. There was a warmth about her that drew him in, and a sprightly intelligence that challenged him. He liked that in a woman.

She looked disconcerted, but before she had a chance to answer, her cell phone rang. She looked at the number. "It's Chris," she said. "I have to answer it."

He moved away to give her a little privacy. Still, he heard a bit of the conversation.

"I did get some sleep. I'm going to see Mom now."

He couldn't hear the detective's reply. He wondered how close the two were. He didn't like the unexpected jolt of resentment that struck him. He tried to ignore it.

Kira lowered her voice, but he could still hear the words. "You don't have to come. Max drove by. He said he would take me to the hospital and bring me home."

After another pause, "Not to worry. I'll see you tomorrow."

Jealousy tugged at him again. Stronger than before. Ridiculous, but there it was.

After she hung up, she grabbed a purse.

"Has he learned anything?" he asked.

"No," she said simply.

He wanted to know what Burke had said, but he didn't feel he could ask. She'd been more than a little suspicious when he brought the computer. But then, considering what had happened, maybe a little suspicion was a good thing.

She reset the alarm system. He held the door open and watched as she locked the door behind him.

He put his hand on her arm as they went down the steps, and merely the touch sent new waves of heat through him. He wanted her again. He suspected he would always want her.

He tried to ignore that fact and concentrate on her safety. He glanced around. Nothing suspicious. But he wouldn't be satisfied until his protection people arrived in the morning. Until then he intended to make certain nothing else happened to her. At least from any source other than himself.

It was seven when they arrived at the hospital. Max followed her up, then gestured toward the waiting room. "I'll wait over there," he said. "Take your time."

She nodded, grateful for his presence even as she wanted to dismiss it as unnecessary. She had to admit she was afraid. Physically afraid. Afraid in a way that she'd never been before, and she hated that feeling.

Her mother was asleep when she walked in. Good. The more rest, the better. She doubted her mother had had an easy day after last night's disappointment.

She sat down, and her mother's eyes fluttered open as if sensing her presence. She gave Kira a tired smile, then those electric blue eyes sparked as she studied her daughter's face.

"You look different."

Kira wondered whether her mother was well enough to notice the glow in her. It lingered, and she really didn't want to dampen it. A few minutes of bliss in a year darkened by her mother's illness.

It was breaking her heart to sit back and watch someone she loved fade away, especially when she knew there might be a way to save her.

"I have a new assignment. It's going to give me more time with you."

Her mother's face fell. "You love city hall. I don't want you to lose it. Not for me."

"I won't. I'm just taking a brief break. I've been assigned

to do a series on transplants, Mom. The need for them. The problems involved in organ donations. Kind of like an ongoing diary. I can give a personal view that no one else can."

"Everything?"

"Nothing that will hurt or embarrass you, I promise."

"That's not what I meant," Katy Douglas said with the old feistiness that Kira remembered so well. "You . . . can write anything you want. In fact, I hope you will. If it will help the donor program . . ." She started coughing, and Kira held a cup of water to her mouth as she took a sip.

Kira chewed on her tongue. A habit from childhood when she didn't want to show emotion. She put the water down and took her mother's hand. It looked so fragile. "You're my heroine, you know."

Now her mother's eyes misted over. "The only thing . . . I want to see you fall in love. I want to see your children . . ." Her voice trailed off as if the words were too much.

"You will, Mom. I promise."

But there probably wouldn't be any children. She was thirty-two and had no prospect in sight. Max was certainly beyond her reach, even if they weren't adversaries. Today was a freak event. Neither of them could afford to let it happen again.

Her mother's eyes closed. The conversation had worn her out. It was happening more and more often. She leaned down and pushed away hair from her mother's face. More gray now. Thinner. Her mother's breathing was ragged. The number of tubes going into her had increased. Kira had to talk to her doctor tomorrow.

Fear shot through her, wrapped around her heart. How could she lose her?

She didn't know how long she remained. An hour or so. Memories flickered through her head. Picnics and parks on Sundays. Usually places that didn't cost much. But she treasured them, along with those times she'd helped her mother clean a vacant house. Her mother would take along a radio and would sometimes waltz with a broom. Life should be fun, she always said, and she was superb at making lemonade out of lemons.

"Good night," Kira whispered as darkness started to enclose the room. "I'll be back tomorrow."

She hesitated at the door, not wanting to leave but not wanting to tie up Max all night, either. She really didn't want to owe him, even for something as little as this.

He stood when he saw her.

"How is she?"

"Getting sicker by the moment."

"I'm sorry."

"Everyone says that but not many have a chance to do something about it." The statement was barbed, and from the flicker in his eyes, she knew she'd struck home.

He didn't reply, and that was fine with her. She didn't want false promises. She'd slept with him knowing the conflict between them. She could only hope that over time he could convince Leigh. He wanted to. She felt that, though he hadn't put it into words.

But she wanted more. She wanted them to feel the urgency she did.

She hesitated as he guided her to the door. How could she have dinner when her mother was so sick? How could she relax when time was slipping away?

Convince him so he will convince Leigh.

They walked to Lucchesi's. The owner greeted them with a smile. "Happy to have you back." He guided them to a secluded table in the back and lit the red candle on the table.

Pavarotti was still singing his heart out.

Lucchesi beamed at them, then poured Chianti in their glasses. "Ready to order? Or would you just like to look at each other for a while?" His voice was definitely fatherly.

Was she that obvious? How could she even think about Max, about sex, when her mother was fighting for her life?

"We're ready to order," Max said, and she realized he knew exactly what she was thinking. It was disconcerting the way he did that.

"My usual," she said.

"Steak Lucchesi," he said.

Lucchesi touched his lips with his fingers as if blowing a

kiss. "It is *bellissimo*. You will love it." He left the table, a broad smile on his face.

Max leaned back in his chair and regarded her carefully. "You look exhausted."

"Surprise," she said wryly. "It happens when you don't get much sleep."

"You also look delectable."

Oddly, she felt delectable even through the weariness and anxiety. Her body still hummed from his touch.

She tried to shake away the feelings crowding in on her. They shouldn't have come here. It was romantic and intimate and . . . the last place she should be tonight.

"You said there were things to talk about," she reminded him, trying to break the hypnotic hold he had on her.

He took a sip of wine. "We complicated things today."

Classic understatement. "I know."

"We could end up on opposite sides."

"We *are* on opposite sides," she replied. "We will be until Leigh gives the kidney if she's a match."

"Even if you're right about the DNA, she may not be a donor match," he warned. "And if she is, she may not consent to a transplant."

"Can't you convince her?"

He met her gaze directly. "There's nothing more I would like than to see her donate a kidney to your mother, and not only for your mother. Leigh always believed she was unwanted. By everyone. It's messed up her life, just like the accident made her terrified of blood and hospitals. You're asking her to do the one thing she mentally cannot do. Not now. Not yet. Maybe if she met your mother . . ."

"I don't want my mother to know about the switch. It could kill her."

"You have to make some decisions," he said. "You can't say no to everything I suggest. We have Leigh's agreement to the DNA test. It's going to take some convincing to take the next step. Right now your mother is a stranger to her. There's no emotional connection."

His words struck her like a bullet. She *would* have to make

a decision. If there was a match, she would have to tell her
mother about what had happened in that maternity room years
ago. She'd hoped that Leigh could be an anonymous donor,
but that wouldn't be fair to anyone.

"And if she doesn't agree?" she asked after a moment's silence.

"I represent her," he said without emotion, but his gaze
didn't leave her face. "I've represented the family all my
working life, and as an attorney, I'm bound by her wishes."

"Then I'll file suit. I don't care if she's afraid of blood. I
don't care if her life has been tragic. I'm sorry, but that doesn't
mean as much to me as Mom's life."

His eyes cooled. "The more you push it, the more she'll
resist. Leave it to me for a few days. You can't force her to
give a kidney even if she is a match."

She broke a roll into small pieces as she fought her frustration. "Isn't this dinner a conflict of interest?"

"Not if I bring about a negotiation," he said. "That's what
an attorney does."

"Was that what this afternoon was about?" she said, unable to stop the sharp reply. She regretted her comment nearly
the moment it left her mouth.

"Is that what you think?"

"I don't know what to think."

"I don't do negotiations in the bedroom." His voice was
like ice.

She wanted to trust him, but she couldn't. He'd just made it
plain where his loyalties were.

"What are we going to do about today?" she asked.

"Try to forget it happened." His voice was flat.

"No ethics violations?"

"No. Bad judgment maybe." A muscle twitched in his jaw.

"I would say terrible on both of our parts," she said. "I
don't usually sleep with enemies." Lord, but she hurt inside.
She'd been so hopeful he would understand, that he would
convince Leigh. Instead, he was saying, "Wait."

She couldn't wait. Her mother couldn't wait.

"We're not enemies," he replied after a moment.

"Aren't we? I thought you just made that plain." She wasn't sure why she was doing this. Exhaustion. Frustration. Disappointment. Grief.

Or the fact she wanted him to be something he couldn't—wouldn't—be. *Her* advocate. Not Leigh's. Not the person who might be standing between her mother and death.

Unfair? Yes. But she was punishing herself as much as him. She had fallen in bed with him almost immediately. She never did that. Never. There was always a courtship before. An old-fashioned word, but it conveyed what she felt. She'd always prided herself on knowing someone well, or at least liking them very well, before having sex.

She'd practically thrown herself into his arms. She knew nothing about him except he was known as a ruthless and effective attorney and was named bachelor of the year. That usually meant someone who was a player.

The food arrived, breaking the awkward silence. A waitress placed a steaming platter of spaghetti in front of her, asked whether she wanted cheese. She nodded. She wasn't hungry any longer, but she needed to eat.

Max smiled at the waitress and thanked her. It was a small courtesy, but she was always struck by how many people neglected it.

He was perplexing. Enigmatic in many ways. He kept surprising her, but never more than earlier today at the apartment. She should have known he would be an accomplished lover, but she hadn't imagined how accomplished.

Dammit. Her spoon sliced down through the pasta.

"That's a string of spaghetti, not a snake," Max noted.

Had he read her mind? She looked up from the plate and saw the corner of his lips turn up.

"I'm angry."

"I've noticed."

"I'm angry at myself. I shouldn't have—"

"If anyone has a right to be angry with oneself, it's me," he interrupted. "I broke one of my cardinal rules. Never get involved with someone associated with a case. On either side. I'm angry because I've obviously made you unhappy. I didn't intend that. I didn't go to your home planning to make love to you. Dammit, it was the last thing on my mind. I'm still not quite sure . . ."

She couldn't take her gaze away from his. Good Lord, but his eyes were green. At the same time, his words kicked in. So did the almost bewildered way he said the latter ones.

The admission broke some of the tension. For the first time, she wondered if she was getting the first real glimpse at what was inside the well-dressed exterior.

"I'm sorry," she said. "I shouldn't have questioned your . . ." She stopped, looking for the right word. Reporters always looked for the right word.

"Intentions?"

"Motives," she corrected.

"Good," he said simply. "Now eat."

She slowly started to relax. She wasn't ready to shed all her reservations and suspicions, but for the moment it didn't matter. They were two people out to dinner. The candle flickered lazily between them. The wine was seductive. The room warm. The corner intimate. His face intriguing. His eyes deep and intense. Willing her to believe him.

God help her, she did.

21

Leigh paused in front of the full-length mirror in her bedroom.
She rarely did that. She'd even thought about taking it down.

Her grandmother had the mirror put there fifty years ago. It was exquisite. And revealing.

Leigh usually avoided it. She still carried scars from the accident. She had some plastic surgery to cover the worst of them, but the scars on her left leg had been too extensive. She'd had a bone transplant and several other operations to repair it.

She'd trained herself to walk normally, although the left leg was a little shorter than the right, and she usually wore long-sleeved blouses to cover the remaining scars on her left arm.

When angry, her ex-husband had told her how ugly her body was. *Why would any man want to touch you?* He'd seen it before they were married, but within a few months of their marriage she realized he'd married her for her money. Or what he thought was her money.

She bit her lip as she turned away and dressed.

She wasn't sure why she'd agreed to meet the detective. Max had told her not to talk to anyone about this. But curiosity had won out. She kept looking at photos of her mother and comparing them to herself, and to the reporter.

She touched one of the photos. Traced the figure with her fingers. Karen Westerfield Howard had been a tall woman. She was striking on one of the horses she loved. Leigh had always longed to be tall like her. Instead, she was small. Five foot two.

She should be more excited about the new horse that would arrive tomorrow. And she was. But she also realized that the horse wasn't going to fill the huge empty space in her life. In a rare moment of introspection, she realized her obsession with the horse was only to cover the fact that she was lonely.

Max cared, but it was with an exasperated affection that precluded any real relationship. Her housekeeper had been in the Westerfield employ for nearly thirty years. She'd even tried to mother Leigh in her own austere way, but she'd always maintained a certain distance. Her grandfather had been mostly disapproving.

She was probably closest to her second cousins, but David was completely absorbed with his medical practice, and Seth with his political career. And they were family. They *had* to like her.

She stopped herself. She hated those spells, those introspective moments that made her look inside and see the bad stuff. Why did she pick losers as husband material? Why was she so afraid of succeeding at anything? She'd gone through months of therapy to find the reason, and the reason turned out to be the worst possible truth.

Kira Douglas had reopened old but still very raw wounds. Leigh ached as she recalled the love with which the other woman talked of her mother, the way she'd been not only willing but anxious to give a kidney.

It was self-destructive to want to know more. She didn't think she could voluntarily go into a hospital again after the many pain-filled months she'd spent there. The horror of the accident . . .

Even if the kidney was compatible.

And if it was, her entire life had been a terrible joke . . .

She changed blouses. A long-sleeved green one. Fully clothed, she looked elegant. The blouse and slacks covered the ugly parts.

She looked at the clock. Ten till four.

Leigh put on just a touch of lipstick, a brush of powder.

The doorbell rang. Mrs. Baker would answer it, would know that she heard it, too.

She waited a moment, then went downstairs. She met Mrs. Baker going out. "You'll be okay?" the housekeeper asked.

She nodded and went into the library. The man had his back toward the door and was looking at the titles.

"My grandfather collected books. He thought they made a good impression for guests. I doubt if he read any of them."

He turned. "A waste."

She knew from what Kira Douglas said that he was a former police detective. She hadn't known what to expect, but it wasn't the face of the man who turned toward her.

He smiled easily, and his eyes were a warm brown. He wasn't handsome, not like Max, but it was a compelling face with interesting trails around his eyes.

"You like books?" she asked.

"Very much."

"Anything in particular?"

"Histories. Mysteries. Some classics. There are always truths in them. Human nature hasn't changed in a thousand years."

"That's cynical."

"Not really. There's been good guys and bad guys throughout history."

"No one in between?"

"Probably most people fall in between. Shades of gray are the norm. Mother Teresa and Charles Manson are the exceptions."

"Which are the most prominent?"

"Unfortunately the Mansons fascinate more than the saints."

"I don't know if I accept that."

"I hope you don't. It's a cop's perspective. We tend to be gloomy about human nature."

"You're not a cop anymore."

"No, but there's some residue left."

She studied him for a moment. He was a big man. Not fat.

She didn't think there was an ounce of fat on him. Tall. Big boned. And relaxed. Much more relaxed than she felt. She thought he would look relaxed anywhere. He had an air of self-confidence about him. Of authority.

She liked his eyes. Unlike Max's always-wary ones, this man's were open. Friendly. Not like a cop's eyes at all. Or what she thought a cop's eyes would look like. She'd had very little experience with them on a social basis.

"Would you like a drink?"

"Yes, but I have something to ask you first."

"What?"

"I just picked up my dog from the vet. I didn't have time to take him home. He's next to my car with a water bowl. Is that okay?"

"He won't wander away?"

"No. He's decided he found a good thing in me. He's not going to do anything to risk it."

"He can come inside out of the heat."

He looked around the elegant room. "He's housebroken, but are you sure?"

"Now that Mrs. Baker is probably gone, yes."

Now why did she say that? It sounded pitiful. She owned the house now, but she'd never been permitted to have a dog while her grandfather was alive. He always said they were messy, dirty animals. Useless with no real purpose.

But the detective's smile was worth breaking the protocol.

She followed him outside. The dog, his tail wagging madly, stood when they approached. A most peculiar-looking dog of many colors and only one ear.

"Found him alongside the road," the detective said. "Someone had cut off an ear and left him to bleed to death."

She stooped down to pet him and he fell to the ground, turned over, and exposed his stomach to her.

Leigh leaned down and scratched it, and was rewarded by groans of utter pleasure. "What's his name?"

"Archie. And you've just made a friend for life," the detective said.

Feeling awkward, she stood. "Let's go inside."

The dog trotted beside her as they reentered the house and went to the study. Archie sat down next to her feet.

"You're a natural with dogs," he said. "Archie's pretty easy with people now, but he usually doesn't adopt them like this."

"I like animals," she said.

"I read about it in Kira's story. You have horses and a donkey."

She reached down and touched Archie, and he tried to lick her hand. "I thought about getting a dog, but . . . I'm gone a lot during the day." *Excuses. Excuses not to break out of a habit.*

She loved her horse and Maude, but the real responsibility belonged to Rick.

"You said you would like a drink?"

"A beer?"

She flushed. "I think that's the one thing we don't have. Bourbon, Scotch, wine?"

"Bourbon and water, thanks."

She went to a bar in the corner and returned shortly with a glass of bourbon for him and a small glass of wine for herself. "Now what can I do for you, Mr. Burke?"

"Chris. Everyone calls me Chris."

"You wanted to talk to me," she said abruptly.

"Yes."

"Go ahead."

If he was surprised by the sudden change in the conversation, he didn't show it. She'd wanted to surprise him, wanted to shock him out of the pleasantly amiable presence.

"I wanted to tell you something about Katy Douglas."

"Maybe I don't want to hear anything about her."

"Not even a tiny spark of curiosity?"

"Why should I? My mother died twenty-six years ago."

"The mother that nourished you, loved you, did. What if you had a second chance?"

"I don't want a second chance."

"Because you don't want the pain associated with loss?"

"What do you know about loss?"

"Too much. My wife died eighteen months ago after a long illness."

She glanced down at his hand. He wore a wedding ring. "Have you remarried?"

"No."

"Can't find a good replacement?"

He looked surprised, then gave her a crooked grin. "Touché."

"I don't want to replace my mother. Or my father," she said.

"A disclaimer," he said quietly. "I'm not just an investigator for the family. I'm doing this pro bono because I've been a friend of the family for years. Mrs. Douglas—Katy Douglas—often looked after my wife when she was dying of cancer. Her company—a small housekeeping firm—took care of the house for the last four years. There's no one I admire or respect more. She was eighteen when she had a child. A very sick child who nearly died, and would have, if she'd not found a surgeon who performed a very risky procedure."

He paused, then continued, "Her husband couldn't face the pressure and left. She kept the baby, worked as a housekeeper sometimes fourteen hours a day. When Kira was old enough, Katy went to night school, earned a two-year degree in business, and started a maid service, something she could do at home and still spend time with Kira. She's a remarkable woman."

Leigh found herself soaking up the information. She didn't want to. She wanted this to go away. She couldn't give credence to the story because that would invalidate everything she knew. Everything she was.

"I told Max I would give you a DNA sample," she finally said. "It won't be what you want."

"Thank you," he replied. "But time is of the essence. The doctor feels Katy's other organs will start shutting down soon."

She was oddly drawn to him, to the quiet conviction and persuasion in his voice. She looked up and saw his gaze on her. She hadn't imagined the sympathy. Or warmth.

She was beginning to have second thoughts about the invitation, but then she'd had them from the moment she'd uttered it. Yet she had a curiosity about the Douglas family she hadn't been able to admit to Max. She knew from experience that he told her what he wanted her to know. He felt she couldn't handle some stuff. And that had been right in the past. She was trying to change that.

"Have you found out anything about the attacks on Ms. Douglas?" she asked.

"No. Except it wasn't a simple burglary. The thief really tore up her home and destroyed what he didn't take. Paintings. Clothes. Furniture. He was obviously angry."

"I'm sorry."

"I am, too. She didn't need this now."

"And the assailant at the MARTA station. Have you discovered who did it?"

"Someone got a brief look but not long enough for an accurate description. The witness swears, though, that he'll recognize him when he sees him."

"What next?"

"The police took fingerprints. They're checking out the area to see whether anyone saw anything. We're also checking all the stories Kira has written. Maybe she just made someone angry with one of her reports."

"But you don't believe that?" She couldn't stop asking questions, although she knew how risky it was. Still, she had to know what the police knew.

"No."

She tried again. "Why not?"

He smiled. "Now you sound just like her. You question like a pro. I went through all her stories for the past three months to see if anyone might be angry enough to do harm. Nothing there. I don't think someone waited months and then in one day tried to kill her and burglarized her house."

She returned to the original topic. It hurt, but she was becoming obsessed with the question. "Did Katy Douglas have any other children?"

"No. Kira's the only one. Now I have a question," he said. "Why did you agree to see me?"

She hesitated before answering, then thought a half-truth would do. "Because I wanted to know what happened yesterday.

I wanted to say that I agreed to the DNA test because I know it will come back negative."

"Then we'll all fade away and be but a bad memory," he said.

"What about Mrs. Douglas?"

"She'll die," he said flatly. "She won't be viable for a new kidney much longer."

"I'm sorry." And she was. Katy Douglas was no longer an unknown threat. His words had made her real.

He finished his drink and put it on the table. "I should go."

She could only nod. She led the way to the door, Archie trailing behind.

"Thank you," he said.

"That's it?" she asked.

"I told you I wouldn't pressure you."

"I'm not used to people saying what they mean."

"I'm sorry about that," he said.

Sorry again. An easy word to say that often didn't mean anything. But she thought he really meant it.

She opened the door, and Chris Burke and Archie stepped outside. She couldn't afford to let him linger. He made her want to confide in him. She'd done enough of that today.

"Good night," she said.

He hesitated for a moment, then said, "G'night, Ms. Howard."

She closed the door behind him and leaned against it. "Dammit," she muttered. "Dammit, dammit, dammit."

She wanted him to come back.

22

Chris couldn't stop thinking about Leigh on the way home. It had been a long time since he'd felt an attraction for a woman. His heart had died with Risa.

Yet there was something about Leigh that touched him. He suspected there was a very complicated soul under that elegant facade.

She really was a beautiful woman, but nothing like Risa. Risa's hair had been short, dark, and curly, and her eyes nearly black. She'd been a fiery Italian who bubbled with life and never met a stranger. He'd been surprised that she had chosen him. He was big and quiet and even a bit shy with women, which made his cop buddies roll over with laughter.

Risa's exuberant personality brought out the best in him. The decline of her body, if not her will, broke his heart, and he thought—no, knew—he would never love like that again. Not with his entire being and soul.

He'd been drifting these past two years, earning enough as a PI to pay his bills and even save a bit over his police retirement. Archie was just enough company. But Kira's quest had awakened him from the somnolent state he'd retreated into. At first, it was repaying a debt. Now it had become much more than that. It was a puzzle he had to solve. He wanted to save a life rather than clean up after a life that had been taken.

And now there was Leigh Howard.

Her eyes were a Caribbean Sea color, a mixture of blues and blue greens that was striking. He'd never quite seen anything like them before. Her face was flawless, and her blond hair had never seen a coloring agent. But what made her appealing was the wistfulness he saw in her face. And a sadness that ran deep.

She'd surprised him today with her frankness, her graciousness. She'd agreed to a DNA test but nothing more. Yet her curiosity about the Douglases was a good sign. She was thinking about them. She hadn't just dismissed the possibility of a transplant.

Or, the cop side of him pondered, was this just a con job?

Someone had tried to murder Kira, and Leigh Howard had the best motive. Was that why she'd agreed to the visit? She wanted to know what he knew?

He didn't think so, but then, he'd been fooled before. He'd known personable murderers and crooks. Most sociopaths were likeable and appealing.

And Leigh Howard—like Max Payton—had a great deal to lose.

Max drove Kira home. When they arrived, he went inside with her and checked out the rooms. Then he went to the door. They stood there awkwardly.

He wanted to stay. She wanted him to stay. But both of them knew it was a bad idea. He saw it in her defensive stance even as her eyes said something else.

His body certainly wanted to stay. The most excitable part was already rebelling against his briefs. It was remarkable the way she caused that reaction.

The problem was the desire didn't reside only in his friend down there. He wanted to wrap his arms around Kira and blend into her until he couldn't tell where he ended and she began. He wanted to kiss her and hold her and taste every part of her. He wanted her to trust him, but then, he couldn't let her do that.

"Thank you," she said. "For dinner. For taking me to the hospital."

"My pleasure," he replied, and meant it. He paused. "You probably should have someone here tonight."

"I have my super-duper alarm system Chris had installed." She took a step back. It could have been a mile for the emotional distance it put between them.

"Alarm systems can be breached."

"And you would know this, how?"

"Believe me, I know," he said grimly.

"I'll have my cell phone beside me all the time," she said lightly. "Chris promised that the police would patrol often."

"Okay," he agreed. She obviously didn't want him to stay, and he sure as hell knew he shouldn't.

He left before he said anything else. He walked to the car, wondering how she'd so dismantled the cool, calm, and analytical Max he'd built so carefully.

He looked at his watch. Ten p.m. The security company he'd hired would have someone here at 7:00 a.m. He would stay around until they arrived. He didn't have her faith in security systems.

Kira didn't sleep. She tried. She went to bed. Mussed it up with her tossing. It wasn't fear. At least not of unknown bad guys.

She feared her own uncertainty. She'd wanted to ask Max to stay. Wanted it more than anything other than her mother getting well. She ached for him. Her body kept reminding her of what it was missing.

She didn't want to remember that all she needed to do was hold out a hand to him. She didn't want to think how close she had come to doing that.

She got out of bed and went to the computer. Then she remembered that hers was gone, and Chris had the one Max had brought. He wanted to make sure there were no spyware programs. He promised to have it back later today.

The television had been destroyed. She usually watched late at night after returning from a visit to Mom. She was always too emotionally depleted to sleep, so she usually found some mindless show and allowed it to put her to sleep.

A mental list: Get computer. Buy television. Check on insurance claim. Start the diary for the newspaper. Her editor had given her a gift of time. She needed to use it.

She finished the list and stared at it. Scenes flickered through her mind like a kaleidoscope. Max. Leigh with her horse, Silver Lady. The painting of Leigh's mother. And photos of Kira's mother. Both today and as she remembered her three years ago. The attack at the MARTA station. Her house after the burglary. She wanted to stop the spinning images, but she couldn't. She closed her eyes tight as she thought of Karen Westerfield. Had she been happy until her death? Had she loved her child?

Had she known that Leigh was not her natural child? Had she tried to exchange a sickly one for a well one? Or had she been an innocent victim as well?

So many questions whirled around her head, all of them starting with why. Why had a baby exchange taken place? Why was she attacked? Why was her mother's home trashed?

Why? Why? Why?

She finally fell into a restless sleep. It was shattered when the phone rang.

She looked at her watch. Eight a.m. She picked up the phone. "Hello."

"Hi. Wade here. I know I told you that you could have the next several weeks free. But I need you tonight. Diane's baby is sick and she can't cover the public forum on the budget tonight. You're the expert on it. Can you possibly make it?"

"Of course," she said. "I'll be there."

"Oh, and the managing editor approved the diary idea. He thinks it's a great idea. So after tonight, you're free."

"Thanks, Wade."

He hung up without answering.

She looked outside. The sun was climbing high in the sky. She called Chris.

"Can I get the computer back?"

"Yeah. I didn't find anything suspicious, but just in case, I installed a firewall program. It'll disable any spy program."

"Great. I'll drop over and get it, if that's okay."

"Sure. I have some stuff to tell you as well."

"Important?"

"I'm not sure. Just some impressions. I saw Leigh last night."

"I'm on my way," she replied.

She hung up, showered and dressed quickly, and was out of the door in twenty minutes. She would eat later. Any news was welcome.

Chris's home was only ten minutes away. He opened the door as she approached. Archie must have warned him.

Archie greeted her ecstatically. He danced around, chasing his tail and looking ridiculous.

Chris shrugged. "What can I say?"

"He's perfect," she said. "I would take him in a New York minute if I was at home more. Maybe when Mom comes home . . ."

"You'll have to find another. We've gotten used to each other. It wasn't easy for either of us. Come in. Have a cup of coffee. You look hungover."

"Thanks," she said wryly.

"No sleep?"

"Not much. The clock keeps ticking. I feel so damned helpless."

"I'm sorry the donor kidney didn't work out."

"It seems fate is working against us." She changed subjects. "You saw Leigh. Will she go ahead with the DNA test? Do you think there's any chance she might give a kidney?"

"She said she would take the test," he said as he scooped coffee into the automatic coffeepot. "She says she'll do it because she knows it'll prove she *is* Karen Westerfield Howard's biological daughter. Still, she did ask some questions about you and your mother. She also wanted to know what I knew about the attacks against you."

"Do you think she could be involved?"

"I don't think so, but then, I've been wrong before."

"So we're nowhere."

"Not really. I said I had some 'impressions.' I think she really is thinking about the possibility of your mother being hers. She doesn't want to admit it. Maybe she doesn't even realize she's doing it. But the curiosity is there. That's a step forward."

Not much of one.

"Max Payton took me to see Mom last night," she said. "He said he didn't want me to go there alone."

"He's right. I don't want you alone, either. Call me when you have to go somewhere." He hesitated, then added, "Be careful with Max Payton."

"Why?"

"Just be careful. He has a pretty big stake in what happens with the Westerfield fortune. There's also precious little information on him before he joined Ed Westerfield."

"What do you mean?"

"No birth records, at least not in this state or any surrounding ones. No information at all until he started college at twenty. I couldn't find school records. There's a certain mystery about him."

"Shouldn't the college have high school records?"

"If they did, they've disappeared."

"Maybe he was overseas. There're lots of possible explanations," she suggested, even though she saw him raise his eyebrows.

"Maybe," he said doubtfully. "But I really think you should have someone with you all the time now. Someone other than Max Payton."

She shook her head. "I won't be careless, but neither will I have a guard around me twenty-four hours a day."

"What about today?" he asked.

"I'm going to see Mom. Buy a television and a few other things I need. Then I have to work tonight. A city council forum where they present the budget to the public. After that, I can work at home for the next few weeks." She told him about her new assignment.

"Sounds perfect."

"It's a lifesaver. It means I can spend more time with Mom and keep up with the nationwide shortage of kidney donors. Maybe we can convince more people to designate themselves as organ donors and make their relatives aware of their wishes."

The coffeepot beeped. Chris poured them both a cup, and they sat at the round breakfast-room table.

"What about Payton? Did he say anything?"

"He thinks she'll eventually agree, too, but I don't think either of them is aware that we have only days left."

"I tried to emphasize that."

At least he didn't make the excuses for Leigh that Max had. Still, she heard a faint strain of sympathy in Chris's voice as he talked about her.

She had no sympathy. Her mother could die because Leigh Howard was diddling. If only she could legally force her . . .

"Have you found an attorney for me? Maybe if she thought she would lose the house and horse and clothes and everything else, she would reconsider."

He held out a card. "I already talked to her. Agnes Blackwell. She's expecting you to call. I explained most of it, and she's intrigued with the legal questions involved."

She'd heard of Ms. Blackwell. She was considered one of the most accomplished attorneys in Atlanta.

"I can't afford . . ."

"She'll do it on contingency. If you win, she'll take ten percent of the settlement. If not, well, her loss."

"Ten percent is low, isn't it?"

"Yes, but it's a case that's certainly going to garner press. And more business."

"And if I want to drop it because Leigh agrees?"

"I mentioned that. She'll charge for the time spent, but you can take your time in paying it back."

More bills, but she had no choice. Hopefully just the threat of a suit would spur Leigh Howard to act.

"I'll call now."

A secretary answered and put her through to the attorney. In minutes, she had an appointment for 1:00 p.m. At least she was doing *something*.

"Okay, I'm off," she said.

"I'll go with you."

"No. I'll be out in public most of the time. You have other things to do. I will be very, very careful. No lonely MARTA stations. No walks at night alone, or even in lonely places in the daylight. I will stick to other people like glue."

She stopped at the door. "Thank you, Chris. I can't say that too many times. Not only for what you're doing on the case, but for being a rock for me to hold on to."

"Your mom was that for Risa."

"For me, too."

She said good-bye then. She had things to do.

She reached her mother at three. She'd spent an hour and a half with the attorney, who was practically salivating at taking the case. It would be high profile.

If it went further than Kira desired. She warned Agnes Blackwell that her one motive was a kidney. Not money. She wasn't sure the attorney had listened. How long did she have before the news broke?

Her mother was awake. The television was on, but her mother was looking out the window to the hall. She saw Kira, started to smile, then it faltered. "What's wrong, baby?"

"I want to manufacture a kidney for you, and I can't," Kira said.

"You always did want to conquer the world. Nothing less would do."

She held out her hand and Kira took it.

"You look tired," her mother said. "Much too tired." Then her eyes focused. The old sharpness returned. "Something else is wrong. You were worried before. There's more, isn't there? Is it money? Your job? You've been spending so much time here."

Kira didn't want to lie. But now there was a moral dilemma. Could she tell the truth and risk the shock to her mother's health? Her mother always knew when she lied, or shaded the truth. It was as if she wore a big placard around her neck reading, "Liar."

But it wouldn't be long now before the media started a feeding frenzy. The lawsuit would be all over the news—local and national. It was far better coming from herself. She took a deep breath.

Kira squeezed her mother's hand. "I know you didn't want me to donate a kidney. But I had the tests taken, anyway. I hoped you would change your mind if there was a match."

Her mother's gaze didn't move from her. In fact she looked stronger than she had in days. As if she'd been saving her strength all day to confront her. She still wanted to be the mother, not the child.

"I thought you would," she said. "But then you didn't say anything so I thought the tests didn't give you a match."

She was close. But she could never guess at the entire truth. No one could.

"I did take the tests. And no, I wasn't a match." She hesitated. "There's something else, though."

Her mother stared at her. "That bad?"

"Maybe. Maybe good. Maybe really good."

"Go ahead, kitten. Spill it."

Kira had no idea where to begin. But her mother's fingers tightened around hers.

"We're a team, kitten. Always have been. Nothing you say can change that."

While Kira knew that, she also knew that she would be turning her mother's world upside down just as hers had been.

"I'm not your genetic daughter, Mom."

23

Kira didn't think her mother's face could age any more than it had during the past two months. Now she watched it do exactly that.

"Are you sure?" Katy Douglas whispered after Kira related the details. Or most of them. She purposely left out the burglary and suspected attempt on her life.

"I had a second DNA test taken after the first said I wasn't your biological daughter. It was sent to a different lab. Same results. I'm not your blood daughter, but you're my mother in every way that counts." Emotion welled up in her throat. Maybe the truth hadn't seemed real until this moment. She'd heard that when someone died, loved ones felt a numbness akin to a state of shock. Emotional and mental self-protection. She realized her mother was going through the same process. *Disbelief.*

"I love you," Kira said softly. "I didn't want to tell you until I fixed it."

Her mother smiled wanly. "My little crusader. You always want to make everything right. Didn't matter if it was a neighbor's broken bike or a kid that was bullied. How did you think you would fix this?"

"I don't know," Kira said. She didn't want to say she was

trying to blackmail her mother's real daughter into donating a kidney. She knew exactly what her mother would think of that.

"How could it have happened?" her mother asked.

"I don't know that, either. It could have been a mix-up in the delivery room."

"I never had any trouble in my pregnancy," her mother said. "Never. And I had all the tests. I couldn't understand . . ." Her voice trailed off, then she started again. "Who is she? Do you know?"

Kira nodded. "Her name is Leigh Howard."

Her mother didn't react. She obviously had no connection to the name. "I want to see her," Katy Douglas said after a moment.

"I . . . don't know if I can arrange that right now. She doesn't . . . think it could be true."

"What about her family?"

"There isn't any left. Her . . . parents were killed in a car crash when she was six. Her grandfather died two years ago. She doesn't have any siblings."

Her mother's eyes filled with tears. Her hand pressed deeper in Kira's. Kira felt the flood of emotion passing into her, the sudden pain of loss that was raw and excruciating. It was just hitting her mother now and would take her time to digest, just as it had taken Kira time.

"You'll always be my daughter," her mother said. "Always. And I couldn't ask for a better one." She shifted on the bed. "So much. You've had so much on your shoulders. You've always been my Kira, my light. You will always be my daughter. Oh, Kira, I love you so much."

"I know," Kira whispered. "And I'm so lucky that someone gave me to you."

Kira didn't know how long they stayed that way, clutching each other's hands in a world turned upside down. Her mother's eyes finally closed, and Kira leaned back, reluctant to go, even more reluctant not to be there when her mother woke.

A nurse came in to take vitals, and Kira looked at the clock. It was getting late, and she had to get to the meeting.

Her heart heavy, she went outside and waited for the nurse to come out.

"How is she?" she asked.

"She's hanging in there."

"She's tough," Kira said. She paused, then added, "I gave her some bad news today. She took it really well, but can you check her frequently tonight?"

"Of course. I'm on duty until midnight."

"I'll call and see how's she doing." She already knew all the nurses by name and the number from memory.

The nurse placed a comforting hand on her arm. "She's one of our favorites. We're all praying for that new kidney."

"So am I."

Kira hurried down the hall. She had thirty minutes to get to city hall.

Seth decided to call Leigh. He'd been fuming ever since she told him that someone was claiming to be a Westerfield cousin. An heir to the estate.

It had galled his grandfather, father, and himself that his great-grandfather—Dan Westerfield—had left nearly everything to his second son, Ed, and very little to the first son who had been raised by his mother's family. They'd been the poor cousins, part of the family but only on the fringes.

But his resentment had always been aimed at Ed, just as his father's was. Leigh was a victim of Ed Westerfield as much as his family had been. In truth, he'd been a little in love with her during her wild, reckless days. He knew, though, that society would never approve and even in his teens he'd planned to go into politics, just as his father had. Unlike his father, who had never gone beyond state politics, Seth intended to to be a U.S. Senator someday. Maybe even go higher.

He'd always hoped that when Ed Westerfield died, he would make right a fifty-year-old wrong. No such luck. Seth had received a small stipend, and Leigh had been tied in knots by a trust controlled by an outsider.

He hated Max Payton. The attorney had stepped into a

seat that should have been occupied by a Westerfield. By himself. Instead, Max lorded over all of them, handing out a dollar or so when he was in a good mood.

Leigh could break the trust if only she tried. He was very close to the probate judge. He'd been responsible for his appointment to the post and then for his continued reelection. But Leigh wouldn't take those steps. Not yet. Soon, though, if he had anything to do with it.

But now . . .

He didn't think the story was true. The Douglas woman was a con woman. Had to be. Babies didn't get switched in hospitals. And Dr. Michael Crawford, David's father, was the most competent, rigidly correct man he'd ever met.

But even a bogus claim could tie up the estate for years, ruining any chance he had to bring down Max.

He called Leigh's cell.

"I'm checking out the new horse," she said, a rare excitement in her voice. "She's wonderful."

Seth didn't give a fig about the new horse. "I was hoping you would drop by the campaign headquarters today. We can use you."

"I'm sorry. I didn't sleep well last night, and then the horse came, and . . ."

"So Max came through for you."

"Partly. It's a lease. But I'm sure he'll end up buying her. One look at her and he'll understand."

"Anything new on that Douglas woman?"

"I've agreed to the DNA test. A technician is coming over tomorrow."

"And that's okay with you?"

"No. But it's not going away. That much is clear. If I don't, she'll file suit and force it. It may take months, even a year, but it will be hanging over my head. I would rather disprove it immediately."

"What if . . . ?"

"There is no 'what if,'" she said with a surety that surprised him.

"Still, I don't think you should take it."

"Why?"

"Results could be switched. A lot could happen."

"Max is arranging it. Not *her*."

"Are you sure he's on your side?"

"What do you mean?"

"I decided it might be a good idea to look into this Kira Douglas. I sent one of my aides over to take photos of people coming and going. He had met Max. When he saw her leave with him, he followed them to a hospital, then to a small restaurant. They were there for two hours."

There was a silence. "He told me he was going to meet with her."

"I don't like it," Seth said. "You know I've never trusted Max."

"I can't talk about it now," she said.

"I don't have a meeting tonight. Why don't you come over for dinner? Susan would love that."

"Sounds good," she said.

"I'll ask David to come, too. Seven?"

"Okay." He thought she sounded reluctant.

"Don't do anything until you talk to us. Don't let them take a DNA sample."

She didn't answer.

"I'll see you then." He hung up before she changed her mind about dinner and started making other calls. He'd dropped his bomb about Max. Now he would sit back and see what happened.

*The meeting dragged on seemingly forever. The council pre-*sented the budget, and an overflow crowd complained about bits and pieces. They all wanted lower property taxes and more police services, more fire stations, and more streetlights.

Part of Kira absorbed what was being said. She jotted notes on the small notebook computer, even writing part of the story when nothing more than petty stuff was being argued. The other part of her brain was back with her mother.

She could write the story at home tonight and have it to the paper for the first edition in the morning. She would return to the hospital then. Her mother would have even more questions. Questions she dreaded answering.

Kira sat with Nick Whitten, another print reporter—a big, bulking guy she knew well and liked. At the meeting's end, she turned to him. "Where are you parked?"

"I walked from the paper."

"I'll give you a ride back," she said.

"I can walk. Need the exercise."

"It's dangerous out there."

"I'm bigger than most victims."

"I'm not," she said, hating the vulnerability the words couldn't disguise.

He glanced at her with surprise. They'd both covered the city hall beat for more than a year, and never once had she said anything that indicated a weakness.

"Then I would appreciate a ride," he said. "I don't like exercise anyway."

They walked together down the street to her car. Many of those at the meeting left earlier once their particular agenda item had been considered, and now the remaining attendees and city council workers filtered out with them. She felt safe among them.

They were almost to the car when pain ripped through her side. She stumbled, then was pushed to the ground by Nick, who covered her body with his. She was aware of a shout, then a scream. More screams. Pandemonium. The sound of shoes pounding against the pavement. Nick nearly suffocated her with his weight as more screams rang out. Then moans. Nick rolled off her and knelt at her side. He quickly unbuttoned her blouse and checked her wound, then used his cell to call 911.

Blood stained her white blouse crimson. Pain replaced shock. She felt as if a searing-hot poker had been jabbed into her side.

Nick took off his short-sleeved shirt and pressed it against the wound.

"What . . . happened?" she gasped between her teeth.

"You've been shot. So have others."

"How many?"

"I don't know," he said.

She tried to sit up, but the pain intensified.

"Stay still," Nick said. "Let me keep the pressure on the wound."

She looked at him in an entirely different way. "The others . . . maybe you can help them. I can hold the bandage in place."

"You might go into shock. Others are helping." He continued to press down until a uniformed security guard from city hall knelt beside them. "Ambulances are on the way," he said.

"How many others?" she asked, reverting to reporter mode despite the agony rolling through her in waves.

"Three."

"What happened?"

"Looks like a sniper with a noise suppressor," the guard said.

"Did anyone see who was shooting?"

"Not that we can find," the guard said with disgust.

Distant sirens grew louder. Two different kinds. She knew them both. Police sirens. Ambulances. The noise was suddenly earsplitting as they neared.

The pain was growing worse. She heard other groans. Crying. Then paramedics were there, and police, and two men she'd never seen before.

A police officer talked to Nick as one paramedic applied a pressure wrapping to her wound and the other asked her standard questions. Name. Age. Allergies if any. Next of kin. Not her mother, and there was no one else. Finally, she mentioned Chris and gave the paramedic her cell phone with his number in it. Her memory was fuzzy and getting fuzzier by the moment.

She heard an ambulance leave, the sound of the siren fading as it headed for the hospital.

The paramedic finished his examination. "Another couple of inches and you would be dead."

"That's helpful to know," she said, feeling extremely exposed in front of the gathering crowd.

He grinned at her. "Good attitude," he said, then stood. "I

have two others in worse condition than you," he said. "They'll go first."

"Were they all women?"

He looked startled. "Yes."

A policeman took the medic's place at her side. "Do you remember anything, ma'am?"

"Just being hit by a thunderbolt."

"Looks like a sniper. Seems like he shot at anything that moved."

But she had been the first.

Another coincidence? Three attacks in four days.

The Westerfields. It had to be a member of the Westerfield family or one of their retainers. But she didn't have any proof. It could just as well be some unhinged soul shooting randomly. She wanted to believe that. She really, truly wanted to believe it.

She thought about telling him about the MARTA station incident. *This isn't the first time.* But her mouth stayed stubbornly closed. He was a patrolman. She wanted to talk to Chris before saying anything more.

She also wanted to talk to Max. She wanted Max there to tell her everything was under control.

But maybe Max already knew about this.

She didn't think Leigh was capable of finding a sniper, a burglar, and an assailant to knock her onto the MARTA tracks.

And she wouldn't believe Max had been involved.

The second paramedic returned. "Got in touch with your Chris Burke. He's going to meet you at the hospital." He looked at his partner. "Ready to go?"

She looked at a stretcher they placed next to her.

"I don't need that," she protested. She tried to stand and immediately felt dizzy.

"You don't want us to get in trouble," the paramedic said.

"My car? It will be illegal in the morning." She knew it was a dumb worry, considering the circumstances, but she had to focus on something other than the pain. And the ramifications of what had just happened.

"Give me the keys," Nick said. "I'll park it at the newspaper. My car's there."

She hated to be without her car. Even for a few hours. It was her independence. It gave her the illusion of always being in control.

But a wave of fresh pain washed over her as she located her purse next to her. She surrendered. "What hospital?" she asked the paramedic. Any but the one her mother was at. Word traveled too quickly within a hospital. Her mother didn't need to learn about this so quickly after the news she'd heard this afternoon.

Two pairs of arms moved her efficiently onto the stretcher. She shouldn't be here. She had a million things to do. She didn't want to go to the hospital. And she definitely didn't want to think someone wanted her dead.

Her. Kira Douglas. She couldn't wrap her mind around it. *Concentrate.*

She was loaded into the ambulance. It sped through the night, the siren wailing while a paramedic sat next to her, keeping an eye on her vital signs.

Who? Why?

She moved, and jolts of pain surged through her, each one greater than the last. But the questions were more painful. She'd been flippant back there, but that was always the way she confronted anything serious.

She tried to tamp down her fear. There was no doubt now that someone wished her dead. She could give the MARTA incident the benefit of the doubt, even the break-in could have been a coincidence, although that was a stretch. Now she knew that not only did someone want her dead, but they were willing to kill others to do it. She hated fear. And she hated feeling so much fear.

She'd heard no sound, which meant a silencer. No, a noise suppressor. She knew that from covering a hearing on gun control. She also remembered suppressors were highly regulated. Difficult to obtain.

A couple of inches, the paramedic said.

And this time she wasn't the only victim. A crazed killer.

Or someone trying to make it look that way. Was she responsible for others being wounded, even killed?

Oh God, her mother! She closed her eyes. This would surely be in the papers. It would be on the police radio, and the *Observer*'s police reporter most certainly would pick it up. A sniper outside of city hall would be big news.

Dammit, dammit, dammit. The world was crashing down on her.

And her mother.

24

The trip to the hospital took only a few moments. Kira's side felt as if it were being consumed by a brush fire spreading ferociously through the upper part of her body.

She was wheeled into a treatment room, and nearly immediately a trauma surgeon was by her side and inspecting the wound. "In and out," he said. "You're lucky. No major bones in the way, but it nicked a rib, and it's going to hurt like hell for a while. The bullet sucked in pieces of your clothing. It'll have to be cleaned and you'll need a series of antibiotics."

The curtain was shoved aside and to her shock Max Payton stood there. She'd expected Chris.

Her first thought was how glad she was to see him.

How did he know? Chris's words came back to her. Max had as much to lose as anyone if she was named heiress.

Max studied her for a moment, then turned to the doctor. "How is she?"

The doctor looked at him. "Husband?"

"No. A friend."

"Then you'll have to wait outside."

Chris walked in with Nick.

The doctor raised an eyebrow. "Family?" he asked again.

"Friends," they said in unison.

"You'll have to wait outside, too."

"How is she?"

The doctor sighed and turned to Kira. "How many more are there?"

She was already light-headed. Now her head swam. She shook her head. "I don't think . . ."

A nurse ushered the men out and returned.

The doctor turned back to Kira. "The nurse will give you a local to freeze the area and clean the wound. She'll also give you another shot, an antibiotic and a painkiller. I'll see if we can't find a room for you tonight."

"I don't want to stay."

"Do you have someone living with you?"

"No."

"You shouldn't be alone. If it starts bleeding again, or you have a reaction . . ."

"I can get someone."

He frowned. "You're going to be weak. You really need bed rest for two or three days." He sighed, giving up. "I can't make you stay. You *will* need someone to drive you home."

Just as he walked out, a fourth person popped his head into the room. "I'm Detective Cal Perkins," he said. "I saw Chris outside. He says he's a friend."

"He is."

"He's a good one to have." He took out a notebook. "Chris filled me in outside on a previous attack and burglary. You reported one, not the other."

"Because I wasn't sure the first *was* an actual attack. I think I wanted to believe it was an accident."

"But you don't now?"

"Oh no. I stopped believing in coincidences a few hours ago."

"Did you see anything tonight?"

"No. No sound. No indication. Just a fire running through my side. It knocked me to the ground."

"Any idea who did this?"

Before she could reply, the nurse shooed him out as she had the others. A shot numbed Kira's side while the nurse cleaned her wound and bandaged it.

Kira left with several prescriptions. The four men were waiting outside.

She went to Nick first. "Thank you. You didn't have to come here."

"I wanted to give you your keys."

"You could have left them in the newsroom."

He grinned. "And go into the halls of the enemy?"

"Is that what you think the *Observer* is?" she said.

"Close to it. Anyway, I'm glad you're okay."

"I might not have been if you hadn't fallen on me."

"Hell, it's a good story, and now I have to go write it."

He escaped, obviously embarrassed.

The detective stepped up. "Ms. Douglas?"

"I've told you everything I remember. Can you come over in the morning if you need anything more?"

"In the morning, then," he agreed.

She was left alone with Max and Chris, and they looked none too happy with each other. She tried to get to her feet and nearly fell. She clung to the table. She was weaker than she'd thought.

She looked at Max. "How did you know what happened?"

He gave her a chagrined look. "The truth?"

"That would be nice."

"I had two men following you. I was worried about you. The agency is well-known and reputable. They were supposed to keep you safe. It didn't work that well, and someone will be fired in the morning."

"You shouldn't blame them. No one could have expected this."

"They sure as hell should have seen something."

Then the words sank in. They should have registered quicker, but her mind had gone as feeble as her body. "You hired someone to follow me without bothering to share that information?"

"You would have said no."

"Maybe," she admitted. "Maybe not."

"You should go home, if you aren't being hospitalized," Max said. "I'll take you."

So late. And she was so tired. But she didn't want him to

take her home, or maybe she did, and that made her not want him to. Damn, if she ever wrote that sentence for publication, she would be fired.

But the fact was that she couldn't afford to like *anyone* at the moment. Particularly anyone belonging to the Westerfield clan, and most certainly Max did.

His eyes demanded an answer. Demanded a trust that she didn't have. Not now.

Chris stepped closer. "I'll take her."

"Kira?" Max said.

She knew the question was about more than taking her home. It was about trusting him. She wanted to. She wanted it with all her heart. But she couldn't. Despite his impact on her life, she'd only known him a few days. Something like a week, and that week had been tumultuous. Too much had happened to think logically. Too much was at stake to fall in love . . .

Or had she already done that? She hadn't considered the word before. Not in connection with Max. Lust. Desire. Extraordinary attraction. But love? How can you fall in love in a few days?

You can't, she told herself. Not now.

His eyes shuttered, like the first time she'd seen him. He gave her a half smile. "As you will."

He left without another word. It was as if life drained from the room.

She stood. She felt weak on her feet and dizzy, and her side hurt. Not like it would without the painkillers, but she definitely knew it had been injured.

Chris looked at the empty doorway, then at her. "I must have missed something."

"No."

"Something between you two?"

He'd been too much help to lie to him. He was her friend. Probably the best friend anyone ever had.

"Not now."

"Okay. But if you ever want to talk about it, I have a good ear."

"You have a good heart, too."

"A lot of people would scoff at that."

"I want to know how the other people are before I go," she said. "I feel responsible."

"All right," he said, "but you'll do it in a wheelchair."

She agreed. Her side was hurting more by the moment. But she felt responsible for the others who'd been injured. Maybe it was random, but maybe it was because she had pursued Leigh Howard.

Chris quickly returned with a wheelchair and pushed her down to the information desk.

He identified himself as a former police officer and current private investigator and asked about the other victims in the city hall attack. The woman hesitated, then made a call.

"One died," she said. "The other two are stable."

Kira closed her eyes.

"It's not your fault," Chris said.

But it was.

"Did you have any idea you were followed?"

"No," she said. "I probably should have. I did try to pay attention to what was going on. I did as you said. Stayed with someone. I almost got Nick killed."

"I'll check into the agency Payton said he hired."

"You don't think he did?"

"Oh yes. I'm just not sure what their orders were." He paused. "I really have no reason to say that. It's just that too much about Payton's youth is missing. And he does have a stake in what happens to the Westerfield heiress."

"Thanks for telling me that."

"For a reporter, you're too damn trusting."

She made a face at him, but her silence agreed.

He didn't say anything, just turned the wheelchair toward the door.

"What did you do?" The voice rose on every syllable.

"I did what you told me to."

"I didn't tell you to kill anyone. I just wanted you to scare her away."

"That's not the impression I got."

"Well, end it."

"I don't think so." The voice was full of amusement.

"I'll go to the police."

"No, you won't. I'll tell them you planned the whole thing. Besides, you owe me. You owe me a life."

"Not this."

"This and more. Much, much more."

Silence on the end of the caller. "Why? Why shoot so many?"

"You didn't want the target to be obvious, did you? You wanted to scare the hell out of her, but not draw the cops your way."

"Don't you think they're going to look at all of us now?"

"Maybe you. Not me. But there's no proof. And you'll go on protecting me."

He hung up.

The caller's blood froze. He was out of control. And now there was no way to stop him.

25

"Dust in our eyes. That's what this was about," Chris said when they reached her house.

"What do you mean?" Kira knew her voice was slurred. She tried to reason, but reasoning disappeared a few hours ago when she was shot.

"The shooting of the others. Someone was trying to throw some doubt that you were the target."

She looked down at her lap. Blood again. She'd been seeing too much of it lately. "It's pretty obvious to me."

He looked grim. "Yes."

"Same thing happened to a friend of mine last year," she said. "Kirke was a paramedic. A sniper with a rifle shot her and a fellow paramedic."

"Maybe someone reads the newspaper," Chris said. "Copycat."

"But the other people? One died. That's so . . . callous."

"It's worse than that," he said. "This was at city hall. It's not only vicious but blatant. There's going to be one hell of a police response. Expect any number of cops at your house tomorrow. I got you a brief reprieve because you didn't see anything, and you were obviously exhausted and wounded, but now that there's murder involved, you have to tell the police about the Westerfield connection."

"It's all going to get out, isn't it?"

"Yes."

"I'd better warn the newspaper. If I am scooped on this, I'll be out of a job."

"Want me to call them for you?"

She shook her head. "I have to do it."

She called the night city editor, told her what had happened and that she would have a piece on the shooting in the morning. She also asked her to have Wade call her as soon as he came in.

"You're going to bed," Chris said when she completed the call.

"Okay," she agreed. He walked behind her as she went into the bedroom.

"Lie down," he said.

"My nightshirt," she said. "It's in the top drawer."

He found it and handed it to her. "Can you manage?"

She nodded.

"I'll get some water for your meds."

"I don't want any more pain pills."

"You will, believe me," he said. "When that shot you got at the hospital wears off, you're going to hurt like hell. And you're going to hurt worse tomorrow."

"I have to see Mom. This will be on the news."

"You have to talk to the police first. They'll be mad as hell when they hear what we have to say in the morning."

"Will you get in trouble?"

"Not any more than I can handle."

He left, and she slowly, painfully stripped. She managed to pull on a robe and limp to the bathroom. She tried to wash, then leaned against the vanity.

He found her there. "Dammit, you shouldn't have gotten up."

"I'm nasty."

He brought a bowl and washcloth and stood outside as she hand washed herself, then he helped her into bed.

She was grateful, but part of her wished it was Max standing there, and his expression wouldn't be just concern.

Forget it!

Why, she wondered, couldn't she be attracted to Chris? Honest. Open. Kind. Attractive.

Yet there was no electricity between them, just a friend helping a friend. Nothing like the surge of desire that ran through her like lightning whenever Max touched her.

"Thank you."

"You're welcome."

"I do have to see Mom tomorrow," she said.

"You won't be able to move much tomorrow."

She wasn't going to argue with him. She would, and she could. Her mother had to see she was all right.

Even if she wasn't.

He was at the bedroom door, ready to leave. "I'll be in the other room," he said. "Call if you need me."

"What about Archie?" she asked, not really wanting to be alone.

"He'll be okay for tonight."

"You can't stay here forever."

"No. But I'm going to make a few calls to some retired cops," he said grimly. "Let them take turns watching you. This time you'll know they're there and where to turn."

He didn't give her a chance to protest. He left.

She closed her eyes but couldn't sleep, even with the painkillers. She couldn't stop thinking that at least one person died tonight, probably because of her.

Max used his key to go into the main Westerfield house. Mrs. Baker wouldn't be there yet.

Lights had been on in several rooms when he'd left for the hospital. That meant Leigh had been up and probably wandering about the house. Now the house was dark except for the faint light in Leigh's room.

He was beyond angry when he stepped inside. Angry, and jealous as hell, too. He'd seen that moment of distrust in

Kira's eyes, the way she'd turned to Chris Burke. He hadn't thought something like that could hurt as much as it did.

His immediate target, though, was the security company. The two men on duty said they'd immediately gone to Kira Douglas rather than trying to find the shooter. Someone else assisted her, and then and only then had they looked around. He couldn't really quarrel with their priorities. Kira came first. Still, they were supposed to be professionals. They should have seen *something*.

He'd broken every speed limit to get to the hospital. He'd felt great relief to find her walking and talking and wanting to go home.

What he hadn't expected was the suspicion and reserve in her eyes when she saw him. Nor the rejection when he offered to take her home.

He'd left quickly. He wanted to kill whoever had shot her, and he didn't want her to see that part of him. He'd worked hard to harness a temper that once threatened to destroy his life. But now it was like a raging bull inside.

Worse was the unexpected ache he felt in places he thought well guarded . . .

Everything was silent in the house. He went into Ed's study. It was just as the old man had left it. He went to the wall gun cabinet. Ed's rifles were still there, locked by a chain. He counted them. One was missing. Then he went to the safe located in a large closet behind the desk. He used the combination to open it. He didn't know if anyone else knew it, but he doubted whether Ed wanted them to know it. He had grown paranoid in his last years.

Ed kept his handguns in the safe. A .45-caliber had been of particular concern. It was a heavily regulated weapon, and Max had never updated the registration. He'd been uncertain what to do about the weapons. The house and its contents belonged to Leigh. And she'd changed nothing in her grandfather's study. She'd made very few changes in the house itself. She hadn't seemed to care, almost as if she continued to live in someone else's house.

He went through the weapons. The .45 wasn't there, either.

The sniper last night wouldn't have used the .45, even with a noise suppressor. Too inaccurate. But it worried him that it was gone. He closed the safe. He didn't doubt that the police would be here. Burke and Kira would have to tell them about the connection to the Westerfields now.

He doubted they would come with a search warrant. They wouldn't have enough probable cause, but they would be here and might well ask about weapons.

They would check his answer against ATF records. He would have to tell them that the .45 and one rifle were missing or let them discover it for themselves. Either way, there would be questions. Lots of them.

He knew Leigh wasn't involved in the shooting. She didn't have the skills, nor the mind-set.

He also knew where suspicion would point.

He went into the kitchen. He filled the coffeepot with water, then coffee, and turned it on.

He thought about the first time he was in this kitchen. He was seventeen, green as could be, and thought it the most wonderful house in the world.

Maybe that was the reason he didn't move away. The Westerfields were the only family he had.

He started upstairs to wake Leigh up when he heard a noise at the kitchen door. Mrs. Baker came in. She stopped in surprise when she saw him.

"You're up and about early," she said.

"There's been another attack on Kira Douglas."

She dropped the purse, spilling the contents on the floor. "Oh no!"

"This time someone was killed."

"Ms. Douglas?"

"No. Someone shot her and three other people at city hall last night."

"Maybe it was a coincidence," she said hesitantly.

"I don't think so. Neither will the police. It wouldn't surprise me if they were here in a few hours."

She gathered the belongings on the floor. "But why?"

"Surely they couldn't suspect Miss Leigh."

"Mrs. Baker, I think they will suspect everyone in and

around this family, including me." He paused. "I'm going to wake Leigh and tell her. You might make some tea for her."

Her face had paled, but she nodded. "I'll do it right now."

He left her for the stairs. He hated to barge in, but he wanted to see her before she saw the television. Or maybe she'd heard something last night. He hoped to hell not. He wanted to see her reaction. He had to know whether she had anything to do with the shooting. It would be the only way he could help her.

He knocked at the door. No answer.

He tried again.

"Mrs. Baker?"

"No, it's Max."

"Just a minute."

It was more than a minute, but less time than he expected. She opened the door and peered out at him.

Her eyes were red, swollen, but her hair was brushed and she wore a long robe. Alarm was in her eyes.

"Max?"

"May I come in?"

"I'm not sure. You have that frown you wear when delivering bad news."

"I didn't think I was that transparent."

"You usually aren't, but occasionally displeasure breaks through."

"You look like you had a sleepless night."

"That transparent?" she said with a teasing note born, he thought, of tension.

"You usually are," he replied.

She stepped aside and went to one of the big lounge chairs in the room. She sat in the chair, drawing her legs under her. She looked far younger than her thirty-two years. And innocent.

"There was another attack on Kira Douglas," he said abruptly.

There was no mistaking the surprise in her eyes. "Is she . . . ?"

"No, but another person was killed. She and two others were wounded."

"How?"

"Someone started shooting people leaving a meeting at the Atlanta City Hall."

She looked dazed for a moment. "You're sure it was her he was after?" she asked.

"Yes," he said. "And I think the police will as well."

Then she caught the meaning of what he was saying. It was in her eyes. "You don't think I had anything to do with it?"

"No." And he meant it. He knew her too well. She couldn't feign the emotions that crossed her face.

Yet he had another question. "Have you been in your grandfather's gun safe?"

"No. I was there when you took everything out and showed them to me." She gave him a wry look. "I didn't pay much attention. Grandfather trusted you and so do I. I know you put the guns there, and that was fine with me. I never liked them."

"Did you know the combination?"

She shook her head. "You know how I am about numbers, and I had no reason to want to know."

"Did anyone else? Seth? David?"

"If they did, they never said anything about it. Besides, neither of them hunt."

"There are two guns missing. A forty-five and a rifle. The police will surely check because they're registered." He let that sink in. "Who else has been in the house in the past week?"

"Seth. David. Mrs. Baker." She stopped. "You can't possibly think any of them are involved. Can you see Mrs. Baker with a gun?"

"No," he admitted. He'd always marveled at the way Mrs. Baker always remained "Mrs. Baker" despite more than thirty years with the family. Ed had been scrupulous about calling her "Mrs. Baker," and she had always called him "Mr. Wester-field" and Leigh "Miss Leigh." His death had not changed long-ingrained habits.

"Are you sure it was there? There were so many. I never understood why he wanted so many."

"He was a collector. He liked having what no one else did. And I think he liked the control a gun gave him. Much more powerful than a golf club," he said. He didn't have to elaborate. Ed Westerfield always liked being in control. And he relished owning a .45, otherwise known as an assassin's gun.

He paused. "My security guys said there had to be a noise suppressor."

"Your guys?" Her eyes had grown larger.

"I didn't want anything else to happen to her," he said simply. "It would lead back to us."

She gave him a sly look. "Is that the real reason? She's pretty, but she doesn't look like your type."

"And what is my type?"

"Sleek and beautiful. At least, that's who you always brought to my grandfather's parties."

"You're right. She's not my type," he said shortly. "Now back to the safe. You're going to be asked about the gun collection."

"I haven't opened it."

"You will have to tell the police who might have had access."

"I don't think anyone but you has the combination."

"But you don't know."

She shook her head. She obviously realized what he was saying, but it was also evident she didn't want to implicate anyone. "Maybe it's not the gun that was used."

"Probably not," he tried to assure her. "I just want you to be aware of everything."

She was shaking. He put his arms around her. "Just answer the questions," he said. "Insist on me being there, but I won't interrupt unless it's necessary. You'll do okay."

She straightened. "Yes, I will." She gave him a wan smile. "I'll get dressed."

He paused. "The DNA technician will be here at two."

She made a face. "It's not going to go away, is it?"

"No."

"I suppose I hoped it would, if I delayed long enough. I wanted to believe she was a fraud."

"I'll call Chris Burke. He should be there."

"Why?" she asked.

He saw a blush start in her cheeks and wondered why.

"A representative of Ms. Douglas should be present. He might well want to run a sample through another lab."

"I'll be here."

"There's something else," he said.

"More bad news?"

"I don't think this whole . . . baby-switch supposition will be under wraps after this morning."

He watched as the words sank in. She stiffened.

"Kira Douglas hasn't made it public. She wanted to do it all quietly. But now murder's involved. And the police. They will certainly ask her whether she has any idea of who is behind this . . ."

"Surely she doesn't think I . . ." She paused. "You said several people were shot. It could have been one of those crazies . . ."

"I doubt anyone else had their home trashed in the past few days, nor had someone tried to push them in front of a train. She'll have to tell the police about everything that happened in the past few days, and suspicion will be aimed right at us. The police have never been known for being discreet. I imagine Ms. Douglas, as a reporter, will be writing her own story. The fact is you'll probably be hounded by the media soon. Just say, 'No comment.' I'll send a couple of people to man the gates and make sure no one gets to the house."

"My friends . . ."

"Tell them I said you can't discuss it. I don't want anything being misconstrued and repeated."

She nodded.

"You'll be okay," he said. "You're a lot stronger than you think."

"I'm not sure about that. What if I lose everything?"

"I won't let it happen, okay?" He stood. "I'll tell Mrs. Baker to start breakfast. What do you want?"

"I don't think I can eat anything."

"Yes, you can. You need to keep up your strength."

Her shoulders straightened. "Okay. Maybe some fruit. A piece of toast."

"I'll tell her."

He left, satisfied that she could hold her own when questioned.

His mind went to those who might benefit from the revelation that Kira Douglas was really Leigh Howard. Seth had been pressuring Leigh to file suit and try to end the trust. The Crawfords—Michael and his son, David—had never expressed an interest in getting anything but the nice bequest Ed had left them. He wondered whether Seth could bear closer scrutiny. Maybe he'd been using his own money for the campaign.

Yet as far as he knew there had never been a hint of scandal around him, and God knew he would have heard if there was one.

He knew one thing. They would all be investigated now. Seth. Leigh. Himself. How deep would they go?

Chris made coffee at six the next morning after grabbing a few hours' sleep in an easy chair. He'd peeked in at Kira several times.

He'd spent much of the night waking friends with phone calls. Six retired officers agreed to take turns watching her. After last night, he sure as hell didn't trust Payton's private cops.

After they talked to the police this morning, he would head for the hospital himself. He could reassure Katy about Kira, and he wanted to talk to her about the doctors who treated her and Kira thirty-two years ago. He also wanted to know what nurses were on duty that day. They should be in hospital records someplace.

Maybe he'd been looking in the wrong direction. He'd been thinking the attacks came because someone today thought they would lose, or gain, something if Kira was proven to be the granddaughter of Ed Westerfield.

Maybe the attacks weren't about money or inheritances at all. Maybe someone was trying to cover up a thirty-two-year-old crime.

26

"Drink this," Chris ordered. He handed Kira a large glass of orange juice.

She sat up in bed. She didn't want it. She was a little nauseated, but he had insisted.

"You lost blood yesterday," he persisted. "You need it."

"I need to get up."

"After the orange juice."

She was still drinking it when she heard the doorbell. She knew instinctively who, and why.

She also knew she needed to make some very long explanations.

Chris knocked at the door, then came in. "Two detectives are here. It's time now to tell them everything. Your mother. The baby switch. The attacks. Suspicions. Everything," he stressed, then left before she had a chance to answer.

A moment later, he ushered two men inside, then fetched two chairs for them to sit in.

"Detective Ray Callum," the tallest introduced himself. "My partner, Jeff Paul. We're both with Homicide."

Detective Callum was younger than the other, though obviously the senior partner. She took note of his suit, his slicked-back hair, and his sharp eyes. His partner, Paul, was probably in his fifties.

Chris stood at the end of the bed.

"We would like to talk to her alone," Callum said.

"No," Chris replied easily. "I'm a friend."

"What kind of friend?" Callum said, his eyes narrowing.

"Not that kind," Chris said. "She and her mother took care of my wife when she was sick."

"You know the procedures," Callum said. It was obvious he disliked—or resented—Chris. "We talk to witnesses alone."

"I also know I can remain here unless she's under arrest."

Callum ignored him and took out his notebook. "You told an officer yesterday you didn't see anyone."

"No. I just felt . . . this blow, like being hit with a sledge-hammer. A friend shielded me. I heard shouts. Screams. People running. Ambulances."

"You were the first hit," Callum said. "Maybe the shooter was aiming for you."

"I thought about that," she said. "It's possible. There've been several . . . incidents in the past few days."

She related everything that had happened since she discovered she was not her mother's biological daughter. As she retold the story, Callum's frown turned into a glower. "Westerfields?" he said. "Isn't one of them running for some office?"

She nodded. "He's a state senator now. He's running for Congress."

"Dammit," the detective said. "If we'd known this last night . . ."

"She was out of it last night," Chris said, exaggerating.

"*You* weren't. You were supposed to be a good cop, a real hotshot. Once upon a time. We wasted time yesterday. Maybe we could have found the killer if we'd known that."

"And when were you assigned to the case?"

Callum didn't reply.

"This morning, I would guess," Chris said. "Maybe at seven. Everyone was busy last night interviewing witnesses, searching for bullets, looking for anyone with a gun. I'm not sure how this information would have helped just then."

"That's not your decision."

"Why don't you just do your damned job now," Chris said.

The detective's face flushed. Then he turned back to Kira. "Why didn't you report the attack at the MARTA station?"

"As I said, I thought it was probably an accident."

"And when your home was trashed?" He looked around. There were still signs of the invasion. A torn curtain. Holes in the walls.

"I reported it, of course."

"Don't you think you should have mentioned the other incident?"

"I still didn't know they were connected. The Westerfield name would have been all over the press."

The mention of press had an effect. He straightened.

She exchanged a look with Chris. He nodded. The detective would probably be on the phone before he reached the station.

"Who have you talked to about this 'switched babies' theory?" It was obvious he didn't really believe it.

She glanced at Chris. He nodded.

"Just Leigh Howard and her attorney—the company's attorney—Max Payton."

"Anyone else know about it?"

"I don't know," Kira said. "I don't know whom they might have told. The only people I've discussed it with are my mother and Chris. Chris is doing some work for me."

The questions went on, but most were repetitive. He kept asking about the man on the train platform. She kept saying she didn't see the attacker's face.

"Nothing about his body that stood out?"

"No." She'd been over that with Chris over and over again. She didn't think she should tell the detective that, though. He was already furious.

The two detectives were on the way out when Callum turned to her. "Don't hold anything else back."

"No," she said meekly. She didn't like anything about the young detective. He was rude and supercilious.

She sat up after they left. Every movement hurt like hell.

Chris stepped back into the room. "What are you doing?"

"I'm calling in a story, then I'm going to the hospital." She looked at him stubbornly. "I want my car."

"You still have too many drugs in you to drive."

"Then I'll take a cab."

"I'll take you," he said. "Some friends of mine—retired cops—will accompany you when I can't be here."

"You must really be using up your friends."

"Most of them are tired of fishing," he replied. "Now make your call to the newspaper. I'll be ready when you are."

He went out, closing the door behind him. She called Wade and dictated a short sidebar about being in the midst of a shoot-out. She looked longingly at her pillow. God, she hurt.

Her phone rang. She grabbed it.

"Hello." The deep voice belonged to Max. Her heart flip-flopped. She told it to behave.

"Hi."

"How are you?"

"Sore." She paused, debating whether she should tell him her discussion with the detectives. He probably knew what was coming.

"Two detectives just left," she said. "I told them about the baby switch."

"I expected that," he said evenly. "You didn't have a choice. Not after being shot at."

Her heart fluttered faster. She should have known. Max Payton was a realist.

"What about Leigh?"

"She's still going to give the DNA sample. Today. In fact, that's one reason I called. Burke might want to be at her house. Two p.m."

"I know you had something to do with it. Thank you."

"It's my job to give my best advice to a client," he said curtly.

There was a silence.

"I'm glad you're doing okay," he finally said in a cool voice.

"I wish everyone there had been that lucky. I feel responsible."

"You don't know what motivated the shooter."

"Yes, I do. In my gut, I know. Maybe if I'd gone to the police earlier . . ."

"Don't ever play that game, Kira. Ifs, buts, and maybes don't change anything. Neither does regret."

Her fluttering heart stilled. Was he telling her something? That he had some kind of regrets. About her?

His voice took on a clipped note. "I just wanted to know how you were. And your mother."

"She's not dead yet, thank you," she snapped.

"I would be very sorry if she was," he said quietly, then, "I still want you protected, but this time I won't do it without your permission."

"Chris has already arranged for protection," she said.

"Good. Good-bye then." The phone went dead, and she felt a huge emptiness inside. Why had she acted so cool when every ounce of her wanted to ask him to come over?

Kira knew the answer only too well. He'd crawled into her thoughts and emotions and, God help her, her heart. She'd told herself she would never be used as her mother had been used. Pretty words, then desertion after the first sign of trouble. She'd hated her father for years, then decided he wasn't worth it. But his desertion had colored every male/female relationship she'd ever had.

She put the phone down and stood. She swayed for a moment, then made her way to the chest. She pulled out a loose pair of jeans and a big shirt that just needed to be buttoned. No bra. She went into the bathroom. She was a fright.

She ran a brush through her hair and added a dab of lipstick.

She slowly made her way into the living room. The wound in her side pulled and burned, but the big problem was the bruised rib. Every movement was pure pain.

Chris looked up from the television. A camera was scanning the front of the courthouse.

"Nothing new?"

"No."

"Max Payton called," she said. "He thought you—we—might want to be there when Leigh is having DNA samples taken this afternoon."

"I do."

"Maybe that will stop whatever is going on," she said hopefully.

His expression was thoughtful. "That would be reasonable," he said slowly. "I don't think this person is reasonable. You don't shoot up a crowd if you just wanted to scare off one person or even to kill that one person. You don't keep escalating the violence. You don't murder strangers."

"What do you mean?"

He shrugged. "It just doesn't make sense. The first attack, yes. Scare off an imposter. Even the burglary. Someone looking for whatever proof you have. But last night? Why bring so much attention to the Westerfields? It was bound to bring the baby switch to public view. I don't think the Westerfields wanted that."

"Then who? Why?"

"Damned if I know."

27

To Max's surprise, no one from the police department ap-peared at the Westerfield home the morning after the city hall shooting. No calls from the media, either.

Max lingered at Leigh's home, expecting an onslaught from both at any time.

He left at eleven for a noon board meeting. "Call me if the police come," he instructed Leigh. "For God's sake, don't say anything. Just tell them your attorney insisted that he be here."

"Won't that make me look guilty of something?"

"It'll make you look smart, and don't let them tell you anything different. I'll be back at two."

"You're not going to let me slide out of it?"

"No." He didn't want Leigh to have second thoughts. He hoped that once the results were in, the violence would stop. There would be too much of a spotlight on the story.

Leigh was evidently thinking of that as well. "Won't they need a sample from my mother as well? Otherwise, how can Kira Douglas claim to be my mother's daughter? God, that sounds ridiculous."

He liked the wryness in her voice. She would need a sense of humor in the days ahead. "A sample from Seth or, better yet, from Dr. Michael Crawford should do," Max said. "If necessary, we might be required by a court to disinter Karen's remains."

"No!"

"You may not have a choice."

"You keep saying that. It's your job to give me choices."

"I can't perform miracles," Max said.

"You were good at making husbands, and potential husbands, disappear."

"Neither was good enough for you," he said. "You always undervalued yourself."

"You're the only one who ever thought that. Grandfather didn't."

"Yes, he did. He loved you. He just wasn't good at expressing it."

"You were the son he wanted."

"No, I was never that. To be honest, I wanted to be. But you were his granddaughter, and I was hired help."

"But I may not be his granddaughter."

That was the first time she admitted the possibility. He tried not to show any reaction. She had to reach the decisions on her own. "Doesn't matter. He loved *you*."

"I would really like to think that. It was lonely growing up here."

"I know."

She looked at him. "I always thought you were cold and unfeeling."

"I am," he said, straight-faced.

"You seemed to be on *her* side."

"I'm sorry you felt that way. I did believe her, though. And I didn't think you could evade the issue forever. You would drive yourself crazy wondering whether you were Katy Douglas's child. And always regret not knowing until it was too late."

"You *want* me to donate a kidney . . . if it's true?"

"It's not my decision and I'm not going to try to make it for you, sport."

"You haven't called me that since . . ."

"You went to college," Max finished for her.

"Have you ever been really, really attracted to anyone?"

The question came from left field, and he didn't know how to answer it. Of course he'd been attracted to women, but probably, as she said, not "really, really." Not until this past week. There had been brief alliances, even affection, but nothing that tempted him into long-term plans. He'd thought he was missing something inside, that there was an emotional block that made him back away when anyone threatened to get too close.

She was waiting for an answer. "Yes," he said simply. It wouldn't have been true a week ago. He surprised himself by admitting it today.

"I had a terrible crush on you," she admitted.

"I know."

"You could have seduced me."

"I knew that, too."

"Why didn't you? Because of Grandfather?"

"I liked you," he said simply.

She smiled. "Thank you. I think you were the only one who did. I was a brat."

"I was a lot worse," he admitted.

"I can't imagine that."

"Anyway, I'm proud of you. I think your grandfather would be, too."

"You say he may not be my grandfather."

"He'll always be your grandfather," Max said. "But you might also have a mother. Think about that, Leigh. Katy Douglas is a good woman, a warm and loving one from everything I know. You might get what you've always wanted."

"And what's that?" she asked, a bit of the old defiance back.

"A living parent who loves you."

"She doesn't know me." That she didn't deny his statement spoke volumes.

"I think she would be delighted with you."

Her face reflected doubt.

"Trust me," he said.

"I'm not good at that."

"I know. I'm not, either, sport," he said. "Maybe it's not too late for either of us."

Kira walked into her mother's hospital room. Her chest hurt like the furies of hell. She tried not to show it. This visit was necessary, though. Her mother would have heard of the attacks. The news would be everywhere this morning.

The television was on. Kira's face was plastered on it.

Her mother uttered a cry when she saw Kira. "Thank God."

"I'm sorry," Kira said. "I asked the nurses to keep the television off until I got here. I'm fine. Please don't worry."

Her mother frowned. "It's a mom's job to worry." Her eyes were fueled with worry as she did an inch-by-inch visual inspection of Kira.

Kira winced as she sat down. Her wound burned and her rib felt as if someone were pounding on it. "I know."

"Was that a random shooting or did it have something to do . . . with me?"

"Why would you think that?"

"You've been worried, and it's not just about my kidney." Her mother sighed. "Although I'm . . . ill, I still have powers of observation." She paused, then added, "Don't hold anything back from me, baby."

Kira knew she would feel the same way. She would have hated it if her mother tried to protect her from something she had every right to know.

"How much has been on television?" she asked.

"Only that a shooter fired on a crowd leaving city hall. Three people injured, one killed. You were one of the three."

"No leads?"

"They say not."

"I think it does have something to do with you," she said, "and whatever happened in that delivery room thirty-two years ago."

"I still have a hard time believing that you are not my biological daughter," her mother said. "I loved you so much from the first moment I saw you in the nursery. You were so small, and there were all these tubes . . ."

"Were you awake when I was born?"

"No. Dr. Crawford thought there was something wrong, that the baby was in the wrong position. He gave me something . . . I was in a haze . . . Then the doctor told me my baby was sick, and I couldn't hold her. I kept asking for you . . ."

"Dr. Crawford?"

"He was the nicest doctor . . . so helpful over the next few weeks. He didn't have to be. It wasn't his fault you were sick, but he kept stopping in the nursery, and he found me a pediatric surgeon who would operate."

Bells were ringing in her head. Why hadn't she asked her mother these questions earlier? Dr. Crawford. Dr. Crawford was a cousin of Karen's. He'd probably been her obstetrician as well.

No wonder that her mother's medical records had been lost. She and Chris should have asked those questions first.

Dr. Crawford. Dr. Michael Crawford. He had to be the key to the whole puzzle. The caring Dr. Crawford who'd found a surgeon who would work for free. Or had he?

What would be the statute of limitations on deliberate baby switching? Certainly, his reputation would be destroyed, and maybe even his son's would be tainted. Enough to commit murder?

Her mother was watching her face. "You suddenly thought of something." It was more question than statement.

"I was just wondering if Dr. Crawford was responsible for the switch."

"No," her mother said. "He wouldn't." She closed her eyes for a moment. "It must have been a mistake."

"No, Mom, I don't think so. Apparently, I was so sick they rushed me to intensive care. They would have known the moment I left your—Karen Howard's—body that I . . . was a blue baby. That something was very wrong."

"But why . . ."

"Dr. Crawford was the cousin of Karen Howard, the mother of Leigh Howard, the woman I think—no, I know—is your daughter. Maybe she didn't want a sick baby. Didn't you say that everyone thought I would die?"

"But he's a doctor."

"He's also a member of that family."

Her mother's breathing was more labored. "What about the . . . DNA test?"

"She's agreed to do it today."

"It has . . . to be very hard on her."

"Yes," Kira said simply.

"How long will . . . it take to get results?"

"A couple of days."

"Do you have a picture of her?"

Kira had been waiting for that. She'd had copies made of the photos Dan took at the Westerfield house. She took them from her purse and handed them to her mother. It was a strange feeling, almost like handing the right to be Katy Douglas's daughter to someone else. She felt a sudden ache very different from physical pain.

Her mother stared at them, and Kira knew she was looking for features similar to her own, and maybe even to her husband. Kira had done the same thing with the painting of Karen Howard in the Westerfield home.

"She's very pretty," Kira finally said.

"Yes, but so are you." Her mother knew exactly what she was thinking, just as she always did. She held out an arm discolored from needles. One line was attached to it.

Kira took her hand. It seemed almost transparent. Yet there was still strength there, and that strength clung to Kira.

"You'll always be my daughter," Katy Douglas said. "Always the best thing in my life."

Kira leaned toward her, and an explosion of fresh pain surged through her.

"Go home, baby," her mother said, then, "Will you be safe there?"

"Chris is providing me with my own policemen. He brought me here, and one of them will take me home."

"Stay there. Take the prescriptions."

Just like her mother. Sick with a terminal condition unless a kidney was found and here she was, worrying about Kira's minor wound. "You said I would always be your daughter. You know you will always, always be my mother. And I *am* going to get you a kidney."

Her mother fixed a stare on her. "You haven't asked her to donate a kidney?"

She squirmed under that stare.

"Kira?"

"Kinda," she admitted.

"I know what 'kinda' means. Hog-tying her and dragging her kicking and screaming to the hospital."

"No. I just . . . gave her a little tug. No more. I swear." Blackmail qualified as a tug.

"I won't do it, Kira. If anything happened to her remaining kidney, I couldn't live with myself."

Kira clasped her hand. "It's so little risk, Mom. It really is. You're just fifty. You deserve to live long and well."

"I didn't want to take one of your kidneys, and I certainly don't want to introduce myself to Leigh Howard by asking for one of hers," her mother said with the glint in her eyes that said she wouldn't change her mind. "Drop it, Kira. I won't give my consent for a transplant under those circumstances. I won't do it, so go back to her and tell her it's all been a terrible mistake. Let her go on with her own life."

Kira looked at her for a long moment. "I can't do that. It's gone too far. I can't undo what's been done. And both she and I are old enough to make our own decisions."

Her mother's expression softened. "Go home, baby," she said again. "For me. Get some rest so I can get some."

Katy Douglas had not ceded. Not yet. She'd merely changed the subject.

But Kira knew they both needed rest. And she badly needed another one of those little white pills. "Okay. I'll see you tomorrow."

She ducked out the door before her mother could protest and ran into a burly man in his sixties.

"Ms. Douglas? Kira Douglas?"

"Yes."

"I'm Bob Harold. A friend of Chris's. I'm here to take you home."

Her own personal bodyguard.

"What about my mother? I don't think she should be alone."

"Chris has already talked to security. They're to keep an eye on her. No visitors other than you. No information will be given out about her room number."

Was she being paranoid? Probably. Her mother had not been targeted.

"I would rather you stayed here," she said. "I can take a cab home."

He smiled. "Chris would flay me alive if I let you do that. Look, let me make a few calls." He moved out of her hearing and spoke into a cell phone. In minutes he came back. "Someone will be over here in an hour. Good enough?"

She thought of what Max had said yesterday, that he had hired bodyguards. It hadn't helped her last night.

"I'm parked a fair distance away," the retired policeman said. "I'll get the car and meet you at the entrance."

Kira nodded. "I'm going to say good-bye."

He took the elevator down, and she peeked into her mother's room. Katy was already asleep. The visit had worn her out.

She hurried down the hall and caught the elevator. As she exited on the first floor, she glanced at the people crowding into an elevator across from her. One man caught her attention, and she wasn't sure why. He wore a florist's jacket and carried flowers. Her reporter's mind sized him up. Overweight. Mussed brown hair. Thick glasses. He glanced at her, then turned and moved into the elevator.

An ordinary visitor.

She started for the front door, but something nagged at her. The way he'd turned. Lighter than his bulk would indicate. She retraced her steps, waited impatiently for an elevator. Both were stopped at upper floors.

Maybe the stairs. But with her aching chest, she might never make it. One of the elevators started down. Fourth floor. Stopped. She took out her cell and punched the button for her mother's nurse's station. It rang. And rang. The elevator started back down again. Third. Stopped at second.

She wanted to scream at it.

A nurse on her mother's unit finally answered. "My mother's room," Kira said in quick gasps. "Check my mom's room. Now. Someone . . ." The elevator stopped and she impatiently waited for a crowd to leave. "Dammit," she yelled into the phone. "Someone might try to kill her."

Everyone stared at her as she stepped into the elevator and the signal died. Others followed. "Please," she said to the other passengers. "My mom might be in danger. Please don't press a button for another floor."

Two stepped out. Three others nodded their heads, standing away from her as they might from a deranged person.

The elevator stopped at the second floor anyway, and she had to wait for someone to get in. They started to punch the button for three when she said, "No," and pushed the hand away.

The elevator reached her mother's floor. She stepped out and ran to her mother's room. The door was open, and a nurse leaned over her mother. The IV had been pulled from her arm.

She looked down. Bloodred flowers spilled across the floor.

28

The nurse glanced up. "After you called, I came in to look. A man was leaning over the IV. I screamed. He knocked me aside and took off. I immediately pulled the IV."

Panic exploded in her. Kira watched as Julie, a nurse she knew well, took her mother's vital signs.

"Heart and pulse okay," Julie said. "I alerted security. Told them we had an intruder wearing a florist's uniform, but I doubt whether they'll find him."

"Thank God you got here," Kira murmured, although she hated the thought of the man getting away.

"Thank God you called," Julie replied. She paused, then added, "I heard the news about you today," Julie said. "I've been trying to keep an eye on her, but we got really busy all of a sudden."

Kira glanced down at the bed. Her mother still slept. The good news was that she didn't know what had just happened; the shock of someone leaning over her might have killed her. The bad news was that she hadn't woken up. She was slipping more and more into sleep.

"I left instructions that no one, absolutely no one other than myself, was to be allowed in her room," she said. "No one, but myself and hospital personnel."

"I know. We were going to put a sign on the door."

"A sign isn't much of a deterrent."

She turned to the room phone and dialed Chris's cell number. He answered immediately.

"Someone just attacked Mom," she said without preamble. She quickly told him what happened.

"Are you there now?"

"Yes."

"I sent someone over to watch over you."

"I know. He came up to Mom's room, then went down for his car. He thought I was right behind him. I was, until I saw someone getting on the elevator. Something about him seemed . . . out of place."

"Maybe you've seen him before . . . on a train platform."

"Could be, but the hair . . . was different. So was the build."

"Both are easily changed. Additional clothes. A wig."

She hadn't had time to consider that.

"I would come over and get you, but I'm due at the Westerfield house for the DNA sample."

"I want to go with you. Then your guard can stay with Mom."

"I thought you decided to let me do it."

"That was then. This is now."

"You must be hurting like hell."

"Maybe a little," she admitted.

"You should be in bed."

"I'll take a pain pill. I have them with me."

"Leigh Howard may not want you there."

"Then I can stay in the car, but this is too important . . ."

"I'm still not sure that's a good idea," he said.

"I'm going. Even if I have to take a cab."

"I'll be there soon," he surrendered.

"Maybe if this is settled, then the violence will stop."

There was a pause on the phone, and she realized he didn't agree.

"I'm on the way," he said.

She stood by as two nurses came in with a new IV. Julie took vital signs again. Blood pressure. Temperature. A blood sample. Oxygen.

"Everything seems okay," one nurse said. "We'll keep checking signs until we get a report back on the IV bag. They've tightened security."

"A former policeman will be here shortly. I want him at the door."

"You can take that up with security," she said.

Pain or not, she was ready to do battle. She was outraged that someone could just walk in her mother's room.

Just then Bob Harold appeared in the door of the room. "Chris filled me in," he said. "He asked me to stay here."

It was alarming that her mother hadn't awakened. But then, she'd been awake longer than usual today. She was filled with drugs now.

Helpless.

Kira's heart took a nosedive.

Ordinarily her mother would have heard them, would be sitting up in bed, figuring out ways to defeat the bad guys. Her eyes would sparkle with the light of battle. Her mother never gave up. She wasn't giving up now, but time was running out for her.

She wanted to see the DNA taken, but more than that, she wanted another chance to convince Leigh to consider a donation if she was a match.

It would be twenty minutes before Chris arrived. She sat down next to her mother. Took her hand. Wondered what she would do without her. Katy Douglas, biological mother or not, was the one person in the world that loved her unconditionally. The one person she trusted completely.

She touched her mother's drawn face. A kidney. One small organ that could be easily replaced if only there was another available.

Why would Leigh Howard hesitate to save a life? Even for a second?

After Max left, Leigh left the house and walked to the stable.

Rick was just leaving. "Cleaned out the stalls and fed and watered the horses, Miss Leigh." Her name was said with something close to a sneer. If it wasn't for Mrs. Baker . . .

The housekeeper had been so grateful when Leigh agreed to take on Rick and help him get other grooming jobs as well. He'd spent summers working with horses at a stable near her sister's home, she said, but had a hard time getting a job after returning from Desert Storm.

She would have preferred taking care of the horses herself. "How are they?" she asked Rick. "Getting along?"

"Yeah. I woulda let them out in the pasture, but I thought you might want to go riding."

"Not right now. But I have some apple pieces for them."

"Then you don't need me to stay?"

"No, thanks. I have to work on the horse show auction."

She went into the stable. Silver Lady was snorting. That wasn't like her. Something had upset her. Leigh checked the water. Clean. The grain in the feed bucket looked fine. Yet Leigh was attuned to Lady far more than the new horse. Maybe it was a little jealousy on Lady's part. Or maybe it was her own anxiety that Lady picked up on.

Leigh held out the piece of apple in her palm, and Lady took it. Then she moved to the next stall. Samara stuck her head out and neighed for attention.

"Pretty girl," Leigh crooned as the horse took a piece of the apple, then another. She moved on to Maude, the little rescue donkey who almost took her fingers along with the apple.

She longed to ride. But she knew her apprehension would be only too clear to the horses. Maybe later today.

What if she didn't have them next month? What if Kira Douglas was entitled to everything she had?

Everything she had. None of it really meant anything but the animals. She couldn't bear losing them.

Her cell phone rang. She checked the caller identification. One of the board members of the horse show. She winced, then answered it.

"Leigh, darling. I just heard the news on the television. It isn't true, is it?"

"I don't know. What did you hear?"

"That someone is claiming to be you?"

Her heart dropped. She knew it was coming. After she

heard about the attack last night, it was bound to happen. Kira Douglas had said she wouldn't say anything until the DNA tests, but she was no longer in control.

None of them were.

"True," she said. "At least the fact that someone is making that claim."

"But can it be true, dear?"

She went outside, only to see a car approaching. The police, no doubt. "I'm sorry, Anne. I have to go. I have company."

"Well, do keep us advised," Anne Mitchell said. "If you have to take some time to resolve this, let us know."

In other words, if she wasn't a Westerfield, forget it.

Leigh hung up and walked to the front of the house as a car stopped at the gate, and the driver leaned out to talk to the newly arrived guards ordered by Max. The gate opened. She waited as the driver parked in front of the house and two men got out.

"Ms. Howard?"

"Yes?"

"I'm Detective Callum. This is Detective Paul. We would like to talk to you."

"About last night?"

"Yes, and a few other events."

"Of course," she said graciously. "I just have to call my attorney first."

"That's not necessary," Detective Callum said. "Unless you have something to hide."

She smiled. "My attorney said you would say that. He also said only a fool would believe it."

She punched Max's button. He answered immediately.

"The police are here."

"Be charming and offer them tea. Most cops hate tea."

She had to smile at that. She hung up and led the way inside.

Mrs. Baker met them in the hall. She wore her usual reserved expression but her gray eyes were red rimmed. Tired-looking. She was being affected as well.

"Please bring tea to the living room," Leigh said. The

living room was large and, she always thought, stuffy. Not the sense of intimacy that there was in the library. "Mr. Payton will be here soon."

Mrs. Baker nodded and disappeared. She didn't deign to recognize the officers.

"Who is that?"

"Our housekeeper, Alma Baker."

The lead detective noted it in a notebook he'd pulled out.

She led them to the living room and offered the most uncomfortable seats. She sat across from them.

"Mr. Payton told me about the attack last night," she said. "How are those who were wounded?"

"One is in serious condition," Callum said. "Ms. Douglas was released early this morning. One woman was killed."

"Do you have any leads?"

"A few."

"Good," she said flatly.

"I understand you have some guns registered to your grandfather."

"Nice try, Detective," she said pleasantly. She never would have been able to do that five years ago. She would have been resentful. Fearful.

Mrs. Baker returned and set down a tray in front of the detectives. An elegant teapot and four fragile cups. Lemon. Cream. Sugar. Small, dainty cookies.

"Please help yourselves, Detectives," Leigh said.

They regarded the pot and cups warily. "Do you have coffee?" the younger one asked.

Leigh looked at Mrs. Baker.

"Certainly," the housekeeper replied.

Leigh busied herself preparing a cup of tea, very carefully adding lemon and a spoonful of sugar. She chose a cookie. "Gentlemen, what about a cookie?"

Callum looked disgusted, and he glanced at his watch. Good. They were on the defensive.

She could see the grandfather clock in the corner. Max should be here in ten minutes. Maybe less.

"Maybe you can tell us who lives in the house," Callum tried again.

"Sure. Myself."

"That's all?"

"That's it."

"What about the housekeeper?"

"She has her own home several blocks away. She's only here during the day."

"How long has she been in your employ?"

Answer no questions, Max had said. These were surely harmless ones but she knew she should listen to him. She hadn't before and paid for it. "I don't really know the exact number," she said. "She worked for my grandfather a number of years."

She sipped her tea to forestall any additional questions. Still, the older detective persisted. "Nice house," he said.

"Thank you."

"Be a hell of a shame to lose it."

She wanted to throw the tea in his face. At one time she might have done it.

"I don't know about that," she said. "There's a lot of places to go and things to see."

"But they all take money."

"I'm not exactly helpless, Detective," she said. She regretted the words the second they left her mouth. She'd wanted to be the helpless, not-very-bright, aging debutante. Now she knew why Max didn't want her to say anything without him.

Callum eyed her speculatively. "I can see you aren't." He looked down at his notebook. "I understand a number of weapons were registered to your grandfather. And I see you have a gun permit. We checked at several gun ranges. You were once a customer." He paused. "Would you like to tell us where you were last night?'"

29

Max strode into Leigh's living room. Two detectives were
seated in the large room. One young and dark-haired, the
other older and nearly bald. A pot of tea along with dainty
cups had been placed on a coffee table before them. They
looked untouched except for the one Leigh held.

Leigh stood as he entered. "These two detectives have
been very patient," she said. "I explained that you told me you
should be present and I couldn't say anything but hello until
you came."

She sounded like a bubblehead, and he knew she was anything but.

"Gentlemen," he acknowledged.

"Why can't she talk if she doesn't have anything to hide?"

"Would you?" he asked, giving him a pained expression.
"Even if you didn't have anything to hide?"

"Yeah, I would," one said. The other just shrugged and
took out a small recorder.

"Max," Leigh said. "Detective Callum just asked about the
gun permit that I have, and the firearms course I took."

He wasn't surprised. When they hadn't appeared immediately, he concluded they had been doing some homework

before showing up at the home of an influential family. Not to mention the up-and-coming politician who was Leigh's second cousin.

He assumed from the way she posed the statement that the question had been asked, but not answered. Good for her. "She took lessons a number of years ago as a favor to her grandfather. Ed Westerfield had two passions in his life. Business and hunting. He wanted to see what she was made of. Leigh took lessons to please him. Unfortunately, it didn't work out very well. On the first hunt, she couldn't—or wouldn't—shoot a deer. He killed it, and she refused to go again. She doesn't like guns and she doesn't like hunting."

"I assume Ms. Howard can speak for herself," one detective said, and turned back to her.

"Mr. Payton is right. I hated guns. They scared me then, and they scare me now, but my grandfather was insistent. He thought I was . . . too soft. He also said I needed to be able to take care of myself. I took lessons, but as Mr. Payton said, I wasn't very good at it."

"Ms. Douglas, one of the victims last night, said there might be some bad feelings between her and the Westerfields."

"Did she now?" Max said. "Exactly like that?"

The detective shrugged. "Close to that. Seems she might be the heiress to"—he spread out his arms—"all of this. Money makes people do some strange things."

"You can rest assured that Ms. Howard had nothing to do with any of these incidents. She was home last night."

"Can anyone verify that?" The detective stared hard at Leigh.

She shook her head. "Our housekeeper left at five p.m. I went riding late in the afternoon, then came inside. I was supposed to have dinner with my cousins, but I decided to stay home. I looked over the program for a benefit auction preceding a charity horse show in two weeks."

"Did you make any calls?" the dark-haired detective said.

"Several."

The detective looked at Max. "We would like to look at the call logs."

"Help yourself."

The detectives exchanged glances. "Back to the firearms course," he said. "How long did you take lessons?"

"Twice a week for a few months," she said. "I don't remember exactly."

"It certainly doesn't qualify her to shoot a silenced rifle from a hundred yards away," Max broke in.

"How do you know how many yards?" the detective snapped.

"I had hired someone to look after Ms. Douglas. Two of them were present last night at city hall."

"You need better talent," a detective observed.

"I remedied that," Max said curtly.

"What did they see?" Callum asked.

"Very little. They saw Ms. Douglas go down. Then two other people. Their first interest was to get to Ms. Douglas, not to find the shooter. I told them to go to the police department and tell them exactly what they saw."

"I'll make sure they did that," the detective said. He changed course. "Before we came, we checked on gun registrations. There were a number registered to Ed Westerfield."

"He was a hunter and gun collector," Max said.

"May we see them?"

He nodded. The detectives didn't have a search warrant, but they could get one, and the ATF could walk in at any time and demand to see the weapons. It would only make them all look more suspicious if he refused.

"I can tell you two are missing," he said. "After the shooting last night, I knew you would pay us a visit. I checked the gun safe and rifle cabinet. A Remington Model 700 rifle is missing along with a forty-five. And to answer your next question, I don't know when they disappeared. I haven't looked in two years."

"Why do you have access?"

"I'm administrator of the estate. Ms. Howard was left the house and all its contents. It was my job to catalogue them and make the weapons safe. I felt they were."

"Show us the cabinet and safe," Callum said.

Max walked them to the study and opened the gun safe. They compared copies of registration forms to the weapons.

"Did he have a silencer for the rifle?"

Max nodded. "It's on the list. Mr. Westerfield never did anything in a small way. He was a hunter. He was fascinated with guns and their history."

The detective frowned. "Who might have had access to the guns?"

It was a question Max had dreaded. "I don't know," he said. "I haven't seen his guns since I took inventory after his death. I can tell you those two weapons were there then. I made sure then they were locked up until Leigh decided what to do with them."

The detective turned to Leigh.

"As Mr. Payton said, my grandfather tried to interest me in hunting. I hated it. I didn't want anything to do with his gun collection. I certainly haven't checked on it."

The detective looked at his notes again. "Anyone else have access to the guns?"

"Possibly," Max said. "Locks weren't changed on the house. I don't know who may have had access to the gun safe. Westerfield had several hunting buddies that met here."

"I want their names as well as those of anyone else who has access to the house," the detective said. "Let's turn to money. It seems Ms. Howard stands to lose a great deal. What about this charge of a baby switch thirty years ago?"

Max shrugged again. "I think the question has something to do with a possible mistake, nothing criminal. Ms. Howard is taking a DNA test to erase any doubt. She is cooperating in every way. She wants this settled as much as anyone does."

"Not what we were told."

"I don't care what you were told." He handed the older officer a card. "That's the lab that's sending over a technician. Call him yourself if you want."

The detective ignored him and turned all his attention to Leigh. "Isn't it true you could lose everything if the charge proves true?"

"Ed Westerfield left his estate to the granddaughter he knew," Max interrupted. "Even if there is any truth to a possible mistake in the delivery room, Leigh Howard is still the person Ed Westerfield meant to inherit his money. Now is there anything else?"

"Not for the moment."

Max stood. "Then I think this visit is over."

"For now. We'll be back with a search warrant."

"If you have the probable cause for one," Max said with a slight smile. "I don't think you do."

"We have motive."

"Not much of one since Ms. Howard has agreed to a DNA test, and I think Ms. Douglas will tell you she doesn't intend to contest the will."

The dark-haired officer stood. "We'll be back," he said again.

"It'll be a pleasure to see you again," Max said wryly as he showed them the door.

A small triumph. They obviously had little to go on, and this was little more than a fishing expedition.

But the next hours might change that.

The phone rang. It stopped suddenly and Max supposed that Mrs. Baker had answered it. Before he could finish the thought, she knocked on the door and came in.

"A local television station," Mrs. Baker said. "They want a comment on the . . . the story that babies might have been switched at birth."

"Tell them, 'No comment,'" he said.

"It's started," Leigh said.

"You can handle it," Max said.

"For how long? And how long am I going to be Leigh Howard?"

He saw the questions in her eyes and wished he could answer them. He couldn't. No more than he could answer the questions in another woman's blue gray eyes. God, he wished he could stop thinking about her. Stop wanting to be with her. He wished he could reconcile his responsibility to Leigh with the need inside him for Kira Douglas.

But he couldn't.

In a few hours the technician would be here to take the DNA test. By then, the press would be in full cry.

Kira knew immediately that Leigh Howard was surprised to see her, and none too happy about it. The woman's expression softened as she greeted Chris behind her. Kira saw something pass between them, a connection that surprised her.

She would have thought that Leigh would be the last woman to attract Chris. She was cool and contained and reserved. As unlike the laughing Risa as anyone could be.

But then, she would have thought the same thing about Max and herself. Maybe it really was true that opposites attract.

That didn't mean it was a healthy thing. She told herself that as she saw Max when they stepped inside. Her heart flip-flopped, then did a nosedive. His eyes were neutral, his expression grim. Even if she hadn't seen him, she suspected she would have recognized the scent of sandalwood that always hovered around him and the way her body reacted whenever he was near. There was a kind of intense energy that played between them.

She resented that energy, even as it intrigued her. She liked being in control of her life. She didn't want anyone to have the kind of impact on it that he did.

For the fleetest of seconds, their gazes met and she thought she saw possession in his eyes. It sent a shiver down her spine. Then heat.

She didn't want to feel that heat. Especially since she didn't trust him. He'd been honest about his commitment to Leigh Howard and the Westerfields. Maybe he could live with divided loyalties. She couldn't. Not now.

He stepped back as if burned, then his eyes cooled.

"I didn't realize you were coming," he said. "Shouldn't you be in bed?"

"Someone tried to kill my mother earlier today."

She heard a small cry from where Leigh stood. Max's expression hardened. "I'm sorry to hear that. Is she all right?"

"Yes, but the guy got away. I think it's the same one who tried to push me off the platform."

"You saw him?" Max asked, his gaze focusing on her.

She nodded. "Briefly. He was getting on the elevator when I got off. I think he was surprised when he saw me. He made a sudden turn, just like at the station. Catlike. It didn't go with the stocky build.

"I called the nurse's desk while I waited for the elevator and asked that they check on Mom. The nurse found someone leaning over her IV. Someone who shouldn't be there."

"What did he look like?"

"Overweight, which is a little different from the impression I had a few days ago. Messy red hair. Glasses."

"You said the other man was wearing a cap?"

"This one wasn't. That's why it didn't register immediately. It was only the way he suddenly turned when he saw me. He . . . spun. Just like before."

Leigh moved closer. "That doesn't make sense."

"None of it makes sense," Kira agreed. "My mother's death wouldn't change anything." She looked directly at Leigh. She could barely control her anger. "If she's murdered or dies because someone who could help, didn't, all bets are off. I'll go after every penny. I would probably end up giving it to charity, but not one person liable for her death will benefit from it."

"You don't think I had anything to do with the shooting or what happened today?" Leigh's blue eyes flamed.

Chris stepped between them. His gaze warned Kira. Then he turned to Leigh. "No one is accusing anyone of anything. We're just trying to find the truth."

For a second, Kira felt a profound sense of betrayal. Was Chris taking Leigh's side, too? First Max. Now Chris. He was certainly looking at Leigh with a lot more warmth than Kira felt. "It's obviously someone in this family," she persisted. "Or someone connected to it."

"We don't even know there was a switch," Leigh said stubbornly as she glared daggers at Kira. "You walk into our lives with a lie, then make an outlandish claim. You demand I give a stranger a kidney without proof, then threaten me with blackmail if I don't. You, Ms. Douglas, can go to hell."

Kira took a step back. The litany of sins hit home. Yet she

couldn't back down. Her mother's life was at stake. Why couldn't people understand that?

Max started to say something, but was interrupted by Mrs. Baker, who'd been manning the telephones. "The guard at the gate said someone from a lab is here."

Max glanced at Leigh. She hesitated, then nodded.

"Tell the guards to let him through," Max said.

"They also said that television trucks are gathering at the gate."

"Make it clear to them that we will charge trespassers," Max said. "We will have a statement later. There will be no comment beyond that."

"A statement?" Leigh asked.

"If you give them something, they will go away."

Leigh glared at Kira. "You said you could keep this quiet."

"I didn't know then that my mother and I would become targets for a homicidal maniac," Kira said. "I've been pushed in front of a train, my apartment was trashed, I was shot while an innocent bystander was killed. And my mother was attacked hours ago. And you're upset because I wasn't quiet. Come on. Someone on your side obviously has no interest in keeping this private."

Chris put a hand on her arm, but Kira brushed it off. "I'm sick of all this poor-Leigh stuff." She faced the person she now thought of as her nemesis. "Grow up. The woman who might be your mother is dying. That's the only thing that should matter now."

"I've agreed to the DNA test," Leigh protested as she took a step backward.

"But not the blood tests for compatibility with Mom."

"Your mom. Not mine. I didn't have one. I haven't had one for twenty-six years."

The doorbell rang, and the conversation stopped. Max stepped past by Kira on the way to the door. His face was like stone.

Not for the first time, she wondered whether there wasn't something more than a client/attorney relationship. He obviously held the purse strings of the trust, and he was lead attorney for a billion-dollar company. He was a chameleon.

Someone who turned colors to meld into the background. She'd seen it several times now. He had been a different person at Lucchesi's. Warm. Accessible. Now he was a stranger.

She would never know what he was thinking. He'd been gentle. Even tender. But that Max was gone now. He was in full protection mode of his client, and to hell with her.

To be honest with herself, she didn't even know whether he was a murderer. Or a protector of one.

An hour later, a caller dialed a number from a public phone booth only to receive the message: "This number is out of service."

No way to reach him now.

He was out of control. No one was to be badly hurt, and now a bystander was dead and others wounded.

What to do now? Someone had been killed. An accessory would be held equally guilty.

Never tempt a tiger.

The rage in him hadn't been evident. The offer of five thousand dollars to scare off a pretender had seemed the only way to avoid disaster, to conceal a secret that could ravage the family, and the family's fortune.

No one was to be hurt. Only frightened away. It had seemed the only way to avoid disaster.

Now the caller was probably the most frightened of all.

30

Kira watched as the technician carefully packaged the DNA sample and left. Chris took another. It would go to a different lab.

Max turned to her. "I'll take you home."

"I came with Chris," she said. "And I'm going back to the hospital. I want to make sure Mom's okay." She tried to ignore the pain as she moved. It had worsened, but she didn't know whether it would be any better at home.

She glanced at Leigh. She wanted to drag her to the hospital for blood tests. She wanted to get on her knees and beg Leigh to help their mother. And that's what Katy Douglas was: mother of both of them.

She didn't want to understand what Max had been trying to tell her. That Leigh wouldn't—couldn't—believe it until she saw the test results in black and white, and maybe not even then. Kira hadn't believed it at first, either. It had been her mother's urgent condition that had made her accept the truth more rapidly.

She didn't want to be understanding, and she deeply resented Max for making her feel she *should* be. Understanding could come later. Not now. Not when every moment counted.

Chris, who was standing nearby, looked from Kira to Leigh

and back again. "I have another stop on the way home," he said. "You might want to go with him."

Traitor. Throwing her to the wolf.

She had been thinking just moments ago that Max was one of those with a very big stake in whether she lived or died. Maybe that was why he was showing so much interest in her. Maybe Ted Bundy showed the same tenderness and thoughtfulness before he killed his victims.

Yet deep down she didn't believe it. Neither did Chris, or he never would have suggested she go with Max. Chris must have his reasons for suggesting it.

Or was it Leigh?

The thought was ungracious to the extreme. Chris had been a true friend. A lifesaver in so many ways. He'd practically given up his life for her mother. He certainly had the right to be attracted to Leigh, just as she was—unfortunately—attracted to Max.

She feared they both were going to pay dearly for those attractions.

She shrugged. "Maybe you can meet me there later," she suggested to Chris. A warning. For both Max and herself.

"I'll do that." Chris looked at his watch. "Say in two hours."

Kira saw Chris glance at Leigh. A long, measuring glance that lingered a second too long. Well, Leigh was pretty, even beautiful. Kira had a second of apprehension, then dismissed it. Chris was about as straight an arrow as ever lived.

Instead she forced herself to address Leigh. "Thank you," she said, trying to make amends for her earlier truculence. After all, the woman did finally agree to the DNA test, if not the blood tests.

One step at a time, she told herself.

Max led the way to the door and opened it. He followed her out and opened the door of his car. She barely suppressed a groan as she stepped inside. That darn rib!

"You shouldn't have come," Max said, then muttered something she couldn't hear. It was probably just as well.

He said nothing else as they drove to the gate. The guards opened it as Max approached. The drive beyond the gate was lined with cars, trucks, and portable satellite vans from various television stations. Max drove a few yards and got out of the car.

"Is that Kira Douglas?" yelled one.

"Ms. Douglas, how do you feel about being a heiress?" said another reporter who tried to approach the car.

"Are you going to sue the hospital?" yelled another.

Max stepped in front of them. "We'll have a statement later this evening," he said.

"Who're you?" yelled a reporter.

"Maxwell Payton. I'm the attorney for Westerfield Industries."

"Why are you with Ms. Douglas? Are you representing her as well?"

"What about the kidney?" a television reporter yelled out. "We heard . . ."

"Who's trying to kill you?" That from another reporter in the back of the pack. The question was obviously meant for Kira. She shook her head.

"Come on, Kira," said another. "You know we have deadlines."

Max fought to get back into the car. He started slowly, even as questions continued to fly at both of them.

"Where and when will the statement be issued?" came one last question.

"Seven. At my office." He gave an address. "Until then, there will be no comment from Kira or from any of the Westerfields, so you might as well leave."

He put his foot on the gas pedal and made his way through the gauntlet.

"They won't give up," Kira said.

"I know," he said.

"Who's going to write the statement?"

"You and I. But Leigh will have a say."

The reporters suddenly made her remember her cell phone. She had turned it off while the technician took the DNA sample. She hadn't wanted anything, anything at all, to delay the test. She turned it on and saw she had three messages. All from the newspaper.

Damn. For the first time in her life she forgot about a story. Not forgot, exactly, but just pushed more important things in front of it. The attack on her mother. The DNA test.

Wade would be livid.

She punched the button for the city desk.

"Carlton!" the rough voice barked out.

"Wade, this is Kira. I'm sorry. I should have gotten in touch with you sooner, but someone tried to kill my mother at the hospital and . . ."

"Good God," came the expletive. "Look, we're on deadline. Our police reporter is covering the city hall stuff. Can you just dictate something quickly? All the television stations are going nuts with this baby-switch thing. Apparently someone got a tip from the police department."

For the first time in her life, she didn't get a rush in writing a story. "I'm too close to it . . ."

"Look, Robin Stuart is here. She's the best we have. Can you give her some details, then write something for the morning paper tomorrow?" Before she could reply, he'd transferred the call.

Kira was careful in what she said. She passed over how she got the first DNA sample and simply said that Leigh Howard was one of several possibilities and that she'd been kind enough to give a DNA sample. Nothing was positive yet. She gave a time line of the attacks on her and suggested the attacks could be related to several stories in the past. She downplayed any connection.

When she finished, Robin read back what she had.

"*Atlanta Observer* reporter Kira Douglas, one of several victims shot outside city hall Thursday night, might have been the victim of an accidental baby switch at Eastside Hospital thirty-two years ago. Police are investigating whether the two events are connected . . ."

Fifteen minutes later, Kira finished, satisfied that she'd done as much as she could to report the important facts without pointing an accusation against the Westerfields. She wanted to do nothing that would slow the reluctant cooperation she now had.

Max had listened to her side of the conversation. "Thanks for toning down the Westerfield connection."

"Don't thank me. Until the DNA is official, it would be irresponsible to make any claims or charges. There're other stories, though. The police department report was leaked, and it mentioned the possible connection."

"But your story might defuse it for right now. It might give us a few days, time for Leigh to accept whatever comes."

"Is that possible? Leigh still doesn't want to admit the truth."

He took his gaze from the road and turned to her. "How long did it take you to accept the impossible?" he said.

"A day. Two."

"Longer than that. You said you had to wait several days for the third test to come in. Didn't you, in all that time, want to believe it wasn't true?"

He'd said something similar before. She wanted to debate him. This was a life. Her mother's life.

"Do you love her?" she asked. She hadn't meant to blurt out the question, but out it came. She hoped it was only her roiling emotions and lack of sleep rather than jealousy, but she suspected the truth was all three.

He glanced over at her, his green eyes meeting hers.

"Yes," he said, sounding as if the answer surprised even him. He sounded tired and frustrated. "I probably never admitted it before, even to myself. I've avoided that word like the plague. But, yeah, I do care for her. Maybe even more than I thought."

Her heart plunged.

A muscle tightened in his cheek. "Like Leigh, I grew up without much support. Certainly damned little love. It's something I shared with her. I didn't believe in it and avoided any kind of emotional entanglements. Leigh did the opposite. She ran to any man that promised love."

He stopped. Kira couldn't take her eyes from him. Each word seemed forced from his throat, and that surprised her. He'd always seemed so at ease with himself.

His hands tightened around the steering wheel. "You asked

whether I love her," he said. "You know about the accident she had. I used to drive her to school. She always wore long-sleeved shirts to cover the scars on her arms. She still does. You haven't seen them because she still hides them. I took her to ballet lessons and she always wore tights on the way. Her legs are scarred as well. Not bad. Not as much as she thinks, but the memories of that night make them worse in her mind. We have a pool, but the only time I've seen her swimming is at night."

Kira listened intently as he swerved in and out of traffic. "She accepts me because I never pitied her," he continued. "Never catered to her. I make her angry, but there's a certain respect between us. She knows I won't take advantage of her, that I'll tell her exactly what I think where she's concerned. If she's being a damned fool, I tell her that."

He stopped for a red light. He turned to her. "Ed Wester-field treated her like a piece of property. He was determined she would not marry 'trash' like her mother did, which, of course, drove her to do exactly that. If he cared, he never knew how to express it. In any event, he never gave her the unconditional love she's always yearned for. So I've watched her struggle through a horrific marriage and a gold-digging fiancé. She's just now beginning to find herself, and you throw this at her."

The light changed and he looked back at the road. "So, yes, I am protective. And I guess I love her as I would a kid sister." A muscle jerked in his jaw, and Kira knew exactly how much he cared and how torn he was.

This was a different Max. He'd finally let his guard down, and she feared he would regret it. But for now her heart filled with a bittersweet knowledge of what he was trying to say to her. He not only owed his duty to Leigh, but a piece of his heart. Perhaps even a larger piece than he thought.

She was a fool to fret over it. She had far larger worries than someone who had always been out of reach, even if she was interested in a relationship. Which she wasn't.

"I don't want you to think, even for an instant, that Leigh

could have anything to do with what's happened these past few days. The truth is she wouldn't hurt a flea. Herself, yes. A flea, no."

"Then who?"

"I've gone over it a dozen times," he said. "I keep wondering who would benefit if something happened to you. Especially if Leigh was blamed."

She waited for him to continue. When he didn't, she asked, "What *would* happen?"

"I suspect that other members of the family would step in as potential heirs and contest the trust. None of them is overly fond of me."

"Would they win?"

"I don't think so. Since I was an interested party, I found the best law firm in Georgia to draw the trust. Ed told them exactly what he wanted. But you never know how a judge is going to rule." He paused, then continued, "This kind of trust is rare in that the beneficiary has little or no control. It's to protect her. If Leigh doesn't conform to the terms of the will, the money goes to charity. I would administer that process and could make some very fat fees. So I imagine I would be considered someone who would benefit. There would be few checks on what I could and couldn't do."

"Who are the relatives who could contest?" She knew from Chris's research, but she wanted to hear it from him.

"Leigh's cousins, Seth and David, and David's father, Dr. Crawford. That's all. The Westerfields aren't very prolific."

"There's no one else who would have a claim or benefit?"

He was thoughtful. Silent. Then he shrugged. "Not that I'm aware of."

Before she could ask more questions, they arrived at the hospital.

"You don't have to come in with me," she said as they turned into the hospital driveway.

"Lady, I'm not letting you out of my sight until Burke gets here." The way he said "lady" sent a warm tingle through her.

She was silent as he parked. She didn't wait for him to come around to her side. Despite the pounding on her ribs, she was out of the car and walking toward the entrance before he caught up with her.

They didn't talk on their way to the elevator, but she was only too aware of his body language, especially when he rested an arm on her shoulder. Claiming her.

The tingle grew into a rush of warmth.

Not good, Douglas. He'd just said he avoided emotional entanglements like the plague. He'd told her that he was more than a little on Leigh's side.

But no matter how much she warned herself, her body didn't behave. It reacted to him all on its own.

They reached her mother's floor. She stopped at the nurse's station. "How is she?"

The nurse on duty knew her well. "Holding her own. We're all praying for another kidney." She paused. "I heard what happened. There's a guy outside your mother's room. He's been vetted by our security here, and we're keeping a special eye on her."

Kira smiled her gratitude and went on to the room. She didn't recognize the man sitting in a chair outside the room. He stood as they approached.

"I'm Kira Douglas, Mrs. Douglas's daughter."

"I recognize you, Ms. Douglas. Go in."

"How do you recognize me?"

"Chris sent pictures along. I have one of Mr. Payton as well."

"Anyone else been here?"

"Only staff. I've checked all their credentials. The doctor wasn't happy, but . . ."

She didn't wait for him to finish. She opened the door and went inside.

Her mother was on oxygen. And asleep. She retreated back to the nurse's station. "She's on oxygen?"

"On and off. It relieves the strain on her heart. You can take it off while you're here."

She returned to the room. Max had waited outside, but now he followed her inside. She wanted the company. It took the edge off the despair. The continuing anger at Leigh's inertia.

Her mother's eyes opened as if she sensed her presence.

The smile was dimming, but it was there. "Kira. I'm . . . so glad to see you. I've been worried about you."

"I'm better," she said. Anything more optimistic would warn her mother. "I did ask Carly to take over the books at the Clean Sweep." Carly had worked for the Clean Sweep for two years and had offered to step in yesterday. "It's taken a big load off." She paused, then added, "People are asking about you."

"They know?" She looked distressed.

"Yes. Remember what I told you yesterday. The story is in the newspapers now. A lot of people know—and care—about you."

And someone wanted her dead.

Her mother's gaze left her face and went to Max, who stood in the doorway. Her eyes filled with curiosity.

"This is Max Payton," Kira said. "He's the attorney for your . . . for Leigh Howard."

"I would like to see her." Katy Douglas's voice trembled slightly.

Max stepped closer. "You will," he said softly.

"When?"

"Soon, I expect."

She held out her hand to him. "Thank you."

"You're welcome, Mrs. Douglas."

"Katy. Everyone calls . . . me Katy."

"Katy then," he said easily.

Her mother looked at him with speculation in her eyes. Sick as she was, Katy Douglas was an unrepentant matchmaker for her daughter, and now she had a glimmer of that old fire in her eyes.

Before she had an opportunity to question him further, he crossed the room in what seemed like three steps. "I'll wait outside while you visit." And then he was gone, the door closing softly after him.

Her mother's eyes widened. "Wow," she said. "He's certainly . . . something."

He was that. The problem was that Kira didn't know what kind of "something" he was.

"He seems nice," her mother probed. "Is he married?"

"No, Mom, he isn't." Kira suspected that no matter how sick mothers were, they remained moms. And they had special antennas.

"I want someone . . . for you."

She didn't add that she wanted someone for Kira before she died. She didn't have to. The words were in her face.

It broke Kira's heart.

She must have looked stricken. Her mother stretched her hand out and took one of hers. "I was so lucky to have you."

"I think you will like Leigh, too."

"I know I will. But you'll always be my baby."

"The two of us together. Always." Kira repeated her mother's mantra. Whenever they were low on money, or weren't quite sure where they would live next, Katy Douglas saw it as a challenge, and one that bonded them even closer.

She was rewarded with that smile again. And then her mother's eyes closed.

After Max and Kira Douglas left the Westerfield home, Chris turned to Leigh. "I think someone is trying to frame you," he said.

She looked up at him. "Why?"

"The gun missing from the cabinet, the attacks timed when you don't have an alibi. Someone probably knows you took firearms training. You have a motive. You had opportunity."

"I couldn't hit a blow-up alligator in a kid's swimming pool," she said.

"Whoever is behind this doesn't know that. Nor can you prove it."

"The instructor can."

"You could have gone somewhere else."

"I didn't . . . I wouldn't . . ."

"I know," he said. "But the police will be back unless they find the city hall shooter."

She looked at him with those damn big eyes. God, she was pretty. "I don't know who . . ." she started.

"I can count five on my fingers now," he said.

"No. Not Max. Not Seth. Not David or Michael."

"I said five." He watched as her lips frowned in thought. "The president and CEO of Westerfield Industries. I understand he and Payton have had some differences of opinion, and Payton has control of fifty-one percent of the stock. He holds it only as long as the trust lasts. If Kira dies and you're charged with murder, then the trust ends. The shares will go to charity or, if the will is contested, be divided among any heirs. Control will be diluted."

"You really think Jack Melton could be responsible? I've known him for years."

"I don't know. I'm just looking at possibilities. Who else might have felt entitled to more than what they received?"

"No one," she said.

He looked around the room. He hadn't seen the housekeeper today. "Where's Mrs. Baker?"

"She went home at noon. She wasn't feeling well." Then she stared at him with wide-open eyes. "You don't think . . . ?"

"Would she have had access to the gun closet?"

"No. It was always locked."

Chris paused. "I saw the will in the probate office. Mrs. Baker received a good chunk of money. Maybe she wanted more."

"Mrs. Baker?" she said with surprise. "She was ecstatic that she received what she did. One thing about Grandfather: He always paid his employees well and in return he demanded total loyalty. Mrs. Baker always gave it to him, and to me. We're her family. I think she probably expected a small sum when Grandfather died but she was delighted at how much. She always wanted a house of her own and with what she'd saved she was able to buy a nice cottage with all cash."

"How long has she been with the family?"

"Nearly forty years. I understand she left for a year or so when she got married. Her husband died in the military, and she returned."

"No family then?"

"Only Rick."

"Rick?"

"You met him. He's the groom and handyman for us. He

also works at several other horse farms. He's Mrs. Baker's nephew."

"How long has he been here?"

"Eighteen months. I wasn't too sure about him for a while. Silver Lady didn't take to him, but he seems conscientious enough. He's dependable."

"What do you know about him?"

"Ex-military. Couldn't find a job after getting out, and Mrs. Baker said he had experience with animals, that as a teenager he once worked for a horse farm."

"Does he live with Mrs. Baker?"

"No, he has a place of his own. A small apartment not far from here."

Chris made a mental note to run a check on the nephew. "What's his last name?" he asked.

"Rick. Rick Salter. You don't think . . . ?"

"I don't think anything," he said. "Besides, I'm sure the police are checking out everyone on the estate." He paused, then asked, "Your grandfather never remarried after his wife died?"

"No. He was a workaholic, not very social unless it was business oriented. Mrs. Baker did everything for him."

"I should go," he said, seeing the fatigue in her eyes. She probably hadn't slept much in the past few days.

Her eyes met his. "Do you have to? Can you stay a few moments? I really don't want to be alone."

And she shouldn't be alone. He'd been thinking of Kira and Katy. But no one seemed to have thought of Leigh, who'd had to deal with this mess on her own.

She'd showed courage. She'd agreed—albeit reluctantly—to the DNA test. He would have been reluctant as well, considering the evidence given her. She wasn't only being asked to give up a kidney for a stranger, but to deny everything she believed she was.

She opened the door without waiting for his help and went outside. It was as if she couldn't get out of the house fast enough.

The sun was still hot, but a breeze wafted through the thick canopy of trees that dotted the pasture. The entire estate was surrounded by a picturesque white fence, but the pasture was fenced inside that area.

The donkey was grazing but looked up as they approached and sauntered toward them. Leigh took something from a pocket in her slacks and gave it to him.

"You try it," she said.

He reached out and gave the donkey the cube of sugar. It quickly disappeared, and the donkey nuzzled him for more.

"Later, greedy one," she said.

He was enchanted. He'd thought her lovely before but now there was pink in her cheeks and her eyes sparkled. "Come," she said, grabbing his hand and drawing him inside the stable.

She took out more cubes of sugar and held one out to the white mare.

"Do you always carry those?" he asked.

"Sugar or carrots or slices of apple. Apple is really better, but it's not as easy to tuck in a pocket."

The mare nudged her for more, and she laughed. "It's the sugar more than me," she said.

Then she led the way to another stall. "Pretty girl," she crooned as the mare moved restlessly. "She's new. Not quite sure she's home yet." She reached out and ran her hand lightly down the horse's neck. "I haven't ridden her yet, but tomorrow . . ." She stopped. "Maybe I won't have them much longer," she said, biting her lip. "If the DNA . . ."

Chris took the photo of Katy Douglas from his pocket and held it out to her.

Leigh resisted for a moment, then took it.

The photo had been taken five years earlier, according to Kira. Katy was laughing at something, her face alight with pure joy. Her taffy-colored hair was neatly cut for easy care with a wisp of bangs nearly reaching her eyes.

"She looks . . . nice."

"She *is* nice. One of the nicest, warmest women I've ever met. When my wife was so ill, she stopped in every afternoon with something to tempt Risa's appetite."

He watched as Leigh studied the photo. He wondered if she saw the similarities. The sea-colored eyes and high cheekbones and small ears. The wide lips.

Leigh touched a finger to the face in the photo. Chris watched as the finger seemed to trace the face. Then she looked up, and Chris saw the stark longing in her face.

"My father hated my mother," she said suddenly, softly. "He said so the night he . . . died. He purposely ran the car into an abutment. He wanted to kill all of us. He believed my mother cheated on him. He'd had a blood test, he said, and I wasn't his. He demanded to know who the father was. I didn't remember those words until I went under hypnosis with a psychiatrist, but they were there, deep inside."

Horror filled her face as she suddenly realized the implications of what she'd just said. "They died . . . because someone made a mistake?"

31

"I'm not so sure it was a mistake," Chris said slowly.

Leigh stiffened as the import of the words sank in. "Oh God, you don't think someone intentionally switched babies?" Total incredulity was in her voice.

"When Kira was born, she had what was then almost always a fatal heart condition. The obstetrician would have instantly known something was wrong." He paused. "Dr. Michael Crawford was your mother's obstetrician."

She stared at him for a moment, then asked in a trembling voice, "Was he also Mrs. Douglas's obstetrician?"

"Yes, and you and Kira were born within minutes of each other. According to Katy Douglas, he also found the pediatric surgeon who repaired Kira's heart. An anonymous donor paid at least part of the bills."

"Not Uncle Michael," she protested. "He's someone special. He retired five years ago to join Doctors Without Borders. He's been in Africa almost constantly."

"Perhaps because he feels guilty about something," Chris said.

"No," she said adamantly. "He wouldn't do that; no way would he switch babies."

"Maybe he thought he was doing everyone a favor," he

said. "Katy Douglas was barely eighteen and her husband left soon after the baby was born. He might have known the marriage was in trouble. Your mother, the one who brought you home, was thirty-five. There were no other children."

She blinked, then looked thoughtful. "I once asked why I didn't have any sisters and brothers. She said she was waiting for me, how precious I was. But Seth told me she'd had several miscarriages."

"This might have been her last chance to have a child. When her child appeared to be in critical condition, maybe your uncle thought this was the best thing."

"But how could . . . anyone play God like that?" Her voice broke and her eyes filled with tears. The horse behind her neighed and moved restlessly.

Leigh leaned over and soothed her. "Sorry, baby," Leigh said. Her voice resumed a normal tone as she assured the mare, but when she turned back to him, her eyes were wide with confusion. "How could anyone . . . ?"

He touched her face. Traced the cheekbone with a finger and pushed back a blond strand of hair. "I'm sorry," he said. "It's only speculation. I don't know. No one knows how this happened but the person responsible. You know your uncle. I thought you should realize that it's one avenue we're exploring."

She looked up at him. Her eyes were bright with unshed tears. "I *should* know. Thank you for telling me. But I really don't think . . . not Uncle Michael."

"It's just one of many possibilities," he said.

"But you think it's the right one?"

"It had to be someone in that operating room," he said. "I've been talking to some physicians and most don't think a mistake is possible under these circumstances. A critically ill child would be taken to the neonatal care unit immediately."

She clung to him. She had more guts than he'd first thought. From what she'd said a few moments earlier, she'd been living all these years with the fact that her father killed her mother and tried to kill her. There was really no one to help her come to terms with that fact. No loving family. Only a cold, hard grandfather who had expected entirely too much. He wondered if Ed Westerfield ever knew what happened in that car all those years ago.

He realized why she'd been so reluctant to believe that she was not a Westerfield. All that pain during her growing-up years; according to Payton, she was finally coming to grips with it. Then someone comes along and pulls the rug out from under her feet again.

That still didn't solve the immediate problem, though. Dr. Michael Crawford may have been responsible for switching the babies—or not—but he certainly wasn't responsible for the attacks on Kira. Two crimes separated by thirty-two years. What was the connection?

"I want to see her," Leigh said suddenly. "I want to see Katy Douglas."

He took a step back. Looked at her face. Unshed tears glittered and made those spectacular eyes even more vivid. He and Risa had taken a Caribbean cruise after she was diagnosed. A short one just before surgery. It was something she'd always wanted but he'd never had time to take.

Leigh's eyes looked like that sea, the incredible shades of blue meshing together.

The reminder of that vacation wasn't as excruciating as in the past. Some of the pain was receding, replaced by good memories. Regret was still there, but it, too, was fading. He couldn't change the past. But he could deal with it better.

Leigh Howard was doing that now.

"You're thinking about your wife?" she said.

"Yes. I wish she'd known you, and you her. She was a brave soul. You have a lot in common."

"I'm not brave at all. I've been a coward most of my life. Poor, pitiful me. I made every wrong decision that could be made. I married someone who wanted my money and . . ."

She didn't have to continue. He'd seen that look in other women's eyes. He wanted to kill the bastard.

Leigh fed the horse another sugar cube, then ran her hand along its muzzle. "It wasn't until Max forced me to go into therapy that I realized what a total mess I was."

He took her in his arms and leaned down. She was a small

woman, smaller than Risa, and yet she fit well against him. His lips touched hers with tenderness.

He'd thought it gone after Risa's death, that no one could touch his soul again. He hadn't thought he wanted it touched again. The pain was too agonizing.

But now the need to touch, to comfort, to feel again was even stronger.

She stood on tiptoes. Her arms went around his neck and her lips were eager against his. There was a sweetness about her kiss, the tentativeness of her touch, that was intoxicating.

He knew she'd been married before, but her responses seemed like an awakening. He wondered whether anyone had been gentle with her before.

His fingers ran through her hair, releasing the clasp that kept it back, and it fell around her face, the silken strands tumbling over his hand.

Bad move, Burke. She's vulnerable. She needed a friend, not someone who had another loyalty, not someone who wanted to take that blouse off and run his hands up and down her body.

Yet he didn't stop the kiss. Instead he deepened it, his lips opening slightly. His need was strong and deep, and for a moment he allowed himself to revel in being alive again.

One of the horses whinnied, wanting attention, and he suddenly jerked away. Her hand dropped from his neck but caught his hand. "Don't go away," she said in a low voice.

The plea cut through him like a knife.

"I won't," he said. "But I promised to meet Kira and Payton at the hospital."

"You're sure she—Mrs. Douglas—is my mother, aren't you?" she said hesitantly.

"Yes. I'm the one who took the cup and hair sample to the lab. I know Kira probably went about it in the wrong way, but she didn't want to spread her anguish to other women without proof." He paused.

"*And* she was in a hurry," Leigh added caustically.

"Yes. I probably would have done the same thing had it been my wife. Or mother."

She absorbed that. "You really think I look like her . . . Katy Douglas?"

"Oh yes."

Her gaze bored into him. Then her fingers curled around his. "I'll go with you."

He squeezed her hand. "Are you sure?"

"Yes."

His free hand touched her face. Wiped away a wayward tear that had slipped from her brimming eyes. Something shifted inside him. Maybe no one else would believe what she was doing took courage, but he knew. He knew from the struggle in her face. In those amazing eyes.

He'd tried to put himself in her position, and he couldn't do it. He honestly didn't know what he would do. Although giving a kidney held little immediate risk, any major operation carried some danger and if anything happened to the other kidney, she would be in trouble. He wanted to think he would do it, but he didn't have Leigh's history weighing him down. She wouldn't be risking just a kidney but what little sense of belonging and home she'd managed to carve for herself.

"You're a brave lady," he said.

"I think that's the nicest compliment anyone has ever given me, though I don't think it's true."

"Oh, it's true, Leigh Howard. And you're also . . . very pretty." Damn, but he was lousy at compliments. And he was getting in trouble. Deep, deep trouble. The last thing he wanted to do was pose more problems for her and create more conflicts of interest for himself.

"Do you have another of those cubes of sugar?" he asked. A diversion of sorts. For himself.

She took one from her pocket and gave it to him. He held it out to the white mare and felt the softness of her mouth as she daintily took it from his palm.

Leigh gave him an approving glance and took his hand. "Let's go before I change my mind."

Kira and Max waited in the visitors' room for Chris Burke. Kira was already regretting asking him to meet her there.

Max faced her. "You look tired . . . and damned desirable."

"Always the diplomat. Or the attorney who wants to win."

"Right now, I'm neither. I don't want one side to win to the detriment of the other." He very carefully did not touch her. He wanted to. She was so obviously exhausted. And sad. Even hopeless.

But she would misconstrue whatever he did. He hadn't missed the wariness in her eyes at times. Not always. They had definitely softened when he talked to her mother.

"I understand why you love her so much," he said.

"Do you?" she challenged.

He paused. Considered his answer, then admitted, "Maybe not. I'm not good at families. I don't understand that kind of . . ." He stopped.

"Have you never had a family?"

He shrugged. "The Westerfields came closest to it."

"From what I understand it wasn't a *Brady Bunch* family."

He smiled slightly. "No."

"No mother or father? No brother or sister? Not even a distant cousin lurking somewhere?"

"None of the above. I lost my mother when I was nine. I spent the next few years in various foster homes, none of which were that eager to have me there. Money, yes. Me, no."

She rested her hand on his knee. "I'm sorry. It must have been lonely."

"Not so. There was an independence that appealed to me. No one cared whether I was at a certain place at night. I learned a number of skills on the street."

"How did you become one of Atlanta's most eligible bachelors?"

"The PR firm I hired to promote Westerfield Industries. They didn't quite understand I wanted the corporation publicized, not me. I fired them, but I was stuck."

"Ah, a retiring lawyer."

She was at her cynical best. He liked that side of her. Not particularly the cynicism, but the challenge in every word. She had learned not to take everything at face value. Well, so had he.

She wanted to probe deeper. That was obvious to him. But he didn't want to go deeper.

She might understand. But she was a newspaper reporter, and his past was something he'd carefully concealed all these years. She was open. Probably the most open woman he'd ever met. She wore her emotions on her face. He didn't want to see pity there. Or horror. Or even fear.

"Are you from Atlanta?" she continued to probe.

She was in full reporter mode, and he'd learned she was a very good one.

"No." Hopefully the answer was short enough, and curt enough, to cut off any additional questions.

His hopes were quickly dashed.

"Where, then?"

"A place that no longer exists. It's been paved over and made into industrial properties. It's not a place I like remembering."

It was a warning. Hell, it was like hitting her over the head with a hammer. His voice had chilled in a way that usually sent people scurrying for the door.

"Okay," she said. "I'm sorry. Questions are instinctive for me. Even if I wasn't a reporter, I would always want to know everything about everyone. I'm told it can be a very annoying trait."

He was disarmed, and he didn't want to be disarmed. He had no question but she would try to find out more about him. Thus far, the police had only talked to him about what he knew about the shooting, which was damned little. But they would be back with more questions.

"You said you didn't think Leigh's cousins could be involved. Why?"

"Seth Westerfield has a promising career. He's the favorite for Congress. He'll probably make a good one, as politicians go. He knows nearly everyone who counts in his district, has done favors for many of them. He wouldn't do anything to risk his campaign. His father ran, and lost. Seth has something to prove."

"He needs money to run," Kira ventured.

"He's being supported by the national party. He's also

raised a lot locally." He hesitated, then added, "If Seth has a soft spot, it's Leigh. He wants to break the will, but he wants to do it for Leigh. If he gets something, fine, but he would never hurt her or try to blame something he did on her."

"You say that with certainty."

He shrugged. "He loves her. If she wasn't his cousin, I think . . . he would have gone after her."

"And the other cousin?"

"David? He doesn't care anything about money. Never did. Not that he needed to. His father made a lot of money and had a great money manager. In fact, I think David gave his Westerfield inheritance to charity."

"But maybe he knew his father was involved in some way . . ."

"I thought about that, but I doubt he has any of the skills needed to do what's been done these last few days. All he knows is medicine, and that's all he cares about except his family."

"And the housekeeper?"

"Mrs. Baker?"

She nodded.

"She was with Ed forever. He trusted her completely."

"Is there anyone else around the house?"

"Just Rick. He's Mrs. Baker's nephew. But he has no motive."

"Did you check his references?"

"I asked one of my staff attorneys to do it. He said Rick came up clean. And he *is* Mrs. Baker's nephew."

"Why does everyone call her Mrs. Baker? Why not by her first name?"

Her questions were defusing the tension between them. He wondered whether she was intentionally doing that.

"I don't know. Ed always called her that. It was never Alma. Always Mrs. Baker. The rest of us followed his lead. It became a habit. And she never asked us to do anything else."

Max knew now why she was such a good reporter. She was relentless.

"Maybe the nephew thought she should get more."

"I don't think they're that close, and I know that Mrs. Baker was more than pleased with what she received."

"That leaves us back at square one," she said, disappointment in her voice.

"But you did a damn good job in summarizing. Except for one thing."

"What?"

"Me. I might have the best motive of all. I get rid of both of you, and I can do anything I want with the trust."

"You can shoot?"

"Yes. I could also hire someone fairly capable to try to frighten you off."

"And make love to me at the same time?"

He found a smile forming. Dammit, but she got to the heart of the matter.

"No," he said simply.

She took his left hand in her right one. "I suspected as much."

"Just suspected?"

"Okay, I knew as much."

"From the beginning?"

"Now you're asking too much," she said. "I was certainly attracted to you, but I couldn't understand why you might be attracted to me."

He raised an eyebrow. "Why? You're pretty. Smart as hell. Gutsy. Interesting."

"Interesting?" she echoed just as he had a few seconds earlier. She would have been insulted if anyone else had said it, but she sensed it was a rare compliment from him.

He drew her hand to his mouth and kissed her palm. "I like interesting."

He put his arm around her shoulders and she relaxed into it. She liked being pretty, smart as hell, gutsy. Even "interesting." She liked being next to him. She liked the warmth of his body next to her. She liked talking to him and she liked his touch. Liked? Greatest understatement in the world.

He'd been so good with her mother. Katy had liked him. And her mother was a great judge of character.

Admit it. She trusted him. She hadn't wanted to. He was too close to the Westerfields. He'd made it clear his loyalty—or duty—was first and foremost to Leigh Howard.

He had been open and honest about it. Just as she had been about her mother. So how could she complain? Although she'd skittered away several times, she realized it was more the fear of falling in love with him rather than actual distrust of him. There had been a certain ease between them almost from the beginning. An ease spiced by the sexual electricity that had been there from minute one.

She still didn't know that much about him. He'd hinted at secrets. And her natural curiosity wanted to press him, but now was not the time.

She'd just started to relax when she saw Chris and Leigh approach. Leigh's blond hair was pulled back in a long braid and she looked as elegant as ever. But her eyes were slightly red with dark rings underneath. She, too, was obviously having sleepless nights.

Kira rose and went to her. "Thank you for coming," she said simply.

"How is she?"

"She's sleeping now, but she would want me to wake her," Kira said.

Leigh started to turn. "Maybe later."

"No. Please," Kira said. "It would mean so much to her. She keeps asking about you. I showed her a photo." She didn't know how Chris had convinced her to come, but now it was up to her to get her to stay.

Her heart was in her throat as she watched Leigh's face. She recalled everything Max had said, and her heart went out to her. "It would mean a lot to her," she said in a ragged voice.

Leigh glanced at Chris, who nodded.

"I'll wait until she wakes," she said.

Kira's breath evened out. A miracle. Now she needed just one more. Just one more.

32

It took every ounce of Leigh's strength to go into the hospital and up to Katy Douglas's room.

She'd seen it many times in her memories. In her dreams. The endless surgeries, the pain, the sorrow, and particularly the guilt that had never left her. She was the reason her mother and father died.

Chris took her hand, squeezed it. He didn't know the deep-seated guilt she'd felt all these years, or maybe he sensed it. But his touch gave her strength. She could do anything with him next to her.

She waited as Kira went into the room across the hall. Her heart was moving spasmodically in her chest. Why had she agreed? She'd surprised herself by doing it. But looking at the photo of Katy Douglas was like looking at herself.

In seconds, Kira was back, waving her in.

"Do you want me to go in with you?" Chris asked.

"No," she said. "But thank you."

He nodded approvingly and she felt a new surge of confidence. She went inside and closed the door behind her.

Kira stood next to the bed. Protectively, Leigh thought. The woman in the bed had turned her head toward the door, and she broke into a smile as Leigh neared the bed. Stood there. Unsure. Beyond nervous.

Katy Douglas was small, and the disease had probably made her seem even smaller. She was wan, her eyes hollow, but the color was an intense dark blue. A darker shade than her own.

"Sit . . . down," the woman said. "Near me, please."

Leigh took the chair next to the bed. She was grateful for it. Her legs weren't working very well, and her heart was pounding.

"This must . . . be very hard," Katy Douglas said. Her eyes were full of compassion, and Leigh's mouth suddenly felt thick.

"For you, too," Leigh replied after a moment.

"No. It's not hard gaining another daughter. It's a . . . joy."

And Leigh saw that it was. Not because of a kidney. She looked into the kind, compassionate face and suddenly understood why Chris had wanted her to meet Katy Douglas.

It felt disloyal, though, to the mother who had sung to her and sat beside her when she was sad or sick or afraid.

"I'll go outside," Kira said.

"No . . ." But it was too late. The door closed behind Kira Douglas as she left the room.

Katy Douglas seemed to be able to see right through all Leigh's uncertainty. "Thank you . . . for coming." Her voice was growing weaker.

"I . . ." Leigh began.

"Don't say it," Katy said. "I think we've all gone through some . . . denial about what happened. I probably have the least adjustment. I get a new daughter. If you'll let me."

Except it might not be for long. Leigh didn't want a new mother if she was just going to lose her again. She wanted to flee the room.

"Will you tell me something about yourself?" Katy asked. "Anything. What you like. What you don't like."

What to tell? Kira Douglas was smart, had a great job, and was obviously respected, while she'd made one mess after another.

"I like horses. I'm involved in a horse show."

The woman in the bed smiled. "I always wanted to ride. So did Kira, but there was never time or money. I'm so glad you had the opportunity."

Katy held out her hand. "I don't want to push you . . . Leigh . . . but there may not be much time. I want you to know me . . . and Kira. You're like sisters."

"I would like that, too," Leigh replied. "But you look tired. Maybe another time."

"Just a few more minutes . . ."

Katy Douglas was fighting exhaustion. That much was obvious.

"This can't be good for you . . ."

"It's wonderful for me. At first . . . it hurt. I had a daughter I'd never held, never knew. I love Kira with all my heart but to know there was someone out there . . ."

There was so much love and tenderness and understanding in a body ravaged by disease that Leigh's heart started to crack.

"No," Katy said shortly. "No regrets. No tears."

"You need a . . . a kidney."

"And I'll tell you what I told Kira. I still have my senses about me. I still have to sign a consent for surgery. And I won't sign it. I told her I wouldn't take her kidney, and I won't take yours. It's too dangerous."

Leigh touched the hand lying on the cover. "I'm glad I came."

"Kira was right," Katy said. "You're lovely. And nice."

Kira had lied. She hadn't been nice at all. She was suddenly very grateful.

"She loves you very much," Leigh said.

"Maybe too much," Katy said. "She thinks . . . she knows what's best for me. She doesn't."

The kidney, Leigh knew immediately. Pain rushed through her. She might have the means of prolonging this woman's life. Prolonging the time she could get to know her.

The fear rushed in after that. The white walls of the room did it. The sound of heels on the hall floors outside did it. The drip stand did it, along with the other sounds of a hospital room.

"What is it?" Katy Douglas asked softly.

"I don't like hospitals. I was in an accident when I was young, and I was in and out of the hospital—hospitals—for several years."

"I'm . . . sorry." Empathy shone in eyes too much like her own.

"It was a long time ago," Leigh said.

"Not so long ago for you." The voice was soft, understanding.

"No. It revisits several times a week at night. My mom and dad died at the same time."

Katy Douglas's face paled even more. "Kira told me your . . . parents died in a crash."

Leigh didn't know what to say. She didn't know what to do. She had wished to have her mother back for years. Now she was offered a new one. It was all too new, too strange to accept.

She stood. "I was told not to stay long."

"Will you come back?"

"Yes."

"If you have any photos . . . when you were young . . ."

"I'll bring them."

"Thank you."

"I don't know what to call you."

"Katy. Everyone calls me Katy."

To her own surprise, Leigh leaned down and clasped Katy's hand. "I'm glad to meet you, Katy."

Katy's fingers clasped hers. And she nodded.

Leigh left before her eyes gave her away for the second time today. Until now she hadn't cried in a long time.

Thoughts and plans were floating like flotsam through Kira's mind. She had wanted to listen in on the conversation but in the end she had too much respect for her mother.

She needed to write a better story for the paper, but there was little she could say now. Too much she didn't know. Too many people who could get hurt.

She hadn't really considered that in her career. News was

news. Now she was learning the personal toll of some news stories. Fingers would be pointed toward an important family. Seth Westerfield's political campaign could be affected. So could Dr. David and Dr. Michael Crawford's reputations. She didn't want to be responsible for that.

Max was talking to Chris in a corner. She walked over and joined them.

Chris moved to make way for her.

"Thank you for bringing her. I don't know how you did it, but . . ."

"It was her decision. She brought it up. She offered to come."

"It's a change."

"I think she's been thinking about it."

"Will she give a kidney?"

"I don't know. That wasn't discussed."

"Maybe after meeting her . . ."

"Katy is still a stranger to her," Max warned. "And even if the DNA proves to Leigh's satisfaction she's Katy's biological daughter, that doesn't mean she's compatible."

"I think she's already accepted that she's Mom's natural daughter or she wouldn't be here," Kira said hopefully.

Their eyes met. Kira's and Max's. She felt the now-familiar sparks inside, the tingling in the pit of her stomach that presaged even stronger reactions. Her face warmed as she remembered the hours they'd spent . . .

Dammit. Not now. She stepped away, trying to break that intimacy that so suddenly had enwrapped them.

She glanced at Chris. Saw his raised eyebrows as he obviously understood what was happening.

Just then the door to her mother's room opened. Leigh walked out. Slowly. Hesitantly.

Kira went over to her. "Thank you."

Leigh merely nodded, then said haltingly, "I'll have the blood tests for a kidney match. That doesn't mean . . ."

Kira nodded. It didn't mean Leigh would go through with it. Kira understood the woman better now. She was taking it step-by-step, and that was all she could expect. It was what Max had been trying to tell her.

Chris put his arm around Leigh, and she leaned into him. So that was the way it was.

"Let's go down to the cafeteria and work out the statement," Max said.

Twenty minutes later, they agreed on a statement along the lines of what Kira had reported to the newspaper.

"It's not going to satisfy anyone," Chris said. "And Kira is really going to be under pressure from her newspaper."

"I know," Max replied. "But if we stick together and insist that's all we're going to say until DNA test results come in, they won't have much to run with. At least for the moment." He paused. "I think it's best if it comes from both Kira and myself. That way they can't run to the other side."

Kira nodded. "Put my name on it."

Max nodded. "I'll have my secretary fax it to all the news media immediately." He looked at Kira. "It's time for you to go home."

She knew that. She'd been running on adrenaline and pain-killers, and now it was catching up with her.

Chris's cell rang. He flipped it open. Listened. Turned away and spoke in a low voice, too low to be heard. Then he turned back.

His gaze went to Kira, then to Max. "I'll take Kira home while you see to the statement." He turned to Leigh. "Why don't you come with us?"

"Yes, come with us," Kira said to Leigh, sensing something very big was not being said. So, apparently, did Max. His green eyes turned cool, and a muscle throbbed in his neck.

Leigh looked bewildered, so Kira continued, "I'm staying at Mom's house. We have a lot of photos you might like to see."

Chris turned to Max. "Your investigators may have sources I don't," he said. "Can you try to get information on Richard Salter? He's a cipher."

"Of course," Max said easily. Yet his eyes told another story. He was being locked out, and he didn't like it. "I'll be in contact with you. Maybe breakfast in the morning."

Chris nodded. "I'll call. In the meantime, some of my

friends are watching the house so Kira should be safe enough. Someone will stay with Katy, too."

"I'll keep guards at Leigh's house," Max added.

Kira caught his hand. "Thank you," she said simply. He would know she meant Leigh's change of heart.

His lips turned up on one side. "You're welcome."

After he left, she turned to Chris. "What was that about?' "

Chris glanced at her, then Leigh. "The police are focusing their investigation on Payton. They think he's behind everything."

33

Kira went into momentary shock. The police focusing on Max?

"Why?" she asked.

"Yes, why?" Leigh echoed.

"I don't know exactly," Chris said. "My contact just said they found something in his background."

"I don't believe it," Kira said.

Chris didn't reply.

"The police are wrong," Kira said flatly. "They are wrong all the time."

"Maybe," Chris said. "In the meantime I don't want either of you with him alone. Leigh, I want you to stay with Kira."

"I've been with Max a thousand times," Leigh protested. "I never once feared for myself. I would never tell him, but he's been my rock for more years than I want to remember."

"I'll try to find out what evidence they have," Chris said. "But I want my people guarding you. Not his. After the city hall shooting, I don't have any faith in them."

"Someone has to make sure Maude and the horses are fed and watered," Leigh protested.

"You have a groom to do that."

"I know but . . . I like to make sure."

"I'll drive you over tomorrow."

They all fell into silence as Chris drove them to her mother's house. Kira ran over every conversation she'd had with Max, every tender moment. Every small revelation. She realized now how seldom Max had talked about his past, how little she really knew him.

But she wasn't afraid of him. She could never be afraid of him.

Why did the police suspect him? And were they close to an arrest?

She'd been optimistic a few moments ago. Leigh had met her mother, might even donate a kidney if there was a match. She was in love for the first time in her life. Her career was surviving despite her inattention.

Max couldn't be involved.

Kira couldn't believe it. She wouldn't believe it.

There was silence the rest of the way. She had gotten in the backseat with Leigh. There was a connection now. Kira's gratitude had deepened during the afternoon.

They had something else in common. Max. Leigh looked stricken by Chris's news. Lost. Kira leaned over and took Leigh's hand and squeezed it.

Leigh bit her lip. She shook her head slightly, still denying what Chris had said.

When they reached the house, Kira saw two men sitting in a car outside her mother's home. Chris parked in the driveway. He got out and went over to the men. Then he returned and opened the door for Leigh.

Kira exited on her own side and they silently walked to the house. Kira unlocked the door and, once inside, punched in the alarm code. Leigh followed her inside.

"Can I get you something?" she asked Leigh, instinctively switching into hostess mode. "Coffee, tea, a glass of wine?"

Kira was surviving only on adrenaline. She was exhausted. She was heartsick. Her ribs hurt like hell. She hadn't had a pain pill in hours now, and she needed one.

Chris interceded. "Go to bed, Kira."

"I will," she promised. "Just let me show Leigh where stuff is."

"Then bed," he insisted. "Leigh, make sure she does it. I'm going to the police department. I can find out more in person than over the telephone. In the meantime, I don't want either of you to leave the house. You'll be safe here. Those guys are retired Atlanta cops. Good ones." He hesitated, then said, "Promise me. Promise you won't leave this house. If you need anything, call me."

Leigh hesitated, then nodded. "Just until you get back. I have to call Mrs. Baker and Rick. Otherwise they will worry."

Chris nodded, his lips thinned into a straight line and his eyes hardened.

He left without another word.

"I'll show you where everything is," Kira said, leading the way to the kitchen.

She noticed that Leigh stopped at the fireplace mantel to look at family photos. She stopped. Waiting.

After a few seconds, Leigh joined her at the doorway leading into the kitchen.

She showed Leigh around the kitchen: coffee, tea, bread. "There's wine in the fridge and some salad stuff and cold cuts. Help yourself. My house is your house."

"Thank you," Leigh said. "Now will you do as Chris said? Go to bed. You look like you're ready to drop."

"I don't know if I can sleep," Kira said.

"I think you're ready to pass out," Leigh said. "And I'll be here."

Kira held out her hand. "I'm sorry all this happened to you. I know it's been really hard."

"You, too."

"I meant it when I said I don't want anything but Mom to get well."

"We can talk about that later."

Kira felt as if she was going to pass out. "I'll show you to Mom's room. You can use one of my robes and nightshirts. They will be a bit big—"

"Anything will be fine," Leigh cut her off.

Kira used the railing to help her upstairs to the bedrooms. She was that tired. When they reached her room, she found two nightshirts and handed one to Leigh along with a robe. "Mom's room is across the hall," Kira said, grateful that she'd replaced the mattress.

"I'll bring some water," Leigh said. "Are the pain pills in your purse?"

Kira nodded. If felt good to have someone take care of her. Really good. She was so tired . . .

Leigh went back downstairs. She hesitated at the mantel again and the photos. Frames might have been smashed, but some of the photos survived the burglary.

Regret tugged at her. She didn't know what it was like to be a part of a real family. Hers had been a disaster.

Even that, though, was falling away beneath her. Each time she thought she had found footing, another piece fell, just like some of the earthquake movies she'd seen.

Mrs. Baker and Max had been the only two constants in her life. Mrs. Baker, though, always kept an emotional distance. Grandfather had been a distant, disapproving figure. And Max? Max had been her nemesis as well as protector. And scold. He would scold in a quiet, commonsense way that often reduced her to tears but also made her think. She'd hated his fingers on the purse and yet eventually she usually got what she wanted, but in a reasoned manner, not a haphazard one. It had taken her a very long time to learn that. He'd wanted her to think about why she wanted something and whether she was willing to take care of whatever it was.

And now Max was suspected of murder. She shoved away the idea. Someone was just plain wrong. She returned to the kitchen even as she continued to look around the interior. The home was small but cozy, or it would have been if much of the furniture hadn't been split or scratched. The remnants looked as if they had been comfortable.

She compared it to her house. Hers was much larger. Much more luxurious, but it never had the warmth this house must have had.

She should have changed the house, refurnished it, added

her own taste, but she'd remained cowed by her grandfather, even two years after his death. Just like she still didn't have a pet. He'd have none of it while he was alive.

Maude and the horses were as close to defiance as she ever got, even after his death.

She filled a glass with ice and water, then found Kira's purse. She found the pills and took both water glass and pills back upstairs.

Kira took one pill and gulped it down. "Thanks," she said.

Leigh turned to leave.

"Stay for a few minutes," Kira said.

Leigh lingered. She looked around the room. It was small, the bed a single. Built-in bookcases lined one side of the room, and they were filled with a combination of books and teddy bears.

"What can I say," Kira said, apparently noticing her interest. "I was a sucker for teddy bears. And I never could get rid of any of them. So they stayed here when I moved. They kinda welcomed me back when I moved in."

"You don't seem like the teddy bear type." Leigh continued looking and noticed a photo tucked away at the end of the counter. A black-and-white photo of a band.

"The third from the left is my long-lost father, or your father." Kira gave a mirthless laugh. "Confusing, isn't it?"

"Tell me about him."

"Not much to tell."

"Is he still alive?"

Kira stiffened, and Leigh knew suddenly it was a sore subject. Still, she kept a photo. Something else in common. Neither of them could quite let go of the past.

"I don't think so," Kira said. "He left less than a year after I was born. Mom thinks he died in an accident."

"Did you ever think about looking for him?"

"No," Kira said sharply. "Why should I? He left Mom when she needed him."

"Were they married?"

"Mom thought they were. She was months from high school graduation. She loved music. You might say she was a groupie.

His band played at her prom, and he singled her out. A week later they were married by a JP. At least she thought they were. Later when she decided to get a divorce, she couldn't find any record of the marriage. Apparently it never happened."

"Her parents?"

"My grandfather died when she was young. Her mother disowned her when she married a musician. In later years she and Grandma made peace."

"Is she still alive?"

"No. She died five years ago."

"How did your mom manage after you were born?"

"She refused to give up on me. She kept trying to find a pediatric surgeon, then suddenly one appeared. She didn't have any money, but she vowed to pay the bills if it took the rest of her life. She made several payments, then suddenly no more bills were sent. She asked, and the hospital business office said someone had paid the bills. An anonymous donor."

Leigh was silent, thinking. An unwelcome thought knocked on a mental door. She tried to dismiss it.

"How did she provide for you?"

"She moved in with another single mother. They both worked several jobs, each taking care of the children when the other wasn't there. Mom graduated from high school, but she couldn't get much of a job, especially with me. So she started cleaning houses. Eventually she took night college courses and started her own cleaning business.

"She would take me along when she could, and later I would help out." She continued, "So we spent a lot of time together."

Kira's eyes started to close.

"I'm going to go to bed now," Leigh said. "Good night."

"G'night. And thanks for seeing Mom."

"You're welcome," Leigh said as she picked up the few garments she'd selected and turned out the light.

Restless, she prowled through the house, taking note of what was left after the burglary. She realized she had accepted the fact that she was Katy Douglas's daughter, and now she wanted to know everything she could about her.

She thought about the recent events. The one thing she didn't believe was that Max was responsible. Neither was Seth or David.

Someone took care of the hospital bills when Kira was born. They would have been enormous. She didn't like thinking the thought that hammered at her. Uncle Mike was the kindest man she knew. He attended her when she was born. He had mentioned that several times.

If it was possible . . . if he did switch babies, he couldn't have anything to do with what was happening now. He was someplace in Africa, Senegal, she thought.

Or was he?

*Max had known instantly that something had changed be*tween Burke and himself at the hospital. It obviously had to do with the phone call.

So he wasn't surprised when he reached home to see police cars there. The guards at the gate apologized. "We thought we had to let them in," one said.

"Did they have a warrant?"

"No, sir, but . . ."

"You were right to let them in," he said. "When did the media leave?"

"An hour ago."

"Okay. Has Ms. Howard returned?"

"No, sir."

He nodded and drove through to his house. He remembered the time Ed had given him the keys to the house. It meant he was family. He could have bought nearly any house he wanted. A sleek condo downtown, a minimansion in horse country. But this was home. The only one he'd ever had.

He locked his car and walked to where detectives waited on the porch. They were not the same ones who had been visited him earlier.

"Mr. Payton?"

"Yes."

"We would like to talk to you."

"Come in."

"We would prefer you come down to the station."

"I prefer to stay here unless you have a warrant."

They glanced at each other and nodded.

He led the way inside to the living room. He'd redone it in masculine browns and tans. The furniture was all leather and bought for comfort. He headed toward his favorite easy chair and waved his arm toward the sofa and other chairs. "Sit anywhere you please," he said, knowing in that one act he'd gained control. They knew it, too.

So they threw the question right at him. "Does the bar association know that you've killed before?"

34

Although he had expected it, Max's stomach churned when he saw the police waiting for him at his house.

After the look in Chris's eyes, he'd realized someone had found something. But maybe it was time. Maybe he had learned from Leigh you couldn't hide forever.

There should have been no records, though the story had been in all the papers. He'd believed, hoped, that he'd built enough walls to hide his secrets.

The detectives didn't mince words. "We ran a background check on all the people connected with the Westerfields," one said. "Yours started at Georgia State. We couldn't find a Maxwell Payton before that. Georgia State had a high school transcript, but one of our people acted on a hunch and decided to check on it. Lo and behold, the school burned down, and all its records along with it. Yet one apparently survived. Yours."

"Really?" he observed. "Your point?"

"It interested us. We had someone check your car for fingerprints when you were at the hospital. We had an interesting match. Joe Cantwell. A runaway who disappeared from a foster home thirty years ago."

"So?"

"He was in foster care after killing his father."

"Did you read the complete file?" Max asked.

"Not yet. It's not computerized. They're faxing us copies."

There was no sense in lying or avoiding the past. It would all come out now. "You will find I was ten. My father went after my mom with a knife. I shot him to keep him from killing her. He died. I didn't mourn him."

"Why change your name?"

"I hated it. So did my mother. She suffered every day she was married to him. After he was killed, I was sent to a group home, then a series of foster homes. I didn't do well. I didn't like the rules, and they didn't like me, so I took off when I was sixteen. I adopted another name because too many people remembered the story. I made it legal at twenty-one."

"What about your mother?"

"She died eight days after my father attacked her."

"Did Westerfield know your background?"

"Yes. In fact he helped me change my name legally."

"You have access to the gun safe?" the other detective said, changing the subject.

"Yes. I told the other detectives that I inventoried them after Mr. Westerfield's death. That was the last time I checked."

"And you don't know anyone else who might have the combination."

"No." God, he was tired of answering the questions over and over again.

"And you know firearms?"

"We went over this before, too. Yes. I went hunting a couple of times with Mr. Westerfield. He loved hunting. I didn't."

The older detective's eyes bored into him. "You don't have an alibi for the city hall shooting."

"But I do for the attempted murder of Mrs. Douglas and the attempt on Kira's life."

"You could have hired someone."

Max knew that only a fool represented himself. But he also thought things would be worse if he didn't cooperate. So much for not saying anything.

"I could have, but I didn't. And there's no reason to do so.

I don't need money. I've made a lot of money in the past ten years and invested it. You can have the account numbers."

"We'll also want to look at the trust records."

"Anytime," Max said. "You'll find them in great shape."

"Do you mind if we look around?"

"No." He did, but he also knew that one could call and get a warrant within moments. Better to cooperate.

Two hours later the detectives left. He wasn't sure whether he was a person of interest or not, whether he would see his past in the newspaper tomorrow.

And whether Kira and Leigh would ever look at him the same way again.

Kira woke to sunlight streaming in the window. She turned and her side ached. Maybe a bit less, but not much.

The pain brought back all that had happened yesterday.

Leigh. Leigh was here somewhere.

What time was it? What time had she gone to sleep last night? Had anything happened?

She tried to stir herself.

Her body felt leaden.

She managed to turn and look at the clock. Eight a.m.

Kira forced herself to sit up. Her head pounded. She looked down and saw that her shirt was red where it touched the bandage. She needed another pain pill, but she couldn't afford to feel fuzzy.

Maybe coffee would help.

She found a pair of jean shorts and a T-shirt. She felt dizzy as she pulled on the clothes and had to sit down again.

Max. Where was Max? And Chris? She stood again and went to the window. The car from last night was still there. So the whole nightmare was real.

Max a person of interest? A suspect?

She went downstairs. Leigh was at the kitchen table reading the paper. She was wearing the same clothes from the night earlier. She looked up. "I made coffee and got the paper from outside. I hope you don't mind."

"Of course not. Consider this your house." And it was to some extent. It belonged to Kira's mother. And to Leigh's.

Kira poured herself a cup of coffee and sat down. Leigh apparently had finished the front section. It was on the table, folded to reveal the lower half of the front page.

Her brief story was there along with her staff photo. There were five other stories. The hospital, queried about a possible baby switch, offered "no comment." A police source merely said the city hall shootings were under investigation and the department was looking into "related incidents." There was a mention of the Westerfield family as possibly being connected and a history of the family, along with the photo of Leigh taken a week earlier.

Kira winced at the coverage, but of course, the paper had to do what it had to do.

The phone rang. Kira looked at the caller ID. A television station. She didn't answer.

"It's been doing that all morning," Leigh said. "Chris called, suggested that I unplug the phone in your room. I did. I hope you don't mind. I've been monitoring the phone here. I would have called you if your paper called or . . ."

"I don't mind," Kira said. "Thanks. I needed that sleep."

"How are you?"

"Still sore. Still feeling like I'm living a nightmare."

Leigh didn't say anything, but her hollow eyes agreed.

"Did Chris say anything more? Anything about Max?"

"Just that there seems to be something in his background that made the police look twice," Leigh said. "He was going to get some sleep, then start researching on his own."

Then her gaze held Kira's. "He's not involved," she added flatly. "I would bet my life on that."

"Me, too," Kira said.

Leigh glanced at Kira. "Are you falling for him?"

Kira started to protest, then shrugged. "No. Yes. Maybe. A bit."

Leigh laughed for the first time since Kira met her. A pleasant, throaty sound. "I understand. I had a crush on him for a long time. I have to warn you, though, he's never been serious about a woman. He would bring someone to one of Grandfather's parties, but it was never the same one. I asked him about it, and he said he's too much of a workaholic to make a good husband." Leigh looked at her. "That much is true."

"Do you know what 'something in his past' could mean?"

"No. But he had his chance to get his hands on Grandfather's fortune. He could have married me, which I hope would have been a more palatable prospect than killing people. I know Grandfather always wanted it." The amusement in Leigh's face faded. "And I would have said yes. I always said yes," she added wistfully. "To my great chagrin, I married the first person who asked, maybe to spite both Max and Grandfather. Big mistake. Then I almost made the same mistake again. Max bought him off, too."

Sympathy flooded Kira. "I'm sorry."

"Don't be. I've been concentrating on improving my judgment. I finally realized that I was looking at surface stuff like good looks and at least a smattering of surface charm. I think I finally graduated from that school."

"I saw you look at Chris," Kira said. "He's a really good guy."

"I detected that. You're not . . . interested?"

"Not in that way. He's been a good friend. Nothing more. Not now, not ever."

Kira saw relief on Leigh's face. She liked that. She switched to another subject. "Do you have any idea as to who could be behind this?" Kira asked.

"I can't imagine anyone in the family being involved. Seth has too much to lose, and we've always been close." She gave Kira a weak smile. "Besides, he would be far more effective. He's never tolerated sloppiness or incompetence."

Kira raised her eyebrows at that.

"David is too preoccupied by his patients to care. He might think about protecting his father, but he abhors violence and would have absolutely no idea how to go about it. Same with Mrs. Baker. Uncle Michael is in Africa. I don't like the CEO of Westerfield Industries, but he, too, has too much to lose. There's some part-time employees. Rick, our groom and handyman, but he's Mrs. Baker's nephew and has no motive. Then there's a cleaning agency."

"But someone tried to kill me and Mom. It certainly looked as if they were trying to set you up," Kira said.

Leigh tipped her head. "Which means whoever it is wants to get rid of both of us."

Kira nodded. She was beginning to like Leigh.

"So what do we do?" Leigh asked.

"Maybe try to draw whoever it is out."

"I don't think either Chris or Max will agree to that."

Neither did Kira. But she couldn't continue to live her life this way. She had to do *something*.

Kira made breakfast. Toast and jam. Orange juice. Those had been her staples since her mother went into the hospital.

Leigh took a bite, then put the toast down. "I'm not very brave."

Kira was beginning to think she was very brave. Leigh could have gone somewhere else last night. A thousand miles away if she wished. She could have asked Chris to stay. She could have resisted the DNA test. She could have continued to fight against the possibility she might lose everything.

Kira had always wanted a sister. Or a brother. Too early to tell whether Leigh would really be one, but she definitely had promise.

The phone rang. She looked at the ID. *USA Today.* She let it ring. Another ring. A television station. She let it ring again. The third call came from Chris. Kira picked it up.

"How are you feeling?" he asked.

"Like a rag doll. What about Max? Did you find out anything?"

"Everyone's damned closemouthed. The police think they might have something, but they also know Payton is a damned good attorney. They're not going to rush into anything and they are not sharing."

"They're not looking at anyone else?"

"They've run financial checks on everyone else. They are looking deeper into Seth Westerfield's campaign accounts, but so far both he and David Crawford look clean."

"Anything on the bullets at the site?" Kira pressed.

"Not unless they find the weapon."

"You'll keep us posted?"

"Yes, but you stay put," Chris said.

Kira didn't answer.

"Kira?"

"Okay."

"Let me talk to Leigh."

Kira handed over the phone with a few qualms. Would Leigh say anything about their conversation?

But all she heard was, "I'm not planning to go anywhere. No, I haven't thought of anyone else." Then, "I'll wait for you."

Kira raised an eyebrow in question.

"He'll be here this afternoon."

Leigh wanted to go home. She wanted to be with her horses. She wasn't even sure why she was here except she now had an overwhelming need to learn more about Kira's parents. She'd been honest with Kira. She wasn't brave. And she didn't think she was smarter than the police.

She did fear, though, that if the culprit wasn't discovered, they would all live under a cloud for years and she would never feel safe again.

She hadn't slept well last night. Strange bed. Ever stranger day. She kept going over her meeting with Katy Douglas, the connection she'd felt almost immediately, the sudden knowledge that she would give a kidney if she could. Oddly enough the fear of hospitals faded in the face of Katy Douglas's need.

"How long will it take to get the blood results?" she asked suddenly.

"The doctor is expediting it," Kira said. "We might know something today." She studied Leigh. "Max told me a little of what happened to you after the automobile accident," she said softly. "I know this is difficult."

"More like terrifying," Leigh said. "What if your—our—mother refuses to accept the kidney?"

"Appeal to her better side," Kira said. "Right now she thinks she's protecting us. It's a mother thing. She doesn't want to deprive us of anything. What she doesn't understand but what we can make her understand is that it's incredibly selfish of her not to let us—you—do this for her, not to get to know her, or spend time with her." She paused. "If, that is, you're willing to go on."

Leigh met her eyes. "I wouldn't have agreed to the test if I hadn't decided to go on."

Gratitude filled Kira. And hope. For the first time since she'd learned the results of her own test, she had hope. She leaned over and hugged Leigh. "Thank you." She moved back, paused, then asked the question haunting her. "Your . . . my biological mother and father," she asked, "can you tell me something about them?"

Leigh didn't really want to go there. No way did she intend to tell Kira that her father tried to murder both her and her mother because he thought his wife betrayed him.

Especially now. A murder and suicide happened because someone switched babies—accidentally or purposefully. It made the tragedy that much worse. It hadn't needed to happen. And she certainly didn't want Kira to live with the kind of guilt she'd lived with.

But she saw the raw need in Kira's face. "I don't remember much," she said. "I was young, but I remember her singing to me . . ."

"I saw the portrait of her at your home," Kira said. "She . . . was beautiful. And . . . my father? Do you remember anything about him?"

Leigh hesitated. There were no photos of her father in the house. Not even one with members of a band. Neither she nor Kira lucked out on the father factor. "Very little," she finally said. "Both he and my mother were horse people. I remember a pony. But when they died, Grandfather sold the horses. He wouldn't let me have any . . ."

"But you have them now," Kira said.

"I always thought I inherited a love for horses but . . ."

"It's confusing, isn't it," Kira broke in. "I suspect we will be second-guessing ourselves for years, trying to figure out what is real and what isn't."

Leigh nodded. "I still can't get used to . . ."

"Me, either." Kira stood. "Can you draw a family tree? I think I have everything straight, but I'm not sure."

Leigh nodded. "Some of the history is complicated. And it's family lore, so I don't really know the right and wrong of it all. I can say today's history started with Dan Westerfield—our great-grandfather." She smiled wryly. "I think the best way to describe our families now is 'our' rather than 'yours' or 'mine.' It gets confusing." She bit her lip. "Dysfunctional doesn't begin to describe our family."

"What about Ed Westerfield?"

"He was a hard man. Disciplined. Righteous. Ruthless but honest. He would tell someone before he stole their business."

"What was your relationship?"

"I was an obligation. He tolerated me. But I kept disappointing him. I married a guy who . . ." She stopped. What in the hell was she doing telling Kira all this stuff?

"Who what?" Kira prompted. Her eyes were warm. Interested.

Kira would learn one of these days. Seth and David both knew about it. And Max knew better than anyone. "He . . . was sometimes violent. He started . . . abusing me physically when he learned I didn't have cash lying all over. He'd wasted his time on a . . . well, not a particularly nice word." She paused. "God, I was stupid. I thought I deserved it."

"I'm sorry," Kira said. It was obvious she meant it. There was something about her that invited confidences, and there was some information she had every right to know.

"Max found out and practically killed him. He told him if he ever tried to see me again, he *would* kill him. I thought he might. Instead, he gave him two hundred thousand dollars and told him to disappear. He did. Right after signing divorce papers."

Leigh saw Kira's eyes sharpen at the earlier words and cursed herself.

Kira's phone rang, interrupting what she was going to say next.

Reprieved.

For the moment.

Kira answered the phone, then handed it to Leigh. "It's for you. He says it's Rick, and it's an emergency."

Leigh's heart dropped. The only reason Rick would call is if there was something wrong at the barn. Or with Mrs. Baker.

Her hand trembling, she put the phone to her ear.

"Silver Lady is colicky," Rick said in a rush. "She's walking around biting her side, getting up and down, sweating." He sounded panicky.

"Have you called the vet?"

"No. I called you first."

"I'll call her."

"Got her number right here," Rick said. "Just wanted your permission."

"Okay. You call. Describe the symptoms to her. I'll be there as soon as possible." She hung up, then turned to Kira. "I can't wait for Chris to return. My horse is sick. Maybe really bad."

35

"I'll drive," Kira said. She'd realized from the first that there was a strong bond between Leigh and the white mare.

Leigh, her expression stiff with anxiety, nodded. "Thanks. She's really all I have."

Kira immediately thought how sad that was. Not that Leigh loved a horse, but that she felt there was no one else for her.

Leigh could have so much more now if only she would grab it. A mother. Even a sister if she wanted one. And probably Chris if she was any judge of people.

"I'll drive you over, but the guard out in front won't be happy."

"Max has guards at my home," Leigh replied. "We'll be safe enough from here to there."

"Maybe we should call Chris."

"I don't want to waste time arguing with him. I want to be home when the vet arrives."

Kira understood. She recalled the way she felt when her mother fainted at her house. Complete panic. Maybe you couldn't equate a human with an animal, but then again, maybe you could. Empathy flooded her.

She grabbed her purse, glanced inside to make sure the pepper spray was there. She turned to Leigh. "I have some pepper spray, though it's old." Then she darted out the door, Leigh behind her. Her car was in the narrow drive.

"I'll start the car," Kira said. "You tell the guard where we're going." For the first time—or maybe the second if she counted the other night—she wished she had a weapon. And knew how to use it. Maybe she would get someone to teach her.

Who? Chris? Max?

She kept remembering the cool look in Max's eyes as he'd left yesterday, and he hadn't called. He believed that she thought he had something to do with the attempts on her life. With murder.

Cool but caring Max. Not in a million years.

She would call him on the way. Let him know what was going on. But in the meantime she had to get Leigh to her horse.

She drove out to the end of the drive. Leigh was talking expressively with the guard, her hands gesturing. Then she ran over to the car and stepped inside the passenger's side door.

"I think we should call Chris," Kira said again.

"I think the gentleman behind us is doing just that," Leigh said grimly.

"Then Max," Kira said. She was getting a bad feeling about this.

"Not till we get there, and I know something about Lady."

"I thought you said you're not afraid of him?"

"Physically, no. His disapproval, yes."

"Tell me more about him," Kira said as she pulled onto the interstate.

"Like what?" Leigh asked.

"He's never been married?"

"Not that I know of," Leigh said. "But Max never talks about Max."

She should stop asking questions. She was being a wee bit more than obvious, and she hated being obvious.

She turned her attention to driving, but she couldn't stop the nagging thought she should call Max. She would do it the second they arrived at the Westerfield home. He might even be there.

God, she hoped so. She wanted him to know that she was tired last night. That she regretted that reflexive reaction immediately.

She only hoped he would give her that chance.

Max looked at the clock and yawned. He had been at his office all night, and it was now nearing eight.

After the police left his house last night, Max called in a computer specialist and arranged to meet him at his office. The man worked for the company that took care of Westerfield security. After the failure at city hall, the firm was ready to do anything to keep his business, even pull all-nighters.

Sam Abrams was said to be a great hacker. Max put him to work on the only person who hadn't undergone scrutiny: Richard "Rick" Salter. His only real information was that Salter said he'd been in the army and the Social Security number Salter had given the business office.

Sam found several Rick Salters in army records, but none seemed to fit their Rick Salter.

The longer it took, the more Max's chagrin grew. He should have checked the man's background when he came to Atlanta. But he trusted Mrs. Baker. He hadn't thought she would do anything to hurt Ed Westerfield's granddaughter.

By five in the morning, they'd discovered that one Corporal Richard Salter had received a discharge other than honorable. Age and description fit. Abrams was able to bring up a photo. It looked like a much younger Rick Salter. So the man had lied about an honorable discharge. A discharge other than honorable could mean any number of things, none of them admirable. It was often a red flag for employers. No wonder he couldn't get a job.

Max wanted to be sure, though. None of the military records included Salter's Social Security number to confirm that this Corporal Rick Salter was the one employed by Wester-field Industries. Abrams kept hacking. He finally located the Social Security number for Salter when he was in the army. It was different from the one Salter had given the business office.

Abrams found a second Richard Salter. A sergeant. Honorable discharge. Home in Denver, Colorado. Same general description as the other.

"Find out more about both Richard Salters," Max said. He was getting a very bad feeling about this.

In three hours, he had more, thanks to the agency, which was proving superb in digging up information. The Richard Salter whose photo marked him as Mrs. Baker's nephew had been stationed at the army's personnel center. Apparently he'd been suspected of using his position to harvest Social Security numbers and sell them to a partner. Not enough proof to convict him, but he'd broken enough rules to discharge him.

As for the other Richard Salter, he was a dog trainer who'd left the army two months after their Richard Salter. No next of kin mentioned in the record. No wife. No family to ask questions. When the investigator tried to find him, he didn't seem to exist. He apparently just disappeared.

Dead? At Rick's hand?

He and Abrams looked at each other. Mrs. Baker's nephew had access to Social Security numbers. When he knew his plot was about to be discovered, he probably started looking for someone with his name, someone without a dependent.

But why? Certainly not to get a groom's job.

Abrams ran a routine credit check on Rick Salter under the Social Security number Max had on file. There were a few small credit card accounts, all paid on time, and little else. The charges started three weeks after the Colorado Salter's discharge.

Max had occasionally wondered why Salter had taken part-time employment as groom and general handyman. He mentally slapped himself for not checking when those thoughts had first surfaced.

That brought him back to Mrs. Baker. How much did she know?

He didn't like the way his thoughts were going.

"Keep tracking his movements," he told Abrams. "I want anything you can find on either of them."

He wanted to confront Salter himself. Then he sat back down. He was only too aware of his temper when someone threatened someone he cared about. He'd almost killed Leigh's husband after he saw her in the hospital.

He always tried to remember his father's blood ran through him.

At least Leigh and Kira were safe under Chris's protection

He reached for the phone. He would give Chris what he had. In the meantime, he would keep Abrams digging.

*Chris grabbed a few hours of sleep, then went to his old sta-*tion. He took donuts with him. It might well be a joke but cops really did live on donuts. During an all-nighter, they needed the sugar for energy. His former partner, Matt, was there. His cheeks were dark with bristle and his eyes were red-rimmed. The detective looked up in surprise.

"Busy?" Chris asked.

"Yeah, not like some old retired folks I know."

"You have your twenty years. You can quit anytime you want."

"I can, can't I," Matt said. "Thanks for telling me. How's the PI business? Enough for another damn no-good private dick?"

"Anytime, Matt."

"Been a bad night," Matt said. "Pressure's on because of that shooting you were asking about. The mayor's gone nuts. He put all of us on the case, and there's nothing there."

"You said last night that Payton might be involved."

"If the shooting's connected to the Westerfield mess, he's the one with the biggest motive . . . Always look to the money." He glanced at Chris. "You're working for the reporter, aren't you?"

"Yeah."

"Not much I can tell you. We thought we had a lead with Payton. He had motive, opportunity." Matt stopped suddenly.

"What else?"

Matt hesitated, then shrugged. "Payton's not his birth name. He changed it. It was Joe Cantwell."

"Should that mean something to me?"

"Maybe not. Thirty-six years ago he killed his father. Maybe even his mother. He claimed then he was protecting his mother. Both parents ended up dead."

"How?"

"One multiple knife wounds, the other a shotgun."

"How old was he?"

"Ten."

"Christ, he can't be blamed for protecting his mother."

"Unless he was a bad seed. He'd already been in trouble. Stealing stuff. Then he disappeared from the system when he was sixteen."

"I think you're on the wrong track."

"Could be. But he's our best bet."

"Anyone check the financials on the other Westerfields?"

"Yeah. They look clean. The politician has plenty of money in his account and is beginning to look like a shoo-in. He's not going to do anything to upset that applecart. The doctor's rich and has given large sums of money to various charities, not to mention his father is with Doctors Without Borders."

"Wonder if the elder Crawford has been notified of all this?"

"I don't know."

"You might want to get a message to him. He might know something about what happened thirty-two years ago. It could be important."

Matt raised an eyebrow. "More official from us than from you?"

"Something like that," Chris said.

"You always were damned good at getting someone else to do your dirty work."

"You'll let me know if he replies."

"Yeah. Maybe."

"A crime might have been committed three decades ago. It would be a real coup if you solved it."

"By arresting Dr. Do Good? I don't think so."

"You never know," Chris said. "I would appreciate it if you hear anything you can pass on."

Matt hesitated, then nodded.

"I'll be in touch," Chris said.

He had another stop. The hospital. More sweet-talking to someone in the records department. They didn't have to give him personnel records, but the threat of a multimillion-dollar suit might help. He wanted the names of the nurses on duty that day. Hell, he'd wanted them several days ago but hadn't had the time to pursue the subject with the administration.

Then he should be back to Kira's for lunch. He would take Leigh to her home to check on the animals, then gather some clothes. Even with guards, he didn't want her out there alone.

Max called Chris Burke after debating other actions first. He wanted to beat the hell out of Rick Salter for lying to him.

Burke answered on the second ring.

"Burke, this is Payton. Ask the police to look at Richard or Rick Salter, who is employed by the Westerfields. I just had someone check and discovered he received something other than an honorable discharge. He's also been using someone else's Social Security number. I couldn't get anything else."

"Will do," Burke said. Hesitation, then, "Have you talked to either Kira or Leigh this morning?"

"No," Max said shortly. "Keep me posted if you learn anything. I'll do the same." He hung up.

He sat there staring at the phone.

He wanted to call Kira, but her eyes last night . . .

She wouldn't want anything to do with him when she learned the complete truth.

He sat back in his chair.

The news about Kira and her mother had been leaked by the police. He wondered how long it would take to leak the news about Max's background to the papers. So much for one of Atlanta's most eligible bachelors . . .

Hell, he'd stopped feeling sorry for himself decades ago. He wasn't going to start now. He would go back to his house. He wanted to keep an eye on Rick. He just might have to stop himself from tearing him from limb to limb. Whether he was involved in the murders or not, Rick Salter had lied to him. Had lied to Leigh.

He wondered how much Mrs. Baker knew.

36

As Kira drove up to the Westerfield house, the guards who had been at the gate were gone. The bar was down.

"What happened to the guards?" Leigh asked.

"I don't know. Could Max have dismissed them since the press have apparently given up for the moment?"

"Max? No. Not on your life. He wouldn't do that while your attacker is still loose. Especially without telling us. Maybe they went inside for some reason. Maybe coffee."

Kira had a bad feeling. "I'm calling Chris."

She'd turned off her cell phone, aware that Chris would not approve of what she was doing. Now she wondered whether that was a mistake. She turned on the cell and punched in a number.

"Chris's line is busy," she told Leigh. She looked around. "Where's the guards' car?"

"They always park in back," Leigh said as Kira punched in the numbers at the gate.

"Maybe I should drive in back and see if the car is there," Kira suggested.

"You can do that. I have to see about the horse. The vet's truck isn't here, and colic can kill a horse quickly . . . I should have been here." Leigh opened the car door and hopped out before Kira could stop her.

Kira parked and started to follow her inside. Then she remembered the pepper spray in her purse. She retreated to the front seat and rummaged in the purse until she found the small canister and tucked it in her pocket.

She couldn't shake the feeling that something was very wrong. Leigh was right. Max wouldn't have called off the guards, no matter how he felt. She'd learned one thing about Max. Despite his outward cool, he cared very deeply about Leigh. That had been so evident yesterday.

Her cell phone rang. She looked at the identification. Chris. She answered.

"Where in the hell are you?" Chris demanded.

"Leigh and I are at the Westerfield house. Her groom called and said her horse was down. But the guards aren't at the gate."

"Is Leigh with you now?"

"No, she went into the barn."

She heard him curse under his breath, then he said, "Get the hell out of there."

"I have to get Leigh."

"No. Go. Now. I'm on the way and I'm calling the Fayette police."

Fear welled up in her. His urgency, the sound of real worry in his usually calm voice, frightened her. She stared at the barn. The door was still open, but from her angle she couldn't see anything.

Then Chris came back on the phone. "I told them a citizen was in danger. They're on the way."

"Why . . . ?"

"I talked to Payton not long ago. There seems to be more to Rick Salter than anyone thought."

"Oh God."

"Get out of there," he said again.

"You think he's the person . . . ?"

"I don't know. Could be."

"He wouldn't try anything here. Everyone would know . . ."

"Dammit, don't argue with me. Do as I say."

She turned off the phone. She couldn't leave now. Maybe he was wrong. But if he wasn't, Leigh was in terrible danger.

She didn't want to be a stupid heroine but neither could she drive off and leave Leigh alone. She just couldn't. And the police were on their way. And Chris.

She backed up and turned the car so that the driver's side faced the barn. She rolled down the window and called, "Leigh."

Nothing.

Fear grew in her. Her breath seemed to solidify in her throat, and her heart beat wildly. Something was very, very wrong.

She looked to the pasture. Maude stood silently. Alert, as if she sensed something wrong. There was a stillness as she waited. A stillness as if the world had stopped.

What was happening to Leigh? What should she do? What if she was being harmed now? In just a few hours Leigh had become very important to her, and not just because of her mother. There had been something touching about her honesty.

She heard a scream come from inside the barn.

Then she saw the groom at the door, his arm around Leigh's throat. A gun was at her throat, and blood was running down the side of her neck.

"Join us," the man said. "Unless you want me to kill her. Now." The edge of the gun played along Leigh's neck. "Get out and come over here."

"No!" Leigh cried out. "Go! Get out of here."

"I'll kill her," the groom said. "Right here and now. Just think . . . if you come in, you might save her life. And your mother's."

"Why?" Kira asked, playing for time.

Another scream was torn from Leigh as he jabbed the barrel of the gun into her neck, breaking her skin again. "I swear I'll shoot," the groom said. Terror was written all over Leigh's face.

"Okay," Kira said. "Okay, I'm coming. Just . . . be careful with the gun."

Stupid words. But she had no choice. She didn't doubt for a moment that he would do exactly what he said he would. There was a tinge of madness in his voice. Leigh would die, along with any chance her mother had. She had to play along now. He couldn't know she had called Chris and that he and the police were on the way. She felt for the pepper spray in her pocket and was only mildly comforted by the feel of it. He had a gun.

But if she could get him to talk . . .

She held out her hands in front of her as she moved toward him.

As she neared the door, he stepped back, still holding Leigh.

Where were the sirens? Or had it been only a few seconds? It felt like hours.

He moved behind the door as she walked in, her hands still up. Then the door banged shut behind her. Leigh was pushed to the floor, and he turned the gun on Kira.

"Why?" Kira said as she looked around the barn. She wanted to leave as much distance between Leigh and herself as possible.

"Not another step, or you both die right now."

"You were the shooter at city hall?"

"How astute of you."

"And you pushed me?"

"No, I would have succeeded. An acquaintance of mine earned a few dollars doing that."

"And your aunt? Does she know . . ."

"My mother, you mean?"

A small noise came from Leigh, who sat where she'd been pushed down against the wall.

"Yeah, my mother. And old Westerfield was my father. Not that either claimed me." There was a vicious hatred in his voice. "This should have been mine. It will be mine."

"You can't get away with it . . ."

"You don't think so? Who's going to stop me? You were visiting with the princess here when you both were attacked by Mr. Payton. He tried to start a fire to hide the crime but was caught in the flames."

"No one will believe you."

"They will when they find certain evidence left by Mr. Payton, along with his body. After all, he's the only one who had access to the gun closet, to the rifle that killed that woman at city hall, to this gun. His fingerprints will be on both. Not mine. Not only that, I have an alibi. I was with my dear mother. Helping with the shopping. We came home to find a killer burning the barn down."

Keep him talking. "No one will believe Max turned into a crazed killer," she said, risking his wrath.

"Of course they will. He's killed before." He smiled suddenly. "You didn't know that. Well, I did. I made it my business to know everything about this family."

Max? Killed before? "I don't believe you."

"I don't care what you believe. Needless to say the police do." His eyes narrowed. "Move closer to the princess."

She took one step closer. "What happened to the guards?"

"They were fired a few hours ago. The call was made from Payton's home. When I finish with you, I'll call him. A small problem with my mother."

Talking. Keep him talking. "No one will believe he's that stupid."

"Oh, I think they will. He got away with murder before. When you showed up, he saw his gravy train derailing."

Kira's heart dropped. She didn't believe it. She couldn't. But he obviously did. She exchanged glances with Leigh. She had to keep him talking. "You said Mr. Westerfield was your father? That can't be."

"You don't think so?" he said with a mirthless grin. "Well, meet your newest relative. Too bad we won't have a chance to get to know each other better."

37

Max was halfway to the house when he answered a call from his secretary.

"After you left, I received a call from the security company. They said their men had been called off the gate at your home. They wanted to know if something was wrong . . ."

"Called off?"

"They said you called them, talked to the secretary, and said they'd done a, quote, 'piss-poor job,' and they were fired."

"They left?"

"Yes. I knew you wanted guards there, and you didn't say anything to me about canceling the contract. So I thought you should know . . ."

"You thought right. Call Mark Peeples and tell him I *am* displeased now, and to get his people back there."

"I tried. He's out of town."

"Who called?"

"A Mr. Billings."

Max hung up and cursed. He didn't know the name. Probably some low-level manager who panicked while the boss was gone. Even as he pressed down on the gas pedal, he called Chris Burke on the cell phone. When the man answered, Max said simply, "Someone using my name called off the guards."

"I know," Chris said. "Kira and Leigh went to the Westerfield home. Some emergency with one of the horses. Kira called to report the guards were gone and said Leigh had gone in the barn. I've already called the police. I'm on the way, too. Probably fifteen minutes away."

"I'm about ten."

Rick. It had to be Rick.

Stupid. He'd been blind. He'd never considered Rick as a suspect because there didn't seem to be a motive. Nor had he considered Mrs. Baker. She'd been part of the family forever.

Maybe Rick held something over her. Maybe he had blackmailed her or threatened her into doing something . . .

The why didn't matter right now. He sped up, passed a car going the speed limit. Icy fear twisted around his heart as he swerved in and out of traffic, running a red light and barely missing a turning car.

He would welcome a police car but he saw none, even though he was going over seventy in a forty-five speed limit. He finally got out of the main traffic and onto the road leading to the house. He listened for the wail of police cars heading toward the estate, but heard none.

This was the county, not city, and the response time was slower. How long ago had Burke called the cops?

He *had* to get there in time. He was only too aware he had no weapon with him, but probably Rick didn't expect anyone from the agency to call his office. If he could just throw him off . . .

He hadn't realized until this moment how much he cared for Kira, how much life she had brought into his. And Leigh? Pain coursed through him as he thought how many obstacles she'd faced and battled.

For the first time in his life, he prayed.

Leigh tried to think as she heard Rick's mocking words. Blood ran down her neck from where the edge of the gun barrel had scraped her skin. Terror threatened to paralyze her as she glanced from Rick to Kira.

He'd been waiting just inside the door as she entered the barn. He had jerked her head back and jabbed the gun into her neck as he forced her outside to lure Kira inside . . .

Kira entered the barn first. Rick motioned her to the side of the first stall and shoved Leigh down on the floor. She landed between two bales of straw he was to have put in the stalls this morning.

Then he picked up a rifle standing against the wall and tucked his pistol into his waistband. She recognized the rifle as one owned by her grandfather, the one that had gone missing.

She wasn't going to be a victim. She'd played that role far too long. Rick was staring at Kira, obviously believing her to be the greatest risk. She noticed that Kira had moved slightly to the left, away from her.

Trying to give her a chance.

Had Rick noticed it?

She tried to look cowed as she searched for something she could use as a weapon. It wasn't hard. She was terrified. She prayed Kira had that pepper spray with her. Her gaze fastened on a muckrake leaning against the wall. It should have been hung in its place. More evidence of Rick's carelessness. Why had she kept him on?

For Mrs. Baker. No other reason. Where was Mrs. Baker? Was she involved? And Rick? Her son? She couldn't wrap her mind around that thought.

"Why?" she asked, starting to rise. "Why are you doing this?"

Rick stiffened, then turned to her. "Ah, the little lamb has found some guts. Maybe this will be more fun than I thought."

"Why?" she asked again.

"Because you have what should have been mine," he finally said. His gaze bored into her, but his rifle remained trained on Kira. He was concentrating on the real threat. "Useless princess."

"You said Grandfather was your father. That's crazy."

"Crazy, maybe, but true. The respectable Mrs. Baker was nothing more than a whore to your grandfather."

Kira took a step forward, and Rick jerked the rifle back toward her. "Move over to the princess."

Kira didn't move. "You're delusional," she said, taunting him.

Leigh knew Kira, too, was playing for time, but it frightened her. She saw Rick's jaw tighten, his fingers caressing the trigger. He was itching to use it, but he wanted to gloat even more. He wanted to vent his anger against her family. He wanted power he'd never had. It was all in his eyes.

"Westerfield fucked her, then told her to get rid of the baby," Rick said. "Like a piece of garbage. And she did. She dumped me on her sister. I found out when Ma died."

"That doesn't mean Grandfather was your father."

"Ma claimed he was."

"Did Mrs. Baker confirm it?" Kira asked, again drawing his attention.

He scowled, and she knew the answer.

"Because he wasn't." A familiar voice came from the shadows in the barn. *Mrs. Baker's voice.*

All three of them turned toward the sound. Mrs. Baker must have entered through the back door that led to the pasture. She'd obviously been listening. How long had she been there?

Alma Baker appeared from the dim light. Rick stood still in shock, his gaze riveting on the woman who stood in the shadows. "You said you were going to visit a friend." His voice was accusatory.

"I came back early. You seemed too eager to get rid of me."

"And you wanted to join my little party. Now you'll have to die, too."

"I don't care now," Mrs. Baker said. "You killed innocent people. You want to kill Leigh. I won't have it."

"You started it," he said with a strange smile.

"I wanted you to scare off a fraud. That's the only reason I told you about Kira Douglas. I didn't want you to kill her. Or anyone else."

"Who's going to believe you?"

A tear ran down Mrs. Baker's cheek. Leigh had never seen Mrs. Baker cry, or even show much emotion.

"Mr. Westerfield wasn't your father," she said again. "I never told you he was."

"But Ma said . . ."

"I never told Susie who the father was. She might have thought she knew. She didn't. It was wrong of her to tell you about me, to speculate about your father."

"You're lying!"

"No. No longer. I welcomed you when you came here. I was happy that Susie told you that you were my biological son, not hers. My chance to make up for so much."

"Then who was my father?"

Rick's face had turned ugly, his eyes glaring at the woman.

"I don't know. I was raped. I was stupid. I accepted a ride from someone I didn't know after my car broke down. When it happened, I was ashamed, too ashamed to admit it to anyone, much less to Mr. Westerfield. He was a stickler on morals. I told him I was leaving to marry a soldier. A year later, I said he died on a special mission, and I wanted to come back."

"I don't believe you," Rick said flatly.

"I never told you or Susie that Mr. Westerfield was the father. I didn't tell you about the rape. I thought it would hurt you." She hesitated, then added, "For God's sake, if you were his son, he would have claimed you. He was desperate for a son."

"Ma told me you loved him. Admitted it to her."

"She was right," Mrs. Baker said. "I did love him. That's the reason I stayed so long. But he never saw me that way. He loved his Isobel until the day she died, and he never stopped. I was never more than a housekeeper to him."

"He left *you* money."

She looked at him with amazement and horror. "That's why you thought . . ." She stopped, then started again. "He left Max money as well. He rewarded loyalty and service."

But he wasn't listening. Leigh realized he'd convinced himself so thoroughly that he'd been wronged that no one would convince him otherwise.

Mrs. Baker saw it, too, and she, too, was trying to play for time.

Through the corner of her eye, Leigh saw Kira lower one of her hands.

Rick's full attention was on the woman whose usual straight back was bent in grief. Her cool facade was melting like an ice sculpture in hell.

She'd known Mrs. Baker all her life. That she would have a child . . . that she would be any part of the attempts on Kira's life . . . It was devastating. She stared at the person she thought she knew so well. "You knew he was involved in the attempts on Kira's life. You couldn't—"

"Hell, it was her idea," Rick said.

Mrs. Baker turned to Leigh. "It was for you. I just wanted him to scare her away . . . you had already gone through so much." Tears were coming faster now. Silent. "I never thought . . ."

An acute sense of sadness filled her. Mrs. Baker had been the constant in her life. Even more important than Max because she'd been there when Max hadn't been. She'd nursed her through her recuperation from the accident and through kid illnesses. She's always maintained a certain aloofness, but Leigh had known—thought—she cared.

"For you," Rick mocked as he turned toward Leigh. "For the princess. Not for her son. A son she didn't even acknowledge after the master was dead." He looked at Mrs. Baker with real hatred. "But I saw opportunity," Rick said. "The would-be heiress dead, the princess charged with murder. And I step in. But that reporter wouldn't die. I had to change plans. Luckily I heard that the damned attorney has a past, and the police are looking that way." He swung the rifle toward Leigh.

"All the police will find is a burned barn with two bodies inside and the body of the family attorney and a gasoline can outside. Too bad he got caught in his own fire. He has motive."

"No one's going to believe that," Kira said. Leigh stayed quiet. She wanted Rick to forget about her as she edged toward the rake.

"You're just going to ask him nicely to cooperate?" Kira said.

He shrugged. "I had Special Forces training. I can handle him."

"Special Forces," Kira mocked again. "Bet you washed out."

The sudden tightening of his face told her she was right. "Smart mouth. Maybe you should be first."

He swung the rifle toward Kira.

"No," Mrs. Baker said. "I won't let you shoot Leigh. Either one of them."

"You think I care what you think, old woman? You gave me away."

"Susie was a good mother."

"She was trash. You had this, and I lived in a goddamn trailer. I joined the army to get away from her. I could have been a Westerfield . . ."

"I told you Mr. Westerfield was not your father. Several times."

"You lied." Rick swung the rifle toward Leigh. "Hey, princess, you get it first. How high and mighty are you now?"

Bone-deep fear settled in the pit of her stomach.

"You weren't at the MARTA station," Kira said desperately. "Nor at the hospital when someone tried to kill Mom."

"An army buddy of mine," he said. "But I was the sniper. Almost got you then . . ."

"The police would know I couldn't be the sniper," Leigh said desperately, trying to get his attention again. "Nor could I have pushed Kira at the MARTA station."

"You had someone to help. You and your attorney."

"But he would be a witness . . ." She stopped suddenly.

"My buddy is already dead, unfortunately. He botched the job."

The questions had diverted him. He had power now and he was enjoying it. Rick had been too caught up in his anger to order them to move together. And Leigh knew he didn't think she was a threat. She had to become one.

Kira caught her eye and said, "Why did you wait two years?"

He turned and looked at her. "Opportunity. I was waiting for the right time. You gave it to me. Two bitches fighting over an inheritance. If one of you killed the other, then I could step forward."

"And now?" Kira asked, keeping him talking.

Leigh grasped the handle of the muckrake and got to her knees, using it to stand. Rick was still intent on Kira.

"Hell, Payton killed before. My *mother* told me about it. His fingerprints will be on this rifle, the same one that was used at city hall. His body will be next to a gas can. Too bad he misjudged the speed and strength of the fire."

He'd apparently forgotten about Leigh and concentrated solely on Kira.

She had to give Kira a chance to get to the pepper spray. She tightened her grip around the handle of the muckrake, then threw it as far as she could behind him. The clatter caused him to turn all the way around. Away from Kira. He cursed, swung the rifle toward Leigh, his fingers tightening against the trigger.

A movement. Then a body landed on hers.

The room exploded with the sound of a gunshot. The horses went crazy, striking at the boards and whinnying in panic. Acrid smoke filled her nostrils. No pain other than the weight bearing down on her. She opened her eyes.

Rick was on his knees. Coughing. Cursing. Disbelief and shock replaced the sneer.

Leigh felt a dampness and she tried to gently push Mrs. Baker off. Blood gushed from a wound in the housekeeper's chest. She'd thrown herself in front of Leigh.

Kira tightened her hold on the small spray can. Rick had dropped the rifle as he tried to cover his eyes. She sprayed again, directly into his face.

She dived for the rifle, grabbing it with her hands, praying it wouldn't go off. Then she stood, holding it gingerly but determined to fire it if necessary.

Leigh cried out, and Kira glanced at her. Leigh cradled Mrs. Baker's head with one arm and held a blanket to her chest with the other.

Kira looked back at Rick. He was getting to his feet. He coughed again, then lurched forward, a hand reaching for the pistol in his waistband.

Kira stepped back, using both hands to hold the rifle steady. Her finger started to squeeze . . . hesitated . . .

The barn door opened and fresh air rushed in. Then Max was at her side, a tire iron in his hands. He stopped next to her, dropped the tire iron. He grabbed the rifle from her hands. "Don't move, Rick."

"Hell I will." Rick brought up his pistol.

Max fired.

Rick went down, his body twisting around with the impact. The pistol went skittering across the floor. Max handed the rifle to her and stooped next to Rick; blood was pouring out of him. Max tried to stanch it, then stopped as the flow slowed. He felt the pulse in the neck, then shook his head. "Dammit." He stood slowly. "He's dead."

"No!" Mrs. Baker moaned even as the breathing grew harsher.

Max went over to her. "I'm sorry," he said.

Kira followed him. Leigh was still holding the blanket against the wound in her chest. "Keep holding it there," Max said. "The police are on their way, should be here any minute." He took out his cell phone and dialed 911. "We have a critically wounded person, and one dead one," he said. He gave the address, then took off his shirt and substituted that for the blood-soaked blanket.

Mrs. Baker moaned again and tears ran down her face.

The wail of sirens reached them. It grew louder with every second. Kira ran over to Leigh and kneeled beside her.

"Sorry . . . I'm so . . . sorry," Mrs. Baker said in a weak, raspy voice as cars screeched to a stop outside. Her face was contorted with pain.

Two officers, guns drawn, ran inside followed by Chris. They stopped.

"What in the hell?" Chris asked. His eyes panicked as he looked around and saw Leigh, blood staining her clothing.

"Leigh's okay," Kira said, "but Mrs. Baker needs an ambulance. Fast. Max just called, but maybe another call would speed things."

Chris's face didn't change as he went to Leigh, looked at the cut on her neck, then looked to Mrs. Baker.

"What happened here?" one of the officers said.

"I'm not sure," Max said. "I was running toward the barn when I heard a shot. When I came in, I saw . . . the man on the floor. He was waving a pistol, threatening to shoot. Ms. Douglas was holding the rifle. I took it from her, told him to put his gun down."

"And he was doing what? While you were switching guns?" the officer asked.

"He had a hard time seeing. Ms. Douglas sprayed him with tear gas after he shot this woman here."

The officer looked to the others for confirmation.

"He would have killed us all," Kira said. "He said as much. He'd aimed at Leigh Howard. Mrs. Baker got in the way."

More officers poured through the door. An ambulance arrived, and paramedics worked on Mrs. Baker first, then the cut on Leigh's neck.

Max led Kira outside. One officer stopped them.

"We'll be right outside," Max said.

"No one leaves the premises."

Max nodded.

Once outside, he took her in his arms. She started trembling and couldn't stop, even when he tightened his hold. "Rick is—was—Mrs. Baker's son, not her nephew." Max's eyebrows went up.

"He planned to kill us and blame it on you," she explained. Her hands trembled. Her entire body trembled. "He was going to kill you, too, and burn the barn."

His arms went around her. "Shhhh . . . you're safe. I never should have let you out of my sight."

She hesitated, then said, "Mrs. Baker was involved to some extent. She just wanted to scare me off. Unfortunately, Rick had other ideas. He believed he was Ed Westerfield's son. He thought if he could kill me and blame it on Leigh, then he could step in and claim everything. Then he heard there was something about your background and decided to include you in the mix."

"And Mrs. Baker?"

"She threw herself in front of Leigh when he fired," she said softly. "She . . . did it to save her."

He was silent, but she saw a muscle move in his cheek. She knew from what he'd said about Mrs. Baker that he'd liked her. That she had been part of his life.

"I don't think she wanted anyone harmed," she hurried on. "Just scared. She was trying to protect Leigh. Go and speak to her," she said, knowing that was what he wanted to do.

"I don't want to leave you."

"She needs you more. You're all she has now."

"I killed her son," he said, and she heard the numbness in his voice. "And Ed's?"

"She said not."

She followed Max back inside to where the paramedics were loading Mrs. Baker onto a stretcher. He stooped down. "Alma," he said, taking her hand.

The paramedics had inserted a tube and her breathing was harsh, but she reached a hand out and touched his. Her eyes pleaded with him.

"I know," he said softly.

Kira saw a tenderness deepen his eyes. She'd experienced his gentleness, but this was still another facet of Max Payton. As if he knew exactly the heartache Mrs. Baker felt. "Don't say anything," she heard him whisper. "I'm your attorney."

More police arrived. Leigh and Kira were questioned while Mrs. Baker was loaded into an ambulance.

"I want to go with her," Leigh said. "She saved my life."

The paramedic looked at the officer who seemed to be in charge. Chris spoke to both for a moment, and the officer nodded.

He went over to them. "I'm going in the ambulance as well. Leigh needs some attention for the cut. A detective will meet us there."

Kira was a reporter. She should be jotting down words in her mind, later to be delivered on paper. But she couldn't. She was stunned by the emotional overload, by the tragedy of a mother, Leigh's courage, the fear that had not entirely faded.

Her mind was beyond muddled.

Max returned to her side as the ambulance pulled away.

Put his arms back around her and held her tight. "For a moment—several moments—I thought I was going to lose you."

"I have six of my nine lives left."

"More like five. Not nearly enough with your penchant for trouble."

"I'll try to do better."

A muscle flexed in his cheek. "I love you," he said, then looked startled that he had said such a thing.

"Good," she said simply.

He caressed her cheek. Then touched his lips to hers. "My warrior," he said. "Here I came charging to the rescue and you were well on the way to rescuing yourself."

"Not really. I hesitated. I couldn't . . ." She took a deep breath. "I think you made it just in time. And Leigh was the real heroine. She threw a rake behind him and distracted him."

"I'll never mock pepper spray again," he said.

His arms tightened around her. They felt so good. So right. She was where she belonged. She knew that now. And she knew everything was going to be all right. More than all right.

Chris wouldn't let go of Leigh's hand, and that was fine with her. She never wanted to let go again.

Her gaze kept going to Mrs. Baker, who was on the next stretcher. She reached over to her housekeeper. The woman to whom she was now deeply indebted. No matter how this all started, Mrs. Baker had risked her life for Leigh.

Mrs. Baker looked at her through tearstained eyes.

Leigh said softly, "I'll be waiting for my Mrs. Baker."

"I wouldn't . . . let him hurt you," Mrs. Baker said.

"I know," Leigh said.

Chris's fingers tightened around hers in a strong grip.

"I'm so damned proud of you," he said, brushing back a strand of hair that had escaped her clasp.

No one had ever said that to her before. But it was a lie.

"I've never . . . been so scared . . ." She stopped. She *had* been as scared. Decades ago.

But then she was helpless. And alone.

She looked up into those steady brown eyes and knew that she was neither now.

And never would be again.

38

Kira stepped into Max's arms just inside her mother's house.
They had been at the police station until 6:00 p.m. While
there, she'd called in the story to the newspaper and promised
to have a first-person story the next day.

On the way home, she started shivering. She was still shivering. In the past six months, she'd lived with the possibility
of her mother's death. In the last few hours, she'd lived with
the possibility of her own.

She had to change clothes before she left for the hospital to
see her mother. Hers reeked of gunpowder and blood. And
emotionally, she was a wreck, a condition her mother would
immediately recognize.

So much to do. She wanted to check with the hospital
about her mother, with Chris about Leigh.

But now she just wanted to stay where she was. In Max's
arms. She wanted him to repeat what he'd blurted out in the
barn.

Max was not a man to blurt out comments like that.

She looked up at him. "Did you mean what you said in the
barn?"

His arms tightened around her. "I always mean what I say."
He leaned down and kissed her. Gentle. Loving. Seeking.

Then, finding what he sought, he kissed her harder, almost punishing before he lifted his head. "God, you scared the hell out me."

He leaned back and searched her face with an intensity that made her blood warm. "When I heard that you had gone to the Westerfield estate, and I knew Rick was probably the one behind the attacks, I nearly lost it. Pedestrians and drivers are probably still in shock from the way I drove out there."

"Leigh got the worst of it."

"Knowing you, I doubt that. I think you suffered as much by having to watch. Chris said he told you not to go inside that barn."

"Rick had a gun at her throat and threatened to kill her then and there. I couldn't leave her."

"Most people would."

She frowned at him. "I don't think so."

"You see, love," he said, "that's a fundamental problem between us. You're the perennial optimist and I'm the perennial pessimist."

There was that word again. Love.

"Maybe we just balance each other," she said.

Then he kissed her again.

She wanted more. She wanted down and dirty. She wanted to revel in the fact she was still alive. She put her hands around his neck and stretched upward. Her body pressed against his, and his kiss deepened.

All the fear, all the horror of the last hours faded. Nothing mattered now but his lips playing with hers. The air cracked with electricity. His body was like a furnace and she felt every bit of the heat.

The tenderness of the kiss erupted into the explosiveness she'd always sensed in him. Her mouth opened and his tongue entered her mouth, teasing and searching but still with a tenderness that made her heart sing. His arms drew her hard against him as their tongues played love games of their own.

Her hand went up around his neck, touching the thick dark hair that curled ever so slightly around her fingers.

Her gaze met his and she saw a raw, aching longing in them, a yearning that was only part passion. She felt it in his hands, in his lips, in his possessive arms. Then his eyes closed again, as if he realized he had revealed something private. She closed hers, too, absorbing the almost magical closeness of intimate feelings shared.

Her mouth tightened against his. His body shuddered. His lips left her mouth and moved along the contours of her cheek, hesitating at the corner of her eye. His tongue feathered her cheek, his lips caressing skin now burning at his touch.

"Kira," he said in a ragged whisper.

Desire ripped through her as his lips moved again, nuzzling her ear, her neck, until she knew nothing but this consuming need for him.

She couldn't stop a low moan coming from deep in her throat. She'd thought she wanted down and dirty. But this was so much better. An exquisite building of sensations. She shivered with expectation and her hands moved with a fierce tenderness along the side of his neck.

Then, to her shock, he picked her up. She was no lightweight, but he did it easily and carried her into her bedroom. He carefully placed her on the bed, then gently undressed her. As he took off each piece of clothing, he massaged the skin beneath until every part of her was on fire. He was ever so careful about the wound still healing on her side.

She drew a shaky breath, trying to restore calm to a body possessed by a firestorm. Raw lust charged through her, and she put her arms around his neck, pulling him closer until her body strained against his. She felt his arousal and reveled in his soft moan.

Not enough. She wanted more. She withdrew her arms and started unbuttoning his shirt. He unzipped his slacks. Finally he was down to a pair of dark blue briefs. He left her for a second, slipping off his briefs and taking a package from a pocket in his slacks.

He sat down as she lay on her side, watching him. He ran his fingers through her hair, then leaned down again, his mouth caressing her breasts, his tongue leaving a hot wake as it moved from one to the other.

He then arched his body above her, entering with a deliberate slowness that created an aching, agonizing need that made her move against him in instinctive, circular movements, drawing him deeper and deeper inside her.

She felt waves of pleasure wash over her, not only the physical reaction but the unexpectedly exquisite bliss of just being with him, of having him so near. She wanted to capture that feeling forever.

But then his strokes increased in rhythm and power. Her body responded wantonly to his, moving as he did in a sensuous dance that became more and more frantic as they rode an incredible wave that rushed them headlong into an explosion of sensations.

He plunged one last time, then collapsed on her and rolled over until they were both on their sides, both still locked together in the aftermath of their lovemaking. She relished the warmth of his body as aftershocks continued to rock her body.

"Wow," she said. "I was thinking down and dirty, but that was down and glorious."

He chuckled. "I never would have thought of it that way."

She sighed with contentment and snuggled closer to him. "I hope not."

He kissed her. "You always surprise me."

"That's good. I hope."

"Oh, that's very good." He hesitated. "Feeling better?"

"I feel like I've been in a tornado, tossed from one momentous event to another."

"I'm not sure I want to be linked by both events."

"Oh, there's something to be said about going from the bottom of the valley to the top of the mountain."

"God, I love you," he said. He paused, then said, "I've never said those words before."

She wouldn't believe that coming from anyone else. She did believe them now. She touched his face. It was just a wee bit bristly with late-afternoon beard. It was really quite beautiful. And sexy. But then, everything about him was sexy.

She kissed him slowly, very slowly. This time it was all her being the seductress.

He made her feel sexy. Very, very sexy.

He took her hand as she came up for air. "There are things you should know . . ."

She squeezed her fingers around his. She wanted to show him nothing would make a difference.

"Do you ever do anything halfway?" he asked.

"I try not to. Don't you?"

The phone rang. She didn't want to answer. She had to answer it. It could be the hospital.

She reluctantly rolled away from him and answered the bedside phone.

"Kira?" It was Leigh.

She straightened up. "What is it?"

"I had to turn off my cell phone when I was at the hospital. When I turned it back on, I had a message from the hospital. My blood tests show I'm compatible to give a kidney to your mother."

Stunned, Kira couldn't even answer for a moment. Everything she wanted, prayed for, wished for, even lied for.

"Kira, did you hear what I said?"

"Yes. What . . . what are you going to do?"

"I said yes. All we have to do is convince your . . . my . . . mother."

"When?"

"In the morning. I already talked to the doctor. He needs a few more tests. He's arranged to take more blood first thing in the morning. Has something to do with making sure there's no infections, et cetera."

"Bless you," Kira said.

"I think I already am—blessed."

"Where's Chris?"

"Standing next to me. And now he says I have to go to his house and get some sleep. I couldn't be . . . home tonight. Not alone."

"Good. He and Archie will take good care of you."

"I'll like that." She sounded tired and sad.

"What about the horses?"

"Seth found someone to see about them. He likes horses, too. He'll be careful . . . more careful than I was."

"Does he know?"

"Everything? Not yet. I have to tell both Seth and David that they have a new cousin."

"Good." She hesitated, then added, "Leigh, thank you. You'll never know how much this means to me—"

Leigh cut her off. "Thanks for not driving off today. I think he would have killed me. He apparently was obsessed with being a Westerfield, not that it's made many of us content. It's not a happy legacy, Kira."

"I'm beginning to understand that. I have Chris's number. I'll call if I learn anything."

"Tomorrow then."

"Good. Meet you there at eight a.m."

She hung up.

Max sat up. "Leigh . . . is she okay?"

"Better than okay. The lab tests came in this afternoon. She's a match, and she'll donate a kidney."

He just smiled. "I had a feeling she would. She just had to do it in her own way."

"This will make us sisters of a sort. I always wanted one."

"Well, now you'll have cousins as well."

She shook her head. "I still can't believe it. So much, so fast."

Then she came back to the present. "You were saying . . . before the call . . . ?"

"That can wait. You wanted to see your mother."

She nodded, suddenly mortified that she had been so distracted from doing what she always did. "What time is it?"

He looked at his watch. "Nine. Is it too late for visiting hours?"

"They'll let me peek in. She'll be worrying about me . . . especially if she's heard anything from staff or on the tube."

He massaged her back. "I think we both need showers first."

"Together," she said.

"I like that idea."

So did she when he stood and she led him into the bathroom. He was beautiful, if a man could be called that. Lean and muscled. She was still amazed he wanted her. Had even said the L word. But then, they had been in a life-and-death situation. That did strange things to one's psyche.

Once inside the shower, he turned on the water and held

her. She was still a little self-conscious about her naked body.
She wished it was more perfect. Yet he touched her as if she
were pure gold and every bit as wondrous.

Steam filled the bathroom and filtered through her as
well. Their bodies fit as the water washed away the bad memories and refreshed the very nice ones. Her body started
reacting to his again, and his to hers. But she had to get to the
hospital tonight.

She took the soap and washed his back, then his chest. He
in turn did the same. Nothing in her life had been so seductive, so incredibly intimate. He was the one who cut off the
water, then toweled her down.

When he finished, he wrapped the towel around her and
combed out her damp hair. "My God, but you're beautiful.
Your eyes are always so alive, your smile so real. You take on
the world, but on your own terms."

"I lose a lot of battles."

"I don't think you ever lose. You merely have setbacks."
He kissed her on the tip of her nose. "Let's go."

They hurried then. She found a pair of slacks and a dark
blue blouse that deepened the blue in her eyes. He caught her
hand as they left.

No more guards. Her fingers tightened around his. He
stopped, leaned down, and kissed her, slowly and possessively.

"Ah . . . what you do to me, lady," he whispered.

She didn't have time to decipher that remark. He ushered
her to his car. They were on the way.

It was ten before they reached the hospital and went up to
the acute care unit.

She led the way to the nurse's station. "I know we're past
hours but . . ."

"We heard about the shooting, Ms. Douglas," the duty
nurse said. "No one said anything to your mother about it, but
I'm really glad to see you. I think she lives for you."

"Thanks for not saying anything. I just didn't want her to
wake and worry about why I haven't been here."

"Go on in. Just don't stay long."

"How is she doing?"

"Holding her own. I expect she'll be a lot better after seeing you."

"We may have a kidney," she said, unable to contain the news. "I found her biological daughter. She's been tested and she's a match." The words just exploded from her. She wanted to run out and down the hall announcing the news.

"Have you called the doctor?"

"Yes. I just found out an hour ago. They're conducting the last tests tomorrow morning."

The nurse beamed. "I'm really happy for you. Mrs. Douglas is one of our favorite patients."

Kira went into the glassed-in room of the pod. Her mother's eyes were open over the oxygen mask. Kira lifted it. "Hi," she said.

"I was worried about you."

"I know. Something happened today." She had to tell her mother something. Not everything. Not the tense life-and-death moments in the barn, but that Leigh had been attacked and incurred some minor wounds.

"Then it's over," her mother said.

"Yes."

"I'm so glad you're both okay."

"Mom, she's a match. She wants to give you a kidney."

"No!"

Kira had already prepared her speech. She'd prepared it ten days ago when she'd been tested.

"I never thought you were selfish," she said.

"Don't try to play me," her mother said. "I told you . . ."

"When I thought I might be able to give you a kidney, it was one of the happiest moments I've ever known. My worst day was when I discovered I couldn't. It's incredibly selfish of you to deny either of us that chance. It's particularly selfish with Leigh. She never knew you. She hasn't had a mother since she was six years old. No father, either. Are you going to let yourself die, never knowing her or allowing her to know you? It's not fair to her."

A tear started down Katy's cheek. "It's *not* unfair. She's young. If anything happened to her remaining kidney . . ."

"Then we will find another one for her. She's going to be here in the morning, Mom. Don't break her heart."

Her mother didn't answer, but Kira knew from her eyes she was at least reconsidering her position.

Kira leaned over and kissed her. "The nurses said I could only stay a moment. Just wanted to say I love you."

*They all met at the hospital early the next morning. The doc-*tor had already looked over the results. "We need to do more testing on Ms. Howard, but it does seem we have a match."

Leigh went into the room. Katy Douglas—her mother—was awake. Kira had already filled her in on the conversation she'd had with her—their—mother the night before.

Katy was sleeping. Leigh touched her hand, and Katy jerked awake, then focused on Leigh. She held out her hand. "I am so glad you're safe, you and Kira. I'm so happy you're friends."

Leigh took it. It was so frail. It was her mother's. Her heart beat rapidly. She had a chance to save this woman's life. A sense of wonder spread through her.

She suddenly understood that all the guilt she felt all these years didn't belong to her. It belonged to mistakes other people made. As she looked around the room, she didn't feel the fear that had haunted her for so many years.

"You know I'm a match for a kidney."

"Kira told me. I told her I didn't want it."

"You're going to take away my chance to know my mother?" Leigh asked. "I barely remember my mother—oops, this gets messy, doesn't it? Anyway, I always longed for a mother, for a family. You'd be doing me no favors by taking that chance away from me."

"You and . . . Kira conspired together," Katy charged.

"Yes, and . . . we're formidable."

Katy searched her face. "You're sure?"

"I've never been so sure of anything in my life."

Katy smiled. It was a smile that melted Leigh's heart. Full of love and pride. The latter made her heart warm. She impulsively leaned down and kissed the woman on the bed. Not just a woman now. Her mother.

"I'll go out and tell Kira," she said.

She left the room and went over to where Kira waited. "She'll sign the consent forms."

The three of them—Chris, Max, and Kira—huddled together in the surgical waiting room awaiting news of the transplant. They had been there three hours.

Kira was restless. She'd never been good at waiting. Neither, apparently, was Max. He hadn't stopped pacing, or wandering down the hall, or getting coffee for them. He was not a still man. Chris, on the other hand, simply sat stoically. Years of police work, Kira thought.

She stood. Things had moved quickly once Leigh was found in good health and determined to be as perfect a match for her mother as anyone could be.

They'd both been wheeled into the operating room three hours ago.

It had been an incredibly busy few days. She'd written four stories so far on the events. Now she was working on a series about organ transplants.

With Leigh's support, Max was representing Mrs. Baker, who had been charged with accessory to murder. With the agreement of Max and Kira, Leigh planned to use trust money for bail when she was released from the hospital. Mrs. Baker wasn't a danger to the community. She'd started a string of actions that resulted in murder, but murder had never been her intent. And Kira suspected that Rick hadn't needed that kick. That he'd just been waiting for an opportunity.

But in the days since the shooting, the explosive lovemaking between Kira and Max hadn't been repeated. It was as if Max had looked into an abyss and backed away. Maybe he still worried that she would take Leigh's inheritance, although she had absolutely no interest in it. She hadn't earned it, and it was tainted by generations of tragedy. She had what she wanted. A kidney. Her mother back.

"It won't be long now," Max said as he held out yet another cup of coffee.

But it was. Probably another hour. And her anxiety deepened. What if there were complications? What if the kidney didn't take? What if . . .

She looked up, and Max's eyes were on her. They were expressionless, just as they had been when they first met. She didn't even want to think what emotion her eyes held. Hurt. Anger. He'd awakened something in her, given her a hint of what they could have, and now seemed to be withdrawing away.

"Let's go for a walk," he said.

"I don't want to leave . . ."

"Chris will get us." Chris had gone from being Burke to Chris in the past several days. He'd worked on Mrs. Baker's case and felt as they did—that a prison term wouldn't do anyone any good.

Kira didn't want to go with him. She was glad he was here. No, her body was excited that he was here. It was acting in irresponsible ways. It was her brain that was trying to be responsible, that warned her that she'd known from the beginning that he would be short-term. She didn't want to trust him with her emotions again.

But he took her arm and guided her out, and she didn't want to make a scene. Not now. Not here.

He led her down a hall to a small room. She suspected he'd scouted ahead. She'd discovered he was always prepared. Once inside, he closed the door.

"I've tried to stay away from you," he said. "I can't. But you have to know everything about me. It will probably come out eventually, and I don't want you touched by it."

"Touched by what?"

"Payton isn't my real name. I legally changed it when I was twenty-one Ed Westerfield helped me do it."

She didn't ask why. He was about to tell her. Her breath caught in her throat.

"I was Joe. Joe Cantwell. The name probably doesn't mean much to you, but it was all over the newspapers years ago. I killed my dad. Some police officers thought I killed my mother as well."

The floor started to fall under her. "Was that what pointed the police toward you?" she asked. She hoped her voice didn't tremble as much as she feared it did.

"Yes."

"What happened?"

"I was ten. My dad was beating the hell out of my mother. He turned on me, and Mom hit him with an iron. He took out a knife and stabbed her. I grabbed his gun and shot him." He said the words coolly. Dispassionately. As if it had happened to someone else.

She hurt for him. Desperately. For him. For that boy all those years ago.

She waited for him to continue.

"My father had a long, violent record, and I had a juvenile one. He would disappear for weeks, leaving us without food or money. I would sometimes lift a package of hotdogs or a box of cereal. I was caught twice."

"You were only ten."

"Yeah, but my mom died, and no one wanted me. I was a troublemaker. I was put in a group home. Then a series of foster homes, each one worse than the last. At sixteen, I ran away. Lived on the streets, then a streetwise con told me how to get a new identity. Max Payton. It sounded like class to me.

"By then I discovered I didn't want to be a petty thief. Or drug dealer. I found a job as a janitor at Westerfield Industries, went to night school, and got my GED. Ed discovered me reading when I should have been scrubbing floors. Instead of firing me, he took me under his wing."

"I think he got a good deal on his investment," she said, her voice trembling.

"If it becomes public . . . Westerfield attorney murdered father."

"I don't care about that. You were a kid."

"There's another reason," he said quietly. "I come from a long line of abusers. My dad. His father. From what I hear beyond that. It seems it's passed on from father to son."

"Not always. Not even usually," she said. "I've done some articles on it." She peered up at him. "Is that why you never married?"

He shrugged. "I never met anyone I really wanted to share my life with. Until now."

"And now you want to scare me away?"

He smiled then. "No. But you had to know."

"Why now?"

"I was going to wait until after the surgery, but I want you to . . . know that I'm here for you. If you still want me."

That was like asking her if she wanted the moon and stars. She'd always been attracted to him. More than attracted. But now she admired him more than ever. She reached up and kissed him, long and hard. "I want," she said simply.

A knock at the door interrupted his reply.

Chris opened it, looked from one to the other. "Glad you guys got things straightened out. You both have been looking like hell."

"Is there news?"

"Both came through just great," Chris said with a grin.

Max put his arm around her shoulders. "Let's go see our family."

She looked up at him and blinked. A few weeks ago she had a dying mother. No one else in the world. Now her mother would be with her for a long time. And she had a sister. Of sorts. Probably a brother-in-law of sorts, too.

And Max.

She wrapped her hand in his. "Let's go do that," she said.

Epilogue

Kira Douglas Payton stood hand in hand with Max as they watched the sign go up over the driveway into the Westerfield estate.

Westerfield Riding Camp, it read. The sign itself was made of wood with the words burned into it.

Kira smiled at Leigh, who stood in front of the sign, studying it from every angle before nodding her head.

The sign had taken the place of the forbidding gate that once regulated visitors. Now it welcomed them.

The camp would officially open in two weeks. It would offer day classes during much of the year and a weeklong camp experience during the summer, mostly for kids with disabilities. The Westerfield trust financed the expansion of the stables and renovation of the big house. The first floor had been transformed into rooms for the kids, as well as a kitchen, dining room, and physical therapy rooms. Katy Douglas had a suite of rooms above with her own kitchen. She'd claimed the title of House Mother.

The trust also would provide funds for staff as well as scholarships for kids who couldn't afford the experience.

After the sign was up properly, the small group of attendees trooped inside Max's house for lunch.

Congressman Seth Westerfield turned to Leigh. "Good job, Cous. But you should have let me notify the media."

"I think we've had enough publicity, thank you," Leigh said wryly.

Seth shrugged. "But this is *good* publicity."

"No," Leigh said sternly, then glanced at Kira.

Warmth filled Kira as her fingers tightened around Max's. Leigh's confidence had grown noticeably in the past months, and never more so than the day four weeks earlier when she'd married Chris, three months after Kira had wed Max.

Chris smiled down at his new wife. He hadn't stopped smiling in the past months. The grief in his eyes had faded, though Kira knew Risa would always hold a place in his heart.

The relationship hadn't been easy for Leigh in the beginning. It was hard for her to trust, to believe that he wouldn't come to hate her scars, both physical and emotional. Leigh had surmounted far more obstacles than Kira. And now they were like sisters, the sister each had always wanted but never had.

Mrs. Baker was an invisible presence. She had been invited but declined. The prosecution had decided not to press charges after hearing all the facts, and she'd retired to her cottage.

Kira's mother came into the room carrying a large casserole she'd made earlier, along with a bowl of salad. Max opened a bottle of champagne and another of sparkling cider. He poured the contents into flutes, then raised his own glass. "To Leigh's dream."

Kira took a sip and looked around. David and his wife were there. He raised his glass but his eyes were somber. His father had flown back after receiving a telegram about the events. He'd confessed to all of them that he'd been responsible for the switch.

It had been a momentary decision that had haunted him the rest of his life. His cousin, Karen, had already had three miscarriages and this had been a risky pregnancy. Michael had always loved Karen, and when he saw that her child had what he believed was a fatal illness and would live no longer than a few days, he made the decision to switch the child with one born at the same time to a very young girl who had no money and whose husband obviously didn't want a child.

The young mother—Katy Douglas—would have other opportunities. His cousin wouldn't. He made sure Katy Douglas and the ill baby had the best medical care possible, and he paid the costs.

When Karen and her husband died and Leigh was so badly injured, he stayed to make sure she had the best care, then joined Doctors Without Borders. He'd thought then about confessing his action, but he feared he would make everything worse.

Kira and Max, Leigh and Chris held a meeting. They'd already informed a grateful hospital administration they had no intention of suing. They didn't need the money, and it would hurt the hospital's spiraling insurance costs. They decided to let everyone to believe the switch was an accident rather than drag the Westerfield name through the papers for months, maybe years.

Then there was the trust. Kira said she would not contest her grandfather's will. She had been the lucky one, not Leigh.

Max turned over control of the trust to Leigh, but she asked him to stay on and manage the funds as well as the stock. He'd concurred with her plans for the ranch and even joined enthusiastically in the planning. He'd suggested that they also save several weeks for inner-city kids.

It was also time for him to leave the Westerfield compound. With Kira's enthusiastic approval, he'd donated his house to the project. Leigh and Chris would live there, while the big house would lodge Katy and the campers. Kira wanted Leigh to have time with their mother, and their mother was ecstatic about working with kids. She was always a natural-born caretaker.

And Kira and Max? He'd purchased land not far away, and the contractor was finishing a stone-and-glass home they'd designed together. A house of light and warmth. He had lived in the Westerfields' pocket too long. He would continue to be Leigh's attorney, but he would accept other clients as well.

He stood again. "Another toast," he said, his eyes twinkling. They had been doing a lot of that lately.

Everyone looked toward him. He clasped Kira's hand and drew her up next to him. He put his arm around her and pulled her close.

"We're going to have a baby in exactly six months."

Katy Douglas stood. Tears rolled down her face. "I never thought . . . to see . . ."

Kira bit her lip to stop her own tears. She hadn't thought her mother would see a grandchild, either.

But as she looked at Leigh's delighted face, and the way Chris pulled her to him, she knew it wouldn't be long before there was another child in the family . . .

"To the family," Chris said. "To our complicated, confused, and altogether wonderful family."

And they all raised their glasses.

In 1988, **Patricia Potter** won the Maggie Award and a Reviewer's Choice Award from *Romantic Times* for her first novel. She has been named Storyteller of the Year by *Romantic Times* and has received the magazine's Career Achievement Award for Western Historical Romance along with numerous Reviewer's Choice nominations and awards.

She has won three Maggie awards, is a six-time RITA finalist, and has been on the *USA Today* bestseller list. Her books have been alternate choices for the Doubleday Book Club.

Prior to writing fiction, she was a newspaper reporter with the *Atlanta Journal* and president of a public relations firm in Atlanta. She has served as president of Georgia Romance Writers, as a board member of River City Romance Writers, and as past president of Romance Writers of America.

**SOMETIMES DOING THE RIGHT THING—
IS THE WRONG THING...**

CATCH A SHADOW

By *USA Today* bestselling author
PATRICIA POTTER

When paramedic Kirke Palmer agreed to the deathbed request of a hit-and-run victim, she thought she was doing the right thing. Little did she realize that her goodwill gesture would make her the target of a cold-blooded killer...

penguin.com

M316T0708